THE SUMMONING

Other books by Robert Towers

THE NECKLACE OF KALI
THE MONKEY WATCHER

THE SUMMONING

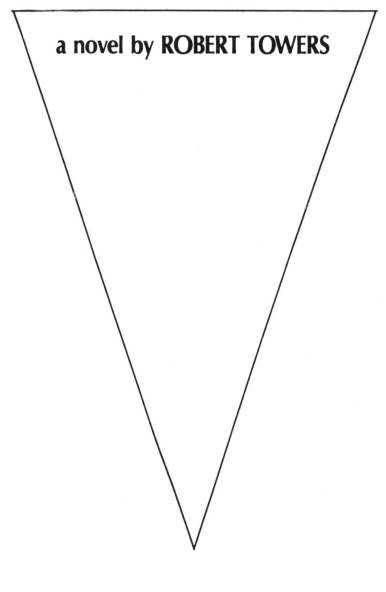

a novel by ROBERT TOWERS

1817

HARPER & ROW, PUBLISHERS, New York
Cambridge, Philadelphia, San Francisco, London, Mexico City,
São Paulo, Sydney

FIRST EDITION
Designer: Ruth Bornschlegel

Library of Congress Cataloging in Publication Data

Towers, Robert, date
   The summoning.

   I. Title.
PS3570.O88S9   1983   813'.54   82-48686
ISBN 0-06-015168-4

83 84 85 86 87 10 9 8 7 6 5 4 3 2 1

To Pat

Acknowledgments

I want to record my gratitude to Yaddo and to the New York Society Library, both of which provided (in different ways) a quiet and sustaining refuge for the writing of much of this novel.

PART 1

Chapter One

A man named Lawrence Hux sat reading within a cone of yellow light that fell from the only decent lamp in the room. As he read, he would reach from time to time into a five-pound bag of pistachio nuts on the floor next to his chair. Then, laying down his paperback book, he would open the nuts, dropping most of the empty coral-red shells into the bag but letting a few of them slip into the lap of his bathrobe. By ten o'clock his right thumbnail was sore from prying open the nuts. Though indolent in posture and movement, he did not seem relaxed.

Hux's robe, which was fading from maroon to rust, had become his nighttime refuge from the appearance he maintained during the day; stained down the front with beer and smearings of cheese, its pockets lined with trapped crumbs, the robe was no doubt analyzable in some criminologist's laboratory for traces of urine on its skirts and probably semen as well. Hux stared at the red shells in his lap and was tempted to brush them to the floor. Instead, he scooped them up and returned them to the bag. Aware of how many nuts he had consumed, he warned himself that obesity lay ahead if he kept this up; already his suits and shirt collars were becoming too tight. At thirty-seven he had still been able to take pride in possessing the hard, flat stomach of a well-conditioned man of twenty-five; but at thirty-seven and a half, he could clutch two handfuls of loose stomach flesh. Hating what he was doing to his body, Hux used his bare right foot to shove the bag out of reach, thereby dislodging his paperback (a copy of Norman Mailer's *The Prisoner of Sex*), which fell to the floor, where other paperbacks lay scattered. The slap of the book against the uncarpeted floor made him jump slightly, though he had seen it falling and had half tried to catch it.

Hux did not pick up the book but instead raised his eyes to the blank wall over his unmade bed on the other side of the studio apartment. Testing his sore thumbnail against another nail (it hurt!), he thought of Joanna, her small hand nestled in his as they walked down Eighth Avenue below the Port Authority Bus Terminal last Saturday night, the wind blowing grit in their faces. . . .

What sort of man was this Lawrence Hux, sitting thus alone on an evening in late March, 1974? Properly dressed, he was pleasant-looking, with thick, carefully barbered hair the color of tarnished brass, a rounded face with smooth cheeks, and a perfectly straight nose. Though overweight, he was not yet fat. His wide, light-blue eyes were pink-rimmed, as if he were an insomniac or a drinker or both. An angry girl whom he had picked up at one of the singles bars around the corner on First Avenue had called him a "baby-faced killer," and his ex-wife, during a recent quarrel over their son's schooling, had scathingly compared him to one of Nixon's pretty young men, now so much in the news; both descriptions were considerably wide of the mark.

As to his character, an investigator would have had to sort through a rather large file of conflicting views to get even a rough idea. "As you saw, he can turn on the Southern charm when he wants to. Larry's a subtle fellow, a bit devious. He can be ornery as hell, maddening, stubborn, drive you right up the wall. . . . And of course he's *very* bright." So Newbold Jenkins, in his slightly braying, St. Mark's–Harvard voice, had described his associate director for educational projects to a friend over lunch at the Century Club. Despite repeated rudenesses on Hux's part, Jenkins, who was director of the Morrow Foundation, still retained a great fondness for the younger man, but he had long since given up hope of becoming Hux's good friend as well as his boss. While not rejecting any of Jenkins's terms, Hux's ex-wife, Louise, would have insisted that he was also a loser, a bad sport, and a spoiler; she was, to be sure, bitter—and had every right to be. Hux's son Tony, a polite and troubled boy of ten, would never have articulated, even to himself, an opinion of his father, with whom—on the few occasions when they now met—he was increasingly secretive and wary. The views of his associates at the Foundation would have varied: "Nice enough guy, very capable, but I really don't know him"—or: "I can't stand the way he sucks up to Newbold Jenkins. I don't know exactly why, but I've never trusted Larry Hux." Fran Duffy, one of the researchers at the Foundation, might have said, shrugging, "I've given up trying to understand Larry. In some ways he's a very sweet guy. But really screwed-up. And I mean *really*, at least when it comes to women."

Ten years before, Clinton McPeters, the head of the Princeton chapter of CORE, had described Hux as "committed right up to the eyeballs. Him an' Clark Helmholtz the two hardest-workin' guys we got." And Professor Marvin Beale, who was directing Hux's doctoral thesis (later aborted) at the Woodrow Wilson School of Public and International Affairs at Princeton, had placed Hux's name in the number-two position on his list of candidates for a Procter Fellowship. Five years earlier still, Philip O'Brien, who was then directing *Richard II* for the Carolina Playmakers, told an interviewer for the *Tarheel Daily* that Larry Hux was the best Richard he had ever seen—"even better than Maurice Evans." And going all the way back to the earliest source of all, one might have heard Rachel Stallings Hux—now a widow living in Raleigh—say of her son, "Well, Lorenzo was always a shy little boy. I tried not to spoil him."

None of those who knew him—not even Louise, who had once loved him and had lived with him for eleven years—could have imagined the slovenliness into which he now sank every night when he came home from the office, where he was still the efficient, exasperating, and immaculate Larry Hux they had always known.

The apartment house into which he had moved after the separation was one of those white-brick buildings that had sprung up in the Sixties east of Third Avenue, a building with a marbled and mirrored lobby hung with crimson flocked wallpaper and an opera-house chandelier—a glossy, cheaply constructed container designed for *Cosmopolitan* girls and young PR men with sunglasses and the bell-bottomed suits then fashionable. Hux, wearing one of his dark pin-striped suits and carrying an attaché case, always looked out of

3

place in the lobby, as if he had come for illicit purposes—or else to call upon a particularly disreputable client. When he had first moved in, he had had ambitious plans for the decoration of his apartment. These had largely been inspired by Fran Duffy, the first of the women he had taken up with after Louise had finally given up on him. She had promised to help him choose a rug, curtains, slipcovers, and some pieces of furniture to supplement what he had brought over from the West End Avenue apartment; she had a flair for that sort of thing. Hux expected to have some wild parties—the kind where anything might happen, the kind Louise detested. But with the breakup of the affair, following its complete sexual collapse, Hux had done nothing further with the apartment. The floors stayed bare; curtains were never hung. He had just enough furniture to accommodate himself, in a meager and churlish way, with no provision for guests. So much for the promises he had made to himself and Tony, who had come—shortly after the separation—to spend a couple of experimental weekends with his father and had been so obviously uncomfortable and resentful that Hux had stopped asking the boy to come again. Despite its bleakness, the apartment had been kept fairly clean until recent months, but now siftings and whorls of dust had gathered under each piece of furniture and in the corners of the room. Hux had done little except wipe the tabletops with a blackened cloth.

In contrast to this squalor were the five good suits, from Brooks Brothers and J. Press, draped neatly from wooden hangers in the closet, the carefully stacked shirts in the drawers, and the five pairs of expensive shoes, glowingly polished and fitted with shoe trees; the shoes were lined up on a slanting rack above the closet floor, which was strewn with dirty laundry.

Joanna again came into focus, swimming through the blue haze of a Times Square hustlers' bar called the Goldfish Bowl. She had been nice enough, Joanna—tactful about his behavior when he accompanied her to a room in a flea-bag hotel near Penn Station and paid her fifty dollars just to undress and lie next to him while he fondled her breasts—he could still feel the nub of her rosy-brown nipple between thumb and forefinger. . . . She did not urge him to go further, showed no contempt. Probably she was used to this sort of thing, perhaps even relieved. In any case she had been unlike many of the girls he had brought home from the singles bars—those secretaries and nurses, receptionists and airline stewardesses, who had been tactful neither about their sexual requirements nor their frequent disappointment. Their voices—nasalized or dentalized or full of glottal

4

stops—screeched in his ear like a chorus of parrots. Perhaps Joanna was kinder because she was being paid cash instead of expensive drinks and therefore had a low opinion of herself; perhaps she was flattered that he wanted to listen to the story of her fights with her mother back home, of her running away from Gadsden, Alabama, and the three-week bus trip, with numerous stopovers, to the Port Authority Terminal. Perhaps (the notion occurred to Hux) she was kind because (like himself) she was Southern.

Idly he wondered if he could still make it with that other—and very different—Southern girl whom he had married. He and Louise had not made love during the last months before the separation, but that had been (so Hux told himself) a matter of angry withdrawal on both sides. He knew that sooner or later he would have to do something about the growing frequency of the fiascos—see a doctor, take hormone injections, or, as Louise had insisted for other reasons, go into therapy. Half the people he knew in New York had been in therapy or analysis. . . . But for the last couple of months nothing had seemed urgent. The parade of pickups into his apartment had stopped. Currents of sexual feeling still ran strongly at times, but they now seldom drove him into the streets and bars. A kind of quiescence had descended, an amputee's resignation that was not unwelcome. Probably his visit—on a sudden impulse—to the Goldfish Bowl had been a mistake; it had broken the peace while doing nothing to restore his confidence. The brief stirring he had felt at Joanna's side would come back to tempt him into renewed action—and probable failure—again.

Hux was beginning to feel sleepy. If he could just get soundly enough to sleep, perhaps he could slip past the insomnia that regularly flung him into wakefulness between three and five in the morning. It was this insomnia, more than anything else, that threatened to break down the barrier he had successfully maintained between his cell life at night and his office life during the day; last Wednesday he had fallen asleep at his desk. Perhaps a beer or two would do the trick. While he sipped his beer he could watch the eleven-o'clock news and then go to bed. On his way to the refrigerator he accidentally kicked an empty beer can from two nights ago and sent it clattering across the floor. The sound frightened him, reverberating as loudly to his ear as if a truckload of scrap metal had been suddenly dumped into the room. He was trembling. Back in his chair, Hux thought: it isn't good for me to be so isolated that even the popping of the top of a new can of beer makes me jump. . . . He was trembling.

Though the evidence lay all around him, Hux had not really thought of himself as being in a bad way. He still had Sunday dinner once a month with Louise and Tony on West End Avenue, still occasionally took his son to the movies or to a ball game; but he had no wish to see more of his family, despite (or because of) his guilt about Tony. For weeks now he had seen none of his old friends, who had become tired of asking him to meals only to be turned down; his unmarried colleagues at the office no longer suggested that he join them for an evening on the town. This is the way I want it, he told himself grimly; the thought of other possibilities bored him, filled him with a weariness that was like an interminable wait in a bleakly lit station. Yet he was trembling. . . .

Hux turned on the television and came back to his chair. Congressman Rodino was being questioned about the intricacies of an impeachment proceeding. Then a mug shot of Nixon was shown. . . .

At midnight Hux was still awake. Tired of television, he turned off the set and then picked up *The Prisoner of Sex*, only to put it down. Reaching at random into the scattering of paperbacks near his chair, he drew forth *Zelda*, a book that he had begun weeks before and then put aside—something he was always doing these days, even with the books he liked. He found the place where he had left off—closer to the beginning than he had expected—and began to read about the girlhood of Zelda Sayre in Montgomery, Alabama. Soon he had drifted from the text into thoughts about the bus boycott and Martin Luther King . . . and James Earl Ray. . . . Hux let the book drop and leaned back, closing his eyes, his head resting on the worn and greasy upholstery of the chair top. The lamplight glowed a dull red against his eyelids. His mind seemed to be thickening with sleep. Hux stayed where he was, knowing that the exertion of going to bed might keep him awake forever.

Someone was in the room. Gradually Hux had become aware of the sound of breathing—a heavy, measured breathing that was distinctly within the room, a sound that was not coming, as he had at first thought, from the street outside. He opened his eyes but saw nothing, blinded as he was by the glare of the lamplight, which seemed brighter than usual, an eye-splitting white. The sound persisted—now stertorous, rasping, like the breathing of his father in the last half hour of his life. Leaning forward, so that his head was beyond the immediate cone of light, Hux peered, holding his breath, into the enveloping gloom. Gradually the familiar spaces and props became visible as his eyes adjusted: the kitchen alcove, the open door to the bathroom, the dresser, the rack of ties on the closet door. . . . Certain objects—an empty glass on the dresser, a doorknob—were rimmed by an odd fuzz of light. Along the footboard of the bed—

Hux uttered a cry that was like a groan. A man was sitting on the bed, holding his bowed head in both hands. His figure—broad-shouldered, hunched over—was also outlined by a faint greenish glow that seemed to pulse with the noisy breathing. Despite the shadow in which the man's face was submerged, Hux had the impression—as vivid as if he were only inches away—that the man was frowning, with his eyes closed and his mouth slightly open, a man with a heavy cold clogging his nostrils. Hux knew instantly who the man was.

"Clark!" he cried out, rising from his chair so that the paperback slipped to the floor. "Clark!"

The man looked up and at the same time removed his hand from the right side of his head and held it out, palm upward. In the dim light the hand seemed to be covered with a black, gummy substance like tar; the same blackness matted the exposed side of his head and oozed from the corner of his eye.

"Oh, my God," Hux wailed above the pounding of his chest. "Clark! Oh, Clark!"

He found himself standing several feet in front of his chair, staring at the rumpled bed on which no one sat. Then he staggered backward, lowered himself into the chair, and covered his own face. The lamplight struck the thick golden hair on the back of his head, which was tipped forward as if Hux were expecting a rabbit punch across the nape of his neck. The bathrobe, its sash untied, had slipped from his right shoulder.

Over and over again, Hux told himself that it was a dream, a nightmare—that he had fallen asleep; but the warm flood of relief that he expected never came. Instead, he felt impaled upon a blade of grief that seemed to enter his chest below the heart, pinning him motionless to his chair.

Chapter Two

Like his bedroom, Claiborne Herne's workroom was kept as neat as a surgery. On the long table the implements were laid out in meticulous rows—shining pincers, awls, pliers, swabs, tack hammers, brushes, spools, planes, scissors, knives, razors, boxes of pins, tiny nails, tacks, needles, packets of sandpaper, trays containing little bottles and cans of paint, various glues, varnishes, and shellac. At one end of the table, near the vise and lathe, were delicate strips of wheat-colored wood, carefully stacked or tied into bundles, spools of copper and steel wire, a burner, and a white cardboard box filled with tiny squares of fine canvas, odd bits and cuttings of linen and bright-colored silks. At the end of each work day Dr. Herne—however much whiskey he had drunk during the afternoon—would sweep up all the shavings, every snippet of thread and wire, wash his brushes, and polish each metal implement with a soft chamois cloth. Next, after pouring himself another drink, he would open the windows to dilute the fumes of lacquers and solvents and glue that gave the room a smell as distinctive as the medical combination of green soap and Lysol. Then he would sit for a while in a rocking chair with his drink and stare at the nautical maps, brown-varnished and framed, with which the room was hung. Sometimes he would take from the bookshelf one of the volumes on old ships that he had collected and study a particular plate or diagram.

On this afternoon Dr. Herne sat gently rocking, with an open folio weighing heavily upon his knees. Both windows were wide open, but there was no breeze and the flowered curtains hung limp. Though the warmth of the day—it was more like June than the end of March—made him a bit drowsy, Dr. Herne continued to pore over a picture, in color, of a Venetian state galley, all scarlet and gold, wondering whether he had the patience to undertake such a gorgeous monster as his next project, now that his model of the Acapulco galleon was nearly finished. It was a question of patience rather than competence, for Claiborne Herne's fingers, however unsuited they had become for the practice of medicine, could still knot a nearly invisible rope to a scarcely more visible spar. Eventually the stillness lulled him so that his attention wandered from the galley and his thoughts floated back to a succession of summer afternoons, years ago, when he had supervised the members of his boys' club in the building of a kayak in the stable behind the old house. Some memory trace of an old smell—glue? canvas?—made him lift his head like a stallion testing the air.

He was still an impressive man, almost handsome, his face now darkened to the dull purple-red of a freshly split brick, his eyebrows and hair silky white against his angry skin. His clothes were simple but neat: a white shirt open at the collar, gray flannel trousers with the sharpest of creases, mahogany-red loafers polished to a military gloss. With his black-rimmed spectacles resting upon the jut of his nose, Claiborne Herne had the look—at once fierce and a bit dazed—of a retired army officer whose chin, now thrust forward, might at any moment drop to his breastbone.

The front doorbell rang, tearing Dr. Herne from his reverie. He wondered if his sister would answer it. Isabelle's deafness was unpredictable: if the door to her bedroom was open, she could usually, though not always, hear the telephone or doorbell. But whether she heard it or not, he had no intention of going to the door himself. The wait annoyed him. The bell sounded again, and this time he saw Isabelle scurry past the open door of his workroom, which was the third bedroom of the ranch house the Hernes now inhabited. A moment later Isabelle stood in the doorway, wide-hipped and squat, her face sagging like that of a child struggling against tears.

"You've got to come to the front door, Brother. It's Rooney. He's come back." Her pitch was uncertain, her voice rasping despite the Mississippian softness of her inflections.

"Rooney's at the front door? Rooney's in Detroit!" Glaring at his sister as if he had caught her in a palpably stupid lie, Dr. Herne pressed his feet against the floor to keep his chair from rocking.

"He's back. You'd better come." Isabelle turned and dragged her way slowly back to the kitchen, where she had been preparing dinner.

As he stood up, Dr. Herne tottered slightly. He was over six feet tall, still trim and angular. Then he strode into the narrow, low-ceilinged hall. Framed in the open front door was a silhouette at once familiar and strange against the light—the slender, broad-shouldered figure that Dr. Herne knew so well, but now capped by a huge mushroom of frizzy hair.

"How you doin', Dr. Claib'n?" The man, a light-skinned black in his early thirties, held out his right hand, which the doctor ignored.

9

He then laughed derisively, hooking his thumbs in the waist of his blue jeans, which he wore beneath a lime-green T-shirt. Grinning, he stood with one leg crossed in front of the other, his new sneakers gleaming like fresh white paint. "Ain't you gonna ask me in the livin' room?"

"Stop sayin' 'ain't,' " snapped the doctor. "You're supposed to be an educated man."

Again the black laughed. He followed Claiborne Herne into the living room, where the low ceiling pressed down upon the massive and blackened old furniture like the lid of a plywood box. Sitting at opposite ends of the creaking Victorian sofa, Dr. Herne and Rooney Lee swung challengingly to face one another.

"I thought you were supposed to be in Detroit."

"I jus' couldn't stay 'way from Alhambra. Besides, Vicky hated it up North. Bad environment. Mighty bad. You know how it is."

"I don't know *how it is* and I don't care. All I know is that you've broken our agreement." Dr. Herne could feel his rage hammering like heated pistons in each temple. Wishing that he had brought his drink with him, he had to struggle against an impulse to rush back to his workroom. "If you won't keep your word, I have no intention of dealing with you."

"I guess you got a problem, Dr. Claib'n. You'll jus' have to solve it the best ol' way you can. I got me some problems too. That brother-in-law of mine ain't got the sense he was born with, and that's the truth. He's tryin' to run the parlor like it was a easy-credit furniture store or somethin'. So I figure I better come on home and try to straighten things out before Brother Maddox screws up the place for good. I was a fool to think he could handle it. Like I said, he ain't got the sense he was born with."

"Stop sayin' 'ain't.' I didn't send you to Waldrup College to say 'ain't.' "

Rooney bent double with silent laughter that shook the black froth of his afro. "Dr. Claib'n, you're somethin' else. Here I am, tryin' to be real serious, talkin' about my problems, and all you can hear is 'ain't.' "

Claiborne Herne flexed his fingers in front of his throat as if he had thought of choking himself. Then he stood up, steadied himself by gripping the sofa arm, and walked out of the room. The door of Isabelle's room was open, and he could see her at her desk. Something rigid and unsettled about her position in her chair made him suspect that she had rushed to it and seated herself after eavesdropping in the hall; his suspicion was confirmed by the fact that she was in her stocking feet. *Fool,* he thought as he entered his workroom, *damn fool—she can't hear one word in ten unless she's looking right at you, but she won't give up.* . . . Though the ice had by now melted in his drink, the liquid was nearly as dark as strong tea. Picking up the glass, he took two long swallows while he stood in the middle of the floor, as if afraid to return to the living room. Rooney meant trouble—and the stirring-up of something Dr. Herne had put fiercely behind him. Then, holding his glass against his chest, he shrugged and stepped into the hall.

Rooney Lee was standing at the living-room window. "Come here, Dr. Claib'n. Got somethin' to show you."

Pushing aside the faded mulberry velvet of the curtain—a curtain obviously cut for a much larger window—Dr. Herne glared at a large white Buick parked on the street in front of the house.

"Did you steal that in Detroit?"

"No, suh. I bought it. Paid cash."

"Then the parlor must be makin' plenty of money in spite of your brother-in-law." Dr. Herne took several swallows from his glass, then drew a liver-spotted hand across his mouth. His proximity to Rooney made his skin contract, as if he expected to be stung. "Be that as it may," he said loudly, "I forbid you to park that monstrosity in front of this house again. I don't want neighbors or delivery men or anybody else associatin' *that* car with *this* house. Is that clear?" His voice rose to a falsetto of outrage as he drew away from the window. "What in God's name made you want to buy or steal a flashy nigger car like that? It's the most conspicuous car in Alhambra. The police will never let you out of sight for a minute."

At the window Rooney clasped his hands together, pressing them so that his tan biceps rippled. He gave a catlike yawn and said, "I need a sweetener."

"What?"

"I need a sweetener," said Rooney with a wide smile for the doctor, who had sat down on the sofa. "Tha's why I'm here. Say, like eight hundred."

"What are you talkin' about? Eight hundred! You owe me more than that in back interest. Eight hundred!"

"Easy, Dr. Claib'n. Now you take it easy." Rooney crossed to the sofa and sat down. "I *need* that car. Business reasons . . . makin' the right impression. I got somethin' goin' that stretches down to New Orleans and up to Memphis and all the way back to Detroit. Before long—when it all works out—it's gonna make that ol' funeral parlor look like chicken feed. But right now you might say I'm a little short on the cash flow. I *need* that sweetener." Rooney wrinkled his forehead, extending his fleshy lower lip. "Don't you worry. You'll get it back by July first at the latest, along with the interest. Don't you worry about *that*."

Dr. Herne sat in silence, resting his now nearly empty glass on his knee, his head tilted back. Behind the black-rimmed glasses his watery blue eyes were nearly closed. *No*, he thought, *no—I can't get into all that again....*

"You're my benefactor, Dr. Claib'n. Where'd I be today if it wasn't for you?" Rooney's voice was at once caressing and fuzzy, a peach skin against the lips. "I haven't ask you for nothin' since the big loan. You had it real easy for a long time now. Real easy."

"You haven't paid me one goddamn cent of interest! And you've broken your word about Detroit. You promised me you'd stay away from Mississippi for at least two years and here you are back after—after what?—not even nine months! You're a cheap, swindlin', petty criminal. God knows why I've put up with you as long as I have." But Claiborne Herne, despite his words, was now less angry than resentful—and resigned. He felt unwell—dizzy. Above all he wanted Rooney Lee out of the house. The presence of his former protégé made him as uneasy as if a honey-colored puma—for the moment yawning and playful—had curled up on the sofa beside him.

"I need the sweetener before the weekend," said Rooney, who had crossed his legs and was swinging one white-sneakered foot in a little arc. "You reckon you could get Miss Isabelle to drop you off at the bank tomorrow? I could drop by around five tomorrow evenin' and pick it up."

Dr. Herne looked away for several long moments, then spoke as if just awakened from a drugged sleep. "All right. Come to the kitchen door.... And don't try to come into the house—it upsets my sister too much. And park way up the street, past all the houses."

"You'll have the money? I ain't in the mood for tricks."

"I'll have the money."

"Maybe you be in the mood for a prayer meetin' Sunday mornin'—while Miss Isabelle's in church?"

"No!" shouted Claiborne Herne, snapping his head to the side so that strands of silky white hair fell across his forehead. "I'm sick of all that. I'm through with it. Now get out of here."

"Jes' askin', jes' askin'," said Rooney as he stood up. "Vicky send you her best re-gards." He waited, grinning. "You look to me like a man who need to unburden himself. I expec' one of yo' ol'-time prayer meetin's might do you a whole worl' of good. Git rid of mighty big load of sin that's built up while I been away and couldn't keep an eye on you."

"Get out of here!" Clutching the carved arm of the old sofa, Dr. Herne pulled himself to his feet and stood with his legs spread, a wobbly colossus. His voice was shredded with hoarseness. "If you don't leave this house this instant I'm goin' to—" Suddenly he strode over to the towering secretary in the corner of the room and snatched up a daggerlike brass letter opener. "Now you get out of here. I'm sick of you. Get that disgustin' car of yours off my street!"

Rooney drew back in mock terror and loudly slapped both knees. "Good Lord have mercy! Dr. Claib'n, you're a mess. What am I gonna do with you?" He straightened himself and sauntered toward the door, shaking his head. "Tomorrow evenin' at five. I'll come creepin' up to the back door like a ol' nigger tramp wantin' a handout. And if you change your mind about Sunday mornin'—"

"Out! This instant!"

Chapter Three

On the morning after his nightmare or hallucination or whatever it was, Hux, who had spent the rest of the night in his chair, set about pulling himself together as best he could. He took a long, steaming shower, shaved, and then dressed with special care, forcing his boneless fingers to retie his tie several times until the knot was perfect—with just the right dimple in the heavy silk below the knot. Trying to ignore the ghastly look of his face and eyes, he turned his head several times to examine his freshly combed hair in the mirror, estimating that he had another five or six days to go before a visit to his barber. Even in his present state he derived a subtle pleasure from the contrast between the perfectionism of his grooming and the secret mess he inhabited. But he was troubled by the tightness of his gray herringbone suit, knowing that sooner rather than later his gaining of thirteen pounds—with more obviously on the way—would force him to buy new suits, though the ones he owned were fairly new and in excellent condition. He took off the herringbone and changed into his glen-plaid but there was no improvement. After starting to change back again, Hux sat down trouserless on the edge of his bed, wanting to cry and at the same time telling himself that it was ridiculous to be so concerned about his clothes when he was obviously on the verge of a crackup. The morning light bothered his eyes. Certain things—the empty beer can on the table, the coffeepot on the stove—seemed to retain a trace of the bright fuzz that other objects had acquired just before his vision of Clark. Finally he put on the glen-plaid. Eating breakfast was out of the question—even a cup of coffee would have nauseated him. . . .

At the office Hux crouched over his desk, trying to put together a report on the Cincinnati Conservatory grant, for which he—as the Foundation's associate director for educational projects—was responsible. The bamboo blinds were inadequate defense against the eastern sunlight pouring into the room, high up in the RCA Building in Rockefeller Center; the placing of his executive-size desk had never been satisfactorily worked out to shield Hux and his visitors from the glare in the corner office, where the southern light was just as blinding as the eastern. This morning the aching of his eyeballs made him periodically desperate, as if someone were pressing his thumbs into their corners, between the bony socket and the ball. The pages on his desk shimmered like foil.

Suddenly Hux started, with a hissing intake of breath. The stocky figure of Clark Helmholtz, with a halo of light around his unruly hair, had materialized in the visitor's chair a few feet beyond the outer rim of his desk. Unable to expel his breath, Hux stared at the apparition until he was released by a sudden laugh, followed by a cultivated voice that he recognized—Newbold Jenkins's.

"Sorry I startled you, Larry. This carpeting's absurdly thick. . . . Here, I thought you might like to have a look at this." Except for the sturdiness of his build and his perpetually tousled, schoolboyish hair, Newbold Jenkins did not in the least resemble Hux's dead friend. Leaning over the desk, Jenkins, who practiced a studied informality with his subordinates, held out what looked like a Xeroxed copy of an article.

Hux refused to reach for the article. "Don't you ever sneak up on me again!" he said in a voice vibrant with rage.

"For heaven's sake, Larry, what's come over you?" Newbold Jenkins stared at Hux as if his colleague had been transformed into a wart-covered troll. "I came in here not only to bring you the article but to ask you to join me for lunch. But you're obviously upset."

"I'm sorry, Newbie," mumbled Hux, accepting the article. "Something's wrong with me. I think I may be coming down with the flu or something," he added, not very convincingly.

"Maybe you'd better go home. You look absolutely rotten."

"I'll see how I feel later. But I'd better not plan to join you."

"I quite agree. Perhaps we can make it later in the week."

Alone again, Hux tried to quiet the hum and crackle of his mind long enough to make sense of what had happened last night. But the merest thought of Clark brought back the image of his head, with that black gummy mass, and with it a sharp stab of unendurable pain. He would have to wait until the presence had receded somewhat before he could begin to see it for what it was. Meanwhile, he could only hold on tightly, follow—with as few deviations as possible—the routine of his work, and hope that he could survive the day—and then the next and the next—without splitting down the middle like a chunk of pine wood under an axe.

Picking up the article, he saw that it was written by an assistant librarian at Mississippi State and dealt with university and college library holdings in the Tennessee-Mississippi-Arkansas area. From the opening paragraph it was clear that the author was deploring not only the relative meagerness of the resources but also their scattering and the lack of coordination among holders. Newbold Jenkins had scrawled across the top: "Is this something we might want to get involved in?" *Mississippi,* Hux thought as he put down the article without reading any more. *Mississippi* . . . That on this of all mornings he should be handed an article by a Mississippian was too much to bear. He was angry at Newbold Jenkins, as if the man had deliberately scraped the great wound that had been opened last night. But a moment later he was trembling again, having caught sight of Clark's raised head, and he glanced wildly around the office and toward the open door leading to the little room where Blossom Goldstein, his secretary, sat typing. I can call Blossom if I have to, he told himself— if things get really bad. Reassured, he was able to get back to work on the Cincinnati report.

Though he felt better after lunch and was able to concentrate sporadically on his work, Hux, for the first time in months, dreaded the thought of going home alone to his apartment. Whom could he have dinner with, spend the evening with? He was too jumpy, too shattered still, to endure the idea of going out on the town with any of the unmarried men around the office. What he needed was an old friend—or better yet, a married couple who would invite him to dinner. But systematically, over the years, he had alienated the couples to whom he and Louise, jointly, had been close; Louise still saw them, but they had all given up on Hux. And as for new male friendships . . . he had had no heart for them after the death of Clark. The old friends that he might still claim were all in Princeton or the South—people whom he had scarcely seen or written to in a decade.

In desperation he thought of calling up Louise and inviting himself to dinner there; he might even ask to sleep over in the little room—once a maid's room—where they had often put up guests. But what excuse could he give for such an extraordinary request? And what made him think that Louise—even if she was not going out or having company—would permit such a thing? After all, they had quarreled sharply over Tony's schooling at their last meeting. He could hardly throw himself on her mercy and tell her that he was afraid to go home because of a nightmare!

Hux called his secretary and asked her to reserve a single room for him at the Algonquin or, failing that, the Salisbury. He was prepared to pay dearly for his panic. He would treat himself to a good dinner, go to a movie (maybe a porno film), get moderately drunk at Charley O's or Michael's Pub, and hope to cheat his insomnia in the snug safety of a hotel room where no one was likely to have seen a dead friend.

This decision had a calming effect upon Hux. For the first time that day he was able to approach rather than run away from the question of what had happened. During the long, slow seconds of its existence, the figure of Clark had been more real, more densely tangible, than any actual person he had met or spoken to all the previous day. How, he wondered, could any nightmare or hallucination be so *bodily?* Once, in 1967, he had, despite Louise's disapproval, taken LSD in the company of a City College psychologist who had conducted many trips; but even during his most fantastic visions, a part of him had known that the things he was seeing and hearing—no matter how "real" in their completeness and texture—were merely that: visions. But in Clark's presence last night, there had not been, even slightly, the saving sense of a discrepancy between what he saw and what was actually on the bed. Clark's *presentness* had been total. Even now, as he allowed the image an instant's reappearance before shutting it off, Hux felt a deep vibration of fear run through him, like the plucking of a cello string. In his fright he wondered if he was experiencing a long-delayed after-effect of the LSD, signaling the approach of a still worse trip to come after all these years.

Hux could think of nothing that had happened recently to remind him of Clark, much less to account for the sudden ripping-open of the old grief. For the pain he had felt after the first subsiding of the terror was as raw and open and seeping as it had been a week after Clark's death, when the numbing shock of the news had worn off. He had experienced it again, intensified by rage and frustration, at the time of Claiborne Herne's acquittal nearly eight months later. But that last flare-up had ended it, abruptly. From then on Hux had thought as little as possible about Clark and the whole tumultuous summer and its crazy aftermath; he had left Princeton, moved with his wife and baby to New York, and raised a high barrier, like an electrified fence, across the road leading back to Mississippi. The annual exchange of bland Christmas card messages with Linda Helmholtz (now remarried) was the only reminder of his dead friend that he permitted. Even Louise had learned to avoid the subject, though she missed Princeton and considered the move to New York a mistake.

Hux's reverie led him nowhere. He was very tired. Suddenly Clark seemed close again, so dangerously close that Hux got up from his desk and hurried down the corridor toward the elevators. After several minutes of pacing and a visit to the men's room, he returned to his office, assuring himself that there was no such thing as a fatal nightmare. . . .

That evening, Hux did not go to a movie, pornographic or otherwise. Instead he went to the New York Public Library, which was open until ten, and spent several hours poring over the bound volumes of *Time* for the years 1963 and 1964.

Chapter Four

In the days that followed Clark did not reappear. But his presence was like the gray shadow of an owl on Hux's shoulder, something to be glimpsed if only Hux could turn his head fast enough. Except for that first night at the Algonquin, Hux slept at the apartment but did not get home until nearly eleven each evening, at which time he would drink one beer and go to bed exhausted. While Clark did not recognizably enter his dreams, some residue from that first appearance kept stirring them, night after night, into a bubbling ferment, which alternated with hours of staring insomnia. The combination left poor Hux sour-tongued and red-eyed every morning, almost too weak to get out of bed. Yet he did not miss a single day's work at the Foundation. He took a shower every morning, put on fresh clothes, and continued to keep his suits and shoes in perfect order; his fastidiousness about his person even increased, if that was possible. The mess in his apartment remained much as it was, despite one Sunday afternoon devoted to straightening up.

At the office his irritability was beginning to create problems. A week or so after the flare-up with Newbold Jenkins, he astonished himself by giving Marty Chaikin, the Foundation's business manager, a furious bawling-out for coming into his office merely to waste time. Marty, who was a genial waster of his colleagues' time, told Hux to go to hell and stalked out; a moment later Hux rushed after him, effusive with apologies, which Marty accepted. But a few days later Hux offended his only black colleague, Oliver Marsden, by telling him that his report on the Howard University Library Fund read as if it had been written by Henry James in his final phase. When Oliver left the office in a prissy huff, Fran Duffy, who had come in with him, remained behind to say, "What's the point of hurting Ollie that way? Obviously I'm the one you're really angry at. Don't take out your hostility on Ollie."

Hux was again furious. Ever since their affair, now more than two years past, he and Fran had maintained a polite and businesslike reticence. He now met her eye—something he regularly avoided doing—and said, "That may well be the most purely egotistical remark

I've ever heard." As his anger soared, this attractive and ordinarily pleasant woman became loathsome to him—dried up and shrill, her freckles disfiguring, her red dress all wrong. . . . No wonder his penis finally refused to go through the motions! "Look," he continued, rising from his swivel chair and leaning dramatically across his desk like an outraged executive in an office comedy, "distasteful as this may be to your pride, I happened to be criticizing Ollie's prose style. What I said had nothing to do with you. I don't waste my thoughts or feelings on you and I haven't for years. Now get out of my office."

"Larry, you're disgusting. And pitiful. A pitiful human being." She left.

On the next day he wrote abject notes to both of them. His remorse was acute—and sincere; he could expect no forgiveness. His apology was accepted grudgingly by Oliver and not at all by Fran, who never even acknowledged his note.

All three of his offended colleagues had unwittingly intruded upon Hux when he was in the grip of a new preoccupation that absorbed his vacant hours at the office and made him yearn for the coming of five o'clock. Each afternoon, as soon as he was out of the building, he would hurry down Fifth Avenue to the New York Public Library, his excitement mounting as he approached the lion-flanked steps to the palace on Forty-second Street. At the library he would put in several hours filing call slips and picking up books and periodicals when his number flashed on the screen in the reading room. Sometimes he forgot to go out to dinner, contenting himself with a quick sandwich after the reading room closed. The object of this research was to recover, in as much detail as possible, the events leading up to the rifle shot that had smashed through the skull of his friend. Hux had no clear idea of what was to be gained by this recovery, for he did not think of it as therapy or as a way of understanding his nightmare or of arming himself against its recurrence. What he urgently wanted was to get closer to Clark and to that period in his own life when he had seemed to himself most fully alive. This blind need was enough to turn him into another Public Library crank, a figure as noteworthy, in his highly groomed way, as the wheezing old man in a ragged overcoat who, night after night, sat reading eighteenth-century copies of the *Gentleman's Magazine*; or the thin, gray-haired young woman with darting eyes who sat guarding a pile of unopened books on weaving, lace-making, embroidery, and dyeing. Searching through old copies of *Time, Newsweek, The Nation, The New Republic,* and *Life,* poring over microfilmed columns of the *New*

York Times until his aching eyes gave way, tracking down the exclamatory bulletins and newsletters from CORE, SNCC, the NAACP, and other acronymic organizations, reading through the books on the Movement—what an amazing number of them had been written!—Hux gradually reassembled that whole incredible era, beginning with the Supreme Court decision on segregated schools in 1954 and extending to the late sixties, when "Whitey" was effectively excluded from the radical wing of the Movement. Thus he went far behind and well beyond what remained the incandescent center of his attention—that climactic summer of 1964 which had begun for him with the birth of Tony and ended with the shattering news from Tupelo.

He was disturbed by how much he had forgotten. For he had not only blocked off the road leading back to Mississippi but had apparently taken several deep swallows from some jug of oblivion—not enough to eradicate the big names and the great, recurring climaxes but sufficient to wipe out almost everything that had given the period its living texture. He had remembered, of course, the martyrdom of Chaney, Goodman, and Schwerner but had forgotten the names of that unforgettable sheriff of Neshoba County and his henchman; their faces now populated the long stretches of his insomnia, staring back at him, trying to find voices. Byron de la Beckwith he remembered but not the men charged with the murder of Mrs. Violet Liuzzo. The accounts of the Birmingham church bombing were as full of surprises as if he were reading them for the first time; the little girls in their Sunday dresses had become confused in his memory with the children killed in the Hattiesburg schoolbus bombing. Montgomery, Selma, Prince Edward County, Neshoba County, Meridian—these seemed as remote in their reverberations as had the names of the great Civil War battles—Antietam, Chancellorsville, Cold Harbor—in Hux's Southern boyhood. All the factional quarrels within CORE that had once so preoccupied Clark and Hux remained unfleshed, shadowy. After two weeks of this nightly reading Hux was able to put together most of the buried bones of the period; yet he still could not encase them in skin and muscle or fill them with moving viscera. He could not summon up the look of Mississippi—beyond something vaguely green and piny; it was as though he had never set foot in that state.

The gray owl perched on Hux's shoulder was no longer weightless; heavy now, it dug its claws into his flesh but still whispered nothing that he could understand. As he continued to read, Hux began to brood over the monstrous failure of justice. There had been so many victims—literally hundreds of blacks, several score whites—and they were mostly forgotten. The felonies against them had largely gone unpunished. Even when sentences had been handed out, they were hopelessly incommensurate with the magnitude of the crimes: "Sentenced to three years in prison and fined two thousand dollars for violations of the victim's civil rights" instead of, "Sentenced to death for murder coldly premeditated and viciously carried out." Could anyone claim that James Earl Ray was undergoing adequate punishment? And what about his backers—the oil millionaires or Atlanta businessmen or whoever it was that had hired him? The FBI had not, so far as Hux could tell, shown even a perfunctory interest in tracking them down; it even seemed possible to him that the FBI itself had been involved in the assassination. The injustice sickened him. And yet Hux had always regarded himself as a liberal opposed to capital punishment and would certainly have voted for its total abolition.

There was one area of research that he kept postponing—only dimly aware that he was doing so. Though he had now acquired an almost day-by-day familiarity with everything leading up to that August day in Tupelo, Hux could not bring himself to read about the shooting itself—or about the arrest, trial, and acquittal of Dr. Herne. He rushed headlong to the very edge of the bloodsoaked ground, then backed away and skirted it, rejoining the main road at some distance beyond. Hux knew that sooner or later he would want to take a long look, but for the moment he shrank from it, as if it would entail the close-up inspection of a rotting corpse. He did not want to get close to Clark by that route. Instead, he broadened his reading to include Frantz Fanon and Eldridge Cleaver and imagined that he could now glimpse what the murderous rage of a black must be like.

For all his reading, he felt no nearer to Clark—or to himself as he had once been—than before this immersion. Coming home from the library on a Thursday night, Hux realized that he was lonelier than he had ever been before—bereft of wife and son, bereft of all friends. Overwhelmed with self-pity, he changed into his old bathrobe and fetched a beer from the refrigerator; then he sat in his chair, closed his eyes, and *willed* Clark to reappear. Beneath his close-fitting casque of dull gold hair, his forehead was cut by lines of anguished concentration. *Come,* he thought. *Take any form you like—this time I won't be frightened—but come.* After some moments his brows relaxed their frown, his lips parted, and Hux opened his eyes to the familiar bleakness of his room. He was guiltily aware of the element of play-acting in his invocation; the emotion was too much like what he had been able to induce when performing the part of sorrowful King Richard for the Carolina Playmakers. But the pain was real enough. . . .

22

Suddenly he was seized by the desire to go to Mississippi again, to seek out the people who had worked closely with Clark during those last weeks, to visit Tupelo, to hear, at first hand, an eye-witness account of Clark's death. The idea excited him so much that he jumped from his chair; then, angry with himself, he tried to put it out of his mind, for he knew that it could keep him from getting to sleep.

While he was showering the next morning, Hux remembered the Xeroxed copy of the article on literary holdings in the Mississippi area—the one that Newbold Jenkins had handed him on the morning after Clark's reappearance. Presumably it was still on his desk, buried beneath other documents in his in-box. As he remembered the article, the problems it raised were exactly the sort in which the Morrow Foundation might be expected to take an interest. Might it not be possible to set up a conference, funded by the Foundation, to assess not only library holdings but the entire range of academic resources—laboratories, computers, etc.—of various institutions within, say, a hundred-and-fifty-mile radius of Oxford, Mississippi? By setting such a limit, he would not have to involve himself with the big Tennessee universities to the northeast or Tulane and Louisiana State to the south; he would have a nice, compact territory radiating out from the University of Mississippi—"Ole Miss" herself—at Oxford, a territory that encompassed all the sacred places (and probably most of the people) he might want to see during his secret pilgrimage.

Once again his energies hummed. The next morning Hux, after a troublesome search, found the article. It was all that he had hoped for. Consulting a handbook on higher education, he located eight institutions, white and black, within the chosen area and proceeded to draft a letter which he would send to the president of each. In the official jargon of such communications, Hux proposed that the conference be tentatively scheduled for mid-October, 1974, and that the aim of the regional assessment should be to identify existing resources, to explore the means of increasing their coordination, and to initiate, on a regional basis, a campaign to attract capital gifts in areas of special weakness. Assuming an interest in such a conference, Hux further proposed that he make an exploratory visit to the various campuses in late May and early June to discuss details with the appropriate administrators. When he had finished his draft and had read it over, Hux laughed aloud at the contrast between the high-minded language of the proposal and the secret, personal whim from which it had sprung.

In writing to the presidents without first clearing the plan with Newbold Jenkins and the Administrative Council, Hux was of course far exceeding his authority. But he did not care. He wanted to receive at least two favorable responses to his letter before involving Jenkins. The director, he was certain, would not only go along but applaud Hux on his initiative. Project Mississippi was under way.

Chapter Five

Dressed in the suit which he wore on business trips to Memphis—a dude's suit of burnt-orange shantung with flaring lapels—Rooney Lee bounded up the outside steps to his apartment. There he found his wife, Vicky, slumped in a corner of the white vinyl sofa, watching the Johnny Carson show in color. Except for floppy green slippers she was entirely nude, her huge breasts pendulous over her belly, her crotch totally concealed between the overhang of her belly and the spread of her great brown thighs. She had obviously not expected Rooney home so soon, for he did not permit her to loll around naked now that she had gained so much weight, following the birth of Janey Sue. Without a word he took the pink wrapper dangling over one arm of the sofa and flung it across her. Then, after turning off the television set, he went to the mirrored bar in the corner of the room and poured himself a stiff drink of Canadian Club and 7-Up. Since Rooney was not ordinarily a drinking man, Vicky eyed him appraisingly for several moments before saying, "Dr. Claib'n call right after you lef'."

Rooney spun in her direction. "Yeah? He want you to come over?"

"Want to know is you out for the evenin'. Told him I thought you was. Sound like he mighty drunk."

"Mind your own business." Crouching in his chair, Rooney looked up at his wife sideways. "What time he call?"

"'Bout two hours ago."

Rooney glanced at the ruby dial of a gold wristwatch massive as a manacle.

Clutching her pink wrapper in front of her like a towel, Vicky rose from the sofa. Behind, her lustrous buttocks and thighs wobbled independently with each step she took toward the kitchen. When she came back she was wearing the wrapper and holding in one hand a cellophane-wrapped package of chocolate cupcakes and in the other a can of Dr. Pepper. "They still givin' you a hard time in Memphis?" she asked.

Rooney merely grunted.

"They want more money?"

"None of your fuckin' business."

Vicky subsided into her corner, put the can down on the coffee table, and tore open the wrapping of the cupcakes. "Lord, you make me sick an' tired! When you goin' to stop messin' round with that no-good Memphis crowd? Ain't nothin' good gonna come of it, no more than in De-troit. Same thing. You jus' git in trouble again, same as up there."

"Shut your mouth, Vicky."

She ignored him. "You still payin' them off up in De-troit, ain't you?" After stuffing a whole cupcake into her mouth, she chewed with the cheek motions of a child trying to cope with too much bubble gum. Then she licked the crumbs and smudge of chocolate from her lips and said, "This here business right here plenty good if'n you jus' settle down an' help Maddox straighten it out. No need foolin' round with them bad niggers up in Memphis. You ain't got the talent for that big-time stuff—jus' land you in jail, tha's all—you an' your big ideas. You could forgit all about them an' stop bleedin' that ol' drunk an'—"

Rooney sprang across the room and slapped from Vicky's hand the cupcake she was about to eat. Then he slapped her hard across the face, saying, "How many times I tol' you not to talk disrespectful 'bout Dr. Claib'n? You never understand what that ol' man mean to me and you never will. Next time I ain't just goin' to slap. You hear?"

She looked up at him, rubbing her cheek. Her face was still small and pretty, the face of a doll's head above the vast cushioning of flesh. A sigh that was half a sob rippled across her frame, and her fingers began to dig for the last cupcake in the package.

"You hear?" Rooney half raised his hand.

Popping the cake into the safety of her mouth, Vicky closed her eyes and nodded.

"Now you go on into the bedroom. I got a phone call I got to make if it ain't too late."

Chapter Six

Carrying her cup of coffee—her third that morning—Isabelle Herne went to the living-room window and looked out toward the road. She was dressed for church in a blue-and-white-flowered print which hung gracelessly over her wide hips and sunken bosom. Without illusion as to her face and figure, she nevertheless took pains with her appearance on Sunday mornings, pinning a garnet brooch of her mother's to the front of her dress, carefully combing and parting her hair, which was still mostly brown despite her seventy years, applying a modest touch of rouge to each plump cheek, a dab of coral lipstick to her lips. The effect would have been jaunty, even brave, except for the ineradicable sadness of her eyes. From the window she could not see the big white car she had expected and dreaded, but she felt no relief—it could be lurking just out of sight. In the opposite direction she saw the McCutchin family piling into their car to go to the Baptist church across town—a great cheerful brood as gaily decked out as if it had been Easter Sunday. Glancing at her gold wristwatch with its black band, she realized that she would be late for church unless she left the house in no more than eight minutes. She dreaded going, dreaded leaving Claiborne, but she never permitted herself to be late for church, which was a good fifteen minutes' walk down Granada Street. Isabelle finished her coffee and felt a sharp craving for another cup; it was her one addiction, bad for her sleep, bad for her nerves. She would allow herself just a splash in the bottom of her cup. . . .

Returning from the kitchen, Isabelle paused at the open door of her brother's bedroom. Dr. Herne was sitting in his armchair by the open window, through which streamed the morning light and a breeze that swayed the white muslin curtains. The room was in perfect order. As he did every morning, her brother had made the huge four-poster mahogany bed, pulling the white fringed spread tight as a drum, drawing it over and under the pillows with a precision Isabelle had never mastered. He was wearing a long-sleeved blue shirt, open at the collar, and the trousers to a seersucker suit. With a book propped open against his crossed knee, his black-rimmed glasses astride his great beak of a nose, he looked absorbed, almost serene. *His color's better*, thought Isabelle, who lived in constant fear that his fiery complexion presaged a stroke. Seeing him thus, she began to wonder if she could possibly have misheard the telephone conversation of two days ago—a conversation that confirmed the menace she had felt from the moment of Rooney's return. No, her hearing aid played many tricks on her—there was much that she failed to catch—but there was no mistaking that hoarsely whispered summons she had overheard when she picked up the kitchen extension. She had not dreamed it. Telephone conversations often came through more clearly than the voice of a person addressing her face to face. Furthermore, she had observed something mischievous and slightly furtive in his look—always in the past a signal that one of Rooney's visits was impending.

Dr. Herne raised his face and smiled. "Spyin' on me, are you? Isn't it time you were leavin' for church?"

"Brother, come with me," she suddenly pleaded, putting down her cup and saucer with a small clatter on the marble dresser top just inside the door. "Come with me. Just this once. It's the most *beautiful* mornin'."

Still smiling, he shook his head.

"Won't you please come, Brother? It would mean so much to me." Her thoughts were racing. Did she dare risk his fury by not going? Could she pretend to be suddenly ill? No, he would never believe that. He would be outraged. He would order her out of the house. . . . "It might make all the difference," she added weakly. "Please come."

Claiborne Herne shifted his gaze sideways to the rosewood clock on the wall. "You'd better get started if you don't want to sprint all the way. Now that would be a sight, wouldn't it? Isabelle Herne with her skirts tucked up, sprintin' down Granada Street like a gazelle." He laughed.

Her brother's unkindness made Isabelle wince. He was so often this way before one of Rooney's visits. "I'm leavin' now," she said quietly. "I've plenty of time to walk."

When she came out of the house, now wearing a wide-brimmed navy-blue hat and carrying a white straw handbag, Isabelle saw that the car was there—parked up the street in the vacant stretch beyond the Hutchinsons' house, the last on Granada. Hating the car, she had barely glanced in its direction, and she could not be sure that she had really seen that mushroom crown of black hair silhouetted between the windshield and the back window. Facing now toward the center of town, she set off at a fast pace that was converted by her broad hips and short legs into a kind of waddle. For some time she could see nothing through the bright shimmering of tears.

Isabelle felt helpless and desperate—as if she were standing alone at the end of a dock, unable to swim, watching her brother struggling with a leg cramp in deep water. But Claiborne never called for help; he would push her away even if she managed to reach him. And he was quite unreachable: stubborn and perverse in his wretchedness. As she walked on, she left the new tract houses at the outer end of Granada and entered the old, settled part of the street, with its wide lawns, big trees, and white frame houses. Now she walked with her head lowered, to avoid the greeting of any churchgoing acquaintance she might meet. A quick flash of memory made Isabelle shake her head, as if to drive it away because she could not bear the contrast between its poignant sweetness and the situation she now faced.

But the memory persisted. She was walking to church with Claiborne from the old house on the first Sunday after she returned from her teaching job in New Orleans. It had been a warm, brilliant day of late spring like today. Old friends greeted them, full of questions. And Isabelle, her pride blurting through her shyness, had answered them, saying, yes, she had come back for good, just as Brother had. Alhambra, they both realized, was their true home. Claiborne had given up his practice in Memphis to set up practice here, and she had come back to run the house for him and to take up their joint life where it had diverged a dozen years before. She remembered the *kindliness* of the inquiries, the warmth of the welcome. And the tactfulness: there had been no reference to the divorce, no questions about Janice. Of course the whole town knew the story anyway, but the tactfulness had been genuine all the same. And she remembered the way Brother, who said little, kept beaming down at her from his great height, letting her do all the talking, all the explaining. Though the shyness was still a torture, she had faced their old friends—and the future itself—with a happiness and confidence so exalted that she became a little afraid—afraid that God might humble her.

And had He? No, her faith made no room for a God that played such mean tricks. The humbling had come all right, but it was not His doing. God was still there, just where He had always been, high above the curious workings of human destiny but an infinite resource to those who could reach up to Him. He had been there during that good time when she had been so sure that she could help her brilliant brother—at last free from his dreadful marriage—fulfill in Alhambra (in a quiet, *useful* way) the great promise everyone had felt in him; and He was there now, though she was too weak and discouraged to lift up her hand for His help. Her hope had been foolish to begin with, a childish fantasy, full of a big sister's yearning. Still, for nearly a decade things had gone well enough to sustain her hope that even better times lay ahead. The trial had ruined everything; but for several years before that there were certain signs which she had been slow in recognizing. Now nothing worked. The move to the new house, which she hoped might free Claiborne from old associations, had not helped at all. Her only recourse was to protract the quiet times (which were bad enough) as long as possible to avoid the abrupt plunging into worse times, which seemed bottomless. Now they were plunging again. Rooney was back. The "prayer meeting" had no doubt begun at home.

Isabelle could hardly bring herself to think about Rooney and his transformation. Part of her still saw him as the timid little colored boy who hid behind his mother when she came to pick up or deliver the wash. Or as the bright and ambitious young Negro, so grateful and polite, whom her brother had coached in writing and math and had helped send through college. She and Brother had attended Rooney's wedding to Vicky Covington—the only white people in that little wooden church. How could he have become the smirking presence she most dreaded in the entire world? She had no real idea what went on at those "prayer meetings," as Brother had once referred to them with a sly look that sent a shiver through her. She knew that Rooney brought Vicky along—and that money was involved. But beyond that she did not want to know. In her imagination, which she could usually check before it broke into a wild gallop, the meetings had something to do with blasphemy, with a mocking of the Lord; the money, she imagined, went to one of those evil cults—the kind in California that she had read about. But these were wild imaginings. She really knew only that her brother seemed worse, much worse, for days after one of the meetings. That they were held on Sunday mornings during the hour of divine worship made them all the more intolerable to her. Though a modern Presbyterian who was not even a Calvinist, much less a fundamentalist, a woman who believed in the goodness of God and had no taste for (and little real belief in) the Devil and hellfire, Isabelle was afraid that even the most loving and merciful of Gods would not forever tolerate such a mockery of His Name—*if* indeed (a very large *if*) the meetings involved blasphemy. She still clung to the idea that if she

could get her brother to go back to church *just once,* all might somehow be well again. But Claiborne had not set foot in their family
church for years. . . .

Claiborne had been better while Rooney was in Detroit—there
could be no doubt about that. He had drunk less (though still far
more than was good for him), had seemed less troubled and angry,
had not sunk into one of those awful silences. And for some time
after Rooney's return she had felt that he was struggling against a
resumption of the old ways, that he might be able to hold out. But
that phone call on Friday . . .

The gloriousness of the day mocked her. The worn brick walk at
her feet was dappled with sunlight; whiffs of honeysuckle and cape
jasmine and mimosa reached her from the iron fences and shrubber-
ies of the wide old lawns that she passed.

Her arm was touched, and Isabelle looked up, a startled little girl
of seventy. It was Ben Morgan, her family doctor, and his wife, Stella, both dressed for church.

"Are you all right, Isabelle? Is something the matter?"

In her confusion she became voluble. "Oh, Ben, you took me by
surprise! How are you, Stella my dear? My goodness, I was in a real
deep study! I wish I could say I was thinkin' holy thoughts, but I
wasn't. My mind was somewhere miles and miles away, goodness
knows where. And here I am, practically at the church door and not
even aware of it!"

Chapter Seven

During the week after he launched Project Mississippi, Hux added a new item to his secret agenda—something that in the weeks following came to dominate his whole fantasy of the pilgrimage. On Monday evening he had rejoined the cranks in the reading room at the Forty-second Street library, ready now to explore what he had been postponing. Unwilling to trust his eyes to the scale and shimmer of microfilm, he filed a slip for the bound copies of the *New York Times* for August 27, 28, and 29, 1964, and for the following Sunday edition. There was a long delay, during which Hux had time to observe a young black who was sitting two places away. Sharp-featured and thin, the young man had a look of ascetic concentration which was offset by the elegance of his tan suit and bright orange shirt and the expensive styling of his closely trimmed afro. A scholar, thought Hux, observing the stack of books and periodicals at the man's place—an instructor from City College or even Columbia, probably a sociologist, maybe an urban planner. . . . The book on the top of the stack looked familiar, but it was at such an angle that Hux could not make out the title on its jacket. When at last his number flashed on the screen, Hux—by now intensely curious—walked slowly past the frowning, hollow-cheeked reader and saw that the book was Frantz Fanon's *The Wretched of the Earth. Aha! a terrorist*, he thought, excitedly revising his earlier speculation—*a fellow conspirator.*

Returning to his seat with the awkward and heavy volumes, Hux impatiently flipped the huge pages until suddenly Clark's face sprang out at him—exactly as it had in the general store of the little village of Holderness, New Hampshire, to which Hux had rushed after hearing the news on the radio at the Squam Lake cottage. The photograph was one that had been taken to accompany a piece on his interview with Kwame Nkrumah which Clark had written the previous winter for the *Princeton Alumni Weekly*. How young Clark looked! The photograph had transformed the intellectual and fiercely argumentative graduate student of twenty-six into a college athlete posing stiffly in suit and tie, his normally rumpled hair wet-looking and plastered down, fresh from a shower at the gym. Hux read with little emotion the front-page account and its continuation; there were no surprises for him—he remembered it all. The only part that stirred him was the reference to the unidentified assailant "described by witnesses as a tall, middle-aged white man who walked calmly back to his car after the shooting and drove away before anyone in the confused audience was able to pursue him." Looking up from the page and closing his eyes, Hux very clearly saw the man, later to be identified as Claiborne Herne. He saw the long, arrogant stride, the rifle held with its muzzle down, as if the man had been out shooting woodchucks. But no man out hunting varmints would have been wearing a blue seersucker suit and a tie—and that, for some reason, was how Hux's imagination insisted upon dressing him.

The next day's edition announced the arrest of Dr. Claiborne Herne, fifty-five, a physician and leading citizen of Alhambra, Mississippi. "Herne, who was known to possess a large collection of firearms, surrendered peaceably to state police at his family home in Alhambra this morning. At his arraignment at the Tallahatchie County Courthouse he issued a statement denying his guilt and expressing confidence that his name would be 'cleared in no time flat.'" Again Hux felt a thrill of emotion that was stronger than anything he experienced in reading the rest of the account, which was mostly devoted to tributes to Clark from the president of Princeton, the dean of the Woodrow Wilson School, Clark's thesis advisor (who had also been Hux's) and various co-workers of Clark's who had been present at the rally in Tupelo. One of the co-workers was Franklin Mosby, described as a young black from Laurel, Mississippi, active in SNCC, who was quoted as saying, "Clark is the dead but living brother of every freedom-loving black man and woman in this state, a man whose living spirit we got to rally behind and fight harder than ever." Another was Arnold Bier—also a graduate student from Princeton and member of CORE—who said that "Clark was our brains and our guts. We have no choice but to pick up the pieces and carry on."

Bier's name was the only surprise for Hux. He had forgotten that Arnold had been actually on the scene. The unfortunate phrasing of the statement made Hux smile bleakly; it was typical of Arnold, whom Hux had never liked. There was no need to go all the way to Mississippi to question Arnold Bier, who presumably was living right here in New York. But Hux was in no hurry.

When he finished, Hux closed the volume and rested his arms upon it as he leaned forward. He was trying to bring back details of Clark's funeral in St. Joseph, Missouri, which he had attended, flying out from Boston to St. Louis and back within twenty-four hours. Almost nothing had registered upon his numbed, nearly schizophrenic state of mind at the time. He could not recall whether Linda had worn a black dress or not. He thought he could glimpse the fat-cheeked, Germanic face of Clark's father, a Lutheran minister. Everything else was lost—the service itself, Clark's mother, the meals . . . everything. Two months later, Hux had moved his audience (and himself) to tears by reading aloud Clark's last letter to him from Mississippi at a memorial service for Clark in the Princeton University Chapel; this he could remember very well.

Thus far there had been little that he had not known or anticipated. But when he turned to the next day's paper, he found a background article on Dr. Herne which he tore through as avidly as if he had unexpectedly come across an obituary of his own father. Not only the phrasing but the details and the implications seemed totally new to him; yet he must have read it before—surely he had read everything. The article described Dr. Herne as one of Alhambra's most respected citizens, a member of a prominent family that had owned land in Tallahatchie County and the Delta since the 1840s. As a local doctor he had devoted much of his time to charity work among the Negroes, by whom he was said to be liked and trusted. He was well known also for his work with the white youth of the community, for whom he had organized a service and discussion club just after World War II. Conservative but essentially nonpolitical, he had managed, despite considerable pressure, to avoid association with the White Citizens Council or other anti-desegregation groups that had sprung up following the Supreme Court decision of 1954; it was considered unthinkable that a man of Dr. Herne's background and enlightened social behavior might have belonged to the Klan. Hence the astonishment that had been voiced throughout Alhambra—by detractors (who considered him too "liberal," perhaps "soft on Communism") as well as by much more numerous admirers—when he was arrested for the shooting of Clark Helmholtz. It was said that the arrest had been made on the basis of an identification of Dr. Herne by two eye-witnesses of the shooting, both black, whose names were being withheld and who were under the special protection of the FBI and federal marshals. . . .

The photograph accompanying the article was unsatisfactory. It gave no more than an indistinct impression of a gaunt-looking man with black eyebrows and a beaked nose. Hux read no more that evening, but the article and the photograph lodged themselves in his imagination and kept returning to him during intervals of sleeplessness during the night.

During the next few sessions at the library, Hux carried out as full a research job on Claiborne Herne as the materials allowed. There was little to read during the months between the arrest (and subsequent release on bail) and the trial, but just before the trial began that April, there was a spate of new material. Hux went through every scrap that he could find, not only in the *Times* but in the Jackson and Memphis papers as well, and in the weekly news magazines. There was no doubt in his mind about the conclusiveness of the evidence and the travesty of the acquittal. But something was missing, something that nagged at his memory from nine years before—a clearer image than any of the photographs had provided, some revealing bit of information. At last, on Friday, he found what he was looking for: a two-page spread of photographs, with an accompanying text, that had been published in *Look* just before the opening of the trial. Here at last, in a full-page, color photograph, was the tall man in the blue seersucker suit—shown standing with his sister on the porch of their Alhambra home.

Although Hux had obviously seen the picture before, he had no recollection of the unmarried sister, Isabelle—a squat little woman whose arm was resting in the crook of her brother's and who was gazing up at him. On the opposite page, one photograph showed the famous collection of firearms that occupied one wall of Dr. Herne's bedroom; others showed the attorneys for the prosecution and defense and the minister of the local Presbyterian church, who was quoted in the text. Isabelle Herne was quoted too. "I have absolute faith in my brother's innocence," she had said. "Nobody who knows Brother could imagine for one single instant that he could do a horrible thing like that." Like Dr. Herne, Isabelle was reported to be active in church work and community affairs. She had once taught Latin in a girls' school in New Orleans.

Hux stared for a long time at the two figures standing on the porch. The assassin of his friend stared back, the look in his hooded blue eyes as scornful, as defiant, as if Hux had been one of the reporters hounding him with questions. What arrogance! Trembling slightly, Hux raised his eyes for a moment and looked around the reading room, taking several deep breaths to allay the emotional storm that had burst upon him. When he returned to a calmer scrutiny, he had to admit his disappointment in the house that served as a backdrop for the killer. The columned grandeur of an antebellum

35

mansion would have struck him as more appropriate than the roomy but dowdy-looking Victorian house with the gingerbread scrollwork that reminded him of his paternal grandparents' house in the little town of Warrenton, North Carolina. It suited the sister but not the brother.

Hux's gaze was drawn again to Dr. Herne's eyes, which were glass-clear and pale even in the reduced scale of the photograph. He could imagine the raising of the rifle and the narrowing of one eye and closing of the other as the fatal intersection of hairlines was imposed upon the left side of Clark's skull. He saw the contortion of the features, the scornful mouth gaping open in one corner, as the hooked index finger began its slow pull on the trigger. . . .

Taking a ball-point pen from the inside of his jacket, Hux placed a tiny blue dot between the eyes. Then he pressed harder, and the pen point went right through the page.

That night Hux walked all the way from the library to his apartment beneath a cottony sky glowing pink with the lights of midtown. He hoped that the exercise might slow the whirl of his mind before insomnia made it spin even faster. Weaving in and out of the crowd of young moviegoers sauntering arm in arm along Third Avenue, he was as cut off from their easygoing dalliance as a foreign agent with an appointment to keep. What isolated him was a fantasy that had sprung upon him at the library, after he had returned his books to the desk and was idly looking at the prints in the great third-floor hall—a fantasy thrilling in its seductiveness. The details were still in the process of shaping and clothing themselves, but the central action was already clear. Hux saw himself admitted to the Hernes' parlor in that roomy old house. He saw himself sitting across from Claiborne Herne and his sister, smiling at them, perhaps holding a cup of tea or coffee on his knee while he made some plausible excuse for calling on them. He would ingratiate himself to this aging brother and sister, charm them with his responsiveness and sympathy. Having won their confidence, he would be asked to come back, and he would return as often as his official business let him, bringing them little presents, establishing himself as their devoted young friend. He would worm his way into their hearts, make them love him as if he were their adopted son! Then, when the right moment came, when he was alone with Dr. Herne, he would reveal himself as Clark's closest friend, flash a photograph of Clark before the doctor's horrified eyes, and—

Here the fantasy diverged. Would he lay a curse on Dr. Herne, wishing upon him a disgusting death and eternal damnation? Or would he pick up Clark's photograph, turn on his heel, and stalk out of the house? What *would* he do? Hux did not yet know. For the moment he knew only the blissful excitement of picturing himself face to face with Clark's murderer. He had never seen a murderer, much less been in the company of one. What sort of excuses did a murderer—especially an upper-class murderer, a person of some refinement and (presumably) some conscience—make to himself? Had Dr. Herne been able to maintain the illusion that he had shot Clark in a good cause? Could Hux get to know Claiborne Herne—test him, probe the secret recesses? It was a dizzying idea—nearly as intoxicating as the prospect of revealing himself to the terrified and guilty old man at the end.

Of course, Hux told himself, the whole scheme was crazy. What made him think that he would ever gain access to the house? Surely the doctor was a suspicious, guarded man, not about to welcome a young stranger (so Hux at the moment saw himself) into his house, no matter how ingratiating the fellow might be. Hux was not even sure that Dr. Herne was still alive; even if the doctor's death had been reported—and it might well not have been, assuming that it had occurred naturally—Hux could very easily have missed it. So strong was Hux's fantasy that when he got home he went straight to the telephone and dialed information for northern Mississippi. The operator, whose voice reached him like the parody of a slow-talking, sweet-talking Southerner, confirmed that there was a doctor C. B. Herne listed in Alhambra; she gave Hux the number, which he did not bother to write down. So that was settled. . . .

But, with his fantasy spinning faster than ever, Hux knew that sleep would be impossible unless he could do something to break the whirl. Putting on fresh socks and loafers but otherwise dressed as he had been at the office, he rushed from the apartment as if it had suddenly been filled by an army of fire ants. Outside, the late April night was balmy, soft as a warm breast against his cheek, and Second Avenue was thronged with a noisy crowd of Friday-night bar hoppers. Hux turned downtown, against the crowd, crossed over to First, and had not gone very far before deciding to walk down to P. J. Clarke's. What was Clarke's like these days? It was, after all, the prototype, if not the ancestor, of all the singles bars that had proliferated in his neighborhood. Perhaps it had gone gay; perhaps—such things happened so quickly in New York—it had been torn down. But the little red-brick tenement was still there, nestling among the office towers of Third Avenue, and inside he found the same cut glass, the same carefully preserved (or faked?) Nineties look, the same—or almost the same—sharply dressed and restless crowd that he remembered. Within half an hour he was discussing Nixon with two men from CBS and a gorgeous young black woman who identified herself as the assistant director of a soap opera called "Sandy's Bunch." Propelled by three quick drinks, Hux outlined to them his theory that Nixon would be the first President to attempt suicide. "General Haig will bring Nixon a pistol on a cushion, click his heels, and say, 'Will that be all, Mr. President?' Then he'll salute and go out. Nixon will then tape his last words, cry a little, put the barrel into his mouth, and pull the trigger. The shot will tear through his chipmunk cheek and take off the lobe of his left ear. He'll be too nervous to try again, but that night he'll go on television, wearing a spectacular bandage, and—since he'll be unable to talk because of the new hole in his cheek—he'll use a gadget to flash his words on the screen. And he'll claim to be the victim of an assassination attempt by the CIA."

Hux got a laugh, but he glared around him as if he had expected insults. Within another fifteen minutes the CBS men had wandered out, and Hux was alone with the black girl, who told him that her name was Carolyn Starkie and that she lived with a fashion photographer in Kips Bay Plaza. Carolyn looked like a model herself, with shiny purple eyelids and huge gold-hoop earrings and a blue-green silk shirt cut to expose the inner third of each golden-brown breast. Her boyfriend, she said, was out of town. . . .

Around one in the morning, she and Hux were in bed together—at Kips Bay, in a room full of fancy lighting equipment and huge photo-murals. Hux was lying with his face buried in a silk-covered pillow, while Carolyn sat on the edge of the mattress, her arms clasped around her knees. She had just finished telling him that the reason his body had rejected hers was because her body was black. And when Hux raised his head to protest that color had nothing to do with it, that he had climaxed too quickly out of sheer excitement, Carolyn cocked her head and raised one brow. "Then how come you couldn't get it up again?" she asked. Sodden and miserable, Hux, after mumbling something about having had too much to drink, admitted that he had experienced a certain amount of trouble in "this department" recently; he was willing to wallow in any amount of sexual self-abasement rather than let her (or himself) think that her explanation might be true. He tried hard to convince her. But Carolyn merely continued to look down at him, wrinkling her nose and rolling her eyes as if she had heard his story a hundred times. Then, jumping off the bed, she pranced across the room, her lithe body the color of dark Jamaican rum in the lamplight, grabbed an armful of his clothes from a chair, flung them at the bed, and told him to cut the shit and haul his ass out of there as fast as he could pull on his pants.

Hux left Kips Bay Plaza in a slanting cascade of rain which turned his suit into soggy felt before he could get a taxi on First Avenue. Back at the apartment, he did not bother to hang up his suit but let it lie where he shed it and the rest of his clothes, in the middle of the floor. He had succeeded in breaking the circuit but at a cost. In bed he lay for nearly an hour reliving his humiliation while fighting off the sleep that his body so hungrily craved.

Chapter Eight

The item added to Hux's secret agenda made him want to laugh whenever he thought of it. Meanwhile the official agenda was shaping up nicely. Letters came in from each of the Southern college presidents, their responses ranging from favorable to enthusiastic as they caught a glimpse of green money in the distance. When the time came to lay his project before Newbold Jenkins, Hux did so with the mixture of slyness, truculence, and charm which the older man had come to expect. Hux himself was charmed by his own secret, which, he feared, might at any moment break loose like a grinning lunatic from its place of confinement. As Jenkins turned the pages of Hux's outline, he used his other hand to finger the set of turquoise worry beads he had bought in Turkey for the purpose of distracting himself whenever the urge to light a cigarette became too insistent. Impatient for Jenkins's response, Hux found himself irritated almost to fury by the beads—such a stupid, foppish affectation for this otherwise urbane man! He wanted to snatch the beads from the director's hands and fling them across the room.

Jenkins was full of praise. "It could be very exciting," he said, speaking in that prep-school drawl that sounded as if he were trying to hold a round pebble on the top of his tongue. "And damned important."

Suddenly businesslike, Hux pointed out that they would have to get the Administrative Council's approval no later than the Friday meeting if he was to be able to go to Mississippi by the last week of May. He then proceeded to go over a series of items with Jenkins, who in each instance nodded his approval. Effective though he was, Hux could never discuss Foundation matters with his boss without a strong sense that he was play-acting, doing a clever impersonation. "I figure I'll need about three weeks in Mississippi," he concluded. "Then I might take a week's vacation and go to New Orleans. I've never been there."

"Dreary, overrated, provincial town," drawled Jenkins, twirling his beads. "But the food's good. Galatoire's has held up very well, but you have to wait in line for an hour just to get inside the door."

On the night before he left for Mississippi, Hux went to West End Avenue to pick up some old snapshots and a packet of letters from Clark. Despite the three years of separation and then divorce, Louise allowed Hux to keep a filing cabinet of tax returns and other documents, boxes of old letters, and most of his books in what had once been his study. Hux's own apartment had always seemed temporary to him, a borrowed room in which to play out his scruffy bachelor role; his only real New York home was in this massive old building with its granite façade and heavy canopy suspended by chains. Unlike the singles hive that he inhabited on the far East Side, this was very much a family building in which lived ponderous German-Jewish businessmen and their mink-coated wives, musicians—several of them famous—who could practice securely behind thick walls, writers of TV scripts, professors, and numerous young lawyers, gentile as well as Jewish, most of them destined to move to the suburbs when their young wives tired of coping with all the problems that beset wives with small children in the city.

Having abandoned the West Side bourgeoisie, Hux found it more extraordinary than ever that Louise, with her Richmond background of country club and debutante parties, had become so completely acclimatized to a way of life for which this building served as a fortress as well as a home. Despite the increased money, she had objected to the move from Princeton, urging Hux to stay there and finish his thesis. Yet Louise, whom Hux had first known as a Hollins College senior, attending dances and fraternity parties all over the Upper South, had gotten a part-time job, as soon as Tony was old enough, at the Columbia University Press, where she was now a full-time editor, with a modest salary to supplement her inheritance and Hux's monthly payments. She had trained herself to become an expert cook and gave dinner parties attended by people in this building and from buildings like it up and down Riverside Drive, West End Avenue, and Central Park West; and she went to their dinner parties, where she met divorced lawyers and editors whom her friends (once Hux's) had invited specifically to meet her. Sooner or later she would marry one of them.

But how could Hux continue to think of this building as his one true home when the night doorman did not recognize him and insisted on ringing Louise for permission to admit this stranger who called himself Mr. Hux? Ascending in the paneled elevator, he felt as insubstantial as a vagrant drifting from park bench to gutter.

Louise opened the apartment door. She was wearing what she regularly put on for evenings at home after work: an oversized turtleneck sweater and well-cut jeans. A fair Saxon type, with a fine pink-and-white skin, Louise had dull gold hair that almost matched her ex-husband's; she would have been beautiful except for the tightness of her lips and the perpetual threat of a frown that puckered her forehead. She was actively frowning now. "Hi," she said, as without a smile she let Hux kiss her on the cheek. "Tony's doing his homework. Come on in the living room."

"I can only stay a few minutes. I've got to get home and pack."

"Where are you going?"

"Mississippi. I told you."

"I forgot. God, how can you stand it? I'd expect you to go to any lengths to avoid setting foot there again."

Suppose I told her I was planning to visit Clark's murderer? Hux grinned as he said, "I think of it as a kind of sentimental journey. I'm sort of looking forward to it, actually."

They walked from the entrance hall into a room that Hux had once liked and could not imagine living in again. It was too comfortable, too composed, too strong a reminder of Louise's Richmond side. Yet he had once had a part in that composition, attending auctions with Louise to find a chair that would go with the 1830 rosewood secretary she had inherited from a great-aunt, giving his opinion on swatches of upholstery material brought by the decorator for Louise's selection. It had once been his room too, where he had taken his ease, played with his little boy, offered brandy to guests. Now the chairs, the secretary, even the glorious amber-and-indigo Chinese rug, were mere props, the room itself a set for a play that had closed. Hux crossed to one of the two windows and gazed at the light-beaded sliver of the Hudson visible between the tall apartment buildings on Riverside. Then he turned around and said, "I really can't stay. I'll just say hello and goodbye to Tony, get my stuff, and be on my way."

"Talk a little bit with Tony. He's upset. That gang of boys waylaid him again coming home from school and took all his change. He won't even wear his watch to school any more."

"All right."

Annoyed by this request and ashamed of his annoyance, Hux walked back to Tony's room. The boy was sitting at his desk, a book open in front of him. Leaning his cheek against his knuckle, Tony seemed oblivious of the book and everything else except a patch of bare wall above his desk. He gave a frightened start when Hux said, "Hi, Tony," and then spun around in his chair, a lock of his wheat-straw hair falling across one eye.

"Hi, Dad." Tony politely stood up. The man and boy shook hands.

42

"Hear you had a little trouble today," said Hux as he pulled up a chair. Tony's problems always struck Hux as insoluble—and depressingly familiar from his own childhood.

"It's okay. Not much happened."

"Tell me about it." Hux did not really want to hear. What could he do except feel a little sick? They lived in the city—these things happened. What could he say?

"It wasn't any big deal. Some guys took about eighty-five cents out of my pocket. One of them tried to take my briefcase, but I held on to it and then some ladies across the street started yelling at them and they let me go."

"Black guys or white guys?"

"Black."

"How old?"

"Maybe twelve or thirteen. One of them was real big and looked sort of dumb."

Hux sighed. He felt terribly sorry for the boy, but what could he say? On a previous occasion they had discussed alternate routes home from the school—Buxton—which was on Ninety-sixth Street, just off Central Park West, together with the possibility of organizing a convoy of school friends. But Tony, who was a shy and solitary boy, had brought up objections to each of these plans—objections which Hux was unable to answer. Now Hux could only sigh again, shake his head, and say, "I know it's rough, Tony. Would it help any to take the crosstown bus as far as West End?"

Tony shook his head. "There's an even meaner bunch that hangs out around there. The best thing for me is to head for Broadway as fast as I can. Those kids aren't out there every day."

Hux stood up. "I'm going to Mississippi for three, maybe four weeks. When do you leave for camp?"

"June twenty-first."

"Oh, I'll be back before then. Take care of yourself, Tony."

"Goodnight, Dad. Have a nice trip."

They shook hands and Hux patted the boy on the shoulder, aware of an atavistic impulse to encircle him with both arms. But something paralyzed him. Then Hux went to his old study to get what he had come for. He could hardly wait to get away. When he said goodbye to Louise, she frowned again but wished him a good trip and held up her cheek for his kiss.

Heading east on the Seventy-ninth Street bus, Hux crouched under the weight of a great sadness. With it came a burst of protective tenderness toward his son such as he had not known since the first four

43

or five years of Tony's life. What had happened to it? Where had it been all this time? He had had a good family—a good wife, a good son—and he had not been able to stop himself from throwing them away. . . .

His suitcase packed, Hux got a beer and sat down to look through the snapshots, which he planned to carry in his briefcase. Since the night was warm, he did not put on his old bathrobe but sat in his undershorts, with one ankle resting on top of his knee. He wanted to make a selection to show to Claiborne Herne when the moment came. The first that he looked at showed the two couples—himself and Louise, Clark and Linda—dressed up for a costume dance at the Graduate College: he as an Arab in bathrobe and towel-burnoose, Louise in veil, halter, and harem pants; Clark as Li'l Abner, Linda as Daisy Mae. Another showed Linda with Susie clinging to her shoulders like a monkey. The next shot was of Clark at bat during a graduate students' softball game played (and won, Hux remembered) against the junior faculty of the Princeton Politics Department; it caught the cocky tilt of Clark's cap over his eyes, the dirt and grass stains on his chino trousers. After thumbing through a batch of photographs that had nothing to do with the Helmholtzes, Hux came up with another one taken on the same day—at the picnic after the game on the banks of Lake Carnegie; in it Clark was swaggering and laughing, one hand clutching a beer can, the other resting on Linda's shoulder. Then one more: an enlarged closeup of Clark standing at the entrance to the Firestone Library.

That laugh of Clark's . . . Putting down the snapshots, Hux leaned back and closed his eyes. For a moment he could see—and hear—Clark rocking with laughter during a seminar at the library, outroaring the others in the explosion of laughter he had produced around the table with a spectacular, multi-level pun in the report he was reading; the report, Hux recalled, was on anarcho-syndicalism, but he could no longer remember the pun.

It was impossible for Hux to disentangle his own experience as a graduate student from his friendship with Clark. His own doctoral dissertation had been in some ways an extended conversation—at times an argument—with Clark. Hux had little doubt that it could have been published as a book if he had ever finished it. At one time he had known more than anyone outside the CIA about America's open and secret dealings with Liberia during World War II. His thesis advisor, Marvin Beale, had been enthusiastic about the sections Hux submitted, and Clark, who had read every scrap of his dissertation and was an expert on West Africa himself, had been full of praise, encouragement, and disagreement. But, when Clark was killed, the whole enterprise quickly dwindled into a pointless monologue. Hux had not had the heart to go on with it. When Clark's light went out, Hux's had dimmed. This now seemed blindingly clear to Hux—clearer than it had ever been before. His thesis—his *book*—was like a tiresome ex-mistress, toward whom he felt some obligation but no desire. Louise, however, had never let him forget that he had perversely turned his back on a probably distinguished academic or even diplomatic career, regarding, as she did, the job with the Morrow Foundation as a dead end, as a well-paid betrayal of the promise he had shown at Princeton. But then she had never understood the degree to which that career had depended upon his sustained dialogue with Clark. . . .

Hux drew out another snapshot: himself holding Tony, who was about ten days old at the time. It was one of the few baby pictures of Tony that Louise had not pasted into her album. Again Hux leaned back, shutting his eyes, surrendering to a wistfulness that seemed to sway him in its arms. How little he knew about himself, how little he understood. His sense of loss was oceanic, but sad rather than desperate. Whatever he had had, he had thrown away—and he did not know why, except that Clark's death was obscurely connected with this self-dispossession. How much he had owed to Clark—even the experiencing of Tony's birth. Very deliberately, with his eyes closed tight, Hux began to summon his memories of that extraordinary night at the Princeton Hospital. . . .

Louise's labor had been going badly—hours of contractions, no discernible movement of the fetus. Hux sat by Louise's side, holding her hand, wiping the sweat from her skin. As the pain mounted, his panic mounted with it, and when the nurse came in to check something, Hux mumbled an excuse and rushed from the room, his own shirt sopping wet. From the pay phone outside the waiting room of the maternity ward, he called Clark, who was at home typing up a term paper that was due the next morning. He told Clark that Louise was in a bad way—could Clark come to the hospital for a little while? Clark did not hesitate. "Fuck old Carlton," he said in his Missouri twang, naming the much-hated professor who had assigned the paper. "It'll be late, that's all. Get a good grip on yourself, old buddy. I'll be there in ten—fifteen—minutes." During the interval, Hux returned to the tiny room where Louise lay with her knees drawn up. An intern had joined the nurse, and they were whispering together.

Louise whimpered, gasped sharply, groaned. Hux sponged her face and arms. Then the intern said, "I've got to be here a while. This room's very crowded, so why don't you go back to the waiting room. We'll call you if there's any development." Hux looked at Louise, who nodded. As he went out, he thought, *So much for natural childbirth. She's going to die. . . .*

Clark burst in, his chest swelling the tennis shirt he always wore during the summer. Ebullient, his brown hair tousled, his jaw set in that familiar confident angle, Clark grabbed Hux tightly by the upper right arm and said, "So it's been rough, Larry. You can relax now. I've brought a six-pack. I know it's against the rules, but I walked right past the desk attendant—just said, 'Hello—nice evening'—and here I am." He set down the paper bag containing the beer and said, "We'll wait this one out together. Louise is going to come through in great shape. Nobody dies in childbirth anymore." His brown eyes flashing, he took out a can of Budweiser and popped open the top, sending a spurt of beer two feet across the room. "Ooops, I'm afraid I shook 'em up running from the car. It's a good thing we're the only expectant fathers in the room tonight," he said, handing the dripping can to Hux.

Clark stayed for five hours, while Hux went back and forth between the labor room and the waiting room, too distraught to sit still or talk with any coherence. Clark handed him cans of beer, reserving only one for himself. When a nurse wandered in, saw the empty cans, and protested, Clark simply put his arm around her, drew her into the corridor, and somehow talked her into going her way without making a fuss. Hux had little direct memory of any of this, but Clark had laughed about the episode afterward, filling in the details. What Hux could remember was the way Clark took over, asking questions of the nurse and intern, interpreting what they said to Hux, who was so upset that he could hardly listen, much less ask the right questions.

Then Dr. Moulton, the obstetrician, had come in to say that Louise was being prepared for a caesarean. When he left, Hux nearly went to pieces, convincing himself that Louise would die, that they should never have had a baby, that he was not meant to be a father, and other nonsense of that kind. Clark had sat quietly, letting Hux talk on. Then, in a very matter-of-fact voice, he began to talk about his own fears at the birth of his daughter, Susie, and about his sister-in-law, who had had a first baby by caesarean section, was fine, and had gone ahead to have two more babies by the same method. Gradually Clark's voice reached Hux and he listened. Then they sat quietly together while Hux finished the last of the beers; he was calmer now and a little drunk.

When, around four in the morning, Dr. Moulton, still in his green cap and operating gown, came in to announce that Louise had been delivered of an eight-pound boy, that she was doing beautifully, and that the baby's reflexes seemed as normal as could be expected, considering the anesthesia, Hux could merely stand dumbly and nod, while tears coursed down his cheeks. Then Clark grabbed his hand in a crushing grip, pounding Hux on the back at the same time and yelling, "We've done it, Hux boy, we've done it! We've got our boy, we've got our boy!"

Hux wanted the baby's middle name to be Clark, but Louise insisted that they stick to the name they had earlier decided on for a boy: Anthony Mason Hux. Three weeks later Clark and Hux and two other members of the Princeton chapter of CORE headed south for Mississippi.

Where will I ever find another friend like Clark? Who would stand by me now? Although his eyes watered, Hux's sadness was softened by a sense of Clark's nearness; he *had* succeeded in bringing Clark a bit closer. Once more, open-eyed, he tried to summon his friend into total visibility—and failed. But when he shut his eyes he saw instead the grinning devil's mask of Claiborne Herne.

At some point during the night Hux felt the mattress sag near the foot of his bed. Someone had sat down on it, not far from his own left foot, which was suddenly constricted by the sheet as the weight pulled it down. There was no sound of breathing this time—just the weight and the constriction. After a few seconds during which Hux, paralyzed, thought that his heart would stop, the weight was lifted, and after a few more seconds, he found the strength to turn on the lamp and whisper Clark's name to the empty room. He had no doubt of his visitor's identity; it did not occur to him that a robber or some other intruder might have broken into the room. His sheets were clammy. Even when his terror had subsided and he remembered that he had *wanted* Clark to come back, Hux had trouble convincing himself that he had been dreaming. He fell asleep again with the lamp still on.

47

PART 2

Chapter Nine

On Thursday, May 23, Lawrence Hux flew to Memphis, where he rented a car to drive to Oxford. Instead of one of his dark New York suits, he was wearing a new suit of tan poplin that fitted him well enough to disguise some of his flabbiness. But he looked unwell, with pink eyelids and discolored patches under his eyes, as if he had been weeping all night instead of merely lying sleepless for long stretches. On the plane he had busied himself with his official agenda, going over the latest mail, which he had picked up at the office before leaving, checking once again the schedule of interviews, conferences, and consultations that he had set up in advance. Tomorrow he was to call on the president and other administrators of the University of Mississippi and that evening go to dinner at the home of a Professor Benson of the Politics Department. Appointments had been arranged for all of the following week and well into the next. With that efficiency which—when he chose to exercise it—was a source of wonder to his colleagues at the Foundation, Hux had created an elaborate machine with gears that were already meshed and turning, a machine that could advance almost on its own, leaving its creator free for his secret concerns.

Hux's official identity held firm during the plane ride and the hiring of the car, but once he was on the road, heading southeast toward Oxford, he began to feel unreal to himself, cut loose. . . . Though he had come no further north than Yazoo City during those six weeks in 1964, the landscape of northern Mississippi seemed frighteningly familiar to him; he had seen it all, this landscape of pine trees, rutted red-dirt tracks leading to clearings, vast jungles of kudzu vine. . . . Except for Christmas visits to Louise's family in Richmond, he had been South only once since that summer—to help his mother move into a smaller flat in Raleigh; though Southern all right, those two cities and the suburbs had nothing in common with this suddenly dread terrain. For Hux was anxious, his shoulders tensing every time a car approached or passed. Even the new suit and new, expensive English shoes with which he had been pleased now seemed an absurd disguise—once his car had been forced to the side of the road, he would be recognized instantly as an outside Communist agitator, a nigger lover, a henchman of that son-of-a-bitch Clark Helmholtz. It took Hux almost all the way to Oxford to accept the fact that he was as much the lord of the highway as anyone else, that he had no reason to fear attack from a pickup truck full of rednecks with shotguns or from a cruising cop with a beefy face.

But when Hux was registering in the office of the Holiday Inn, he slipped into an identity much older than either the foundation executive or the civil rights activist: he was a Southerner again, the kind of well-brought-up Southerner who took his time to return the desk clerk's greeting slowly and courteously, to comment on the delightfulness of the weather, the comfort of the flight, and the easiness of the drive from Memphis. Once in his room, he washed up, changed into a red sport shirt and chinos, and placed a telephone call to the office of the president of Ole Miss to confirm his appointment in the morning; the secretary told Hux that the president was looking forward so much to meeting him, and Hux replied that he was looking forward to meeting the president. After trying unsuccessfully to reach Professor Benson at his campus office, Hux called Mrs. Benson at home to announce his arrival and express his pleasure at the prospect of joining the Bensons for dinner on the following evening. "We're just so thrilled you're comin'," said Mrs. Benson, who then commented on the unusualness of the name Hux and wondered if he by any chance was related to the Huxes from down near Greenwood. To this Hux answered that the name was indeed uncommon, so he was probably related somehow to the family she was talking about, though his own family had always lived in North Carolina. In its rhythm, vocabulary, and intonations his speech became the kind that he had heard his parents and grandparents use during his child-hood—a leisurely and fairly elaborate mode that he knew was fast losing ground to the deliberately folksy style of the good ol' boys of the New South.

His duties accomplished, Hux lay back on one of the twin beds. *Well, Clark, here I am*, he said, forming the words soundlessly on his lips. Before arriving, he had expected to check in at the motel, make his calls, and then drive straight to Tupelo, where he would begin his pilgrimage at its most holy and terrible site. But it was now well after four, and Tupelo seemed a long way to go after already having come so far. Travel-weary and dislocated as he was, Hux felt unprepared for the possible impact of a visit to the schoolyard; no, he'd better wait until he was in a more settled and meditative frame of mind. But what about Alhambra, which was much closer? What was to stop him from driving over there? Hux still had no idea how he would begin that part of his mission. But it would do no harm to look around, get the lay of the land, perhaps ask a few discreet questions; his best hope was to leave himself open to impressions, pick up what he could, stay loose, and improvise, improvise. . . . At least he could drive by the Hernes' house—perhaps catch a glimpse of one of them on the porch. Jumping from the bed, he went over to the table where he had left the Mississippi road map that he had picked up at a filling station. This time he studied it more carefully than he ever had before and concluded that he ought to be able to reach Alhambra in no more than forty minutes. . . .

The late afternoon into which Hux emerged from the motel was bright and hot but not humid. The town of Oxford pleased him as he drove through it, especially the leafy old trees that lined North La-mar Street and the defiant look of the old brick courthouse set in its wide square. But once he had found his way to Route 6 and the signs pointing to Batesville, Alhambra, and Clarksdale, he became impatient with the drive before him and was tempted to speed. Since he had no idea how zealous the highway police now were but remembered incidents from the summer of '64 when the slightest infraction of a traffic rule could mean arrest and jailing and worse, Hux made himself slow down from time to time as he continued to check off the diminishing number of miles to his goal. The dull piny landscape had no interest for him until, just beyond Batesville, he crossed a muddy stream moving through a subtropical density of vines and trees on each bank and wondered if it was the Tallahatchie. Just before he reached Alhambra, the wooded terrain began to open into the flat and loamy surface of the Delta, and once more Hux took notice.

The approach to the town itself was so ordinarily American that Hux felt let down: filling stations, a drive-in movie, a used-car lot, a diner, a small shopping center, and then a sign reading "WELCOME TO ALHAMBRA—Pop. 3818." As ordinary as that. Following the highway into the center of town, Hux parked in front of the Tallahatchie Planters Bank (now closed) and got out to look for a public telephone. Downtown Alhambra seemed to have depopulated itself with the closing of the stores after five o'clock; the sidewalks were nearly empty and even the little park had none of the loungers—black or white—that Hux would have expected to find sitting on its green-painted benches or on the steps of the decaying old bandstand. At last he discovered a drugstore that was open—an old-fashioned drugstore with a soda fountain, where two elderly men in loudly patterned sport shirts and Texan cowboy hats were drinking Cokes and joking with the red-headed young man behind the counter. In the rear of the store, near the prescription window, Hux spotted a telephone booth with (what he really wanted) a telephone book on the shelf beside it. As he approached the booth, he nodded and said "Howdy" to the pharmacist behind the window; his greeting was returned but with an appraising stare over half-moon glasses that confirmed Hux's position as a stranger-in-town.

He quickly found what he was looking for in the directory: "Herne, C. B., MD, 128 Granada St. . . . 873-6343." Feeling the pharmacist's eyes upon him as he jotted down the address and number, Hux decided that he should go through the motions of making a call. But why merely go through the motions, why not dial the actual number? Hux did so and then waited, holding his breath, while the phone rang five or six times. Just as he was about to hang up, he heard a click followed by a "Hello?" in an oddly rasping voice of indeterminate sex. After a few seconds the voice, now recognizably feminine despite the rasp, said, "Who did you say it was?" At which point Hux, feeling slightly ashamed of himself, hung up. He got up, nodded to the pharmacist, and left the store as the two cowboy-hatted geezers and the soda jerk turned to watch his exit. Only outside did he realize that he had forgotten to ask directions to Granada Street. He started to go back in but decided against it on the grounds of not wanting to attract too much attention. It seemed important to Hux to maintain his anonymity, at least during the preliminaries to his mission to Alhambra.

Walking along Main Street toward his car, Hux noticed a large sign displayed in a number of shop windows. On it was the photograph of a smiling, moon-faced man of about forty and beneath the picture these words in bright red lettering:

REDEDICATION!

Rev. Archie B. Thurlow
and Other Guest Witnesses
Ephraim Baptist Church
Sunday Services 11:00 a.m.
Nitely Meetings 8:00 p.m.
May 19 — June 2

Hux looked briefly into the evangelist's eyes—such dark, fat, plummy eyes staring from plastic-rimmed glasses. He was in the South, all right. . . . Then he turned his thoughts to the whereabouts of Granada Street, deducing that it must be fairly central—given its association with the name of the town. He would drive slowly down Main, looking for an intersection with Granada, and avoid asking questions if he could.

Granada proved to be the second street beyond the park—a comfortable street of trees with great pendulous branches, of white frame houses (some of them older than the Civil War) and wide lawns, not all of them well kept. Sure that he would soon come to the Hernes' house, which he would recognize from the *Look* photograph, Hux drove at about ten miles an hour, his hands slippery with excitement. Children were playing in some of the yards. An elderly lady in a tentlike dress was watering a newly planted shrub, her face and white hair brushed by the now golden light. He passed the Presbyterian church, substantial and ornate with Victorian brickwork, and felt sure that he was directly on target. In the midst of all this thick cotton wrapping of Southern peacefulness he would find the twisted thing and set to work—but *how*, in God's name?—to make it writhe before he was done. But as Hux drove on, the procession of old houses with their guardians of cedar, oak, magnolia, and pecan trees suddenly stopped, giving way to a new elementary school on one side of the street and a brand-new complex of garden apartments on the other. Beyond lay a few brick ranch houses, designed for a modern and still almost treeless suburbia occupying what had obviously been cotton fields not long before. Hux checked the numbers: 124 on the right, 125 on the left; that could only mean that the Hernes' house was the second that he could see ahead of him on the right.

What Hux experienced was sharper than disappointment: he felt bitter, as if he had been deliberately cheated. The Victorian gingerbread house and all he associated with it had collapsed like a stage set, brought down by some malevolent force determined to thwart his fantasy, to render him aimless and confused. Claiborne Herne had tricked him, had managed to escape. . . .

There was nothing to do but drive on down the street and have a look. The houses—and *the* house—could all have been moved without alteration from a middle-class suburb in Toledo, Ohio, or Camden, New Jersey; only the planting—waxy gardenia bushes, spindly young crape myrtles, five-foot-high magnolias—had anything Mississippian about it. Stopping the car, Hux for the third time took out the slip of paper on which he had written the address. The house was there, all right—a plain ranch house of raw pink brick and white wood trim. Three bedrooms, he guessed, two baths; a living room with a dining el; possibly a small separate dining room or den. The lawn was adequately maintained, and there was a strip of marigolds, geraniums, and petunias on either side of the front walk. Roses had begun to climb the trellis on one side of the house. A Ford Falcon— at least five years old—was parked in the asphalted drive. Windows were open. Someone was probably at home. The only sounds that reached Hux came from children playing ball down the street.

After perhaps five minutes, Hux backed into a driveway and turned his car toward the center of town. With its coalescing lawns, its wide picture windows, and its total lack of hedges and big trees, this neighborhood seemed designed to force visibility upon him and his car, a visibility which his plan, whatever it turned out to be, would have to allow for. Even as he drove away from the place where he had turned around, he could imagine people pressing faces to their windows to watch him. He would need an identity. . . . Minutes later he noticed that he was hungry and remembered that he had seen a café or diner of some sort between the drugstore and the intersection of Main and Granada. He found it promptly—the Cotton Boll Grill—and went in. Given the absence of life in the street, Hux was surprised by the number of people inside: all the booths were occupied and there were only two empty stools at the counter. Choosing one at the end, he was welcomed with a cordial "Evenin', how-wuh yew?" from the counter girl, who handed him a plastic-enclosed menu. "Fresh ham's real good tonight," she said. "You'd recommend it, wouldn't you, Mr. Porter?"

Mr. Porter, who occupied the next stool, looked up from his plate and said, "I sure would. It's real tasty." He was the pharmacist. Again the appraising stare at Hux over half-moon glasses. "Didn't I see you come in the drugstore a while back?"

"Yes, sir, you did," replied Hux with a pleasant smile. "I helped myself to your phone." Turning to the waitress, he ordered roast fresh ham, rice and gravy, black-eyed peas, spinach, and iced coffee. His mind was leaping ahead in anticipation of the friendly but probing inquisition that was likely to follow.

Mr. Porter's pink freckled scalp, which was fringed at the back and sides by lank hair, had a way of wrinkling as he raised and lowered his eyebrows. "Just passin' through?"

"Well, sir, you might say yes and you might say no. I'm stayin' with friends over in Clarksdale, but I reckon I've been in and out of Alhambra a dozen times in the last two weeks." Hux had lapsed, without trying, into Deep Southern speech.

"That right? You by any chance here for Brother Thurlow's Rededication?"

Why not, thought Hux—*why not?* "Yep, you guessed it," he said. "My name's Ainsley Black and I'm here for the Rededication." He held out his hand to Mr. Porter, who solemnly shook it, after a significant wrinkling of his scalp.

"Darn it, Mr. Black, I wish I could git to more of the meetin's. But I have to be at the drugstore till nine-thirty three nights a week. Only way we can compete with the Standard Drug that's opened out in the shoppin' center. I reckon Reverend Thurlow's the most inspirin' man I ever heard. For my money, he even puts Billy Graham in the shade. I reckon it's been four years since his last Rededication in this part of the state, but people are still talkin' about it. And there's been remarkable little backslidin' among the people he helped to find Jesus. Remarkable little. I wouldn't miss the Sunday meetin's for anything—the opener last Sunday was a wonder to behold, I'm certain you'll agree. . . . A wonder to behold. An' I'm goin' to try to git there this Saturday night when the store's closed. Yes, sir, I'll be there." Suddenly shutting off his enthusiasm, Mr. Porter peered at Hux and said, "You say you been around these parts for the last two weeks? How come you got here a week before the Rededication begun, if you don't mind my askin'? You got business dealin's in this neck of the woods?"

Hux thought briefly of telling the pharmacist to mind his own business. But then an idea came which struck him as so funny that he broke into one of his boyish grins, which he immediately suppressed in order to look boyishly solemn. He scratched his head, pulling his hair partly across his forehead, disarraying to some extent its New York styling. "Mr. Porter," he began in a slow drawl, "when you happen to be travelin' on the Lord's business, there's lots of arrangements have to be made." *Why not?* he thought, surprised by what he had come up with but liking it.

Mr. Porter's eyebrows and scalp rose and fell at this. "I see," he said finally. "You must be one of the guest preachers. Hope you won't take offense, sir, if I say I'd never in a million years have guessed it."

Hux peripherally glanced at his red shirt and chinos. *Why not?* "You're partly right and partly wrong. I'm a minister all right, but I'm not preachin' at the Rededication. You might say I'm a forerunner and a messenger." The words sounded biblically mysterious, and Hux was pleased to have thought of them; he could see that the pharmacist was impressed. "There are times," he went on, "when I find it appropriate to disguise my callin'. Sometimes I travel under different names."

"I see." Mr. Porter's nod was grave, accompanied by both his scalpal tic and a thoughtful protrusion of his lower lip.

Maintaining his initiative, Hux said, "How are things in Alhambra these days? I can't recall hearin' anything special about the town since all that trouble ten years ago."

"What trouble you referrin' to, Reverend?" asked Mr. Porter cautiously.

"I mean when one of your most respected citizens stood trial for murder. Dr. Claiborne Herne."

The pharmacist sighed. "Poor man. I reckon you could say it ruined his life."

"How do you mean, sir? After all, he was acquitted."

The waitress brought Hux's plate and his glass of iced coffee, and both men smiled at her, as if they had been talking of nothing more consequential than the weather. As Hux began to eat, he kept looking at the pharmacist, silently urging him to go on. "Yep," said Mr. Porter, "he was acquitted. But you know," he went on, lowering his voice confidentially, "it seems like he never got over the shock and the publicity. We don't see much of him these days. Kind of hides himself away like an animal that's been wounded, poor fella."

"Is that right?" Hux kept his pressuring eye upon Mr. Porter as he chewed the fresh ham, which was tough but flavorful. He was now sure that the pharmacist—once started—would have plenty to say about the Hernes. He was right. What he learned in the next fifteen minutes was that Dr. Herne had given up his practice and become a real recluse. Stopped going to church. Five or six years ago they sold their old house on Toledo Street and bought themselves a new, smaller place out on Granada. . . . Mr. Porter reckoned they weren't so well off since Dr. Herne had stopped practicing, but there was some family money, so he supposed they were still a long way from the poorhouse. "It's a terrible pity, a terrible pity," said the pharmacist, "when you think of the effect that trial had on one of the most— maybe *the* most—prominent people in this town. It's a tragic shame."

"Nobody here thinks he killed that Northerner, do they?"

"Nobody. Not one blessed soul. 'Course those were angry, violent times, an' lots of people got roiled up to the point where they'd do things they ordinarily wouldn't, but Dr. Herne is the last person in this world to take a human life, no matter what the justification. The evidence was all coincidence, what they call circumstantial. Anybody with a brain in his head could see that. But Dr. Herne just couldn't take the glare of that publicity, all the cross-examinations and accusations and all that. He was always what you'd call a real sensitive, high-strung kind of man, and he just couldn't take it. It's a rotten shame."

"Couldn't his pastor help? I seem to recall Dr. Herne was a church-goin' man."

"Old Dr. Blakelock—he was the Presbyterian minister died a few years back—well, Dr. Blakelock did what he could. At least Dr. Herne would see him. The new minister cain't even git inside the house. It breaks Miss Isabelle's heart."

Hux now learned, with a minimum of prodding, that Isabelle Herne was a deeply Christian person who never missed church and carried on as best she could but had to spend most of her time looking after her brother. Since her brother didn't want to see people, she had gradually cut herself off from most of her friends, which was a pity, a terrible pity. Again the wrinkled scalp, the protruded lip. "I still see her," continued the pharmacist. "Not in a social way. We're Baptists and we never did see much of the Hernes in a social way, but she still comes down to the drugstore about once a week, an' you'd never want to see a sweeter, more gracious little lady than Miss Isabelle Herne. She always takes the time to say 'Howdy' and to ask about the wife and the boys—they don't come any nicer than her. And when I ask about the doctor, she always says exactly the same thing. 'It's real kind of you to inquire, Mr. Porter,' she says. 'He's about the same.' And we let it drop at that."

Hux shrugged, sighed, shook his head, and said, "There must be somebody who could reach them, somebody who could help. Do you reckon Miss Isabelle might come to one of Brother Thurlow's meetin's? He might be able to help. At least his word might point the way."

Mr. Porter didn't know. Miss Isabelle almost never went out at night. Besides, you couldn't be sure how a Presbyterian might react to somebody like Reverend Thurlow—they tended to be a little stand-offish where the public workings of the spirit were concerned. Which was a pity. Somebody like Reverend Thurlow might make all the difference in Miss Isabelle's life—and eventually her brother's too. "You know, Reverend, I got a powerful hunch Miss Isabelle's got a soul like a ripe fruit, just ready and waitin' to be plucked by Jesus. I bet all she needs is just a teeny-tiny push in the right direction."

Both men nodded and fell silent. The pharmacist had long since finished his supper, and Hux was toying with the remains of a piece of lemon pie he'd ordered during a gap in the conversation. He now ordered hot coffee. After looking at his watch, Mr. Porter abruptly jumped up, saying he'd overstayed his supper hour and had to hurry back to the drugstore. They shook hands cordially, and Mr. Porter told Hux he was sure his next week would be sanctified by the Lord and that he should feel free to drop by the drugstore any time for a chat—whether he needed to make a purchase or not. "Anyways," he concluded, "I'll be seein' you at one of the meetin's."

Hux watched as the little man hurried out into the orange-pink sunset that had burned its way through the plate-glass windows of the Cotton Boll Grill. "Here's your coffee, Reverend," said the waitress, who had overheard something, possibly a good deal. Suddenly unnerved by his new identity, Hux dribbled scalding coffee over his fingers when he tried to lift the cup.

Chapter Ten

Hux had wanted to spy at the Hernes' lighted windows after dark, but when he left the Cotton Boll, the accumulation of sleepless hours fell heavily upon him. Since he felt like an old man as he walked to his car, he was afraid to trust his reflexes to prowling in that exposed neighborhood, where a weasel-like suppleness—to dart, to flatten himself, to hug the shadows—might suddenly be demanded. Instead, he drove straight back to Oxford, fighting to stay awake in the thickening twilight, his eyes assaulted by the headlights of oncoming cars. He was in bed by nine-thirty, and his sleep that night was like death.

All the next day, as he made his official rounds, Hux kept sneaking back to that attic room in his mind where his secrets were stored. There the scarcely worn identity of the Reverend Ainsley Black hung like a clown's costume on a hook. The thought of trying it on again made Hux grin inappropriately in the middle of a solemn presentation by the chief librarian of the university. Where, in God's name, had Ainsley Black come from? Except for that grin, Hux behaved himself admirably during the whole busy day. A deep night's sleep having obliterated the pouches under his eyes, Hux looked his best: neither the baby-faced killer nor the dissipated cherub but the smooth-cheeked paragon of well-bred efficiency, the young executive who knew his job. When his hosts discovered that he was not—as his appearance suggested—a snotty Ivy League type but a Southerner like themselves, as eager to please as to impress, they outdid themselves in their welcome. All the administrators, beginning with the president, assured Hux that the time for regional coordination was indeed at hand and that he could count upon their most enthusiastic cooperation. An office and a secretary were put at his disposal. Invitations were extended, some of which he found polite reasons for declining; for he realized that, unless he was careful, he would find himself caught up in a professional and social situation that would allow no time for Clark or Alhambra.

His first Ole Miss party was at the Bensons' that evening. He had been asked to come at six so that there would be plenty of time for drinks and supper on the patio before (as Mrs. Benson had put it on the telephone) the bugs drove everybody inside. The earliness suited Hux, who hoped to break away in time to reach Alhambra before the Hernes turned out their lights. Having tucked away this little plan, Hux enjoyed himself for the first two-thirds of the party's duration. Professor Ray Benson—a lanky, sallow-faced man slightly older than Hux—was revealed to be an expert on the state constitution of 1890, which had disenfranchised the Negroes, and he regaled the company—all but Hux Mississippians—with a series of funny and horrendous stories about the legislators of the period, stories which the other guests, who had apparently heard them all before, kept prompting him to tell. Hux could easily imagine that Ray Benson might be a bore on further acquaintance; even now the expression on the face of Mrs. Benson's sister, an angular brunette who sat next to him at the glass-topped patio table, suggested that she had heard the anecdotes at least once too often. Mrs. Benson herself, who was a more conventionally pretty version of her younger sister, had prepared a "real homecooked Southern meal" in Hux's honor: fried chicken with rice and gravy, stuffed tomatoes, okra, and a huge Lady Baltimore cake with whipped cream. When he praised the food, she modestly let it be known that she had taken up cooking only recently, adding that until a few years ago a full professor's wife could have expected to have a colored cook in the kitchen. "But those days are gone forever," she said, declaring that she, for one, had no regrets.

After dinner, while the bugs hurled themselves against the living-room window screens and the scent of honeysuckle and roses wafted in, Hux found himself politely but repeatedly urged to tell horror stories about life in New York. Hux obliged with the story of Tony's recent intimidation but insisted that such episodes, taken in isolation, made life in New York sound far more alarming than it really was. He was assured that things had become worse in the Deep South too, that it was no longer possible to go out at night and leave the front door unlocked the way you used to. When Hux, who was feeling slightly needled, brought up his last trip to Mississippi, in 1964, the company became very guarded in their comments—though a number of liberal sentiments were expressed. It was hard to pin them down as to what *they* had been doing that summer. Hux noticed that several of the guests glanced in the direction of Peggy Benson's sister, whose gaunt face and lively dark eyes contained the merest hint of an ironic smile; she said nothing, however, sitting as impassively as an Indian squaw. Then, after a rather protracted pause, Ray Benson switched the conversation to the great subject of the moment: the coming impeachment or resignation of President Nixon. From then on Hux no longer had to listen to what was being said.

Suddenly the need to get away was overpowering. Though he was looking at Peggy Benson's sister again, he was inwardly staring at the lighted windows on Granada Street. He *had* to see what was happening there. When did they regularly go to bed? Early, he imagined, since they were both old. Even if he left now, it would be nearly ten before he reached the house. Hux could not bear the thought of being too late. "I'm afraid I have to be going now," he said, standing up. "It's been a wonderful evening, but I'm having lunch with the Delta State people tomorrow, and I have to get an early start."

"Don't you dare leave now!" cried Mrs. Benson. Ray Benson was equally appalled at the suggestion. It was only a little after nine, he protested—the evening was still young—Hux couldn't leave now—

Oh, yes I can, thought Hux as he waited for the flurry of hospitable anguish to die down. All he had to do was walk right through that door. . . . Though the tyranny of Southern manners was suddenly hateful to him, he had no intention of being rude. He merely stood his ground, smiling, while Peggy Benson insisted that he just had to stay another hour. Ray would fix him a gin and tonic . . . or maybe Hux would prefer some more iced coffee? After all, Cleveland wasn't so far away—Hux could make the trip in about an hour and a half, couldn't he? Probably less . . . Still Hux refused to sit down. What the hell was he going to do if his hosts didn't relent soon? He was determined to get to Alhambra that night, and just as he was on the point of accepting the necessity of being rude, he was suddenly rescued. Peggy Benson's sister—Annie Slam or whatever her improbable name was—stood up. She hated to break up the party, she declared, but she had to go too. Since she didn't have a car, would Mr. Hux be kind enough to give her a lift to her apartment?

"Oh, Annie, for goodness sake!" screamed her sister. "Don't you dare drag Mr. Hux—Larry—away."

"But you really do have to go, don't you?" said Annie Slam, turning to Hux, her thin face alive with mischief and defiance. "Don't feel you have to stay just to be polite. Ray and Peggy will understand."

"I am *furious*," said Peggy. "But of course we won't insist if Mr.—Larry—feels he really just has to go."

"I really should. I hate to, but I really should."

But before he could escape, Hux was cornered near the front door by another guest, a Mrs. Halsey, who insisted that he come to another dinner party—one that she and her husband, Dean Halsey, were giving a week from Friday. Although he again warned himself against too many engagements, Hux's guilt over his treatment of the Bensons made him accept.

In the car he thanked his rescuer as fervently as he could without giving the impression that he hadn't enjoyed himself at the Bensons'.

"Look," she replied, "you don't have to be polite. I know what it's like to be trapped in that house. Ray and Peg are well-meanin' people, but if you aren't real careful, they'll tie you hand and foot. Not just for tonight but for the rest of your stay in Oxford. Peg is greedy for new flies in her web. Don't let that happen."

"Do you like living in Oxford?" Hux was suspicious of this outspoken and disloyal sister.

"I don't have much choice at the moment," she said flatly. "I'm divorced and I have an eight-year-old daughter. I get practically no child support, so I work at the university library. Which isn't so bad—I can stand it. Anyway, here I am."

"It looks like a pleasant enough old town," said Hux, who was eager to drop her off and be on his way.

"Oxford's a tree-lined cell. I'm one of the less tranquilized inmates."

The distance to Annie's apartment on University Avenue was short. As she got out of the car, she said, "If you get fed up with academic sweet talk, give me a call and come by for a drink." She stood for a moment in the doorway of the building, long-legged and angular, her face again defiant. "Just a friendly drink. No strings. Peg may have designs on you but I haven't."

"All right," said Hux warily. "Thanks. I'll give you a call. What's your last name again?"

"S-C-H-L-A-M-M. Anne Schlamm. It's what I call a real euphonious name." She laughed, tilting her head abruptly so that her dark straight hair fell in a small cascade over one shoulder. "And it's 'Anne,' not 'Annie.' Only Peg calls me that."

"Got it. Goodnight, Anne."

"Goodnight, Larry." She laughed again and pushed open the door with a movement that made her wide red skirt sway like a dancer's.

He was not too late. Lights were on in the living room. Crouching, Hux skirted the front of the house, prepared to throw himself full length on the ground behind the low shrubs in case the headlights of a car approached. He could have peered into the front window but chose to round the corner of the house, where a side window threw a strip of light across the grass. Rising from his crouch like a cat, Hux placed both hands on the sill and slowly raised his head. The window was open several inches from the bottom; insects were crawling on the screen.

Claiborne Herne's face had been replaced by a jagged, tomato-red mask! He had aged at least twenty years since the photograph in *Look*. As he had with the house, Hux felt outrage, bitterness, as he stared at the cotton-white hair and brows, the sagging mouth. Dr. Herne had escaped him by putting on a fantastic disguise, the armoring of a broken old age. Suddenly Hux thought of his own father in his last illness, his face not red but yellowed by cirrhosis, an old man of no more than sixty, drinking his medicine through a bent glass straw.

Gradually the room began to shape itself around Dr. Herne, who was sitting in a battered old Morris chair, holding a tall glass of what appeared to be straight whiskey poured over ice cubes. He was gazing at something in a corner of the room which Hux could not see because of the angle of vision. A television set? A blank wall? Probably not blank, for the low-ceilinged living room of this banal modern house was crammed with oversized furniture, nearly every inch of its walls covered by old prints and brownish photographs—mostly in black oval frames—of bearded men and ladies in high-necked dresses. As Hux watched, Dr. Herne slowly lowered his drink to the flat, shelf-like arm of the Morris chair and from an ashtray on the other arm lifted a cigar with a long white ash. From the rigidly controlled way in which Dr. Herne shook off the ash, Hux guessed that the doctor was either partially paralyzed or else extremely drunk.

Isabelle Herne entered the room—heavier perhaps, puffier, but otherwise little changed from the *Look* picture. She was wearing a pink quilted dressing gown and carrying a book. Despite the open window, Hux could not make out the words she addressed to her brother, who nodded once or twice and noisily cleared his throat. Isabelle reached out hesitantly and touched her brother on the shoulder of his white shirt—like a child patting a horse. Then she left the room. A moment later Dr. Herne got up, clutching his glass, and—with much less decrepitude than Hux would have expected—went to a little table on which stood an ice bucket and a bottle which Hux could identify as Old Grand-Dad. The clink of ice cubes sounded across the room. Next Dr. Herne walked over to a marble-topped console table that stood against the far wall, just within Hux's vision. On it were two models of sailing ships, each very ornate. As Hux craned to look, Dr. Herne, after setting down his glass, bent over one of the ships and adjusted something in the rigging—perhaps a pennant or a sail that had sagged. Then, straightening himself, he stood fully erect, his head nearly touching the ceiling. *Ah, he's not done for yet*, thought Hux, whose own back and knees were aching from his prolonged crouch. He saw the doctor—

A strange light was playing against the side of the house. A car—it was nearly upon him! Terrified that he was too late, Hux darted around to the back of the house. The car had slowed down, and Hux, who did not dare peer around the corner, expected it to stop. But the car passed slowly on, leaving Hux as weak as if he had run a hundred yards. Deciding that he had pressed his luck far enough for one night, Hux did not return to the window but hurried up the street to the spot where he had left his own car. Switching on the motor, he drove several hundred yards with the lights off, fearing that the other car—almost certainly a police car—might have turned around. It was not until he reached the intersection of Granada and Main and turned left that he allowed himself a deep exhalation of relief.

Hux drove back to Oxford pondering the husk of the man whose conscience he had wanted to storm. A burnt-out case, a ruin—still the man was not necessarily beyond reach. Probably he could still be made to writhe like an insect touched by a swab dipped in acid. Hux felt no pity. But how was he to gain access? Could he work through the sister? That pharmacist, he recalled, had said that she was a fruit ripe for the Lord's plucking, or words to that effect. Perhaps she could be approached by Reverend Ainsley Black. . . . But that role would take some practicing. While he was growing up in the South, Hux had had little direct exposure to evangelicals, though he had heard them on the radio often enough. He would need some pointers, a few hints. . . . Why not attend Brother Thurlow's meeting tomorrow night? There at least he could refresh his memory of the language, the jargon, the rhythms. And on Sunday . . . as yet he knew only that he would spend the day in Alhambra. A watchful, hovering angel—that's what he'd be. Loose, improvising, without a plan . . . But ready to swoop when something stirred.

Chapter Eleven

When Rooney Lee saw the prowler—a white man wearing a red shirt—duck around the corner of Dr. Claiborne's house, it did not occur to him to call the police. Any policeman would have been far more concerned with finding out why he—Rooney—was driving through a white neighborhood at that hour than with catching a peeping tom or even a possible burglar. Instead, he continued to drive slowly out Granada, noticing, as he passed it, a beige Plymouth Valiant with Tennessee plates parked by the side of the road beyond the last houses. At the point where the paved portion of Granada ended, he turned off his headlights, pulled off the road into a dirt track, and stopped. Having no gun with him, he took a switchblade knife from the glove compartment and placed it in the hip pocket of his jeans. There was no moonlight, but Rooney, as he advanced down the road, could make out a faint gleam from the roof of the parked car. Beyond were the lights of houses, among them the Hernes'. He made no sound as he padded shadowlike along the edge of the pavement, his white sneakers glowing more dimly than phosphorus in the dark.

When he was less than fifty feet from the car, he heard the rapid slapping of shoes along the road—a man running in his direction. Rooney crouched low and pressed the button of his switchblade, which made a *click* that sounded loud in his ears but could scarcely have been audible even a foot away, so great was the racket of the insects and frogs. Next Rooney heard the opening and slamming shut of the car door, the growl, cough, and purr of the motor, and the scraping of the tires as the car pulled into the street. No lights! Frozen in his cat-man's crouch, Rooney waited until all sounds of the car had died away before standing up. Who the hell was messing around with *his* white man?

Now outside the Hernes' house, he saw that Dr. Claiborne was still up, sitting in his living-room chair. The lights were on in Miss Isabelle's room, but she was working at her desk instead of getting ready for bed. Should he hang around? Rooney had driven to Granada Street with the idea of paying Dr. Herne a surprise nighttime visit to bring up a business matter better dealt with when the old man was drunk rather than moderately sober. He had paid such a visit once before, waiting until Miss Isabelle was in bed and then tapping at the doctor's bedroom window; Dr. Claiborne had been just sober enough to come into the kitchen and open the back door for Rooney. Tonight the old man looked like a dummy sitting in that chair, staring at the wall; it seemed unlikely that he would even make it to his bed before passing out. Well, the business would have to wait until he and Vicky paid their Sunday-morning visit.

Rooney walked back to his car. Though he could make no sense of the prowler's presence, the mere thought of him made Rooney want to hop and skip with rage. *Who the hell was trying to fuck around with his white family?* Since it was still fairly early, Rooney considered driving over to his favorite hangout, a place called the Black Rooster over near Clarksdale. Goldie was likely to be there. But Rooney was so angry that he feared doing something to Goldie that he'd be sorry about later. No, the best time to see Goldie was on a Sunday afternoon, just after one of Vicky's sessions with Dr. Claiborne; for some reason he always felt horny as a billy goat on those afternoons—and in a good mood too, not likely to turn mean with Goldie. He drove back to Waller's Spring, the section of Alhambra where most of the blacks lived. Turning into his drive, he parked next to a black hearse in a carport behind the brick building and then went up the outside stairs to his apartment. Still strung taut with anger, he half hoped that Vicky had already gone to bed so that she wouldn't provoke him into losing control. On the other hand, he wouldn't mind too much if she was still up and did provoke him with some remark or even with one of those sideways looks of hers that never failed to set him off.

Chapter Twelve

During the night Hux was startled into wakefulness by a dream which he then could not remember. After struggling to orient himself, he realized that he was in a motel room in Oxford, Mississippi; for some reason he had thought that he was in his old bedroom in Gastonia, North Carolina, where he had spent his boyhood—a room connected by a sliding door to his parents' bedroom. The threads of light at the top and bottom of the door were much the same. Turning over, Hux tried to bury in sleep the oppressiveness, the anxiety, with which he had awakened. But sleep was now an impossibility. Rolling over on his back again, he stared at the strip of light over the door. . . . *How they had fought!* Night after night he had awakened to the sounds of their rage. But the only voice that now came back was his mother's; the sounds made by his father were muffled, the indistinct sounds of an animal behind a thick wall.

One night his mother, who was prone to melodrama, had pulled back the sliding door and rushed into his room in her nightgown, her long hair, released from its bun for the night, streaming across her shoulders. "Lorenzo, my precious Lorenzo," she had crooned in her throaty voice, "you've got to choose." She carried Hux—who must have been about six at the time, he supposed—to a rocking chair, where she hugged him to her sweat-dampened gown as she rocked back and forth, telling him that she was going to leave Daddy, that she could endure no more, that he would have to choose between them. Through the half-open door the boy could see his parents' bed and his father's bare feet and his pajamaed legs (but not his torso) as he lay on top of the covers, rigid as a corpse.

Hux could not remember how the scene had ended. Presumably his mother, after calming herself with the rocking, had carried the child back to his bed. He could not remember his own fears or anguish—only the strange look of his father's pale feet. His mother of course did not leave. Probably nothing was said at breakfast the next morning. Hux could imagine his father whistling "Oh, What a Beautiful Morning" in his pathetic, off-key way as he set off down the road to the Crawford Mills, where he worked as chief bookkeeper in the accounting department.

The Rededication Service turned out to be of little immediate help to Hux in his new part. In the first place, the star performer and his chief role model, Reverend Archie B. Thurlow, was voiceless, a victim of laryngitis. Word of the preacher's affliction must have been spread beforehand, for when Hux arrived at Ephraim Baptist Church a little before eight, he found a rather meager and elderly congregation. The church itself was as brightly lit as a high-school gymnasium before a basketball game; light glanced from the golden-oak pews, which had been varnished and waxed to a mirroring brilliance, and from the brass strips that bordered the worn red carpeting down the center aisle. This excess of illumination was more depressing than festive, for it merely emphasized the absence of the young, who had clearly decided that there were better ways of spending Saturday night. The prevailing air of dejection was not relieved by a thumping rendition of "Throw Out the Lifeline" on the organ or by the skillfully harmonized singing of the same hymn by the Godspeeders, a trio of young men with very short haircuts, dressed patriotically in deep-blue trousers, short-sleeved white shirts, and bright red ties. Hux would not have been surprised if a cheerleader had come prancing onto the platform.

The most that Reverend Thurlow could manage was to croak out the text for the evening: "Render therefore unto Caesar the things which are Caesar's; and unto God the things that are God's." Then he returned to a chair set a few feet to the side of the preacher's lectern on the carpeted platform in the front of the church. The service itself was conducted by one of Thurlow's associates, identified in the mimeographed program as Rev. Sid DeWitt Covington. Hymns, gospel readings, the offering—all weighed upon Hux with a crushing familiarity—though he realized that he had not set foot in a church since Clark's funeral ten years before. As a boy growing up in Gastonia, he had gone regularly to Sunday school, less frequently to church. Though nominally members of the Mt. Hebron Methodist Church, his parents seldom attended its services. His mother, as the daughter of Raleigh's leading alienist (as she regularly referred to him), prided herself on a scientific, even skeptical approach to religious matters and could barely tolerate the devout and eager ladies of the church who were always pressing her to participate in its many activities. His father, though a believer, was also secretly and sinfully a drinker, an abject figure on Sunday mornings, seldom able to find his way churchward through his private fog of hangover and guilt. Consequently, Hux's chief memories of church stemmed from visits to his paternal grandparents in the small town of Warrenton. There, bribed by peppermints and drawing materials, he had, as a small boy, been squeezed between his stout, sweet-scented grandmother and his even fatter grandfather, whose Sunday suits smelled of diabetic sweat. When he was older, he continued to go with his now-widowed grandmother, for whom he found the hymns and held the hymnbook and for whose sake he sat stupefied during the long sermons, his thoughts straying guiltily into the dark tangles of adolescent sex. Now, re-experiencing the boredom as acutely as if he were still fourteen, he reflected that it served him right for having so recklessly decided to play the part of a preacher....

There seemed little to be learned from the performance of Brother Covington. A raw-boned young man with lank red hair and a yellowish skin, he spoke with a high-pitched nasality, which, combined with a staccato delivery, nearly drove Hux from his pew. The sermon was not what Hux would have thought of as evangelical—perhaps Reverend Thurlow, who sat listening to this substitute with an air of gloomy appraisal, had decided to postpone the harvesting of souls until he could do so in his own voice; instead, the sermon was overtly and offensively political. We should thank the good Lord night and day on our knees, said Brother Covington, that the President of the United States is a Christian, a devoted family man, and the dedicated and proven foe of atheistic Communism. No doubt he had made mistakes—he was only human after all—but if he had—and Brother Covington couldn't help thinking that the charges and allegations were exaggerated—then it was our Christian duty to leave his punishment to the Lord and not to try to take it upon ourselves. "Render!" he half barked, half whined, "unto Caesar! The things. Which are Caesar's! And unto God ..."

Defeated by Brother Covington's logic, Hux stopped listening. Would he make himself too conspicuous if he got up and left? He had spotted Mr. Porter, the pharmacist, sitting with his wife in a nearby pew and decided that it would be unwise, for his future plans, to make a spectacle of himself. The preacher's voice had become the yapping of an agitated fox terrier. Shutting it out as best he could, Hux focused upon the hunched, glowering figure of Reverend Thurlow, trying to connect it with the moon-faced image that had appeared on posters all over town. There was nothing cheery about the squat, barrel-chested man sitting with folded arms on the platform, his glasses flashing in the light. Was he disappointed in his substitute? Or was Brother Covington merely speaking from a script written by Reverend Thurlow, who had, after all, provided the gospel text? Reverend Thurlow's attentive crouch has something potentially brutal about it, reminding Hux of a wrestler or a whip-cracking animal trainer waiting to leap into action. Once Thurlow took off his glasses, wiped them, and looked out over the congregation as if appraising them too—and scornful of the feeble lot he saw. Even from a distance his dark eyes, so genial in the photograph, seemed dark with rage.

The sermon ended with a repetition of the text, accompanied by a gavel-like pounding of Brother Covington's fist upon the lectern. *Inept, miscalculated* . . . Hux thought he saw Brother Thurlow shake his head in disapproval. Then the Godspeeders came forward to sing "The Old Rugged Cross," inviting the reedy-voiced congregation to join in for the final stanza. As Brother Covington pronounced the benediction, Reverend Thurlow came forward and stood beside him, his large head bowed. When it was over, he put one arm around his substitute's shoulder and held out the other like a fascist salute to the congregation. Was it mockery? The members of the congregation stood uncertainly while the organ softly repeated the hymn—were they expecting an appeal to come forward to declare themselves for Jesus? If so, none came. The two preachers, their heads again bowed, left the platform and walked down the central aisle. Slowly the congregation broke up.

As he was leaving the church, Hux felt a touch on his arm. It was Mr. Porter, who had run ahead of his wife. "What a shame," he said, twitching his scalp, "what a shame. The only night when I can git away. But I reckon we have to take the showers with the sunshine, don't we, Brother Black? Will I see you here tomorrow?"

Assuming his Ainsley Black expression and voice, Hux slowly shook his head. "No, sir," he said, "my assignment tomorrow won't permit it. But I have a hunch Reverend Thurlow's voice will come boomin' back. Somethin' tells me you won't be disappointed. Goodnight." And Hux rushed off into the darkness like a man already late.

Chapter Thirteen

Isabelle was nearly late. She had seen the dreaded car again that morning, and she groped her way into the brown gloom of the church as if she had been blinded by the car's white dazzle. Just as the minister advanced toward the lectern in front of the pulpit, Isabelle managed to reach the pew that her family had occupied since the building of the church in 1858. The congregation rose for the opening prayer. Then something unexpected occurred: a man whom she perceived as young—a stranger in a blue seersucker suit—entered the pew at her side and stood next to her, head bowed, as the words "Let us pray" sounded from the pulpit. She gave him a startled timid smile of welcome and then closed her eyes tightly and let her head fall so that the tip of her chin touched the cameo brooch at her chin. When, after the *amen*, the first hymn was announced, the young man deftly extracted a hymnbook from the rack, opened it to the proper number, and handed it to Isabelle. He did not offer to hold it for her—as if such a gesture would have been too familiar—but took out a second hymnal for himself. Side by side they sang "From Greenland's Icy Mountains," she quaveringly, in a key made uncertain by her deafness, he in a tenor that seemed too loud and strained to her, unused as she was to someone singing so close to her ear. During the rest of the service he was attentive in various small ways, picking up her program when she dropped it, patiently holding the collection plate while she fumbled in her purse, smiling at her encouragingly while she adjusted her hearing aid at the beginning of the sermon. Isabelle was grateful for this kindness, but it made her feel so horribly shy that she almost wished he would go away.

"Honor thy father and thy mother: that thy days may be long upon the land which the Lord thy God giveth thee."

No matter what difficulty she might have in following the development of a sermon, Isabelle could always manage to catch the opening text. Her knowledge of the Bible was such that even a couple of words were sufficient for her to assemble the entire verse. She was then able, with the help of sentences or phrases picked up here and there, to improvise a sermon—or, more likely, a detailed reverie that had some tangential reference to what Mr. Munce was saying. Unfortunately, the amplification system which he used clashed violently with that of her hearing aid. Sometimes the acoustical distortion became so painful that she was forced to switch off her device entirely, a situation that she hated, for she had never lost faith in the power of a preacher—almost any preacher—to convey new and helpful thoughts about even the most familiar of texts. No text could have been more familiar to her than today's; yet she could not recall having heard a sermon built upon it in recent years. The fact that Mr. Munce had recently lost his mother (Isabelle had written him a note of condolence) added a poignancy to his topic and made Isabelle all the more frustrated at her failure to catch his words.

She hoped that she had always honored her parents. Her mother, who had come from the little Delta town of Beulah, had been considered one of the great beauties of a region which, socially speaking, reached almost from Memphis to Vicksburg, and the legend of her beauty had been kept alive even to this day. Old Mr. Tom Moodie, who was close to ninety, still loved to tell about the time he had summoned his nerve to ask Florence Buford (as she then was) to dance with him when he was only seventeen and she was already twenty. "She was so gracious," Mr. Tom always said, "so gracious and lovely. She made me feel like a prince, and for a week afterward I still fancied I could smell her perfume on my fingertips." Isabelle was never bored by this story. It helped her to fill out the picture of her mother, to realize that the crossness and distraction that she remembered painfully were really an insignificant part of the whole. Isabelle, who had never been pretty, even as a baby, knew that she could not have been a very easy child for such a mother. Florence Herne had died, suddenly and mysteriously, when Isabelle was only nine. Years later, Claiborne, by then a doctor, had told her that their mother had died of an embolism and that she had been pregnant at the time—information that had, for reasons she could not fathom, made Isabelle so miserable that for days afterward she wanted to die.

Instead, she had now attained the Biblical age of three score and ten! Was this the long life promised to those who honored their fathers and mothers?

Having turned off her hearing aid, Isabelle allowed herself to sink into a memory that still had the power to envelop her in warmth like a goose-down quilt. In the evening after her mother's funeral, little Claiborne, who was only four at the time, had run wild. They had all been startled by the matter-of-fact way in which he had taken his mother's sudden death and the events that followed. He had not cried even when he was lifted to see her lying in her casket. As the stunned and grieving relatives gathered from all over the state and from as far away as Louisiana, he had played contentedly under the supervision of Mammy Norah, pausing sometimes to stare when one of the adults burst into tears. Isabelle could still see that funny, bemused look on the little boy's face. Everyone commented on how well behaved he was. But after the return from the cemetery and the huge supper that followed, he had begun to make a nuisance of himself. Granny Buford, after having been "heroic" for so long, had given way at last to bereavement and exhaustion and had taken to her bed, leaving the child in the hands of Norah, who was unable to control him in his new wild mood. Escaping from her, Claiborne had dragged his hobbyhorse into the crowded parlor and pulled it around the room, bumping into the legs of the mourners. Simultaneously his father ordered him out of the room and Norah came into the room to carry him off to bed. Isabelle remembered that Norah was wearing a black silk scarf around her head instead of the familiar white headcloth. Shrieking with laughter, Claiborne had dodged behind the furniture, evading all efforts to capture him. After what had seemed an interminable chase, during which the whole room was thrown into turmoil, someone—was it Great-uncle Calvin Bledsoe?—had managed to grab the boy's ankle, and Claiborne had been pulled from under the big sofa, limp and hiccuping from laughter. Now came the worst, the most painful part. Before Norah could carry the child away, their father had advanced across the room and slapped Claiborne across the face so hard that he was sent reeling against the rim of the round parlor table and knocked unconscious. If it had not been for the thick fringed tablecloth, his head would have been split wide open. As it was, Isabelle, when she saw the still, white face and blue-tinged eyelids, knew at once that her brother was dead. But then—and she could still remember the surge of relief that swept over her—Claiborne had opened his mouth and begun to scream. After Dr. Cawley, who was sitting with the family, had examined him and pronounced that there would be nothing worse than a nasty lump, Norah had picked up the screaming child and carried him off in her arms.

Isabelle had never blamed her father. Anyone in his distraught state would have done the same thing. He had, of course, struck much harder than he had intended. She could see him, sitting back in his armchair in the now hushed room, his own eyes closed, his white shirtfront heaving up and down as if he couldn't catch his breath. . . .

Meanwhile, Claiborne continued his screaming and fought off Norah whenever she tried to comfort him in any way. The sound of it rang through the stricken house. Then Isabelle, who had been sitting on the carpet at her father's feet, got up and tiptoed out of the parlor and ran upstairs to her brother's room. She found Norah at her wit's end, trying to hold the squirming, kicking, scratching child while tears of angry frustration streamed down her round black cheeks. Claiborne was naked. Although Norah had managed to get his clothes off, she had been unable to slip his nightshirt over his head. When Claiborne saw his sister, he broke loose from his nurse and ran to Isabelle and buried his face in her skirt.

"You can go, Norah," Isabelle said, feeling very grown up. "I'll finish putting Brother to bed."

"Some debble got holt of that chile," said Norah, who loved both the children. Then she mumbled, "Your pa ought to be shamed of hisself."

"Don't say that!" cried Isabelle, clasping the boy's naked shoulders with both hands. "Norah, please go. Right now."

For the next half hour she sat on the edge of Claiborne's little bed, holding him, whispering to him how much their mother, who was in Heaven, wanted him to be a good boy, stroking his hair, kissing his cheeks and the tops of his shoulders, waiting for his sobbing to subside. When finally it did, she continued to whisper that she would always look after him, that he needn't be afraid. And when he, quieted now, murmured that their mother was coming back when she got tired of Memphis, Isabelle said no, that Momma was not coming back, that she hadn't gone to Memphis, that her body was in the cemetery and that her soul was in Heaven, where she was looking down on them, and that she could hear everything they said. Finally she felt her brother's head nod against her shoulder and she got him into his nightshirt and under the sheets. Then she had sat there in the half darkness for a long time, comforted herself but weeping gently and sure that her mother was very proud of her. After that, she had often put Claiborne to bed until he was old enough to do it for himself.

She was still looking after him, she told herself. As best she could. But she could no longer imagine that her mother was proud of her. She hadn't, after all, been able to save him. . . .

A touch on her shoulder. Startled, Isabelle looked up to see that the whole congregation was standing; the sermon was over, the hymn was about to begin. Had her hearing aid gone dead? Smiling down at her, the young man, who was holding an open hymnal, gave a slight nod of encouragement, and Isabelle jumped to her feet. As often happened these days when she got up too suddenly, Isabelle saw spots in front of her eyes and felt dizzy. Swaying slightly, she caught the young man's arm. Something *was* wrong with her hearing aid, though it was not dead: the familiar strains of "He leadeth me" reached her through rasping, hummings, and cracklings, a cacophony that increased her disorientation. Afraid that she was about to faint or be sick and horrified by either possibility, she managed to say loudly, "I have to go. Please let me out." And blindly she tried to push her way past the young man, who seemed intent on thrusting the hymnal under her nose. "I don't feel well," she muttered, barely audible now. In a moment she was in the aisle, her companion having stepped out of the pew. Then she felt his strong hand beneath her elbow and was half lifted, half sustained, as she tottered down the aisle toward the gothic doors.

"In back," she said, still muttering, "in back of the church." Blinking in the hot sunlight, she drew in a head-cleansing breath of leafy air. "There's a bench. . . . I'm all right," she added in a stronger voice. "I really am all right. I just need to sit outside for a few minutes—it was so stuffy in there. I really am all right." Now she looked at him, seeing him clearly, the dizziness nearly gone.

"Your color's comin' back, Miss Isabelle. You suddenly went white as a sheet. But I'm goin' to stay with you for a little while, just to make sure."

She heard every word; whatever had been wrong with her hearing aid seemed to have adjusted itself. Together they followed a mossy brick walk that led along the side of the church to a small garden in the rear. There, sheltered by crape myrtles and shaggy old cedar trees, was the little bench of Tennessee marble that she and Claiborne had given years before when Dr. Blakelock had been so keen on creating the garden. Even in her present state she noted that her refuge was no longer well kept up: the shrubs needed pruning, there were scraps of paper and other wind-blown rubbish lying about. . . . But the bench itself looked inviting in the dappled shade. After brushing away some dead leaves and dirt with her handkerchief, she sat down heavily, and as she did so, she wondered for the first time how the young man had learned her name.

"May I sit with you, Miss Isabelle?"

There it was again!—she had not imagined it. Much too shaken and timid to say that she wanted to be alone, Isabelle could only nod. Then her ingrained politeness produced a rather tremulous smile of welcome as she made room for him on the bench. Sitting down at once, he crossed his legs familiarly, stroked his chin, and asked encouragingly if she was still feeling better.

"Yes, much better, thank you," she said, dropping her eyes, abashed by the stranger's blond handsomeness.

"What a lovely spot. This bench, these trees."

"It used to be kept up better. I'll have to speak to Mr. Munce or the Ladies' Auxiliary about the way it's been allowed to run down. Of course it's so hard to get reliable help these days. . . . This spot is precious to me. My brother and I gave the bench in memory of our parents. Look," she said, moving to one side to reveal a chiseled inscription in the center of the white marble seat.

IN MEMORY OF WILLIAM CLAIBORNE HERNE 1869-1939
AND
FLORENCE BUFORD HERNE 1882-1913
DEVOTED MEMBERS OF THIS CONGREGATION
THEY WALK WITH GOD

While the stranger reverently gazed at it, Isabelle suddenly recalled the question she had been meaning to ask. "But how did you know my name?"

Slowly he turned his sweet gaze upon her. "Someone pointed you out to me. Besides, I'd seen your picture."

What could this mean? Had she heard him properly? "You've seen my picture? Is that what you said?"

"Yes, ma'am. I've known about you—and your brother—*and* his troubles—for nearly ten years. I came to this church today hopin' to see you. I may be able to help your brother—if you'll help me."

Now she was frightened. "But who *are* you? Why—" Looking wildly toward the church, she wondered whom she might call. The congregation would be leaving just now. . . . Should she get up and run to the front?

"I'm sorry, ma'am. I ought to have introduced myself before. My name is Ainsley Black. Reverend Ainsley Black."

Isabelle blinked at him, her mouth slightly open, her hands twisting the handkerchief she had used to wipe the bench.

"Have you heard about Reverend Thurlow's Rededication?"

"You—you mean the Baptists?"

"Yes, ma'am. That's my official reason for bein' in town. But my *real* reason—and I know how peculiar this is goin' to sound—is to get the chance to meet you and your brother."

Isabelle shot a quick glance into the unclouded blue eyes of the plump and smiling young man. Such nice eyes, so friendly, so gentle . . . Yet she was frightened, trembling, for the moment unable to speak.

"What I want most of all," he continued in a slightly nasal, sing-song voice, "is to persuade you and your brother to accompany me to one of Brother Thurlow's services at the Ephraim Baptist Church. There'll be one tonight and one every night this week. The last one is next Sunday, in the mornin'. Will you all come with me to one of them? I think Reverend Thurlow may have a special message for Dr. Herne."

"But—but—we're not Baptists," said Isabelle, hating the lameness of her excuse but incapable of inventing something more plausible. Now that her fear (though not her amazement) was beginning to subside, Isabelle was afraid that she might sound snobbish, that she might inadvertently hurt the young man's feelings. Claiborne, of course, would have had no such compunctions. . . .

"I know that. Baptist, Presbyterian, Methodist, Episcopalian—these labels come to mean so much to us, and they're the merest chaff in the eyes of the Lord! I'd be here with you now, sittin' on this very bench, askin' you to come hear Brother Thurlow, *even* if you were all Roman Catholics worshipin' the Virgin Mary and all the saints."

"Who sent you? Who told you to seek us out? Mr.—Reverend— Thurlow? Why would he—" She broke off, seeing him shake his head in denial. "Then *who*?"

Ainsley Black's expression became very strange. No longer smiling, he continued to shake his head. Isabelle noticed that he was blushing slightly, as if he might be concealing an embarrassing fact. His look was so odd, so mysterious, and at the same time kind, that Isabelle mentally supplied an answer that distressed her: was he about to say "God"?

"Miss Isabelle, let me explain. I'm what you might call a travelin' man. In the South mostly, but in other places too. If it didn't sound too stuckup and conceited, I'd have to describe myself as a fisher of souls. Troubled souls. In every community I visit, I know who they are. Some of them are mighty sinners. Most are victims and sufferers. Makes no difference. Some are the humble poor, the wretched of the earth. Others are distinguished members of their communities, like you and your brother. Some are even black, though mostly I leave them in the capable hands of my wonderful fella agents among their own race. It doesn't matter. All are in trouble, all are desolate, all of them more than anything else need to place their hands, like trustin' little children, into the infinitely mighty and infinitely consolin' hands of the Lord."

Isabelle retreated before his fervor, figuratively raising both hands to ward it off. Some part of her mind reflected that his voice was a bit common, the voice of a hill-country preacher. But what he was saying frightened her, touching as it did upon her constant prayer that her brother might open himself to God.

"Will you come with me to hear Reverend Thurlow? Forget that he's a Baptist. Who he is and where he comes from don't matter one little bit, for he is a vessel of the Lord, an ever-replenished vessel from which pours the livin' Word of God. As for me, I'm a mere errand boy of the Lord, a messenger, a go-between. I am sent to seek out troubled souls that they may drink from the vessel that is Reverend Thurlow and others like him, whose own emptiness is forever filled by the grace of God. Will you come? Will you ask your brother to come?"

"I hardly ever go out in the evenin'," said Isabelle, again hating the awkwardness, the pettiness, of her excuse. "And my brother doesn't go out at all."

"May I talk with your brother?"

"Oh, no!" she cried, horrified at the idea. "He wouldn't see you. He—" But she could not bring herself to speak of her brother's scorn for evangelists, holy rollers, and the like. "He sees no one these days. Not even old friends."

"Miss Isabelle—"

"No," she said, standing up, determined to escape. But once again she had risen too quickly. Black spots danced, and dizziness, tainted with nausea, overcame her, forcing her back to the bench.

After a blacked-out second or two, she heard his voice through the buzzing of her ears. "Miss Isabelle, you don't look well. I'm goin' to take you home in my car."

"No," she said, but already he had caught her under both arms and was lifting her.

"Now just lean on me. I'll have you home in a jiffy, and we'll have the doctor come over and take a look at you."

Isabelle felt much better the minute she was seated in the car. Though she started to protest again that she was perfectly able to walk home, that a walk would do her good, a residue of weakness silenced her. What if she was really ill, if she had had a slight stroke? Who would look after Claiborne? She glanced timidly at Ainsley

Black and he smiled in reply. Already they were driving down Granada. He seemed to know where she lived without her telling him. God's errand boy . . . The word *angel* entered her mind and vanished, giving way to the thought of how furious Claiborne was going to be. Well, there was no helping that. She was unwell, and this kind young man had offered to drive her home. . . . Then another, more horrible idea occurred. What if Vicky and Rooney were still there? She always took her time coming back from church, pausing to chat with old friends, walking home slowly. Once, several years ago, she had returned promptly and had found Claiborne's door still closed; in panic, she had switched off her hearing aid so that no sound could reach her—what sound had she expected? Isabelle could still recall with almost undiminished horror—and hatred—the embarrassed little grin she had received as Vicky, in a nurse's white uniform, had slipped past the open door of Isabelle's bedroom, carrying a black bag like a doctor's. In her weakness Isabelle now fell into one of her violent fantasies: Vicky and Rooney were both dead! A truck had crashed into them, demolishing that dreadful car. She saw the two bodies—one mountainous, one slim—lying side by side beneath a bloodstained sheet on the side of the highway. . . .

As they approached the house, Isabelle fearfully scanned the street ahead. The white car, thank God, was nowhere in sight. Ainsley turned into the drive, stopping just behind her own car. "Here we are. Now you just sit right where you are, Miss Isabelle, and I'll come around and help you out."

Chapter Fourteen

As he held the car door open for Miss Isabelle, Hux felt sensations of infused power and mastery such as he had only fleetingly known before, sensations that an actor sometimes experiences on those eerie occasions when, after weeks of rehearsal, a new role suddenly defeats the actor's own struggling ego and takes over, dictating its own terms, exercising absolute control over voice, gesture, and even the tiniest flickers of expression in the eyes and around the corners of the mouth. A small particle of Hux's consciousness wished that he could watch himself. Only a few times during his performance of Richard II for the Carolina Playmakers had he felt such perfect synthesis—and synchronization—with a part. Ainsley Black had simply absorbed him; all he—Hux—had to do was surrender to the impulses of his tongue and brain. And now the momentum of his performance was about to carry him into the presence of the man who had murdered Clark! Hux was ready for him.

"Just walk me to the front door. I'll be fine."

"No, ma'am. I'm goin' to speak to your brother and have him call the doctor. I want you to go straight to your room and lie down."

"But my brother—"

"Just do like I say, Miss Isabelle. You still look kind of peaked. We don't want to take any chances." Hux waited in perfect confidence while this odd, dumpy little woman stared at him for a moment and then did as she was told—fishing her key out of her handbag, opening the door, calling out softly, "Brother? Brother?" Hux followed her into the front hall and into the low-ceilinged living room, seeing now in unmellowing daylight its clutter of dark old furniture and faded pictures. There was no sign of Dr. Herne. Isabelle went next to a closed door that led from the living room and softly knocked. No response. "Brother," she called, "are you there, are you all right? I need to speak to you."

Hux heard a dull thud, as of feet swung from a bed to a carpeted floor. Then a hoarse, rumbling voice that seemed to force its way up through phlegm. "Isabelle, go away. Don't bother me now." Apparently she had not heard him, for she called out again, "Brother, are you there? Are you all right?"

The door was pulled inward, and Hux saw the murderer standing stiffly, as if wearing a brace, his face flushed and contorted, his neck wattle-red against the open collar of his immaculate white shirt. "Why must you bother me now?" he rasped, not yet having seen Hux, who was standing near the door to the hall.

Miss Isabelle seemed to grow shorter, squatter, in the towering presence of her brother, whose fine white hair glowed like spun glass against his blood-darkened forehead. As her mouth opened soundlessly, it occurred to Hux that she might faint, and he strode forward, his hand extended, saying, "Dr. Herne, your sister had a couple of dizzy spells at church, so I brought her home. She ought to lie down while we call the doctor."

Dr. Herne stepped back into his bedroom doorway, his hands slightly raised as if preparing to beat off the intruder. "Who *is* this man?" he demanded in what was almost a scream.

"Brother, this is Reverend . . ." And Isabelle faltered, having apparently forgotten the name.

"Black, Ainsley Black," said Hux, who was now close to the doctor. Again he held out his hand, which was ignored by the older man, who was staring about wildly, as if trying to find help.

"Brother, Reverend Black was so kind. I don't know what I'd have done without him. He insisted on bringin' me home, even though I told him I was feelin' well enough to walk."

"Much obliged," said Dr. Herne with a slight nod. "Now you can go. My sister will be all right."

Hux, who had just caught a powerful scent of whiskey from the doctor's breath, made no move to leave. The scene had hardly begun; now that he was in the presence of the legendary antagonist, he had no intention of quitting the stage. As the right words seemed to come unbidden to his lips, with the right emphases, the right intonations, he said, "If you don't mind, sir, I'll just hang around until the doctor's been here. You see, I've been right worried about your sister, and I don't want to leave until I find out how she is. The little lady's already feelin' much better, but I'd like to wait till the doctor's been here."

"Go to your room, Isabelle. I'll take care of this intruding fool."

"Brother, Reverend Black's been so helpful . . ."

"Go to your room!"

"Just do like he says, Miss Isabelle. Just lay down and have yourself a good rest."

After a quick, questioning glance from one to the other, Isabelle left the room, with a slightly wobbling gait. Now Dr. Herne lowered his head and thrust his beaked nose almost into Hux's face, drenching him with the odor of whiskey. "I've had enough of this non-sense, Reverend whatever-your-name-is. I thank you for your kindness to my sister, but we do not invite strangers into this house. You don't look like a preacher to me anyway. You're one of those FBI agents who've been sniffing around me for years. I will call Dr. Ben Morgan myself. Now get out."

Hux did not move. What a hateful old man!—his face all twisted, his eyes bloodshot, flecks of spittle in the corners of his mouth. . . .

The doctor, after a moment's pause, said, "Reverend I never thought I'd have to horsewhip a preacher out of my house, but if you don't leave this minute, that's exactly what I'm goin' to do."

"I don't mean to be disrespectful, sir," said Hux in a ringing voice, "but there's just no way you can force me out of this house until that doctor's come and gone. With God's help and my own strength, I can wrest a horsewhip right out of your tremblin' hands. I reckon I'm in better shape at this moment than you are, if it comes to grapplin' with either bodies or souls. Of course you'd be in your rights to shoot me for trespassin', but I doubt if you're all that eager to stand trial for murder for the second time in your life. In any case, I won't go even if you hold a gun to my forehead."

At the word "trial" Dr. Herne winced and abruptly turned his face. For a moment he silently contemplated Hux from an angle, his mouth sagging slightly; then he strode stiffly into the hall, where there was a telephone on a table near the front door. He started to dial, put down the receiver, and muttered something to himself; evidently he had forgotten the doctor's number. After he had looked it up, had dialed, and was waiting for the answer, Hux spoke from the living room. "While I'm here," he said in a less exalted tone, "I'd appreciate a chance to talk to you, Dr. Herne. I've got some news for you, maybe the most important news you'll ever hear."

Dr. Herne raised his hand for silence. After a brief apology to Dr. Morgan for interrupting his Sunday dinner, he reported Isabelle's dizzy spell at church, said that in his own opinion it was nothing, but added that it might be a good idea for Dr. Morgan to have a look at her anyway. Then, with an over-the-shoulder glance at Hux, he said, "I've got a crackpot preacher in the house who's taken up with Isabelle, and the fellow won't leave until you've been here. I hate to hurry you, Ben, but the sooner you get here, the better for all concerned." When he hung up, he went immediately into his bedroom, from which he returned with his drink. From a tray on a marble-top console table he took a bottle of Old Grand-Dad bourbon and poured at least two inches of whiskey over the melting ice at the bottom of his glass. Then, like a man wearing a cast from his neck to his hips, he lowered himself awkwardly into a Morris chair and said, "What kind of a preacher are you anyway? What were you doin' at *our* church?"

"I reckon," said Hux, responding to the doctor's milder tone, "you could call me a freelance preacher of the holy word and seeker of souls for the Lord. My folks are Baptist, but I don't recognize any denomination for what I'm tryin' to do. Right now I've attached myself to Reverend Archie B. Thurlow's Rededication crusade, right here in Alhambra."

"Never heard of it." Dr. Herne drank deeply from his glass.

Watching him, Hux felt his own tongue and throat go dry. "Well, he's a very famous evangelist. Some—uh—many people consider him even more inspirin' than Billy Graham." This sounded lame. The free flow of inspiration had seemingly dwindled, forcing Hux to pump. What if Ainsley Black deserted him? All at once Hux knew what he needed: a good, stiff drink. Did he dare ask for a drink?

A half smile was playing on the doctor's thin lips. As though suddenly recollecting something he had intended to do all along, he leaned forward and said, "You'll have to excuse my bad manners, Reverend. I don't see any company these days, and I've forgotten what it is to be a host. Here I am, sittin' right in front of you, sippin' good whiskey, and it never ever occurred to me to ask if you'd like something to drink."

He's read my mind, thought Hux, to whom the doctor's offer came as a minor miracle. What should he do? His need left him no choice. "Yes, sir, I sure would appreciate a drink. Some of that bourbon would do just fine."

The doctor looked surprised, having presumably expected Hux to ask for ginger ale or a Coke. Recovering, he asked his guest to go to the kitchen for a glass and some ice and to bring back some extra cubes in a bowl. "I've got an ailin' back," he said, "and I'd rather not have to lug my carcass out of this chair until Ben Morgan comes."

Returning from the kitchen, Hux, from whom Ainsley Black had now receded almost beyond reach, poured himself nearly three inches of whiskey, as if fearful that the doctor might at any moment rescind his invitation. It was well that he did so, for when he had taken his first long, restorative swallow, Dr. Herne suddenly screamed at him.

"You goddamn fraud, get out of this house! You're no preacher. No revivalist would let that stuff cross his lips—he'd rather die first. You're from the FBI just like I thought—a cheap, whiskey-drinkin'

Irish cop from the FBI. Now leave this house or I'll—I'll call the sheriff. You have no warrant for enterin' my house. You—"

Hux leaned back against the creaking love seat on which he was sitting and closed his eyes, wishing also that he could close his ears against the doctor's roaring. A trap had been set for him. He had crashed into it with his eyes open and he could see no way of climbing out. Though his situation seemed desperate, Hux did not panic. The chill, damp feel of the glass was reassuring. The first swallow of his drink was already driving out the tiredness, opening the channels of inspiration. Moving his lips as if praying, Hux felt Ainsley Black draw closer. Then he opened his blue eyes wide and said, "I have ample warrant for what I'm doin', Dr. Herne. If you were drinkin' pure poison and asked me to join you, I'd do so, knowin' the good Lord would save me harmless. I'm here to share my news with you, sir, and to do that I'd follow you into a bar or a whorehouse or into Hell itself if necessary."

The doctor blinked at this. "What are you? Are you some kind of hippie revivalist like I've read about—one of those hippie preachers who smokes and drinks and takes dope and speaks in tongues . . . and . . . and advocates free love? Are you part of that breed?"

Now Hux felt able to smile. He had detected, he thought, a glint of horrified fascination in the old man's hooded eyes. Could an all-but-convicted murderer take a high moral line against hippies? It would be tempting to play the old man for a while at the end of that particular rope. But soberness prevailed, and after another gulp of blissful whiskey, Hux said, "Do you think Reverend Archie B. Thurlow would put up with me for an instant if I was like you describe? A man who supports our President in his hour of need—would a man like that put up with hippies and dope and sex orgies? Is that what you think?"

"I know nothing about this Thurlow fellow. For all I know, he's one of—" Dr. Herne was interrupted by the doorbell. "That's Ben Morgan," he said, rising as if slowly hoisted from his chair. He let his colleague in and led him straight to Miss Isabelle's bedroom across the front hall. Returning, he poured more whiskey into his glass, excused himself, and went into his own room. Hux heard the flushing of a toilet through the flimsy walls of the house. Next he became aware of the loud ticking of a Seth Thomas clock on top of a chest; as he looked up at the clock, it struck the half hour: one-thirty. After refilling his own glass, he walked around the room, examining the model ships and the pictures. Already feeling the whiskey (he had eaten nothing since an early breakfast), Hux marveled at his good luck. On his very first try, he had managed to penetrate the murderer's lair, to drink his good booze! It was not to be believed....

The two doctors converged on the living room at almost the same instant. "Nothin' to worry about, Claiborne," said Dr. Morgan, who had given Hux a quick, silent appraisal, followed by a nod. Paunchy and wheezing, Dr. Morgan was an old man, probably in his late seventies, whose medical satchel was in fact a Delta Airlines flight bag. Isabelle's heart was fine, he said—her blood pressure a bit low, but that was no surprise. "I reckon she's picked up a little stomach bug of some kind. Not many of 'em around this time of year but there's always a few. I told her not to take anything stronger than consommé or tea, with maybe a soft-boiled egg for supper if she feels like it."

Dr. Herne nodded. He had made no move to introduce Hux, who was standing by the window. Dr. Morgan kept glancing in his direction, as if waiting for the introduction. Or did he want to be offered a drink? "Ben, it was real good of you to interrupt your Sunday meal," said Dr. Herne. "You better hurry on back while there's still some left."

Looking put out, Dr. Morgan said, "How's your health these days, Claiborne? You haven't been in for a checkup in years. Your color's pretty high. How about lettin' me take your blood pressure while I'm here?"

"No need for that. I'm still capable of taking my own."

"I still wish you'd drop in for a checkup. I don't like your color. Keepin' yourself cooped up in here, it's not right." Dr. Morgan seemed to be digging with his tongue for a food particle caught in a lower molar. "Hard on Isabelle too," he resumed. "You both ought to get out more. She has the church, but that's not enough. It's a right sorry kind of existence if you ask me."

"I wasn't aware that I had."

The older doctor snorted. "Don't you get sassy with me, Claiborne Herne. 'Course it's none of my business how you spend your time, but it's not fair to Isabelle to keep her cooped up too, away from all her friends. You mind what I say."

"Much obliged. You can go now, Ben." Dr. Herne stalked into the hall, opened the front door, and stood beside it, unbending, until Dr. Morgan, after another shrug and snort, went out. "And you can go too," said Dr. Herne as he returned to the living room. "But wait. Before you go I want to know how you happened to attach yourself to my sister in the first place—in a church that wasn't even your church."

Hux turned from the window. He was in a quandary: how far should he try to go with Dr. Herne on this first meeting? Was this the moment to unleash Ainsley Black's evangelical fervor? Or should it be played down until the doctor seemed more receptive? Since Miss Isabelle was certain to repeat to her brother all that had transpired at church, Hux decided that he might as well be forthright. "Like I told your sister," he said, sensing a rising confidence in his voice, "I'm what you might call a professional fisher of souls. . . ."

"Of *what?*"

Undaunted, Hux repeated his phrase. "Whenever Brother Thurlow comes to a new place," he went on, "I sort of fan out over the district and seek out a few people who might have a special need for his message. I'm a kind of scout or outrider for Brother Thurlow's crusade, you might say. A special contact man. I knew about you and Miss Isabelle, and since you don't go out these days, I decided to approach her direct—right on her home ground, right in the church she's gone to all her life." He paused, his face rosy from his effort, to see the effect of his words on Dr. Herne. Hux's glass was now empty, and he longed for another drink.

"And what's so special about us?"

Hux drew a deep breath. "I knew you were unhappy. I knew you could use the message."

"God damn you, that's the—the most presumptuous, most impudent thing I ever heard of in my whole life. Who gave you permission to meddle in our lives?"

There was now no escaping what Hux had to say. "My permission—or authority—comes from the same source as my news. The highest authority there is."

Dr. Herne received this with a twisted grin. "And what is this precious news you've got for me?"

"Sir, may I take advantage of your hospitality and pour myself some more of that mighty fine whiskey?"

After a laugh that seemed to force its way through a chest full of phlegm, Dr. Herne said, "Why, you poor boy, of course you may. Keepin' up this preacher-act must be pretty thirsty work for an FBI agent. I sure don't envy you the job. So by all means help yourself."

"Thank you," said Hux as he went to the drink tray. "But I don't work for the FBI. I'm a special agent for a very different kind of outfit."

"I'll take your word for that. Now give me your news and clear out of here."

For a second Hux couldn't remember the phrasing. He took a

mouthful of whiskey, held it, closed his eyes, and let the whiskey go down in a series of small, stinging swallows. Then, as with the first time when he had seemed to be praying, he popped his eyes wide open. "You know my news. You've known it all your life. It's two thousand years old and it's also the latest thing—hot off the wires. Here it is: 'For God so loved the world that He gave His only begotten Son that whosoever believeth in Him should not perish but have everlasting life.'"

Dr. Herne was scornful. "I had to memorize that verse in Sunday school. I reckon you did too. Looked like you were havin' some trouble recollectin' it."

"The words are ever old and ever new. I repeat them every day of my life." Hux was out of breath. How had he remembered them? Where had they come from?

"And that's all the news you have? That's your message? Do you mean to tell me it was for the sake of this—this Sunday-school stuff that you forced your attentions on my sister and then forced your way into this house? Now that's what I call nerve. And you continue to sit there, with that stupid smile on your face, drinkin' my whiskey, and—"

Just as Hux was about to protest, Miss Isabelle appeared at the doorway. She was still wearing her Sunday dress but had a pair of fuzzy pink slippers on her feet. Turning toward her with a look of fury, Dr. Herne said, "How long have you been standin' there eavesdroppin'?"

"What?"

"Eavesdroppin'! Eavesdroppin'!"

She gave an innocent laugh. "I just got here, Brother. I'm feelin' so much better, and I thought you and Reverend Black might like some lunch. It's after two—you must be starvin'. It's too late for me to cook dinner, but there's some cold chicken and—"

"Don't fix anything for me, Miss Isabelle, thanks all the same," said Hux, who felt suddenly desperate to escape the house. Too much had come too soon, and he was exhausted. "I must go now, but I'll be back."

"Not in this house you won't," said Dr. Herne.

"Oh, Brother!"

"Don't you worry, Miss Isabelle. I'll be in touch with you. I want you to come to Brother Thurlow's with me—it's an experience I wouldn't want you to miss. You'll be hearin' from me in the next couple of days." Walking over to her, Hux clasped her plump right hand in both of his. "God bless you," he said with fervor. Then he

87

turned to Dr. Herne and extended his right hand. To his surprise the doctor accepted it. "Goodbye, sir. I'd like to talk to you again sometime. No preachin', just talkin'. I'm a pretty interestin' fellow when you get to know me. My line of work has led me into some fascinatin' experiences I'd like to tell you about. Think it over, and give me another chance. Goodbye, doctor."

Without a word, Dr. Herne dropped Hux's hand. He went into his bedroom and shut the door behind him. Miss Isabelle accompanied Hux to the front door, where he once more received her thanks, repeated his "God bless you," and then impulsively kissed her on the cheek.

Chapter Fifteen

Though it had been constructed to run almost automatically, the official agenda consumed much more of Hux's time than he had anticipated. In setting up appointments from New York, he had not reckoned on the amount of driving involved. To estimate the driving time from Oxford to Vicksburg with a highway map was one thing; to experience it was not only something else but something belonging to a radically different order of reality. How could he have known what it would be like to be stuck for nearly ten miles on a two-lane highway behind a tanker truck carrying cottonseed oil, a truck so gigantic that he could not see around it, much less pass it? Nor had he anticipated the strain of the constant interviews, lunches, group meetings, and speeches—all of them activities that he had expected to take easily in his stride. The strain was partly due to the need always to pay attention—or at least to give the impression of paying rapt, eye-to-eye attention—at times when his strongest desire was to slip away to that secret attic chamber where Clark, Ainsley Black, and the Hernes awaited him. Added to the strain was simple fatigue, which, when he got back to the Holiday Inn after nine on both Monday and Tuesday, was enough to keep him from telephoning Miss Isabelle or taking up Anne Schlamm on her invitation to drop by for a friendly drink.

During the sometimes dangerously sleepy hours spent on Mississippi's narrow roads, Hux often drifted into a vivid mental replay of the weekend. He had become an actor again—surely the most extraordinary turn his life had taken since he left the Woodrow Wilson School. And he had rediscovered not only the exhilaration, the riskiness, and the sudden funks and drops of the game but also a truth which he had once known and had never articulated: that to be possessed totally (demonically!) by an assumed identity, to "become" Richard II or Ainsley Black, could have the effect of transforming the rest of one's life—the straight parts—into a play. Which was more truly himself, the man playing Ainsley Black or the fellow playing the representative of the Morrow Foundation, the one with the assured manner and all the necessary figures at his fingertips? The amazing thing about the part of Ainsley Black was that he could be both his own director and his own script writer, improvising as he went along.

Where had the words come from? Or the voice, the gestures? Had he really observed a preacher like Ainsley Black? The mysteriousness of the process was a little frightening: what if Ainsley Black suddenly appeared on the scene during a conversation with the president of Mississippi State University, whom he was scheduled to see on Wednesday? Were the compartments of his life secure—or could seepage occur from one to the next?

But it was pleasure, not fear, that dominated Hux's recollection of the weekend, the intense pleasure of having made an opening move that quickly brought results. He should have been an actor, he told himself; he should have listened more seriously to his director at the Playmakers, Philip O'Brien, who tried to convince him that he had a future in the professional theater. At that time Hux, a bright undergraduate with his mind on marriage and a more conventional career, could not be persuaded that his acting, however talented, was more than an enjoyable, even seductive distraction from the main business of life. And at least while Clark was alive, Hux had been sure that his decision for the academy was correct. So strong was his involvement in graduate work that he had refused, despite Louise's urging, to try out for a part in any dramatic production at Princeton; indeed he had felt no desire at all to do so. And since Clark's death? Well, it was possible, he reflected, to see his life during the last decade as having been squandered in a series of unconvincing parts.

Dr. Herne's face often flashed before Hux's inner eye as he drove, a fiery devil's mask, contorted with suspiciousness and rage. In the flesh the old man had proved as hateful as Hux's earlier fantasies of him: a sadistic, drunken bully, vicious to his sister, hostile to the world outside, and probably a bit paranoid as well. All that business about FBI agents . . . Was it possible to reach such a man, to play upon some residue of conscience or honor or fear in order to make him confront what he had done? Hux might have decided that his mission was unachievable—except for one thing: the spectacular success of his first try. There was, of course, the perfectly real possibility that he might never again be allowed into the same room with Dr. Herne, but Hux had a strong hunch that a second try would also succeed. He was a superstitious believer not only in luck but in the momentum of luck.

Luck and Miss Isabelle—together they would see him through. Though he felt sorry for the poor woman, Hux had no compunction about using her. She was a born victim, he had decided, a bit dim, born to be played upon and pushed around. He would be as decent to her as he could, hurt her as little as possible, but he was prepared to exploit her for all that she was worth. On Thursday afternoon, when he had no appointment, he would drop in on her unexpectedly; meanwhile, he would telephone her (if he could get past her deafness) or send her a note. The next big scene in his unwritten script still called for exposing Miss Isabelle (with or without her brother) to Reverend Thurlow's preaching. Though Hux was not entirely sure what he expected to result from such an exposure, he now felt impelled by the logic of his own chosen role to bring about such an encounter if possible. If the Hernes refused to cooperate, so be it: he would have to come up with something else. But at the very least Brother Thurlow had provided him with an excuse to seek another meeting.

Hux wanted to see the evangelist in action. Though his own impersonation of Ainsley Black had not been damaged, Hux was more disappointed than he had realized at the time by Brother Thurlow's failure to preach. A defender of Nixon!—an old-fashioned, right-wing, barrel-chested Bible thumper! The impression of raw power emanating from the crouched figure on the platform convinced Hux that the man would be worth watching, that he would put on a remarkable—probably grotesque—performance. Several times he recalled the moment when the evangelist, having removed and wiped his glasses, stared out darkly over the congregation: clearly a man to summon thunderclouds, to call down God's wrath upon the heads of groveling sinners. . . . Whether the Hernes came with him or not, Hux was determined to see the show.

On Wednesday morning, before leaving for Starkville, Hux sent off a note to Miss Isabelle, a note containing no return address or date.

> Dear Miss Isabelle,
>   Since Sunday I have traveled as far afield as Vicksburg and Memphis and will travel more as the week goes on. I keep no fixed abode but move about as the Lord's business directs me. But always the remembrance of our meeting accompanies me and I pray daily and nightly too that the Lord may soon bring to fruition the blessedness that will be vouchsafed unto you and also the Doctor. With that goal

in mind I again *urge* you and Doctor Herne to accompany me to hear Rev. Archie B. Thurlow and
receive the News he has for you both. Being that his
two last services in Alhambra are Saturday night
and Sunday morning, could you make plans to attend one, maybe both? May the trial you have en-
dured so long soon end!

Before then I shall appear at your threshold perhaps when you least expect me. Tell the Doctor I
won't preach to him, just a friendly visit.

Yours in our Lord Jesus Christ
(Rev.) Ainsley Black

Then Hux, already tired from his previous trips, set out for Starkville
for his appointment with the assembled administrators of Mississippi
State. The conference included yet another of those dragged-out,
napkin-dabbing luncheons, and when it was over, he had to submit
to a tour of antebellum houses in nearby Columbus. While the old
town was pleasant enough, the day was very hot, and Hux took a
strong dislike to his tour guide, a local antiquarian, fat and gossipy,
who giggled when he pointed out the Episcopal rectory where Tennessee Williams was born. By the time he was able to break away,
Hux was worn out, his shirt wet, his suit crumpled. But he did not
return directly to Oxford. He kept seeing road signs pointing to Tupelo, and when he reached the junction with Route 41, he decided to
head north and make the pilgrimage that had now been delayed for
nearly a week. Once in Tupelo, he had a hard time finding the
school, and it was nearly six-thirty before he stepped out of his car
onto what seemed to him holy ground.

A set of weathered bleachers stood in the deserted yard of the
school. Had the speakers' stand been in front of it or somewhere
else? The grass was dry, turning brown under Hux's feet, and the red
clay of the playground was packed hard, just as he had known it
would be. Beyond the playground was the field and beyond the field
a stand of spindly pine trees and a thicket covered with kudzu vine,
now a bronzy green in the dusty hot light. After circling the area of
the bleachers, Hux walked toward the dirt road, hardly more than a
track, that crossed the field and curved behind the pines. When he
reached the place where Herne must have stood, he turned to look
toward the schoolyard, trying to imagine the crowd that had been
there, trying, almost as if he were taking aim, to find the spot where
Clark might have sat. But that involved facing into the sun, which

dazzled and stung his eyes. None of the grand emotions came—only a dusting of sadness that settled over him as he walked back to his car.

But that night, after a late, lonely dinner in the nearly empty dining room of the Holiday Inn, Hux went back to his room and took out the fat packet of letters from Clark. Over a period of nearly four years he had saved every written communication he had received from Clark. They ranged from a two-line postcard greeting from Columbus, Ohio, where the Helmholtzes were spending a month with Linda's parents, to a six-page, single-spaced letter describing Clark's interview with Kwame Nkrumah during his traveling fellowship to Ghana in 1962. Hux had no idea what he would find in the batch of letters, tied with a piece of string, that Clark had written from Mississippi during the last month of his life; as with the public record of the period, Hux had blocked out detail, retaining only the knowledge, like an index tab, that the material existed. Unknotting the string, he realized that he had obliterated even the memory of what Clark had written (in answer to Hux's letter of apology) about the quarrel that had taken place between them on the night before Hux left Jackson to return to his wife and baby in Princeton. If there had been any serious reproach, Hux surely would have preserved some impression, some sense-memory, of the pain, if nothing else. So he told himself; yet his hands were shaking enough to rattle the paper as he took the letter from the envelope postmarked *Greenville, Miss., July 18, 1964.* He needed not have worried. The only reference to the quarrel was these words at the very beginning: "Sorry about the blowup. It was as much my fault as yours. We can talk about it when we're together again—if either of us still feels the need." Thus Clark generously expunged the whole incident, moving rapidly on in his fast scrawl to bring Hux up to date on the rift between the forces of CORE and SNCC at the headquarters in Jackson.

The other letters told of secret and public meetings, of confrontations (sometimes comic) with courthouse registrars, of harassment by local sheriffs and by truckloads of cruising rednecks on country roads at night—the once familiar and now far-off episodes of the Freedom Summer. During his own six weeks in Jackson, Hux had heard reports of such happenings nearly every day, and he had read of them again at the Forty-second Street library; but to read of them now in these letters was to hear Clark's voice at his ear. As Hux pored over the often smeared and cramped handwriting, he began to catch glimpses of faces that went with some of the familiar names, faces that he thought had been lost forever in the pea-soup fog of his own amnesia. Could he really see the frowning, toffee-brown face of Franklin D. Mosby, the young schoolteacher who had come a few times to the Jackson headquarters before moving into northern Mississippi with Clark? Or was the face supplied by his intense yearning to see it again? In his second letter Clark wrote: "I've just decided that Frank Mosby is the bravest and most resourceful man I've ever met"—an opinion followed by an exuberant account of the way Mosby had successfully thwarted the efforts of a New York CORE member to make himself chairman of the rally at Greenwood. Well, he *would* see Mosby again almost certainly on Friday, when he was scheduled to visit Brandon Institute, a small church-supported college for blacks in Greenwood. In going over the material supplied to him in advance by the college, Hux had found Mosby's name listed as director of admissions on the list of administrative staff and faculty. It was as easy as that—no detective work required!

Hux was fairly certain he had never met Anne Sibthorpe, the local white girl who had worked with Clark and Mosby all during that month. In his third letter Clark described her as an "intelligent, quirky, ugly-attractive girl whose so-called 'good' family is convinced that she's literally a nigger lover (i.e., sleeping with Frank)." He had gone on to write that he was reasonably certain Anne was not sleeping with Mosby or anyone else, black or white—"not even with Harry, who's been panting and sniffing at her tail ever since we left Greenville. Funny the way sex looms large when we're all in such close quarters. In other circumstances nobody would give a fuck who was fucking whom." Hux smiled: Clark used the vernacular like the preacher's son he was. . . . But who was Harry? All at once Hux could see him: a thickset, lank-haired slob from Yale whose dirty T-shirts and indescribably filthy chinos had disgusted his black co-workers at Jackson. Now what was the guy's last name?

In his next-to-last letter Clark returned to the subject of Anne Sibthorpe:

> She's a fantastic girl. You can't imagine how she's hated by the local whites. God help her if she ever gets arrested—which of course could happen any moment. Our worthy enforcers of the law would like nothing better than to gang-rape her and then stomp her to death.

Clark wondered what would happen to her in the future, assuming that she survived the present campaign. She would almost certainly have to move North—it was impossible to imagine her living in Mississippi after all this. . . .

Hux picked up the last letter—the one written on the night before Tupelo, the one which he had read aloud at the memorial service in the Princeton chapel. It began with the story of Franklin Mosby's arrest on the steps of the post office in Alhambra. . . . Hux sat back, letting the letter flutter at his knee. Alhambra!—what a detail to forget . . . Could Claiborne Herne have been present? Had he seen Clark then? Hux read on about the frantic efforts to get Mosby released, efforts that succeeded much faster than anyone had expected. The preacher at one of the black churches—"a man with the build of Goliath and the guts of David," according to Clark—had done a wonderful job as a go-between. After Mosby had been set free, the preacher's entire congregation had massed on the same post office steps to sing hymns and shout slogans and the white authorities had not tried to drive them off. Then Clark voiced his exasperation:

> I find myself at a loss among people who talk simply and earnestly about Jesus, despite having been surrounded by them in my childhood. I become annoyed when they ask me questions that assume I share the faith of all the young ministers and theology students who've been swarming all over the state this summer. I'm now so conditioned to thinking (correctly, I insist) that in this instance Marx is right—Christianity is *indeed* the opiate of these poor people, having reconciled them to the intolerable almost (but thank God, not quite!) to the present hour—that I find it hard to accept religious faith as *now* the greatest single energizer of the movement in this part of the country. But so it is. I'm caught in the idiotic position of being simultaneously irritated by all of the naïve Christian assumptions and angry at the scorn some of my fellow atheists can't—or won't bother—to conceal. Despite Arnold and Harry and some of the others, I refuse to consider myself a disgusting hypocrite for singing "What a Friend We Have in Jesus" just as fervently (and badly!) as "We Shall Overcome."

After a short account of the plans for the big rally at Tupelo, where a lot of trouble was expected, Clark ended with a short paragraph that

Hux had not read aloud at the memorial service:

> Though you probably did the right thing (I'm
> more and more convinced I'd have done the same
> thing under the circumstances), I still haven't com-
> pletely forgiven you for pulling out. Not for the
> Movement's sake—the Movement can get along
> without you (or any of us) very well—but for my
> own. There's no longer anyone here who can help
> me get things in perspective, no one who shares the
> same frame of reference, no one to whom I can say
> the things I've just written. It's amazing how much
> of my thinking has been cast in the form of a dia-
> logue with you. For depriving me of that, you're
> still unforgiven.

Then in a postscript that seemed like a real afterthought, Clark mentioned that Linda and Susie were getting along fine in Ohio and
hoped that Louise and the baby were flourishing. His last words
were: "Write again soon, old buddy. I need somebody to catch and
return the ball I've thrown."

Clark's letter had arrived the day after the news from Tupelo. As
Hux folded the sheet and returned it to the envelope, he wondered
what he had written to Clark earlier. He had almost no recollection
of his own letter at all. How, exactly, had he referred to the quarrel?
How fully had he apologized? Whatever he had written must have
been acceptable to Clark—that much was clear. But then Clark was
magnanimous, one of the truly great-souled men of his generation. . . .

When Hux put the letters down, he had the overwhelming sense
that Clark was close, perhaps standing just behind his chair, reading
the words he had written ten years ago, reliving every sensation of that
summer right up to—and including—the shattering of his own skull.
But this nearness was neither frightening nor comforting; it produced
in Hux a need to speak to his friend, to reach out to him, a need so
strong that it drove him restlessly about the airless-seeming room, into
the bathroom for water, and down to the motel lobby and back again.
He had to talk to someone about Clark, talk to someone who had
known him. Should he telephone Louise? No, he could do better than
that: he would call Linda Helmholtz. What the devil was her married
name? Hux rushed to his briefcase, which lay open on the unused bed,
and searched through papers and pamphlets until he came up with his

old address book, which he had, thank God, remembered to bring along.

But after he had already dialed information to get the Vance Johanssens' number in Columbus, Ohio, Hux suddenly lost heart and put the receiver down. What sort of conversation could he expect to have with Linda, catching her off-guard like this? Since they had had for years no other communication than the annual exchange of Christmas cards, a sudden call from Mississippi would be not only startling but perhaps frightening. Still, he had to speak to someone. . . . Hux roamed helplessly around the room, unable to settle, at once stifled and chilled by the air-conditioner, oppressed by the silence.

He decided that he would write Linda a letter. Again rushing to his briefcase, he took out two sheets of paper and carried them to the desk. Once started, he wrote rapidly, taking no time to shape his thoughts.

> Holiday Inn
> Oxford, Miss. 38655
> May 29, 1974

Dear Linda,

Life is so strange. Here I am in Mississippi—it's about 9:30 in the evening and three hours ago I was in Tupelo, visiting the schoolyard where Clark was killed. It wasn't such a moving experience at the time, but since I've come back to my motel I haven't been able to think about anything except Clark— and now about you. I wish we could get together to talk sometime. I'd love to see both you and Susie again—hard to think of her as a teenager. I'm in Miss. on Morrow Foundation business but I'm taking the opportunity to stir up some of the old associations. I can't get the Tupelo schoolyard out of my mind. Such a bare, dusty, uninteresting kind of a place for something to happen that changed our lives in ways we'll never fully understand. Yours more than mine of course, but mine more than I can begin to fathom. And I'm not very far from Alhambra, where Clark Helmholtz goes on living, incredibly enough.

Hux lifted his pen, wondering if he should tell Linda about meeting the doctor. No, it would be too difficult to explain—and possibly upsetting to her. . . .

> Linda, on another occasion I'll write you a *real* letter—bring you up to date on my life, give you news of Louise and Tony, etc. Right now I can't help wondering how Clark seems to you, after all these years and all that's happened. Do you ever dream of him? Do you try to keep his image vivid in Susie's memory? Is he still vivid to you? Do you still love him? Do you judge him harshly or remember him tenderly? I realize, Linda, that I have no right to ask these questions and that they may be offensive to you. Please attribute them to the concern of an old friend whose memories have been stirred and troubled. If you do not wish to answer, I will understand. I'll be at this address another two weeks—after that, New York.
>
> Affectionately always,
Larry

As he read over what he had written, Hux noticed that, in his preoccupation with Clark, he had written "Clark Helmholtz" where he had intended "Claiborne Herne." After making the correction, Hux quickly folded the paper, put it in an envelope, sealed it, and then addressed it, afraid all the time that if he stopped to reflect he might tear up the letter. Next he took it to the mailbox in the motel lobby, where he hesitated for perhaps two seconds before posting it. Afterward, Hux did not return to his room. Instead, he looked up Anne Schlamm's number and dialed, hoping to have a drink with her. Once Hux had succeeded in identifying himself (apparently she had forgotten the name, though not the person), Anne sounded friendly, even cordial. But she pointed out that it was now well past ten and that she had already undressed for bed. They would have to have their drink another time. Then she said that in any case they would be seeing each other at the party Dean and Mrs. Halsey were having on Friday—a party which he had forgotten all about.

Hux thanked her for reminding him of it, asked if he could take her to it, and said goodnight. Disconsolate, he wandered into the motel cocktail lounge, where he drank beer until the bar closed at midnight. Customers came and went, several of them black; the bartender, too, was black, and he talked in an easy way with two beefy white customers in flowered, short-sleeved shirts—exactly the kind of men that Hux (and presumably the bartender) would have been wary of ten years before. The conversation had to do with a real mean dogfight the white men had attended over in New Albany on Saturday night.

Chapter Sixteen

Hux was wrong about Isabelle Herne. Though self-effacing, instinctively conventional, and shy about her looks and deafness, she was in no way dim. Nor was she entirely a victim, seeking more suffering than had already been thrust upon her. During the days following the irruption of Ainsley Black into her life, she went over every detail of the encounter, inspecting every intonation and nuance for some possible danger. Cut off as she was from her old friends and from their sons and daughters and grandchildren, she felt, with some exaggeration, that she had not met or talked with such a young person in years (though she had to admit that, close up, Reverend Black did not look all *that* young). And what an extraordinary person the evangelist was!—at once kind and bold, almost a match for Claiborne's rudeness. The whole experience baffled her. In those moments of near-despair that afflicted her every day when her vitality was low, it seemed probable that Ainsley Black was not an evangelist but a confidence man of some sort, that he had learned all about the Hernes in order to trick them, to get hold of what was left of their money. Or (and this was almost worse) that he was playing a joke on them, a cruel, heartless joke for which she, in her gullibility and need, had fallen. But why would he want to do such a thing to them? Years ago, during and after the trial, they had received hostile letters and threatening telephone calls from civil-rights militants, mostly outside agitators from the North. Still, a joke was different—and harder to deal with. Was it possible that she had offended someone in town? Some Baptist, perhaps, whose feelings she had inadvertently hurt? It did not seem likely, though she knew that people in towns like Alhambra could sometimes hold grudges for decades without saying a word.

But what if Ainsley Black was exactly what he claimed to be: a fisher of souls with a special mission to lead Isabelle and her brother to Reverend Archie Thurlow and through him to a new experience of God? Such a possibility was even more baffling. How should she respond to it? As a good Presbyterian, she had always been distrustful (though never so openly scornful as Claiborne) of what she regarded as "emotionalism" in religion. The well-trodden path of her own church had always seemed best to her. God had thus far sustained her, given her—despite everything—the day-by-day strength to carry on. He had never given her *rapture*, a condition which Isabelle was sure she did not want, would not know what to do with. The only really proper place for rapture was (she felt) in the afterlife. Yet the idea of some extreme bliss, of an ecstatic leap into the fiery furnace of God's love, had teased her ever since her meeting with Reverend Black; it would not go away but hovered on the edge of her consciousness like a slightly shameful temptation. But wasn't rapture exactly what the evangelicals and revivalists had always dealt in, the stuff that made their congregations wriggle and shout so embarrassingly? She had to admit that the Hernes' way, the traditional way, had been of no use to Claiborne in his wretchedness. He was lost to God. Could she be so certain that God might not use extraordinary means—as extraordinary as Reverend Black or Reverend Thurlow—to reach him again?

Often she thought of that look of flushed goodness in Reverend Black's face, the sweetness of his wide blue eyes. God's blond errand boy . . . As she knew from her long-ago study of Greek and Latin, the word "evangelist" meant the bringer of good news, the *angel* of good news. She waited in a kind of subdued terror for his promised reappearance. So little that was thrilling or startling had occurred in their lives for such a long time; even the return of Rooney and Vicky was no more than a sordid repetition—nothing new about *that*. Though she had no idea how she—much less Claiborne—would deal with Reverend Black's invasion of their lives, Isabelle awoke each morning half hoping, half fearing that this would be the day when the blond angel (who might also be a cruel hoaxer) once more came to her door.

Of course none of her fantasies could be mentioned to Claiborne, whose few comments on Reverend Black—mutterings rather—indicated that he still regarded the fellow as an FBI agent, badly disguised. Her brother was in one of the silent phases that so often seemed to follow one of his "prayer sessions" with Vicky Lee. On Monday he had gone through the whole day without addressing a single word to his sister, though he seemed to listen intently to what she said. Since then, he had spoken mostly in gruff asides, as if communicating mainly with himself. It was a lonely time for Isabelle. Brooding over these matters, she went stoically about her daily routine, which began with making breakfast for her brother and a large pot of coffee for herself. No matter how much he had drunk the night before, Claiborne regularly appeared, freshly bathed and shaved, for breakfast at eight. When he left the table, he just as regularly returned to his room and shut the door. Half an hour later he would emerge, carrying yesterday's newspaper, neatly folded, to the kitchen, where he left it on a stack of papers by the back door. Next he went to his workroom and again shut the door. There he would devote three and a half hours to his model ships until his sister summoned him to a light lunch, usually soup or a sandwich.

Meanwhile Isabelle, after washing the breakfast dishes, would make her bed, empty the wastebasket from her room, and make sure that nothing had been left out of place in the meticulous clutter of the living room. She was forbidden to enter her brother's room. For years now he had insisted upon cleaning it himself, making his bed, changing his own sheets, collecting his own laundry in a blue canvas bag that was picked up once a week by the laundryman. He claimed to distrust the black woman named Sally who came twice a week to clean the rest of the house, to wash Isabelle's stockings and underwear, and, incidentally, to provide Isabelle with some much-needed conversation. It had been a decade or more since Isabelle had even sewn a button on one of her brother's shirts. With the household chores done, Isabelle would several times a week set off in her Ford Falcon to do some marketing, take a dress to the cleaners', return books to the library. Passing the liquor store, she would regularly thank God for sparing her the humiliation of having to buy whiskey for her brother. Before local option made it possible to buy liquor legally in Alhambra, Claiborne had always dealt with a bootlegger who brought his supplies to the back door; now he had a standing order for five bottles of Old Grand-Dad bourbon and one bottle of Gordon's gin to be delivered every week by the former bootlegger, an enterprising little woman named Vinny Meaker, who was now the owner of the liquor store.

During this particular week Isabelle observed several indications that Claiborne had begun his daily drinking before lunch; usually he waited until mid-afternoon, following his nap. This increased consumption was another consequence, as she knew from bitter experience, of Vicky Lee's visit. While eating lunch on Tuesday, Claiborne for long moments stared at her with a certain sly expression that she recognized as one of the signs. Already his eyes had begun to redden. The sly expression widened into an almost-smile as she told him about a letter that had come in the morning's mail from the archivist at Delta State University. The letter had been just what Isabelle was waiting for, answering as it did a query of hers about an item in the

Buford family papers that had been given to Delta State. Sometimes Claiborne expressed an interest in Isabelle's project, which was to compile a history of their mother's family, but today he continued to eye her mischievously without once breaking his silence. Isabelle talked bravely on. After all, she had as much right to her hobby, to which she devoted several hours each afternoon (between napping and gardening), as he had to his seventeenth-century galleons, galleasses, and men-of-war. It involved her in a far-flung correspondence with distant relatives in at least three states, who sometimes provided her with fascinating, even scandalous, bits of lore. Gradually, she wound down, defeated by that sly look which more than anything else told her that she could anticipate another of those dreadful nights when she would need all her strength to get her brother from his Morris chair to his bedroom at ten o'clock. Really hard drinking always affected his powers of locomotion. But even when he seemed hardly able to stand, Claiborne would always rally enough at his bedroom door to bar Isabelle's access and make his way to bed—presumably folding and hanging up his clothes—without assistance. Silent now, Isabelle told herself that the mocking quality of her brother's expression came straight from Rooney Lee, who had glanced at her that way when he was hardly more than a child hiding behind his mother's skirts. . . .

Late on Thursday morning Isabelle came into the hall and saw Claiborne standing just inside the open front door, reading a letter. Warm light streamed in, silhouetting him against the delicate eggshell blue of the early summer sky, while a breeze lifted the soft fringes of his white hair from his shadowed forehead.

"Here's a letter from your new beau," he said without looking at her.

"What did you say?"

"A letter from your new beau. The so-called evangelist."

Suddenly Isabelle realized that Claiborne had actually opened and was reading a letter addressed to her. "That's mine!" she cried, snatching the sheet and envelope from his fingers. "Why, Brother, you've opened my letter. You had no right to do that." Sporadically, in certain moods, he did such things to tease her, and she reacted with all the indignation of a small wronged child.

Claiborne ignored her outrage, which was strong enough to make her hands tremble as she held the letter close to her rather nearsighted eyes. "I can't be too careful these days," he said. "All these agents floatin' around, and here you are ready to open the door wide for any one of them who gives you a bit of sweet talk. We ought to go to that revival meetin' just to call that fellow's bluff."

Isabelle had caught only part of Claiborne's sentence. "Did you—did you say we ought to go?" She gazed at her brother in wonderment.

"Do I mean I really might go? Of course not! Don't be an idiot. Furthermore, that man is not to set foot in this house."

"It's my house too," protested Isabelle. Overwhelmed for an instant by the idea that Claiborne might actually attend Reverend Thurlow's meeting, she was perversely relieved by Claiborne's ridicule.

"What's this trial he keeps talkin' about? Does that fool think he's goin' to uncover some new evidence and drag me into court again?"

"That's not what he's referrin' to. You didn't read it carefully. He wants to help, I'm sure he does. Don't close your mind and heart to what he might have to say."

"I'm merely closin' my front door to him. If you want to have a date with him, meet him somewhere else."

"That's mean, Brother, real mean. The young man wants to help. Don't make a joke of it. If and when he comes, I'm not goin' to turn him away."

"We'll see about that," said Claiborne, who stiffly walked past her to his workroom. The slamming of his door echoed painfully in Isabelle's ears.

She reread the letter. As someone who had always remained a schoolteacher at heart, Isabelle noted (with a small sigh) the defects of the preacher's style and promptly dismissed them as unimportant. What mattered was the glow, the incandescence. Again she felt the promise—and threat—of rapture lurking in his words. Shivering a little, she tried again to imagine what some special infusion of God's bliss might mean to her, what reserves of strength and courage she would need to open herself to it, to support it. And Claiborne!—why, he would shrivel, turn black, and crumble into ash at God's merest touch—unless, like major surgery, everything had been carefully anticipated and prepared for. Once more she felt relief that he had no intention of exposing himself to Reverend Thurlow's message, whatever that might turn out to be. Not yet, not yet. But should *she* go, just to see what it was like? Again shivering, Isabelle drew into herself, as if huddling against a sudden streaming of glacial air through the open door.

After a moment she shut the door firmly and returned to her room, ashamed at having surrendered to such a fantasy when she wasn't even sure of Ainsley Black's credentials. Claiborne was right: she *was* gullible, a pushover for anyone who approached her with kindness.

Isabelle was on her knees, not praying but digging at the roots of one of the climbing roses at the side of the house, when she became aware that Ainsley Black was standing above her. She was not surprised to see him there, though she had not heard his approach.

"It's turned into a muggy, steamin' afternoon, Miss Isabelle. May the Lord bless the work of your hands."

She did not hear, and he patiently repeated his words. Then she let him catch her by the wrist to help her to her feet. For a moment she stood a bit unsteadily on her bowed legs, aware that she was sweaty and smudged and that her old brown corduroy gardening trousers were caked with mud. Not daring to take him inside, she pointed to a pair of deck chairs on the back lawn behind the clothesline, where she and Claiborne sometimes sat in silence, gazing toward the cotton fields and the cypress slough to the east.

"Do you think your brother might be willin' to join us?" asked Ainsley Black as she sat down, lowering her thick hips cautiously into the flimsy chair.

Isabelle knew the answer to that, but at first she said nothing, content to smile shyly at the young man, aware that she now trusted him without reservation. Her earlier suspicions had simply evaporated in his presence. There was no guile, no hint of the practical joker or con man in that rounded innocent face. His beautiful hair fitted him like a cap! And such goodness, such kindness in his expression! Despite the fine wrinkles at the corners of the eyes and the slight suggestion of a double chin, the face continued to seem very young to her, the face of a sweet cherub instead of a burning angel—and for this mildness she was deeply grateful. She yearned to see her brother's anger melt in the presence of such mildness. Tentatively she reached out her soiled right hand and for a moment let her fingers rest upon the top of his well-fleshed hand, which lay spread across his knee. Then, as if just remembering his words, she shook her head and said, "Not today. I think we'd better wait."

"Don't you fret about it, Miss Isabelle. We mustn't rush the process. There'll be a clear sign when he's ready."

"You—you mustn't expect too much of him. Of us."

"I know. Don't you worry about it." Suddenly he looked over his shoulder, then again toward the east. "Your brother is watchin' us right this minute. From behind the curtains. He is angry, but there is room in his heart for fear and wonder too. No, don't look around."

Isabelle obeyed him guiltily, for he had guessed her impulse. The sun, still high, was hurting her eyes.

"You're the one I'm thinkin' about now. Will you come with me to the Rededication Saturday night?"

The mere thought of it made her fearful. Suddenly she was a child again, with Norah, watching from a safe distance as a country preacher seized and ducked one white-gowned, shouting, arm-waving victim (as she saw them) after another into the summer-shrunken, coffee-colored waters of the Tallahatchie. But she was being asked to go to a service in a *church*, not to a mass baptism or even a tent meeting. She needn't be so afraid. This kind young man would be with her, to hold her arm, to support her. She would be surrounded by good people, good Christians, not exactly her kind but good Christians all the same, who would sustain her with their hymns and prayers. . . . Then, as if something bat-winged had passed between her and the sun, she sensed another kind of danger and hastened to say, "I don't like to leave him alone at night."

"Then come on Sunday. It's the final meetin'. It'll last about two hours, maybe a little bit more. I'll pick you up about half past nine. We'll need to git there in plenty of time. You'll want to see Brother Thurlow as well as hear him."

Now the two dangers wove a black curtain before her eyes. "I feel more comfortable in my own church," she pleaded weakly. And: "I don't like to leave him for such a long time." She raised one hand to her forehead, shutting out the sunlight. It seemed to her that she had lived forever holding tight, warding off, drawing on more strength than she had, strength meted out to her by God, always just enough but barely. . . . Was it possible ever to let go, to step into the shining river? The water would freeze her, scald her; she would drown. . . .

"There is nothin' to fear. You mustn't shrink from what God offers to all that will come unto him, seekin' him with a pure heart. And you need not fear for your brother. God will station his angels to guard this house. It may be that you are required to go before him, to seek out the path for his salvation."

His words tugged at her gently; his voice summoned her like a distant bell. But for the moment she was preoccupied with a minor miracle: she had been able to hear, easily, every word that he spoke, though she had not watched his face or lips. Not once since they had sat down together had she had to ask him to repeat a single word!

Isabelle began to nod vehemently. "Yes, I'll come," she said. "I'll come with you this time to see what it's like. You mustn't expect anything from me, but I'll come." Now she turned to receive his smile.

"I'm mighty glad you've reached that decision," said Ainsley Black, getting to his feet. "You've stirred the pool of spirit, and there's no tellin' how far the ripples will spread. Now go back to your roses while I steal away. Don't follow me, even with your eyes. Your brother is still watchin' from the window. Just tend to your roses, Miss Isabelle. They need your touch, just like you need the Lord's. The blindin', healin', strengthenin' touch of our Lord Jesus Christ will help you climb and bloom like a rose. Goodbye, Miss Isabelle. I'll call for you on Sunday at half past nine."

"Don't be disappointed if I . . . if nothing happens. I'm pretty old-fashioned when it comes to religion. I—"

"What Brother Thurlow preaches is the most old-fashioned of all. The real ol'-time religion. It's the oldest good news there is."

But just as Reverend Black turned to leave, a sudden noise jarred Isabelle—a gunshot, a thunder clap, the banging of a door—and she swung around in her chair, disobeying the preacher's orders. Claiborne, who must have slammed the kitchen door behind him, was striding like a towering, stiff-kneed stork across the lawn. Isabelle saw Ainsley Black move toward him and hold out his hand, which her brother refused to shake. Getting up too quickly, she staggered for a second, spots leaping before her eyes, and then hurried toward the two men, as if to interpose herself between them.

"You do not have permission to come onto this property," said Claiborne.

"I'm just leavin'," answered the preacher in a soft voice that Isabelle could barely catch, though she had now reached his side and was watching his lips. "Your sister and I have had a real good talk and she's agreed to come to the Rededication on Sunday mornin'. Doctor, is there any chance I could persuade you—"

"She's goin' to do no such thing!" shouted Claiborne. "No, sir! Now get off my property."

Isabelle stepped forward to confront her brother. "Reverend Black is *my* guest. He can stay here as long as he likes. Furthermore, I've told him I'm goin' with him on Sunday and I intend to."

Seldom in her adult life had she so openly defied her brother. Her heart seemed to be thumping against her eardrums. Then as she stood, frightened but resolute, her hand resting on the slope of her henlike bosom, Isabelle witnessed a remarkable transformation of her brother's face. The angry contortion that bared his yellowing teeth gave way to the ravaged but softened look of a tired old man, a man older than Claiborne, older than herself. Slowly he shook his head, as if gently resigned to the follies of the young; a smile, as tender as it was ironic, flickered for an instant across his lips.

"So you've made up your mind to go, have you?" Next he turned slowly toward Ainsley Black, staring at him from beneath hooded lids as if he had beheld something totally new and unexpected and was trying to absorb its elements. "Well, Mr. Preacher," he said at last, after a massive clearing of his throat, "since it looks like you're goin' to be escortin' my sister to church next Sunday, I reckon it's my duty, as her brother and the only male member of this household, to invite you to have Sunday dinner with us when you bring her back."

"Why, Brother!"

"Thank you kindly, Dr. Herne," said Ainsley Black with a quick look toward Isabelle. "That's mighty nice of you. I'd love to stay for dinner."

Her eyes bulging, Isabelle tried to read her brother's expression. Was he planning some mean trick, some mockery? There was no indication of it, no sign of slyness, of deviltry.

"But before I finally accept," continued the preacher, "I better make sure it's all right with Miss Isabelle. After all, she's the one who has to cook the dinner!"

"Of course it's all right with Isabelle," said Claiborne.

"Oh, yes," she cried, "oh, yes! We'd love to have you. Please come."

Ainsley Black thanked them both and once more held out his hand to Claiborne. It was accepted, a bit awkwardly. Then he left them, turning to wave just before he disappeared around the side of the house.

"Why, Brother," Isabelle exclaimed, "what's come over you?"

Claiborne snorted. "Do you realize how long it's been since we've had a young face at our dining-room table? Even if the fellow's a crook, an FBI agent or whatever, it'll be a welcome change from havin' to look across the table at you day in and day out, year after year." Then he smiled. "Cheer up, Isabelle. I didn't mean to hurt your feelin's. I really asked him for your sake."

Chapter Seventeen

On Friday morning, as he was having breakfast at what had become his regular corner table in the motel dining room, Hux realized that he had nearly made a bad blunder. In asking Miss Isabelle to go to the Rededication on Saturday night, he had completely forgotten that the president of Ole Miss had already invited him to a dinner party at the country club that same evening. Thank God Miss Isabelle had decided on Sunday instead. That he had been able to put the president's party so completely out of mind testified alarmingly to the hold that the secret agenda now had upon him. He would have to be very careful, especially on his trip to Brandon Institute today. Because of Franklin Mosby, the official agenda and the personal pilgrimage would merge, and the prospect made Hux nervous. Yet he was immensely eager to see Mosby again, the man whom Clark had described as the bravest and most resourceful he had ever met, the man who had been at Clark's side on the platform at Tupelo. . . . By what route had the young schoolteacher from Meridian risen to be a college administrator? Was he still politically active? Above all, what could he tell Hux about Clark's final weeks and days? The last question was not only the most urgent but potentially the most dangerous, for Hux could imagine himself swept away by it, swept downstream on a cresting flood of emotions past all consideration of the job he had to do. . . .

Hux's regular waitress, whose name, Jackie Sue, was stitched in blue over the right breast of her buttercup-yellow uniform, was standing at his elbow, pressing more coffee upon him. "No use in the worl' drinkin' cold coffee when there's plenty of the hot stuff right here," she crooned. "How 'bout some more hot biscuits?" she urged when he turned down the coffee. Her eager, pinched little face was milky white, her frizzed hair the orange-red of the clay roads outside Oxford. In her unbeautiful way she struck Hux as sexy, bringing to mind the roadside girls, the carhoppers and waitresses of his Carolina adolescence.

"No, thanks," said Hux, who had finished his order of eggs, sausages, and grits. "I'm ready to bust the way it is."

Jackie Sue continued to stand by his table. When Hux looked up again, she jerked her head to the left, indicating something she could not speak about at the moment. Hux glanced around and saw two well-dressed blacks—businessmen by the look of them—in the process of seating themselves at a nearby table. When he turned to Jackie Sue again, she raised her brown-penciled eyebrows and shook her head as if to say, *Would you believe it? Niggers in this dining room! But what can you do?* Hux played dumb, pretending not to understand her signals, which now included a barely audible clicking of her tongue. A moment later Jackie Sue was smiling at the two men as she handed them the breakfast menu, smiling and cooing over them as she stepped on her scruples and obeyed the law of the land. "How-uh are you all this mawnin'?" Hux heard her say. "Looks like it's goin' to be a gorgeous day, don't it? What appeals to you all for breakfast this mawnin'?" Perhaps, he reflected, reminding himself how unthinkable such a scene would have been ten years before, a few outward changes were worth more than a change of heart.

Soon after he reached Brandon Institute, Hux asked the president, a huge man named Bullock, about Franklin D. Mosby.

"Frank Mosby!" exclaimed the president, who was the blackest black man Hux had seen in a long time. "You know Frank? Why, he's just down the hall. He's my director of admissions." And before Hux could explain that Mosby was unlikely to remember him, President Bullock picked up his telephone and instructed his secretary to summon Frank Mosby at once.

From Clark's letters and his own distant memories Hux had retained the image of a flaming young militant with a brow full of pain and anger. He was thus unprepared for—and instantly dismayed by—the suave and slender man in his late thirties who strode into the office, greeted the president familiarly as "Cal," and acknowledged his introduction to Hux with something less than cordiality. When Hux explained that they had met briefly, that he was an old friend of Clark Helmholtz's and had been looking forward to this reunion, Mosby wagged his head and gave a slight smile but said nothing. Now feeling awkward, Hux began to elaborate on his friendship with Clark and his own foray into Mississippi in 1964. Still there was no response from this decidedly handsome man whose face, beneath a modified and carefully trimmed afro, was as silken as a woman's, a delicate mocha brown.

At last Hux paused, whereupon Mosby again smiled slightly and said, "Poor old Clark. I always figured that bullet was meant for my big mouth instead of his."

President Bullock shook his head at this. The yellowed whites of his eyes were like ivory balls in an ebony mask. "Incredible, incredible," he said. "What a time that was. Incredible when you stop to think about it." Just then the business manager came in, and Mosby rose to excuse himself. He was polite but showed no desire to talk further about Clark or even to see Hux again. It was President Bullock who suggested that perhaps Mosby and Hux could get together again for a chat, once the business meetings were over.

"Fine," said Mosby without enthusiasm. "Just drop by my office. If I'm not there, somebody will know where to track me down."

Feeling somewhat rejected, Hux had to draw upon all of his official and social resources to maintain an easy presence during the rest of his visit, but he succeeded. Brandon was a replica in black-face of a small Baptist college he had visited in Holly Springs on his way to Memphis on Tuesday: the same administrative structure, approximately the same level of literacy and aptitude, the same problems (serious ones) concerning money and a declining enrollment. President Bullock, like his white counterpart at Holly Springs, was a windbag, a genial stuffed shirt, a professional optimist who was no doubt effective at a podium or in a pulpit. It was the business manager, Rufus Collins, who had every detail of the enrollment figures, the budget, and the educational resources expertly filed in his mind; he was the one who knew the questions to ask. Hux had a hard time convincing Collins that the Morrow Foundation meant business and that even a little black college like Brandon could expect to benefit from the regional program. In the end they all got along well—so well that after lunch President Bullock urged Hux to return next Saturday to be one of the guest speakers at the graduation exercises—an honor Hux had to decline.

Mosby was seated at his desk when Hux came into the office, and did not rise. "Pull up that chair," he said. "This won't take long." And he returned to his reading of what looked like a stack of application forms. "Now," he said after perhaps five minutes, "that ought to hold 'em." He raised his head, tapped the eraser of a pencil against his slightly protruding lower lip, and looked Hux over. "So you and old Clark were buddies, were you?"

"He was my closest friend. Not only that—I admired him more than any man I've ever known."

"I reckon you could say I *admired* him too. But even if a black man and a white man could be what I consider *real* friends, I'd have a real hard time thinkin' of old Clark that way. He was a born boss, you might say—about as dominatin' as they come."

"Oh, no," protested Hux. "Clark had a strong personality, but I would never call him dominating."

"He was one hard worker, all right," continued Mosby, brushing aside Hux's objection. "Got to give the man credit for that. And plenty bright, far as that goes. And *knew* it, too. But he was Mr. Take Charge from the word go, and finally people got a little *tired* of that, if you know what I mean." He drawled out his last words ironically.

"Judging from his letters, Clark thought of you as a friend. With no qualifications, racial or otherwise."

"Is that right?"

"I'm not kidding you," said Hux with rising anger. "He did think of you as a good friend."

"Oh, we got along pretty well. No use worryin' about that. And I scarcely ever disputed him, exceptin' maybe once or twice. But, man, I sure had to spend a lot of time soothin' hurt feelin's. Not mine so much as some of the other workers'. And that wasn't always easy."

"Then how did you react to Clark's death?" Hux demanded. "You and the other workers." The line of his jaw was tense, his voice full of bitterness.

Mosby raised his eyebrows almost to the crisp wool of his hair. "Man, are you serious? How do you expect we reacted? Look, he was one of us. We'd been through some rough times together. And I mean rough. Man, we just couldn't believe it. Not at first. It was like a movie. I mean, I was actually spattered with bits of his blood and brains. So was the girl sittin' next to me. And I *still* couldn't believe it. Like I say, it was like some movie, some Technicolor movie. Then the next thing I knew, I was beatin' the platform with my two fists and cryin' like a two-year-old. By then everybody was screamin' and runnin' around like crazy. That was one horrible scene."

Hux had turned pale, but he was unappeased. "Did you grieve, did you mourn for him? Or were you secretly glad to have him off your backs?"

Mosby stared at Hux. "Now, come on. You tryin' to get me mad or somethin'?"

"I'm sorry. I take that back."

Mosby dropped his challenge. "I can think of only one person who might have been just a little bit glad when Clark got shot, and that was because he thought Clark was makin' out with his girlfriend.

And I expect even he was mostly sorrowful. You had to be. It was a terrible thing, terrible."

Hux nodded. Across the big uncluttered desk, the two men gazed at each other in silence. As he tried to bring his own grief and anger and disappointment under control, Hux had a sudden vision of Clark's shattered head and felt sick. Closing his eyes for a moment, he shook his head. Then he said, in as matter-of-fact a voice as he could manage, "Do you ever see any of the other people who were there? For instance, Anne Sibthorpe?"

"You talkin' about the white people. They mostly went back North fast as they could shake the red dust off their shoes. Anne went back with one of 'em, one of the worst as far as I was concerned. Married him, too. I *liked* Anne, but I can't say much for the men she kept gettin' mixed up with." Mosby eyed Hux, grinning all the while. "Don't get me wrong," he continued. "There were some good people too, people I wouldn't mind seein' again. But you know how it is. People in the Movement don't keep in touch any more, unless maybe you're still livin' or workin' in the same place. Sometimes I go for months without even *talkin'* with anybody white. Can't say I miss it."

Hux forced himself to ignore this. He was hurt as well as furious, for he had yearned for Mosby to like him. Finally he said, "Why is everybody so pacified around here? Pacified and tame. From President Bullock on down. Has everybody forgotten the early sixties? After all, this *is* Mississippi. Things can't be *that* perfect. Doesn't anybody hate the system any more?" he continued, his voice strident. "Isn't there any militancy? Don't any of your students read Fanon or Eldridge Cleaver these days?"

"Aw, come on, man. Don't you know students got better ways of spendin' their time than readin' that stuff?"

That maddening, superior smile! Hux wanted to hook his hands under the big desk and flip it over on Mosby. "Okay," he said, "forget all about that. Forget all those years of lynchings and beatings and the rest of it. Forget about Medgar Evers and Emmett Till and all the others. But what about *you?* Don't you ever want to run a knife into the fat gut of some illiterate old redneck who still wants to treat you like a nigger?" Suddenly he thought of Jackie Sue and the two men in the motel dining room. "How can you be so goddamn smug? Don't you know they still hate you?"

For a second or two Mosby hesitated. Then he stood up and walked to the door of his office. Turning in his chair, Hux felt a thrill of vindication. Had he finally provoked Mosby into kicking him out?

"I'll give you a quick answer," said Mosby, "and then I've got to get back to work." He placed his hand on the doorknob. "No, I haven't forgotten and the others haven't forgotten, not by a long shot. Mississippi's still got a mighty long way to go before it's a fit place for a self-respectin' black man to live in. Probably not as far as New York," he said, grinning, "but plenty far. But we're not goin' to get where we got to get if we're always draggin' along a whole wagonload of old anger and muck out of the past. But we haven't forgotten."

Hux got up to leave before he was ordered from the room. Though he kept telling himself to stay cool, he was now trembling with rage. At the door he said, "I suppose Clark's death is just part of the muck out of the past."

"Man, are you tryin' to make *me* feel guilty?" Mosby gave Hux a look of weary disbelief, shaking his head slowly from side to side. "Is that what you're tryin' to do? Come on, man, you know better than that." He pulled the door open and said, "How about lettin' me handle *my* past and you take care of yours—okay?"

For a long moment the two men faced each other, the blond in his tan poplin suit and striped rep tie, the light-skinned black in his open-necked shirt and bright blue pants; they were of the same age and of much the same height; they had both known Clark Helmholtz. . . . When Mosby held out his hand, Hux spurned it.

You complacent son of a bitch, he thought, turning abruptly away.

Hux drove back to Oxford in a misanthropic fury. Mosby had upset him badly, leaving him in no mood for polite socializing at Dean Halsey's tonight or at the president's tomorrow. Too many parties, too many people. He wished he had never set foot in Mississippi. . . .

Chapter Eighteen

When Anne Schlamm had returned, with many misgivings, to Oxford five years before, she told herself that she was doing so for the sake of her daughter Prudence. And it was chiefly for Prudence's sake that she continued to live there, a divorced woman of thirty-one with an unchallenging library job and few opportunities to meet the kind of men she found exhilarating. Without the responsibility of the child she would have headed at once (so she told herself) to a city like Atlanta or Houston—or perhaps New Orleans—where she would not have felt so confined. It seemed important to her that Prue grow up with a sense of family, a sense of place, such as could be provided by the Bensons and by the social and physical geography of a university town. Despite the wayward, rebellious streak in her nature that had alienated her father (now dead) and continued to distress (and sometimes frighten) her sister, Peggy Benson, Anne took motherhood seriously and was determined to do nothing that was likely to inflict further psychological damage upon Prudence, who had already (Anne reasoned) been sufficiently hurt by the divorce. She truly loved the child, though she occasionally screamed at her for some trivial offense that served as a pretext for venting a guilt-ridden resentment of her own lot.

Such an outburst had just occurred as Anne was dressing for the Halseys' party. She had gone into the living room and found the floor still strewn with the toys Prudence had been told to pick up at least fifteen minutes earlier. Anne not only screamed at the child but pulled her from the kitchen table where she was finishing her supper and dragged her, then and there, into the living room to pick up every single piece. Terrified, as always, by her mother's sudden and torrential rage, Prue was still sobbing in her room. The sound of it made Anne sick with fury—this time directed exclusively at herself. It had been months since the last outburst, and Anne had been as surprised by it as Prudence. What had come over her? Why tonight, when she was looking forward to going to the Halseys' with a visiting fireman who had impressed her as more attractive than most? As the result of two years of psychotherapy before leaving New Haven,

Anne was accustomed to asking herself such questions, the answers to which were always less clear than she would have liked.

"Okay, honey," she called out. "You don't have to keep cryin'. That's enough now. I'm sorry, and you're sorry, and we'll both try to do better next time." She waited. The sound of sobbing went on. Wearing only her bra and pantyhose, Anne went into Prudence's room and sat down on her bed. The child, who had flung herself across the bed, burst into renewed tears as her mother placed a hand on her shoulder. "I'm sorry. I shouldn't have lost my temper like that." She massaged Prue's neck and shoulders, and after several minutes of this old and reliable remedy, the crying subsided. Prue, whose head was buried in her arms, murmured something.

"What did you say, honey?"

Again something inaudible. Finally the words came out: "Mommy, will you stay home tonight?"

"I can't, sweetie. You know that."

"*Please.*"

"No, darlin', I have to go to a party. Martha Jane's goin' to baby-sit. You always have a good time with her."

"Please don't go."

Exasperated, Anne stood up. "I have to, sweetie. And I want to. You're old enough to understand that. But you'll have fun with Martha Jane."

"Are you goin' with a man?"

"Yes, a nice man. From New York. His name is Mr. Hux."

Prue sat up abruptly. "Mr. Hux! What a yukky name. I hate it."

"But you'll like him. He's real nice."

Anne returned to her bedroom. Larry Hux *had* seemed nice. She had hoped that he would call, and he had. Deciding to dress up for him, she put on her new lime-green dress and looped bright red beads around her throat. Probably he would want to go to bed with her. Probably she would refuse him, though not because she had an absolute policy of never sleeping with a man on their first date; rather, she had come to hate the one-night stands to which she sometimes acceded, driven by a sexual urgency that they almost never gratified. "Five-hour stands" would have been a more accurate term, for Anne, ever mindful of Prudence, had decided that it would be harmful for the child to wake up to find a strange (or even a well-known man) in her mother's bedroom. Meanwhile, liking the company of intelligent and unconventional men, she had a problem in Oxford. The university bachelors—sexually anemic, gay, or alcoholically divorced—could be entertaining at faculty dinner parties but were of little use to her beyond that. The bright men who really interested her were all securely married and off-bounds, and though Anne sometimes flirted with them in public, she was careful not to jeopardize her already marginal social status in Oxford by allowing anything more than bantering friendships to develop with them—mildly sexualized friendships that were enjoyable but led nowhere. That left the occasional strangers passing through town, the visiting firemen as she thought of them, the men of the rare five-hour stands. Larry Hux was the latest in this series.

Though regarded as liberated (threateningly so) by some of the faculty wives with whose husbands she had flirted, Anne did not see herself as an independent woman, self-sufficient enough to take her pleasure with men in a casual way. Nor was she drawn to the ideal of sisterhood—especially with her co-workers and with the women of Peggy's circle. She wanted a husband of her own; and she wanted a loving and responsible stepfather for Prue, who saw her own (remarried) father for only one summer month during the year. As the divorced mother of a fairly difficult child and with what she considered to be the wrong looks and the wrong temperament for most Southern men, Anne did not overestimate her chances of finding the right man in Oxford. She could live without a husband if she had to, but found the prospect dismal. Half accepting her New Haven therapist's diagnosis of a strongly masochistic streak in her psyche, Anne occasionally wondered if her decision to live in a university town reflected not so much her concern for Prudence as a self-destructive impulse of her own, a need to deny herself the possibility of a workable second marriage. Perhaps Houston or Atlanta would have been a better choice—even in the long run for Prue. The answer was never clear.

She had absolutely no expectation that her evening with Larry Hux would lead anywhere, but she had liked what she had seen of him and was inordinately glad that he had called. . . .

He was late. He had said he would pick her up at seven and it was now seven-thirty. Prue had long since finished her interrupted supper, put on her pajamas, and was watching a Charlie Brown special on television with the teenage baby-sitter, who had arrived forty-five minutes before. Had Larry Hux forgotten their date, just as he had apparently forgotten the Halseys' party until Anne reminded him of it? She wouldn't have expected such absent-mindedness in a foundation executive, a man used to dealing in millions. . . .

The doorbell rang. The man Anne let into the apartment startled her, for though he was neatly dressed in a dark suit, his hair still damp from a shower, he had lost the aura of smooth competency that she remembered. Instead, he looked somehow disreputable, even seedy, with a haggard face, a tense, almost petulant mouth, and restless eyes. With hardly a glance in Anne's direction, he looked quickly around the room, as if searching for a way to escape. "Sorry I'm so late," he muttered without further explanation. Then, making what seemed to be a major effort, he held out his hand to Anne, smiled wanly, and said, "I'm afraid I'm sort of a wreck tonight. It's been a rough week, a rough day."

"Sorry to hear that," she replied coolly. "I'd offer you a drink, but we're already pretty late. The Halseys are mighty punctual people, so we'd better get goin'. There'll probably be time for a drink there before they serve dinner." Then, remembering her manners, Anne turned abruptly, so that her black hair swung like a gypsy dancer's, and called out above the noise of the television set, "Prue, honey, come say hello to Mr. Hux."

Prudence, who was habitually rude to any man who came to take her mother out, did not move her eyes from the screen.

"Prue, did you hear me?"

This time the child looked around, raised one hand, flicked her fingers toward the stranger, and said, "Hi."

"Hello, Prudence. Nice to meet you," said Larry Hux.

"Martha Jane, we'll be back no later than eleven—eleven-thirty at the latest," called Anne to the baby-sitter, who was just as absorbed in Charlie Brown as her young charge. The puffy girl, whose hair was stretched tight around a multitude of pink curlers, nodded without looking up. "Let's go," said Anne.

Halfway through the evening at the Halseys', Anne realized that her escort was drunk. It was a fairly large party, with a buffet dinner spread upon the dining-room table and with separate tables, equipped with place cards, set up in the dining room and on the screened porch. Anne had been seated with two Art Department bachelors and Lancelotta Baldridge, who was Dean Halsey's administrative assistant. Meanwhile, Larry, as the dispenser of hoped-for millions, was placed out of Anne's sight with Mary Ellen Halsey and a visiting Faulkner scholar from the University of Arkansas. When the guests reassembled in the living room after dinner, Anne pulled up a spindly chair next to Larry, who had cornered the Faulknerian on a sofa and seemed to be haranguing him about something. Larry's face was puckered like a scowling choirboy's, his eyes glinting mischief. As if poised for possible intervention, Dean Halsey was standing by the arm of the sofa.

Turning to Anne, Larry said, in an absurd back-country accent, "Miz Schlamm, I've jus' been proposin' to Dr. Starkweather here that sump'm ought to be done about Bill Faulkner's body." He lifted his highball glass from the floor at his feet and took a long, gulping drink, smacking his lips afterward.

"His *body*?"

"Yes, ma'am, Miz Schlamm, his body. I been proposin' that they ought to ex-hume it and then hire a team of expert morticians to touch it up so's they could exhibit it. You know, jus' like Lenin's, only in the parlor at Rowan Oak 'stead of the Kremlin. Trouble is, I cain't persuade Dr. Starkweather here that I'm serious."

"I'm afraid I find your humor a little too much on the gruesome side," said Professor Starkweather, who had not yet abandoned his effort to maintain affability. He was a large middle-aged man with rimless glasses and a 1950s crew-cut who looked and sounded (Anne decided) like the manager of a small-town Arkansas bank. He seemed distinctly uneasy, crowded as he was by Larry, who had drawn his chair close to Starkweather's knees, making it difficult for him to stand up and escape. Anne felt a little sorry for the poor man, but, having been bored by the chatter about Florence and fellowships and university funding at her table, she yearned for someone to stir things up, to provide a bit of excitement, and this seemed to be exactly what Larry Hux, in this unexpectedly oafish role, intended to do. If Professor Starkweather had to be sacrificed, too bad. . . . She wondered how Larry—given their late arrival—had managed to drink as much as he apparently had.

"Humor?" he was saying. "Humor? Beggin' your pardon, suh, I've never in my whole life been more serious. Faulkner's body on display—at, say, maybe two dollars per head admission—would bring more revenue to this fine ol' university than ten years' worth of gover'ment grants."

Anne raised her dark eyes to Carruthers Halsey to see how he was taking all this. Faulkner was already big business at Ole Miss. Professor Starkweather had been invited to Oxford as the star of one of a series of "Faulkner Weekends" which the university sponsored during the summer. These weekends were designed to attract schoolteachers, housewives, retired businessmen with a cultural bent, and others who, for a fee of two hundred dollars, were housed in dormitories, taken on tours of the Faulkner country, exposed to lectures by experts like the professor, and entertained at an authentic Mississippi barbecue on the grounds of Faulkner's home, Rowan Oak. "William Faulkner cookouts"—that was how an old townsman, who had known Faulkner, had once described these weekends to Anne, and she had shared his derision. The dean, she saw, was smiling like a good fellow from his standing position by the sofa arm, but his wife, who had come within earshot, was making little motions with her lips, as if trying to decide whether the time had come to pluck Larry from his seat and propel him to another part of the room. Meanwhile, Larry—bless his heart!—had managed to capture the attention of all the nearby guests; there was no small talk going on in this half of the room, no possibility for a tactful diversion. Captivated, partly gleeful, partly disapproving, Anne wondered how far he would go with his act, which could hardly have been endorsed by the Morrow Foundation.

Larry had now, for some drunken reason, dropped his country-boy accent and was speaking in the tones of cultivated inquiry. "Of course much depends on how successful the original embalming was. Perhaps you could give us the details, Professor Starkweather. What has your research uncovered? How, exactly, was the body prepared?"

"Mr. Hux, I believe you're a stranger to this part of the South. I've been listenin' to you as patiently as I can, but I think you should know that the kind of humor you've been indulgin' in is not exactly appreciated down here."

"I agree," said Mary Ellen Halsey, stepping forward as an umpire to part the combatants. "This conversation's gettin' just too maw-bid for me!" She wrinkled her nose. "How about it, Mr. Hux, would you like to come in the dinin' room for a little more coffee?"

"But Mary Ellen," said Anne, "Larry's makin' a serious point. No one's goin' to want to pay out good money to look at a grinnin' skull or a wrinkled old mummy. You can't charge admission for that." An old hand at making her own mischief, Anne generally knew just how far she could go without risking banishment by the Ole Miss hostesses. Now she had endangered herself. Banishment loomed. Let it come. . . .

"That's precisely my point," said Larry, nodding at her, his voice deep, solemn, and a little aggrieved, the voice of a Southern senator speaking for the record. "Precisely the point I've been tryin' to make. There's a limit to what even the most expert cosmetician can do if the original undertakers didn't know their business. That's why I find it disappointin' that our learned friend can't enlighten us on what we're likely to find when they slide back the lid."

"Mr. Hux, I can't bear to hear another *word* on this maw-bid subject. I positively forbid it!" Mrs. Halsey's manner was gay, almost lilting. "If you don't want any more coffee, I'm sure Carruthers would be glad to fix you a drink. Carruthers, see what Mr. Hux would like," she called, retreating across the room. "I'll put him in your safe-keepin'."

Ten minutes later Peggy Benson came over to her sister and said, "Annie, somethin's got to be done about Larry Hux. Since he came with you, maybe you'd better ask him to take you home. He's makin' an awful nuisance of himself, and Ray's afraid he'll get Carruthers really mad at him. Which would be too bad for all kinds of reasons. What's happened to him tonight? He wasn't like this at our house. What's gotten into him?"

"A lot of whiskey, for one thing," said Anne.

But she was wrong. Though he seemed to be almost reeling when they left the Halseys' house together, he looked at her with amazement when she asked for the car keys. "Why?" he asked in a reasonable, undefensive way. "Why do you want to drive?"

"Because you're drunk as a hoot owl. I've got a child at home I have to think about."

"I had one drink before dinner and one after. And one glass of that rotten wine. Did I really seem smashed to you?"

"You sure did!"

He laughed. "It's just a disguise—a useful one when I feel like cutting up a bit. I've had a rough week—too many conversations with too many Starkweathers—and a particularly bad day. So I decided to do my drunken act and let off some steam."

"You were very convincin'. Have you ever done any real acting?"

"Some."

"You've got an amazin' repertory of Southern voices. Can you do Yankees too?"

"Sure," he said, pronouncing it "shurr." "I can talk Amurrican as well as the next guy."

Anne shook her head at him, laughing, though she felt uneasy. So it was all a big joke. What a strange man. Yet she liked him, was glad that he had decided to misbehave. She let him drive, and when they reached her building, she invited him up for a drink. "I'd like to get you really drunk," she said, "and see if there's any difference."

While Anne was paying the baby-sitter, she was aware that Larry was prowling restlessly around the apartment. It must seem pretty crummy to him, she thought, aware that a number of Prue's toys had been returned to the center of the floor. Coming back into the little living room, she saw that he was holding a framed photograph of her ex-husband, which, for Prue's sake, she kept on top of the desk.

"Who's this?" he demanded, fixing her with startled eyes. "I've met this man somewhere."

"It's Prue's father. My ex. He's in the Sociology Department at Wesleyan. Maybe you met him there."

"No . . . I don't think.so. . . . What's his name?"

"Harry. Harry Schlamm."

"Oh, my God!" Laying the photograph on a table, he came toward her and caught her by both arms. "It's the craziest coincidence. I woke up in the middle of the night two nights ago trying to think of Harry Schlamm's last name. I never connected it with yours—isn't that strange? So you were married to Harry Schlamm!"

"Shhh! Your voice carries. I don't want Prue to wake up. Where did you know Harry?"

"I met him in Jackson. Ten years ago. We were both working— Oh, my God!" A look of what Anne interpreted as pure terror contorted his face. "So you were married to Harry Schlamm," he repeated. "Anne Schlamm. Were you—was your name—?"

"Why are you lookin' at me like that?" She asked, freeing her arms from his grip. She was confronting a madman!

"Anne Sibthorpe! You've got to be Anne Sibthorpe! I was talking about you just this afternoon!"

During the next half hour a number of connections were made, but sporadically, in runs and bursts. Now that Anne had poured drinks for the two of them, Larry seemed calmer, though he often frowned, moving his lips even during long silences when he stared at the floor. Anne, on the other hand, grew more and more agitated as Larry told her that he had been Clark Helmholtz's best friend, that he had read about her in Clark's letters, that he had seen Frank Mosby at Brandon that very afternoon. Several times she jumped up from the couch, once to go to the bathroom, twice to go to the kitchen for more ice or paper napkins. "Why did Frank Mosby resent Clark so much?" Larry asked when she had finally settled down. "He made Clark sound like the worst kind of bully. 'Mr. Take Charge'—those were his words. Was Clark like that during those last few weeks?"

Anne was unable to concentrate on the question. What had Clark written to this weird friend of his? How much did Larry know? What, if anything, had Clark told her about Larry? And all the while she was angry at herself for becoming so upset. What did it matter what Larry knew? It was all ancient history, it couldn't matter less. . . . Yet some vestigial prudishness made her reluctant to bring out the simple (not so simple!) fact of her relationship with Clark unless Larry gave some indication that he was already aware of it. Why did she care? Why was the uncertainty making her so nervous?

"Did you hear what I said?" He was looking at her with a quizzical frown, his head cocked to one side.

"Sorry. I was thinkin' about something else. What did you say?"

"I asked if Clark was really like that—bossing everybody around the way Mosby claims."

Glimpsing for a second the beautiful intensity of Frank Mosby's gaze, hearing his voice, so musical even in its urgency, Anne gave a long, wavering sigh. "It depends on how you look at it," she said, now fully concentrating on the question. "Clark couldn't handle opposition very well, especially when he was sure he was right. Which he nearly always was. He could be tactless, he could be—" She broke off, again hearing Frank's voice in passionate argument with Clark on the night before Tupelo, hearing his wail of protest as Clark raked him with the patterned fire of his logic. She had sided with Clark, egging him on, exulting in the defeat of her old ally. . . . Clark, as usual, had been right in his assessment of the situation, but she shouldn't have sided with him so gleefully. . . . "Look," she resumed, "there's something you ought to know. Mosby was eaten up with jealousy of Clark."

"Jealousy?"

If only she could tell him the whole story, lay it all out. . . . But she couldn't, she couldn't, until he gave a sign—the faintest sign would do! Was he playing dumb, trying to force her to say what he already knew? *But why should she care?* "Yes, that's what it was. Plain old jealousy. Of the nonsexual variety," she added quickly, dishonestly. "Frank was used to bein' number one and he couldn't be after Clark joined us in the field. Clark had the great advantage of knowin' the law, backwards and forwards, and he could use it to intimidate the local goons. After Frank got arrested over in Alhambra, Clark had him out of jail in no time flat. A local preacher got most of the credit, but it was really Clark, workin' behind the scenes. Frank couldn't stand bein' dependent on Clark—he thought it made him lose standin' with the other blacks. It's as simple as that. Pure jealousy."

Larry nodded. He's accepted it, Anne thought, once more frantically trying to remember what Clark had told her about Larry. It seemed to her now that there *had* been something—something about a fight, a big blowup that Clark had later regretted . . . ? So much had been going on at that time, so many things crowded into a single day, that in memory the whole summer was like a blurred vision from a speeding bus. "You know," she went on, "Frank made it pretty clear—oh, six or seven years ago—that he wasn't interested in seein' us white folks any more. That's the way it is all around the state. The blacks vote and go almost anywhere they want to—and more jobs are openin' up—but we don't see each other any more. Only the politicians, a few of 'em, still make the effort to keep up with Charlie Evers and the others. It's a rotten shame, when you think of the way we all felt in '64, but I guess it's got to be that way. For a long time at least. I still believe in everything I believed in then, but I guess I'm now ready to settle for a few changes, most of them on the surface. My claws and fangs have been drawn."

Larry was again staring at the floor. Had he been listening to what she said? Suddenly, from nowhere in her conscious mind, a question leapt out: "What was Clark's wife like?"

"Clark's wife?"

Anne felt her face grow warm. Hating her indiscretion, she had no choice but to press on. "I guess I'm just curious, knowin' Clark and all that. Were you and Clark friends apart from your wives or were you involved as couples?"

"We saw each other all the time. Separately and as couples."

"And what sort of person was she—or is she?"

"Linda? Very nice. Sort of a wholesome Middle-Western type. Always organizing picnics and square dances for the graduate students. Didn't drink. Went to church by herself since Clark wouldn't go near one. Being a minister's son," he added with a tenuous smile.

"You don't make her sound exactly appealin'."

"Linda's a good sort. I liked her. My wife tolerated her. We all got along fine. But I don't think she had any real idea of the kind of man she was married to. It's funny you asked," he said after a pause. "Another coincidence. I wrote to Linda the other night—for the first time in years, except for Christmas cards."

"How come?"

Another pause. Then, without looking at Anne, Larry said, "I had just been to Tupelo. I paid a visit to the schoolyard."

"You made a special trip to that schoolyard?" Anne was so moved that she rested her hand for a moment on Larry's shoulder. "Then Clark really did mean a lot to you. Was it miserable for you, bein' at the schoolyard?"

"Not at the time. Just rather ordinary. But afterwards . . ." At last he raised his eyes to Anne's. "I'll confess something to you. My main reason for coming to Mississippi was to visit Tupelo and some of the other places and talk to people who knew Clark. The other business—the whole academic-resources project—is important, I suppose, but—and I'm telling this only to you—it grew out of my personal need to come here, not the other way around. And now I've met you without even having to look for you. It's incredible."

"I think *you're* incredible. After ten years . . ."

"Do you think I'm crazy?"

"Maybe. A little. I don't understand men's loyalties. Let the dead bury the dead—that's more my style. But I'm impressed. I'm sure as hell impressed." Anne stood up, tossing back her glossy hair, and walked into the tiny kitchen. "I'm goin' to fix myself another highball. Do you want one?"

"No, thanks."

The sadness of his voice seeped into an underground reservoir of her own sadness—a dark pool which she often forgot in her daily battle to make a life of sorts for herself and Prudence. But it was there, fed by many streams; Clark's death had once poured into it like a late-summer cloudburst. Sometimes, when she was especially tired or frustrated, she would let herself sink into its shadowy depths. Now, as she measured out the whiskey and filled the glass with ice cubes and water, Anne realized that she was reluctant to go back into the room with Larry Hux. She was a little frightened by the degree to which she had been touched by this strange loyalty or obsession or whatever—surely such loyalty to the memory of a friend ten years dead was overdone and a bit sick? She did not want to be reminded of a time in her life when loyalties had been passionately forged in one single intense conversation held in the basement of some Negro church or over pork-and-greens in a three-room niggertown house, while couriers came and went, and the night outside seemed to crackle with danger. In that exalted time emotions had spilled, sloshed, from one container to the next. In the face of the enemy (who happened to be her own people) distinctions were obliterated, transforming her courtly father into a redneck bully, transforming a political alliance with a black into lifelong (!) brotherhood. Shared rage at racial injustice had infused her lovemaking with Clark, and a desperate effort to climb out of a pit of grief and shock had made even a marriage to Harry Schlamm seem possible. No amount of exaltation had been worth the letdown that followed. And here she was, faced with a living reminder, a yellow-haired stranger who sat in her living room grieving for a friend who had been lost to him for ten years, for a friend who for three weeks had been her lover.

When she re-entered the living room, Larry said, "Were you sitting right next to him at the time?"

Anne knew exactly what he was referring to. "Look," she said as she sat down not on the sofa but in a basket chair facing it, "I was there and sometime I'll tell you all about it if you want me to. But right now I'm not up to it. Don't you think there've been enough amazin' revelations for one evenin'?"

To her surprise, Larry's face relaxed, as if he had won a reprieve. "Right," he said. "And now I'm going to change my mind about that drink. You sit where you are. I'll get it myself."

For the next half hour or so they sipped whiskey and talked sporadically while listening to Anne's collection of Mississippi country music, blues, and work songs. At one point Prudence woke up and appeared at her bedroom door—a plump, scowling, curly-haired child in pink pajamas decorated with blue elephants and monkeys. Anne called her into the room, kissed her on the forehead, and sent her back to bed. When, toward midnight, Larry got up to leave, Anne, who was exhausted by the strain of the evening, did not press him to stay.

At the front door Larry paused with his hand on the knob. "I've got one more question. Do you ever hear anything about the doctor who shot Clark? Is he still living?"

"Last I heard he's still living in a spooky old house over in Alhambra. Lives with his old-maid sister. People say they're both crazy as coots."

Larry nodded but made no comment. Instead, he stepped briskly into the front hall, then turned to face Anne. "I promise I won't talk about Clark the whole time when I see you again," he said. "He mustn't be the chief bond between us. Let's make other connections, like two ordinary people who've just met and like each other."

Anne shrugged. "We can't wipe it all out. If you came all the way to Mississippi in pursuit of Clark, he's bound to pop up from time to time. But I won't mind," she added, smiling, "just so long as you don't let him hog the whole show."

When he moved to kiss her on the lips, she let him. His kiss was very tentative. Oh, come on, she thought—you can do better than that. As they drew apart, he thanked her for sticking by him during the party and putting up with him afterward. Then he said, "In a couple of days—soon as I know my plans—I'll call you and make a proper date. We'll have a night on the town."

"That sounds real nice. I'm always ready to entertain visitin' firemen. Goodnight, Larry."

Leaning over the rail, she watched him go downstairs. She saw the glint of the foyer light on the top of his thick metallic hair. What a strange man, she thought, liking him the more for his strangeness.

Chapter Nineteen

Isabelle stood at the front door, wearing the hat and dress she had worn the previous Sunday and holding over her head a black umbrella so huge that it might have been used by her grandfather's coachman. The size of the umbrella emphasized the stumpiness of her figure, the outward curve of her short legs. Hatless and without an umbrella, Ainsley Black dashed up the front walk, his hair darkened by the rain that dripped across his cheeks; he was wearing a lightweight summer raincoat of tan poplin that nearly matched his suit.

"Mornin', Miss Isabelle," he said hoarsely. "Everybody says this rain is badly needed, but I sure wish it had held off." He seemed out of breath. "I'm sorry I'm late, ma'am, but I overslept. Didn't even have time for breakfast."

Isabelle, who had caught only a few of his words, smiled and held out her hand. "We'll have to hurry," she said, as the umbrella wobbled in her grasp. Resting her free hand on his right arm, she trustingly let him guide and support her past the puddles on the walk to the car. He appeared unwell, she thought, paler than usual, with dark, bruise-colored skin around his sleepy-looking eyes.

"Are you nervous?" he asked.

The question surprised her, and she wondered if she had heard him correctly. When he repeated the words, she nodded, sheltering herself more closely against his protective arm.

"Well, you needn't be, Miss Isabelle. God doesn't require you to feel anything you don't feel in fact. Maybe it isn't His plan for you to receive the Spirit today. Nobody can tell in advance. I'd be real sorry if you felt disappointed because nothin' special happened."

Was she only imagining that he seemed nervous too, that he too would be disappointed if nothing happened? He's afraid he's raised false expectations, she thought, touched by his concern for her, wishing that she could thank him for it, wishing that she could tell him of her hesitations where the dramatic descent of the Holy Spirit was concerned. Above all, she wished that she could restore the glow of health to his face. She felt a tremor pass through his arm.

127

"Just stay real close to me when we're at church," said Isabelle in the rasping whisper of the deaf. As Ainsley was about to open the car door, she caught sight of something that caused her suddenly to sag, letting the umbrella dip to one side. Hardly conscious of the rain that was now wetting her shoulder, she stared up the street, her mouth working as though she were about to cry.

"What's the matter?" said Ainsley Black. "Has something upset you?"

She did not answer but continued to stare at the white car parked a hundred feet away. "Is it something about that car? Get in my car, Miss Isabelle. You're gettin' wet." She obeyed him, and when she was settled in her seat and the umbrella furled and put in back, she heard him say, "Is it somethin' about that big white car that's got you worried? I saw it go past just as I was drivin' up. Couple of blacks in it. Is that what's worryin' you?"

It was easier to pretend not to hear. "What a downpour," she said. "I wonder if it will keep many people from comin'. It's goin' to be a real damp congregation, I'm afraid." She turned her face from him, blinking tears of disappointment—and fear. So they had come anyway, despite the telephone call Claiborne had made. She had caught only part of the conversation: a loud, angry "No, I said no, goddamn it!"—and had leapt to the conclusion that he was ordering them not to come.

"It'll take more than rain to keep people away from Brother Thurlow," he said, and Isabelle was glad that he had apparently decided not to press her about the white car.

The regular pastor of the church was just finishing a speech of welcome when Isabelle and Ainsley Black came in, breathless, and were conducted to a pew with two empty seats on the center aisle. The three young men in red, white, and blue outfits—the Godspeeders—and two guest preachers sat on chairs on the raised platform, facing the congregation. Behind them was banked a funereal profusion of flowers: red roses, blue and lavender hydrangeas, white and orange lilies. Perhaps ten feet further to the rear of the platform, Reverend Archie B. Thurlow sat by himself in deep meditation or prayer, his hand across his face. The organ began to play softly as Isabelle and Ainsley Black took their seats. Like Brother Thurlow, Ainsley Black immediately lowered his head and covered his face, but Isabelle could tell that he was watching her through his spread fingers. As she glanced around the brightly lit church, so glaring, so different from the restful brown and violet gloom of her own, she saw that a number of people in the congregation had recognized her and were nodding and smiling in her direction; among them was Mr. Porter, the pharmacist, who was sitting with his family in the pew across the aisle. She felt ready to sink into the floor from shyness.

The service continued for nearly an hour without the participation of Brother Thurlow. There were three hymns, led by the God-speeders, a special collection, prayers, and addresses by each of the three preachers at the front of the platform. For some reason the Baptist acoustics were better than the Presbyterian, and Isabelle caught much of what the preachers said as they spoke of what a memorable two weeks it had been, of how inspired and comforted they had all been by the words of Brother Thurlow and his fellow evangelists, of what a rich harvest of souls had already been gathered unto the Lord. They wished him success on the new mission which he would begin next Sunday, over in Fayetteville, North Ca'lina. Through it all Brother Thurlow sat with his face covered, removing his hand only when he rose to join in the singing with a rich baritone that sounded throughout the church. And through it all Isabelle struggled to raise her thoughts from the despair in which they had been sunk by the sight of the white car. Claiborne had seemed almost cheerful since last Thursday, as if secretly looking forward to the preacher's presence at Sunday dinner. But now . . .

When at last Reverend Thurlow came forward to the lectern, his face was set, stony, his eyes nearly closed behind his glasses, his body both bent and squatly powerful in a light blue suit that seemed too small for him. He was unrecognizable as the man whose photograph Isabelle had seen in nearly every shop on Main Street. After a prolonged silence, during which something like a collective sighing rose from the congregation, the evangelist's dejected head jerked suddenly upward and his eyes flashed. "I stand before you a humble and repentant sinner," he began in a low, tremulous, nearly sobbing voice, "and I'm goin' to confess publicly to you good people in Alhambra what I've never confessed before except in my anguished prayers to God Almighty. It's your response—the most wonderful I've ever received from any congregation in all my journeyin' for the Lord—that gives me courage to speak what is truly the unspeakable." Resting both hands on the lectern and again closing his eyes, Brother Thurlow sustained a silence that lasted a full three minutes, a silence during which the whole congregation seemed to hold its breath, afraid to sigh, much less to rustle or cough. Isabelle found the pause unendurable and longed for the first word that would blow through the darkening and ominous stillness like the first gust of wind in a summer storm. Without taking her eyes from the preacher, she could feel Ainsley Black's tension at her side.

The words came in what was nearly a scream, so painful to her ears that Isabelle jumped. "I stand before you a drunkard and an adulterer! I stand before you as the destroyer of the happiness and hopes of those who were closer and dearer to me than life itself!"

For the next half hour Brother Thurlow told how the demon of alcohol had first got a grip on him when he was barely twenty, stationed with the navy at Pensacola, already married to a lovely woman who had been his high-school sweetheart back in Shelbyville, Tennessee, and a fine Christian woman; together they had brought forth a wonderful little boy, the very apple of their eyes. As he went on, his voice sank almost to inaudibility and sometimes broke with a yelping sob. He told how, after two years of heavy drinking, he had lost his job with the telephone company in Memphis and how, on the night after he was fired, he had ripped his wife's brand-new dress from top to bottom and struck her across the face in the presence of his terrified little son. Again he paused and covered his face with both hands; then he flung his arms wide, revealed his tear-glistening cheeks, took off his glasses and wiped them, and abruptly bellowed: "Who but the Lord God Almighty Himself could forgive such a miserable, low-down, mean-spirited, drunken wretch? And God *has* forgiven me! In his infinite mercy He *has* forgiven me! And that, my friends, is the message of hope that I, a miserable sinner, bring to you this mornin'!" The voice fell, the account went on—now low-keyed, factual, harrowing. Drunken sprees, fights, encounters with loose women, a car crash, child abuse, divorce, desperation, a suicide attempt—these were related in a deadened voice, a voice drained and exhausted, a voice that could not conceivably have bellowed out as it had just before.

Isabelle listened with mounting distaste, hearing every word, awaiting and dreading the climax that might come at any moment and obliterate all the smaller climaxes along the way. *He's common as dirt*—so Isabelle told herself—*a common, vulgar man, playing on people's emotions like that.* . . . She glanced sideways at her companion. His eyes were closed and his chin rested on the knot of his brown-and-red tie. *He* doesn't think Reverend Thurlow is common, she thought, instantly repudiating her own snobbish response; he believes . . . Suddenly she was tempted to abandon Ainsley, to hurry out of the church rather than submit to the offensive trumpet blast proclaiming redemption and salvation which was bound to come, which was coming now. . . .

"The Lord in His mercy did not let me succeed in killin' myself. He stayed my hand. But believe me, friends, I was already dead. I had been dead a long time. I stunk worse than Lazarus in his tomb. I was dead . . . and . . . I . . . *stunk!*"

Closing her eyes, Isabelle braced herself for the onslaught of regeneration. But she had underestimated Brother Thurlow. As the organ began to sound the strains of Chopin's Funeral March, she opened her eyes to see the preacher leave the lectern and return to his chair behind the flowers, where he sat with his head buried in both hands, with strands of his oily-looking hair now falling across his fingers. Thus he sat while the organ played the entire Funeral March. Then Isabelle could hear nothing, though she could tell from the way the congregation was sitting that they were listening to sounds of some sort. At last, as if from a great distance, the strains of "Rock of Ages" reached her. The three Godspeeders stood up and began to croon the hymn. As the sound of their voices and of the organ began to swell, the entire congregation seemed to yearn toward the devastated figure on the platform, seemed to be waiting for the slightest movement—of shoulders, of fingers, of a strand of hair—that would signal the revival of life. *What a carnival, what a cheap showman* . . . But Isabelle could not push down the emotion now swelling inside her as the music swelled, a feeling that was like suffocation, not blissful at all. She reached for Ainsley's wrist. At the touch, he turned toward her, and she realized, with something like terror, that he was weeping. Then a wavelike movement through the congregation made her face the platform again, and Isabelle saw the preacher arise from his chair and advance toward the lectern with a quick, jogging step—like an athlete, she thought.

"Behold!" he shouted, his head flung back, his chest expanded, his hands on his waist, "I that was dead am now living!"

Isabelle felt a violent tremor run through Ainsley's wrist, on which her fingers were still resting.

After ten minutes of fist-pounding, rhapsodic thanksgiving to the Lord for the miracle of his salvation, Brother Thurlow again retreated to his chair, mopping his forehead, spent. He rested barely a minute, his chest rising and falling, before advancing to the lectern again like a boxer at the sound of the bell. Suddenly humble and gentle, he began his invocation to members of the congregation to declare themselves for Jesus, to come forward and drink deeply of the well of eternal life. The organ played softly while he spoke—"Rock of Ages" again. There was a shuffling of feet, and from the rear of the church came two solemn-faced, blushing boys of about fifteen, dressed in suits and ties. They were followed up the aisle by an extremely tall and thin young woman of about thirty, who wore white gloves and a hat. As each arrived at the platform, Brother Thurlow, now beaming, shook hands in silence, gave each a fraternal hug, and motioned to them to stand in a row just behind him and just in front of the spectacular bank of flowers. "Rock of Ages" droned on, now background music for the reborn, who still came forward, a mixed lot, one of them crying into a handkerchief.

Ainsley Black jumped to his feet. When, after a few seconds, Isabelle realized with amazement that he was stepping into the aisle, that he was going to go forward, she impulsively reached out and caught the hem of his jacket. At the unexpected tug he glanced back, his face streaked with tears, and Isabelle, mortified by what she had just done, let go. For a moment he stood indecisively, one hand resting on the polished knob of the pew; then he sat down abruptly, as if collapsing, and covered his face. Isabelle now saw, to her great alarm, that he was shaking violently, like a man seized with a malarial chill, and that fresh tears were seeping between his spread fingers.

"Are you all right?" she asked, knowing that her voice was too loud. Timidly she touched his shoulder. He did not seem to notice the touch but continued to shudder, hunched over now, his elbows on his thighs. As she looked to the front of the church, wondering what was happening to Ainsley, wondering, in a panic of shyness, whether she should turn to the people on her right for help, she saw that Reverend Thurlow was still standing at the front of the platform, his arms spread wide, a human cross. Above the drone of the organ she caught the singsong of the preacher's voice, and though she could no longer make out his words, she knew that he was calling for more and still more to come forward for Jesus. All at once the congregation around her was rising, for a final hymn or benediction, and only she and Ainsley Black were left sitting. As though trying to comfort a person weeping in bereavement, Isabelle began to pat Ainsley gently on the shoulder and back. Whole minutes passed, and Isabelle continued the rhythmical patting, hardly conscious of what was happening around her. The awful shuddering was, thank God, beginning to subside.

People were now moving down the aisle, leaving the church. Someone stopped at the entrance of the pew. Looking up, Isabelle saw a short, bald man nodding and smiling at them, his eyes twinkling above half-moon glasses. It was Mr. Porter, dressed for Sunday in a powder-blue suit and a yellow bowtie. "The spirit is workin' mightily within him," he said loudly. "It's a gift and an inspiration. Miss Isabelle, I cain't tell you how proud and pleased we all are to have you with us on this inspirin' occasion." The little man's freckled scalp wrinkled and then became smooth, as if a breeze had passed across it.

"Thank you," Isabelle managed to say, paralyzed by his reaction. Mr. Porter gave another approving nod and moved on down the aisle to join his wife. The spirit moving mightily within him! She stared open-mouthed at Ainsley Black. So that's what it was—the working of the Holy Spirit! Mr. Porter had not been in the least alarmed. None of the congregation had come forward to offer help. Only she, it seemed, had been unable to recognize what was taking place, unable to imagine that preachers, too, could "get" religion. Now filled by an awe so intense that it approached holy dread, she removed her hand from Ainsley Black's shoulder and drew back, as if even to touch him in such a state would be sacrilegious.

In a short while he roused himself, letting his own hands drop into his lap. Puffy-eyed, his cheeks still glistening, his face was paler than ever, the bled-white face of a man who has been seriously ill. After looking dumbly at Isabelle for a moment, he turned his gaze to the front of the church, where Brother Thurlow and two of his assistants were moving briskly among the newly assembled flock, separating them into groupings of five or six. Only a few stragglers remained elsewhere in the church. Then, as if rousing himself with a shake, he looked again at Isabelle and mumbled something that she failed to catch.

"What, what?" she whispered urgently.

"We'd better go. I'm—well, I've been through a—through something extraordinary. I don't exactly know what came over me."

"I understand," she hurriedly assured him. "You mustn't feel embarrassed. It was a—it was an *inspiration*."

At the door of the church they were confronted by a curtain of rain. Sheltering beneath Isabelle's umbrella, they made their way over puddles in the sidewalk to Ainsley's car, one of the few left on the street. He seemed preoccupied as he drove, and she respected his silence. Once, as they stopped for a red light, he shook his head several times, a stunned look on his face, but said nothing.

They were nearly home before Isabelle remembered, with an audible groan, the white car and what it portended. As they pulled up in front of the house, she leaned forward to peer through the down-pour, though she did not really expect to see the car still there. Her brother opened the front door while they were hurrying toward it under the umbrella. To Isabelle's amazement—and unspeakable re-lief—he was not only smiling in his crooked, grimacing way, but holding out his hand to Ainsley Black.

"Come in, come in," he said. "Looks to me like your revivalist friend has called down Noah's flood upon our sinful town." Then, speaking loudly and directly to Isabelle, he said, "A visitor came while you were at church, but I sent her away, bag and baggage. Told her I had to get ready to entertain a preacher for Sunday dinner."

PART 3

Chapter Twenty

I that was dead am now living! As if a trumpet had sounded these words next to his ear, Hux was deafened to everything else. And nearly made dumb as well, for he could not trust himself to speak more than a few monosyllables in response to whatever was said to him, for fear of collapsing into convulsive tears. What indeed had come over him? The last hour of the service now seemed to him like some great roiling storm during which he had again and again been transfixed by lightning. Brother Thurlow mounted the storm, his voice thundering, his arms spread eaglelike, his dark eyes blazing. Plucked out of himself, Hux had been swept upward to dizzying heights, poised, in ecstasy and terror, over abysmal depths, and then let down, weak as a child, prone to tears, into a low-ceilinged house—a very ordinary house—crowded with oversized furniture where a fuss was being made over him by two elderly people! Claiborne Herne had poured him a stiff drink of whiskey, which he had accepted but

135

hardly tasted. "I'm assumin' you're still a drinkin' Baptist, Brother Black, " Dr. Herne had said, grinning cadaverously, "or have you taken the temperance pledge as a result of this mornin's service?" To which Hux, recalling the hangover with which he had awakened—was it only this morning?—had responded with a distant smile. Meanwhile, Miss Isabelle was scurrying back and forth between the living room, dining room, and kitchen, setting out food, apologizing repeatedly to Hux for the fact that they were going to have a cold meal since she had not known how long the service might last and had been afraid, in these servantless days, to prepare a real Sunday dinner. At one point she shyly asked if she might call him Ainsley and had beamed like a delighted child when he muttered, "Please do."

Fortunately, not much more was required of him. When they were seated at the table, Miss Isabelle indicated that Hux was to ask the blessing. He did so, recalling one from his childhood, but when he reached the concluding words, "For Christ's sake, amen," he felt a thrilling shudder pass through him, and he sat down abruptly, pretending to cough into his napkin until he had his tears under control. Thereafter, Claiborne Herne dominated the table. As soon as Isabelle had sat down after holding, servantlike, the platter of country ham and cold roast chicken for each of the two men, her brother said, "Well, Isabelle, did you get religion at the revival? Were you filled with the Holy Ghost?"

"It's nothing to joke about, Brother," she replied, blushing and glancing quickly toward their guest. "It was a real impressive service. There were lots of fine people there—mighty fine people. It was not at all like the kind of revival meetin' you're thinkin' about."

"You still haven't answered my question. Were you saved? Were you reborn?"

"Hush, Brother! I can't bear it when you joke about sacred things, things good people take seriously. It's such bad taste."

Claiborne Herne pulled back as if he had been unexpectedly nipped by a white rabbit. "I beg your pardon, big sister," he said. "And yours too, Reverend Agent of the FBI."

"Brother!"

"Our guest knows I'm only teasin', don't you, Brother Black?"

Though he had hardly heard what was being said, Hux knew that a nod was expected. He wondered how he could escape, how soon he could leave without being rude. He needed desperately to be alone with what had happened to him, to try to make sense of it, to come to terms with it. . . .

"Fact of the matter is," continued Dr. Herne, "I'd be mighty sorry if you took what I said in the wrong spirit. I must tell you, Brother Black, it's a great pleasure to have a young face at our dinner table again. It's been a long time. But things were different once, weren't they, Isabelle? Time was when this house was filled with young faces." Suddenly the doctor's own face was masked with pain. "No," he groaned, "no, it was not *this* house. The other house. Our old house. It all seems a hundred years ago." Then, brightening, he said, "Did you know, Reverend Black, that I organized and kept goin' for nearly fifteen years a club for the best bunch of youngsters this town or this county—or, for that matter, this *state*—has seen since the Civil War? Did you know that?" he demanded.

With a huge effort Hux emerged from the swirl of his sensations. "No, sir, I didn't know that. Tell me about your young people's club."

"The best goddamn bunch of youngsters— Reverend, you must forgive an old man's profanity . . . and his boastin'."

"You're only sixty-five, Brother," said Miss Isabelle. "I don't call that very old."

"It's very old, older than the hills. But until I was fifty I had the body and energy of a twenty-year-old. Didn't I, Isabelle? I exercised right along with the boys, coached them, and did everything they did. My stomach was hard and flat as a board. You wouldn't believe it, would you?"

"I believe it," said Hux, who had been trying to recall his secret agenda, to fit together its scattered pieces. Every aspect of it now seemed unreal in view of what had happened. *I've got to pay attention,* he told himself, like someone threatened with overwhelming sleepiness during a crucial briefing.

"I had a kind of gymnasium built in the basement of our old house. Lockers, a couple of showers. It had punching bags, parallel bars—all sorts of equipment. We worked out every afternoon, especially durin' the bad weather after the football season."

"So it was mainly an athletic club?" asked Hux, fetching the words from a far-off place in his mind.

"No, sir-ree!" The doctor seemed furious at this belittlement. "The Tallahatchie Fellowship was *every* kind of a club. Social, athletic, service. Mostly service. I reckon you could say it had a religious side too, bein' based on the idealism of youth. . . . But we had fun too, plenty of fun—you can bet your bottom dollar on that."

"Oh my, yes," said Miss Isabelle, who had been leaning across the table to catch every word. "Such an uproar from the basement some-

137

times. It's a good thing I was already a little hard of hearing, or I would have been driven from the house!"

"No girls allowed," said the doctor. "Lots of roughhouse, specially when we were initiatin' new members. Good clean fun. Boxin' matches, wrestlin', all kinds of contests. Singin', too. Lots of singin'." He shook his head slowly, nostalgically. "And then there were the weekend trips to our old camp on the Tallahatchie . . . huntin' . . . fishin'. All of that."

"You make it sound like a wonderful experience," said Hux.

"It was, sir. It was."

Dinner was over. It had ended with a mixture of sugared orange segments and shredded coconut served from a cut-glass bowl—a dessert called "ambrosia" which Hux had not had since his childhood. The combination of a hangover from the president's party last night and the tumultuous event at church had totally destroyed his appetite, forcing him to swallow unwanted food to placate Miss Isabelle, who kept heaping his plate.

Half an hour later Hux was able to leave, despite pleas from Miss Isabelle that he stay for the afternoon, for supper, for the evening. . . . In order to break away, he invented a scheduled conference with Brother Thurlow, who was leaving shortly for North Carolina.

"And will you be leavin' too?" Miss Isabelle looked stricken.

"Not yet, ma'am, not for a while." But Hux spoke with no assurance. His own future had come unmoored, was drifting. . . .

When he shook hands with Dr. Herne in the front hall, the older man stared at him with a bewildered expression. "You know, Brother Black," he said while still holding Hux's hand in an almost painful grip, "you bear an uncanny resemblance to someone I once knew very well. His name was Fred Wilkie and he had the same kind of dirty-blond hair and the same kind of expression in his eyes—almost exactly the same. Nice-lookin' boy. Clean-cut. Last time I saw him, he'd begun to put on some weight too, which makes the resemblance all the stronger."

"Who was Fred Wilkie?"

"One of the boys in the Fellowship. He'd be about your age now. Son of Curran Wilkie, who owns the hardware store on East Main Street. Respectable people. Last I heard, Fred's practicin' architecture in Nashville. Married, several children. Doin' real well, I heard. I like to think I had some influence on his life." The doctor released Hux's hand.

"I'm sure you did."

"Are you? Don't be too certain." Suddenly the doctor's look was sly, full of malice. "I'm sure you've been well trained to say exactly the right thing. All of you are. Am I right?" he demanded, speaking in a kind of snarl from the corner of his mouth.

Taken aback, too full of his own turmoil to deal with this abrupt shift, Hux could only nod several times and murmur that he really had to go. Dr. Herne picked up his nearly empty whiskey glass and strode into the living room without another word.

Holding the black tent of her umbrella over them both, Miss Isabelle accompanied Hux to his car. "I'm afraid havin' dinner with us must have been sort of a strain—sort of, well, kind of an anticlimax after what you experienced this mornin'."

Curtained off though he was, Hux was touched by her concern. "No, not at all," he said emphatically. "I appreciate your kindness, and . . . and I enjoyed listenin' to your brother."

"He *likes* you. No matter how badly he behaves, that's one thing I'm sure of. I can tell. Oh, Reverend Black—Ainsley—how he needs some of that faith you have in such abundance! Just a little—just a little bit—would make all the difference. I have a feelin' he might listen to you, that he might come to trust you. There's a chance, I think. Oh, please come again soon. Help my brother, help him find his way back to God."

"I'll—I'll do what I can," said Hux in a voice that he could hardly control. "We all need help, all of us. Pray for me too." In another moment he would start crying! What was happening to him? Quickly he leaned forward to kiss Miss Isabelle on the cheek, to pat her on the shoulder; then he ducked into the car. Lowering the window, he thanked her again for dinner and said, "I'll call. I'll call real soon."

"Oh, please. Real soon! Goodbye, dear Ainsley."

For the next hour or so, Hux drove aimlessly around Alhambra in the rain—up one street, then along a connecting street, then down the next. The windshield wipers clicked and squeaked. Driving slowly, he registered little outside except the fringes of green trees behind the veil of rain and an occasional car or traffic light. At last he parked on an unknown street and sat quietly in the car, breathing the wet air, unable to see through the windshield and windows fogged by his breath. But though he kept trying to focus his thoughts upon what had happened, Hux was unable to imagine the church without a suffocating constriction of his chest. Each approach produced terror, a warning of total disintegration, yet with it a temptation to let go, to surrender blissfully to whatever threatened to overwhelm him. The face of Brother Thurlow appeared, came close, and receded, causing a fit of trembling that was almost a convulsion. It appeared again—scowling, ecstatic, agonized—and Hux wanted to flee, to run away as fast and as far as he could.

He turned on the ignition but did not put the car into gear. After wiping the mist from the windows he looked out. Where was he? He had wandered into a section of Alhambra that he had never seen before—a black neighborhood where children were playing, swinging on suspended automobile tires, jumping over puddles on the side of the road. When had the rain stopped? Had it stopped before he left the Hernes? No, it had been raining then; he could summon the sound of the windshield wipers as he drove about town. Taking in the neat bungalows, the blue and pink hydrangeas flanking the steps of porches, the white church, the grocery store, he realized that he was in no shanty town, no rural slum. Well-dressed Negroes, some of them still in churchgoing clothes, were sitting on porch steps, while others stood in a little group at the intersection. He heard greetings, a burst of high laughter. Down the street a man with a bushy afro got out of a large white car and walked toward the rear of a brick building.

Hux slipped his gear lever into drive and proceeded slowly down the street. As he passed in front of the brick building, which was obviously commercial, he saw a neatly lettered sign over the door:

MADDOX C. PERRY, INC.

FUNERAL DIRECTOR

Then he saw the man with the afro—a slender man, light-skinned, with powerful shoulders—standing with his arms and legs stretched out like an acrobat's while he held by one hand the railing of the outside stairs leading to the second story; he was gazing directly toward Hux with a look of blazing intensity. But Hux was so caught up in the whirling of his own thoughts that he did not at first make a connection between what he had just seen and the white car that had passed him that morning at the Hernes'. The man, he now realized, was the same as the driver of that car—so exaggerated a hairstyle could not be mistaken. The image of Miss Isabelle's face—mouth open, eyes bulging with fright or some other version of dismay— now came to him, and he wondered what threat she had perceived in the car and its two occupants, one of them a woman Hux had barely glimpsed. Had there been burglaries in the area? Some other kind of unpleasantness? But Hux had been too preoccupied with his own shattered state to give the matter much attention. As he drove on, both the black man and Miss Isabelle became part of the jumble of images that had usurped his consciousness, making it impossible for his thoughts to cohere. At the intersection with Main Street he turned north.

Hux had awakened that morning with one of the worst hangovers he had ever known. He was also aware that he had behaved badly at the president's party at the country club, but he could remember little beyond a loud argument with some woman over Nixon. Brother Thurlow was a supporter of Nixon's. . . . For a few moments Hux tried to persuade himself that his hangover, with its attendant guilt, had, in some peculiar way, made him vulnerable to the preacher's exhortation and all that followed. Then the notion struck him as absurd, and he began to tremble again. Could it be that the role of Ainsley Black was too dangerous, too unsettling, for him to pursue in his presently weakened condition—that it was this play-acting, and not the hangover, that had laid him open to Brother Thurlow's onslaught? Meanwhile, he had passed the turn-off to Oxford without taking it and was now driving north, at an unsafe speed on a partially flooded highway, toward Memphis. Hunched low over the wheel, Hux found that the need to pay attention to the road at such a speed distracted his thoughts from all that he was leaving behind. Brother Thurlow could not possibly keep up with him—or find him in Memphis.

Chapter Twenty-one

The establishment was called the Tropical Lagoon. There, in a small room illuminated by a phosphorescently green light, Hux lay naked, face down on a broad pad covered by a sheet patterned in gaudy tropical blossoms of orange, scarlet, and pink. He had had a fair amount to drink, both before and after dinner at an expensive steakhouse that featured a panoramic view of the city and the river; but he was not drunk. Kneeling to one side of him was a girl who wore a skimpy beaded apron tied round her loins and a pink-beaded fringe over her breasts, which hung like mangoes as she leaned over him. An artificial pink camellia was fixed in her hair, which was thick and black (with green highlights) and flowed in Gauguinesque coils down her back. Her skin, like Hux's, was pale, with a greenish cast beneath the light.

"Feelin' more relaxed?" Her voice was deep-country, easygoing, and friendly. Her fingers performed a butterfly dance over the small of Hux's back and buttocks. If she did not display a palpable heart of gold, neither did she show any of the anger or self-disgust that disfigured (in Hux's assumption) the psyche of whores.

He responded with a grunt that could have been a sign of either assent or noncommitment.

Choosing the optimistic alternative, the girl drawled out an encouraging "Guh-ud!" and told him to turn over; then she reached toward a glass shelf supporting an array of ointments, creams, powders, and lotions and from it selected a slender bottle.

Lying now on his back, Hux opened his eyes and observed for the first time that the ceiling as well as the walls of the cubicle was mirrored. Such a multiplication of himself and the girl was doubtless intended to have an erotic impact, one that he could easily imagine but could not feel. For him the mirrored images merely added to the dreamy dazzle that afflicted him even when he closed his eyes—as he promptly did again. He felt a pleasant sprinkling down the length of his torso. The cubicle was now beginning to smell like the perfume counter at Bloomingdale's or perhaps Woolworth's. Beginning with his cheeks and then moving to his shoulders and chest, the delicate, slippery fingers glided over his body, avoiding only the crotch, which apparently was not to be touched unless the further fee was agreed upon. As the fingers tickled the tops of his thighs and then gently pressed the pelvic bone, he felt a slight stirring that might have been encouraged; but as the fingers glided on, the spark went out. Earlier, when he had entered the cubicle with a full erection, the girl, whose name was Arlette, had raised her brows and smacked her lips in a professional way but had then immediately proceeded to explain, also professionally, that the basic fee (twenty dollars) included only massage, use of the whirlpool bath and sauna, and free drinks in the Coconut Lounge; anything else involved tipping according to a precisely fixed scale: fifteen dollars for what she delicately referred to as "intimate massage," twenty for "frenching," and thirty for what she referred to as "goin' the whole hog." His potency and confidence suddenly deflated, Hux had replied that he wasn't sure he really wanted anything beside the basic, which seemed steep enough, and that he'd have to wait and see. This led to the massage.

"You decided yet?" asked Arlette after another five minutes. There was little hope in her voice.

"Not yet."

"Well, Stu, maybe you better try the whirlpool bath and then come on back. The whirlpool's real relaxin'." Stu was the name he had given on request to the fat man who sat at the entrance to the Tropical Lagoon.

"All right, I'll give it a whirl."

Hux sat up, smiling. But he was distressed by the image that confronted him on the mirrored wall. He must have gained at least five pounds since coming South. While not actually bulging, his stomach looked as thick as his chest. Had his eyes really sunk so deeply into their discolored frames—or was this another trick of the greenish light?

"Just give me a call when you think you're ready," said Arlette, now free to enjoy a drink, a smoke, and a chat in the Coconut Lounge. "Just relax real good in that ol' whirlpool, you hear?"

Picking up his wallet and watch, which were encased in a clear plastic bag, Hux knotted a towel around his middle (again becoming aware of the spread) and made his way down a short jungle path to a clearing in the rain forest, where, overhung with plastic palm trees, bits of netting, stuffed red and blue macaws, and great, floppy blossoms, he found a round pool surging with milky-blue water. He lowered himself into the luminous maelstrom and sat on a projecting shelf; the warm water, as unreal-seeming as a wizard's bubbling potion, reached the middle of his chest. With a long sigh Hux surrendered to the gently buffeting currents and closed his eyes. Again he experienced a dreamlike shimmering of lights, now soft, now flaring in the colors of the spectrum behind his lids. He tried to concentrate on Arlette with the mango breasts, but her image was fragmented, as if by broken mirrors, and swept into the general dazzle. Though he had been disappointed by his rapid detumescence, Hux felt no humiliation. The day's turbulence had left him too numbed for that. Besides, this was a strictly commercial situation, very different from those occasions when he had lured girls back to his apartment from the singles bars on First Avenue. At least there had been that initial flaring. Was it worth an extra twenty bucks to have Arlette attempt to blow it into a steady flame?

A voice said, "Howdy!" and Hux opened his eyes to see a tall and gangling man lower himself into the other side of the pool.

"Hello."

"Boy, oh boy, this is real nice." He had white hair and a beaked, reddish face, and knobby white shoulders: a tough old rooster pushing seventy. "Are you at the beginnin' or the middle or the end of your session?"

"I guess you could say the middle. Intermission."

The man chuckled. "I ain't even started. All the rooms are occupied at the moment, and my little gal suggested I wait in here until one opens up." He leaned his head back against the rim of the pool, exposing an adam's apple like a baby's fist. "Boy, oh boy, this is the life. Don't git up to Memphis much, so I reckoned I'd give myself a real treat. Nothin' like this back home in Shelbyville. The new permissiveness ain't reached that far yet, but I reckon it will pretty soon. These places just been openin' up in Memphis the last year or so. Drivin' the old-fashioned whorehouses out of business."

"Did you say you're from Shelbyville?" Hux's temples began to throb; the dazzle grew.

"Yep. Lived there all my life."

The impulse was irresistible. "Did you ever know a man named Archie Thurlow from Shelbyville?" Immediately Hux felt a wave of heat flash across his face and chest.

Old Rooster frowned. "You mean the preacher?"

Hux nodded. The coincidence was terrifying; Brother Thurlow had followed him into the Tropical Lagoon, had tracked him down. . . .

"I reckon everybody in Shelbyville knows Archie B. Or heard of him at least. He ain't been back in town for at least ten year, not since before he reformed. But nowadays I hear folks that heard him say Archie B. could win any preachin' contest in the worl' hands-down. Better'n Billy Graham, they say. Myself, I don't much go in for that revival stuff. This here's more my ticket." And Old Rooster leaned back with a lewd grin and let his pink toes rise to the surface of the whirlpool. "How come you innerested in Archie B.? You heard him preach?"

"Yes. This morning."

"I like that. Revival meetin' in the morning, fancy whorehouse in the evenin'. Is he good as people say?"

"Yes. If you go in for that kind of stuff." Hux defied Brother Thurlow to do his worst.

Old Rooster nodded. "Everybody says the same thing. But I'll tell you this, young fella. Famous preacher or not, Archie B. is still ashamed to show his face back in Shelbyville after the way he treated that sweet little gal he married." Then, as if the topic of Archie B. had been exhausted, he swung the conversation back to the Tropical Lagoon. What, he wanted to know, was this business about extra charges? He had thought you paid one fee and that was it. Everything included.

Hux set him straight, harshly, without using Arlette's euphemisms.

Old Rooster turned purple. "You mean to sit there and tell me it's fifteen extra bucks for her just to—to—" His small-town modesty wouldn't let him repeat Hux's words. "Holy Jeez, this place is a goddamn clip joint! Fifteen extra bucks just to— And thirty extra for a plain ol' whorehouse fuck. They must be out of their minds. Good God Almighty!"

Just then a tall blonde, also wearing pink fringes, appeared at the edge of the pool and said, "Don, our room is ready. Come on, honey."

Old Rooster emerged scowling from the churning white waters and grabbed a towel to cover his genitals as if the girl were casting a dangerously avaricious eye upon them. "Now look here," he said as she led him away. "Coupla things we got to git straight right off the bat. . . ."

Hux allowed himself another five minutes in the whirlpool. Less than fifteen minutes remained of the hour reserved for his session. But since the intrusion, so to speak, of Brother Thurlow into the Tropical Lagoon, he had felt once again the need to run. Sex was now out of the question. When he returned with Arlette to the mirrored cubicle of love, he told her that he wasn't in the mood for any of the extras, that he would settle for a five-minute backrub with some of that sweet-smelling lotion.

"That's all right, Stu," she said in her friendly way. "Next time you

145

come, I'll bet you'll be strainin' like a bulldog on a leash that's just seen a pussy cat. I'll bet you'll want to go the whole hog and then some. Just remember to ask for me, Arlette. I'll be ready and waitin'."

She applied herself to the backrub. After two minutes Hux lifted his face from the blossomed pad and said, "What part of the state do you come from, Arlette?" He fully expected her to answer "Shelbyville."

But she said, "Little bitty place called Lizella. You never heard of it. About fifty mile south of Nashville."

"Anywhere near Shelbyville?"

"Not far. 'Bout twenty mile, I reckon."

"Ever hear of a preacher named Archie B. Thurlow?"

She looked down at him with a suddenly suspicious narrowing of her eyes—as if he might begin to admonish her in the name of religion. "Naw, cain't say I ever heard the name. But I left home an' come to Memphis when I was thirteen. How come you askin' me 'bout a preacher?"

"No real reason except he comes from the same part of the state."

The remainder of the backrub passed in cool silence. When it was over, Hux thanked Arlette, gave her a big tip, promised to return with plenty of money the next time he was feeling real horny, and went to the dressing room, where there were lockers, showers, and a sauna. Two clients—one undressing, the other dressing—were joking with the black attendant who opened lockers and handed out towels. The attendant grinned at Hux. "I hope you found everything entirely to your satisfaction," he said in a deep, melodious Jamaican voice.

"This place is a fuckin' rip-off," said the bald-headed client who was pulling on a pair of tan leisure slacks. "But sometimes it seems almost worth it. I reckon that's what you call the inflation mentality."

Hux could barely control an urge to ask all three men if they had ever heard of Archie B. Thurlow. While he was deciding whether to take a quick shower or leave immediately with all that sweet stuff still on his body, the girl assigned to the undressing client (now naked) walked in unabashed and announced that their room had just become available.

"Ready, willin', and able," said the client, an acne-scarred young man, in a nervously loud voice which he accompanied by a grab at his crotch.

"Shower first," said the brazen girl, who was eying both Hux and the bald client. "House rules."

"Hell, I'm clean as a whistle," said the young man in a still louder voice. "I took me a good long shower before I come over."

"You get in that shower, sir," said the black attendant. "House rules are house rules, and it is my obligation to see that they are observed without exception." Almost singing these words, he ended with a good-humored display of white teeth and gold fillings. He was obeyed.

Hux finished dressing and left. The street outside was empty. It was now past midnight, and he had a long drive ahead. He got into his car feeling that Brother Thurlow was still on his trail.

Heading southeast toward Oxford, Hux had to contend with a renewed onslaught of heavy rain, reinforced now by squalls and an almost incessant play of lightning. On the car's radio he heard that a tornado watch was in effect across southern and central Mississippi; presumably he was north of the tornado belt, though he could take no comfort from the menacing look of the weather now assaulting him. Driving very slowly, he had to struggle against sleepiness as well as the storm, an erotic sleepiness that crept over him whenever he let his thoughts drift back to Arlette. She leaned over him, smiling, her arms and thighs glistening, her breasts suspended in their fringe of pink beads. The erection that he had so quickly lost now returned, a slow-burning reminder of all that he had missed. Twice he sank into a dream from which he was jolted awake just as the car swerved onto the shoulder of the road, splashing water from puddles and deep ruts. Badly frightened by his second lapse, Hux turned onto a side road just north of Holly Springs and parked. There, as the sky flashed white and thunder boomed all around him and sudden gusts of wind shook the car, he dealt with his erection the fastest way he could and then napped for half an hour. He was awakened by a rattling of large hailstones against the roof and hood of the car. The fit of sleepiness had passed, and he was able to drive the rest of the way to Oxford sustained by an all-night radio program of country music from Memphis. It had been the strangest day of his life, but Hux was now too tired to recapitulate even a fraction of what had happened. He drove mindlessly, mouthing the words of the sad and monotonous songs that reached him through the crackling of storm-induced static.

Chapter Twenty-two

While he had grown intellectually soft in recent years, lazily consuming whatever caught his eye in the way of reading, Hux still conceived of himself as the same skeptical, questioning empiricist that he had been in graduate school; he would have described himself as a man who took ideas seriously enough to challenge their credentials. Though he had resisted the efforts of his wife and others to lure him into psychotherapy, he had, from his Chapel Hill days onward, read a fair amount of Freud, Reik, Reich, and Fromm and had absorbed even more psychoanalytic theory (both orthodox and revisionist) from the company he kept at Princeton. This absorption had resulted in a vocabulary and mental set that dealt in notions of ambivalence, repression, role playing, and projection and that had canceled, once and for all, the claims of God the Father, God the Son, and God the Holy Ghost—claims already weakened by a chance reading, during Hux's freshman year, of Bertrand Russell's atheistic essay, "A Free Man's Worship." Hux's psychological bias consorted comfortably with a moral stance (acquired unsystematically from the existentialists) that kept him on a constant lookout for small signs of bad faith or inauthenticity. He was consequently suspicious of all proclaimed motives, especially where politics, race, and class were concerned. This suspiciousness was something that he applied proudly to himself as well as to his friends and his enemies. Hence, given his views on civil rights, he had no choice but to go to Mississippi in 1964; to have failed to do so would have been the most flagrant display of bad faith.

A relaxation of the old intellectual rigor had indeed taken place in the years following the death of Clark (keeper of consciences) and the move from graduate school to the less demanding and more pragmatic atmosphere of the Foundation. But Hux was scarcely aware of the change, harboring only a guilty notion that he was not "keeping up" the way he should be. In any case, nothing had prepared him for the shattering impact of Brother Thurlow's performance, and he had no way of coming to terms with it. No matter how often he repeated to himself that he did not believe in a personal God or in the redemptive mission of Jesus Christ, he could not stop himself from trembling or weeping whenever he recalled the image of the preacher as he stood at the lectern, his head flung back, his hands on his waist, and once again heard the great shout: *Behold! I that was dead am now living.* Although he had blanked out most of what had preceded that moment, Hux knew that he had been in an odd, even weepy condition almost from the beginning of the sermon—if that was what it could be called. Several times he tried to account for this condition, but none of his tentative explanations—such as his hangover from the president's party or his play-acting as Ainsley Black— seemed sufficient. Hux was badly frightened, just as frightened as he had been by his vision of the dead Clark months before; and *that*, at least, could be explained rationally, psychologically....

At no point did Hux attempt to analyze his experience in any steady or systematic way. He was afraid to think about it for any length of time—as if he might recall too much and again be overwhelmed. Thoughts came to him in fragments, in phrases and mutterings. At odd times during the next few days he felt an impulse to pray to God. But for what? To be spared another onslaught from His preacher? What he most hoped was that gradually the whole experience would recede and lose its power to turn him into a quivering fool. Afraid that the role of Ainsley Black might indeed be dangerous, that it might soften him up for another invasion of the Spirit, Hux was reluctant to call Miss Isabelle even to thank her for Sunday's hospitality. This avoidance made him feel guilty of more than bad manners, for he had led her along, raised her hopes. Days passed before he could bring himself to call. Meanwhile he kept himself as busy as possible with the official agenda.

On Monday morning he slept right through the buzzing of his alarm clock only to be awakened, shortly after nine, by the telephone. It was Anne, but Hux was so groggy and dislocated from his wild, stormy drive, on top of everything else, that she had to identify herself several times.

"You sound awful," she said. "I tried to phone you last night, but I reckon you must have found still another party to misbehave at."

"In a manner of speaking."

She told him that she had had Sunday dinner with the Bensons, where she heard that both the Halseys and the president's wife were furious—"perfectly furious"—at Hux for his behavior over the weekend. Dean Halsey was even threatening to write to the director of the Morrow Foundation to complain. "You better do some fence mendin' and do it fast," she concluded.

"I'll do what I can." Even in his groggy state Hux was grateful for the ordinary, very human sound of Anne's voice and the ordinary human concerns, even worries, that it conveyed.

"You don't sound in shape to do anything but go back to bed. Seriously though, you'd better send a note of apology to Mrs. Drummond—and maybe drop by to see Carruthers Halsey."

"Have you any idea of what I did at the country club? I've drawn a total blank on that particular evening."

"Blackouts are supposed to be a sign of a real drinkin' problem—you better watch out. Anyway, apparently you insulted one of the Drummonds' house guests whose husband's a big Nixon supporter over in Meridian. Nobody's sure exactly what you said to her, but whatever it was, it drove her to the ladies' room in tears."

"Oh, Christ." Hux felt the stirring of a distant memory. "I think I offered to bet her that Nixon would attempt suicide before the end of the summer—and fail."

"I wish I had been there. But I don't move in presidential circles. Deans are as high as I can reach." Anne laughed. Then, after a sigh that hissed loudly over the telephone, she said, "But seriously, I don't want to see you get in hot water and undo everything you've been tryin' to build up."

"Don't worry." Hux was touched by her concern. "You mustn't forget that I've got a largish sum of money to dangle in front of them. That's always a sure cure for hurt feelings and the like. But I'll be a good boy and try to do a little patching-up later this morning." Now he was the one to sigh. "What a day. I've got four different meetings scheduled for this afternoon."

Before they hung up, Anne invited Hux to a late supper on Wednesday after he got back from Jackson, where he was to spend most of a long day conferring with the administrators of Tougaloo College and Jackson State University. Then Hux ate breakfast and went over to the university campus. There, in the office that had been assigned to him, he telephoned for an appointment with the dean and wrote a note of apology to Mrs. Drummond. When he went to see Dean Halsey, he took along a copy of the Morrow Foundation's annual report, which listed, in handsome figures, the sums granted to various educational projects during the preceding year. Though a bit cool at first, Carruthers Halsey was soon assuring Hux that he had secretly enjoyed the teasing of Professor Starkweather, who, said the dean, had about as much sense of humor as an undertaker greeting the bereaved at a funeral-parlor door; he ended by inviting Hux to lunch at the faculty club. The rest of the day was spent in follow-up meetings with the business manager, the head

150

librarian, the director of the computer-science program, and a representative of the State Board of Higher Education—a schedule that left Hux no time to think about Brother Thurlow. To avoid being alone with such thoughts that evening, he accepted the computer-science director's invitation to a pot-luck supper with his family.

Though Hux had no trouble falling asleep that night, his rest was troubled by luxuriantly detailed and often sinister dreams. In one of them he was back at the Tropical Lagoon, intensely excited, ready to go the whole hog with Arlette. But he couldn't find her; she was not in the assigned room. He wandered down leafy, vine-tangled corridors searching for her. Then he came upon the whirlpool bath, its waters glistening iridescently, and saw Arlette sitting in an unhappy posture at the edge, her legs dangling in the roiling blue water. When he tried to persuade her to come back to the room, she shook her head sadly and covered her face with her hands. Hux was then on the street outside. He saw with relief that he was fully dressed. A long line of men were waiting to get into the establishment, most of them looking sullen or angry. One of the men, his face concealed behind a newspaper, seemed familiar to Hux, who kept staring at him in the hope that he would drop the paper. Suddenly the man stepped out of the line and came toward Hux, his face still hidden. Running down the street, Hux began to scream—and screamed until he was fully awake, lying in a pool of sweat.

At breakfast on Tuesday Hux sat in a stupor, his thoughts still clogged by his dreams. When Jackie Sue, his waitress, brought him his scrambled eggs and a basket of hot biscuits, he blinked at her as if she were a hospital nurse who had shaken him from a drugged sleep. "You look like a man who misses his family real bad," she said with a sympathetic crinkling of her small pinched features. This morning she wore her kinky red hair pulled tight and tied with a big yellow bow that matched her uniform. "Am I right or am I right?"

"Right."

"I can always tell. You git both kinds in a place like this—there's the ones who jes' love the life of the road, got a girlfriend in every town from here to Dallas, and there's the ones eatin' their poor hearts out, almost sick in their beds from missin' their families back home. I spotted you from the very first day you was here as one of the home-lovin' kind. Right?"

"Right."

Jackie Sue filled Hux's cup, smiling and nodding all the while, and went away.

One of the home-lovin' kind. How much thought had he given his former family since coming South? Once—only once—he had thought of calling Louise, of talking with Tony. On his memo pad he wrote down a reminder to send Tony a postcard. Hux was reluctant to finish his breakfast and set out on today's drive to Mississippi Valley State in the oddly named town of Itta Bena; once on the highway, he would have nothing external to distract him—or protect him—from the image of Brother Thurlow. Hux mouthed one of his silent prayers. Then, sipping his coffee, he tried to recollect the significance Itta Bena had for him—something to do with Clark and a protest rally of the black student body. Itta Bena was indeed one of the stops on his pilgrimage route, but it annoyed him that he could not recall what had happened there. If perhaps he could set himself the mental exercise of reconstructing Clark's exact itinerary from the time he left Jackson, he—Hux—should be able to ward off a further onslaught from the evangelist—at least for the duration of the drive.

His thoughts drifted to Anne and the way she had stood by him at the Halseys', handing him his weapons so to speak. She had not laughed at his preoccupation with Clark; she had understood his rage at Franklin Mosby. . . . How long had it been since a woman had seemed a true and trusted ally to him, someone with whom he did not have to wage either sexual or domestic warfare? Louise had been such an ally in the early years of their marriage; there had been no one since. . . .

Brother Thurlow had thrown away *his* loving family too. What a link!

As he felt a shiver ripple across his skin, Hux summoned Anne's image and held it fast in a mental embrace until the shivering stopped. He longed to be with Anne again, to see her before tomorrow's dinner. Perhaps he could invite himself over for a drink tonight, after he got back from Itta Bena. . . . Hux's sexual confidence had been so badly damaged that he hardly dared even the fantasy of starting something with her, though he had a strong hunch that she would be receptive. He liked the way she moved, her legginess, the swirl of her skirt. . . . Could he tell her about Ainsley Black and Alhambra as well as Clark? How would she take all that? Or Brother Thurlow!

"No use in the worl' drinkin' cold caw-fee when there's plenty of the hot stuff waitin' right here," crooned Jackie Sue almost in Hux's ear. She was holding out the coffeepot, waving the spout in her eagerness to pour.

Hux jumped, rattling his cup against the saucer. "No, thanks, I'm late already," he said, standing up and nervously applying his napkin.

Hux did not get back from Itta Bena until nearly eleven that evening, much too late to invite himself to Anne's. The delay was caused by something unmentioned in the correspondence with Mississippi Valley State—an all-faculty barbecue, which was held in a picnic grove outside the town. Hux's hosts, all of them black, had insisted that he stay for it, and Hux quickly saw that their feelings would be hurt if he refused. He had a good time—ate great quantities of barbecued pig and chicken, drank lots of beer, and listened to some extraordinary singing as twilight settled, in dusty pink and gray, over the grove. His hosts hovered around him, a bit formal and awkward but full of good will, asked questions about New York, made sure that he had plenty to eat. No one that he asked seemed to have heard of Clark. No one wanted to talk about the events of '64. Hux left feeling more restored, more nearly sane, than he had for many days. And on the long drive back to Oxford he was able, for the most part, to keep Brother Thurlow at a greater distance than he had expected. But his effort to recover the connection between Clark and Itta Bena was a failure.

At the motel desk he was handed a letter—from Linda Helmholtz Johanssen. Taking it back to his room, Hux removed his tie and shoes and lay down on his bed, reluctant to tear open the envelope. With the experience of Brother Thurlow still dangerously alive, kept barely at bay with much mental effort, Hux felt too weak to fend off another major attack on his emotions from a different quarter. It was one thing to trace Clark's route, to visit the pilgrimage sites; but to endure, in his present state, a new flooding of grief was something else. He wished that he could postpone the reading of the letter until he had recovered further from the shock of last Sunday. But here the letter was. He had asked for it. He had no choice.

> 2015 Woodmere Avenue
> Columbus, Ohio
> Sunday, June 2, 1974
>
> Dear Larry,
>
> What a pleasant surprise to hear from you! It's nice to know that you've been thinking about me—and Clark too, of course. Life seems so full these days that I have very little time to brood over the past but it's always there, full of old friends and lots

of wonderful as well as sad experiences. I expect I'll have a very busy old age just catching up with all my memories.

Vance has been promoted from Assistant Principal to THE Principal of William McKinley High School and you can imagine what a responsibility that is in these times! Willie Mac, as the students call it, is still two-thirds White, but this whole area of Columbus is changing and Vance has to prepare for the fact that it will be at least half Black, maybe more, in the next four or five years. Of course vandalism is growing by leaps and bounds I'm sorry to say, and more and more students are complaining about having their money or watches taken away from them in the rest rooms and things like that, but Vance is doing a terrific job (I think!) and given good will on both sides things *will* work out in time despite all the jolts and setbacks you have to expect along the way (what a terrible sentence!). I do what I can to help—right now I'm chairperson of something called "Concerned Parents for Willie Mac" (CPFWM) which is trying to nip the sore spots of racial conflict in the bud before they get out of hand. I must say there are some *wonderful* responsible Black parents in CPFWM, also a few troublemakers but I guess you always have to expect that, don't you? Also working hard with the churches and the Rotary and Lions and other civic groups who are trying to slow down and maybe even reverse "White Flight" from this area of Columbus to the suburbs and fight "blockbusting." Last Sunday I was responsible for a fundraising supper for 150 people in the annex of the Woodmere Avenue Methodist Church. Then there's the board of the local YWCA and the League of Women Voters (I'm secretary) and *lots* more—you name it! I guess I'm basically the same old Linda you knew—the original Girl Who Couldn't Say No! But I really can't complain, I love it all—*honestly!*

The kids are fine. Susie is now thirteen, can you believe it!—and is beginning to take a lively interest in that mysterious subject known as BOYS. Cheryl is in kindergarten and little Vance is in an excellent nursery school run by our own church. I am enclosing a recent snap of Susie and one of the whole family. I would love to get a real newsy letter from you sometime bringing me up to date about Tony, who was the most adorable little toddler the last time I saw him. It's still hard for me to remember that you and Louise aren't together any more but that's the way it so often is these days and I'm sure you are both making the best of it. Such *difficult* times! Louise was always a great favorite of mine— she has such wonderful taste. Wouldn't it be wonderful if we could all get together some fine day. How I'd love for you to meet Vance and see the kids. But when!?

Lots of love to you and Tony,
Linda

P.S. When I wrote that I don't brood over the past, that doesn't mean that I don't think much about Clark. I do fairly often and I sometimes feel such a great sadness that he never experienced so much that makes life so rewarding—like seeing his daughter grow up and mature. Clark was such an intellectual—sometimes I wonder if he wasn't *too* intellectual and theoretical in his approach to things, so that he really couldn't appreciate the simple things without trying to make them fit some kind of theory. Did you ever feel that way about him? If he had lived longer I feel sure he would have come to appreciate the simple *nice* things more and be more sympathetic to the part that religion can play in our lives. I often think he was handicapped by being the son of a very strict minister and rebelling against all that. But Clark was a wonderful guy in so many ways and I will always feel privileged that we shared those years together.

Love again,
L.

Hux let the four pink sheets and the snapshots flutter to the floor. Write a stupid letter and you get a stupid reply. So Clark was too intellectual, too theoretical!—Clark, who was one of the most passionately involved, deeply caring men that ever lived. The dumb cunt!

After a while Hux reached down from the bed and picked up the two snapshots. The family group were posed around a picnic table—in some Ohio state park, he supposed. Well grown and sunny. Susie was nearly as tall as her mother, but she was looking down and Hux could not get a clear impression of her. Vance Johanssen looked like Hollywood's idea of a stalwart high-school principal—a gigantic, beardless Viking with a friendly smile. Neither Hux nor Louise had been surprised when, about a year and a half after Clark's death, Linda had written from her parents' home in Columbus to say that she was going to marry a wonderful guy she had known ever since high school. So much for poor Clark. . . .

But the other snapshot! Clark had been reincarnated in his daughter—the same curly brown hair, the same serious, level gaze in the brown eyes beneath the prominent brow. Clark was looking directly at Hux through his daughter's eyes; some word of his, some greeting, had formed on her half-smiling lips, which were thick like his. Hux could not bear to look.

Again that night Hux's sleep was a grotesque carnival of dreams, some of them erotic, others full of embarrassment and anxiety. The only one he could remember the next morning had to do with Miss Isabelle, whom he heard shrieking as he approached her house. Sure that her brother was beating her, or even killing her, he rushed into the house and searched everywhere for her, going from room to room, avoiding only her brother's bedroom; when at last he found her, cowering like a small animal beneath her own bed, he was unable to coax her out. . . . As he ate his seven-o'clock breakfast before leaving for Jackson, Hux again felt torn between his obligation to Miss Isabelle and his dread of reassuming the part of Ainsley Black. Behind Ainsley stood the evangelist, his arms spread wide. Once more he decided not to call Miss Isabelle; he would put it off until tomorrow, when his day would not be so crowded. Thank God for the official agenda. . . . But today's long drive loomed before him, and Hux again prayed for God's protection against His preacher.

It was after four when Hux finished the last of his meetings in Jackson. They had gone well, he thought, both at Tougaloo and at Jackson State. The needs of these two institutions were so glaring that even the comparatively small amount that the Morrow Foundation was likely to allocate could make a recognizable difference. He could thus feel happy about the official agenda for its own sake and pleased with his own performance. Again, as at Itta Bena, Hux found the courteous, formal, and slightly skeptical attitude of the black administrators easier to deal with than the overeagerness to please or impress that he often encountered. At no point was there any overt display of hostility in the style of Franklin Mosby. Now the drive to Oxford lay ahead, three hours or more of it before he could find refuge at Anne's.

But Hux did not head back at once. Instead he drove into the black neighborhood of Jackson, where he had stayed at various addresses during the summer of '64, and parked in front of a one-story frame house with a backward-sloping roof; it was only two blocks from the place where Medgar Evers had been shot. This was the home of Junior and Bessie Wilcox, with whom Hux had lived during his last two weeks in Mississippi. The house looked freshly painted and the porch steps, which he remembered as rickety, had been repaired. The whole neighborhood in fact seemed more prosperous, more middle-class, than it had. Because of his experience with Mosby, Hux was somewhat nervous about his possible reception but told himself that things would be different, that the Wilcoxes had not been intellectuals or leaders in the Movement, and that no issues of pride or hurt feelings were at stake. As he was about to press the doorbell, he hesitated, wishing that he had telephoned first; then, bracing himself, he rang.

A boy of about eight, dark-skinned, his eyes rolling white with shyness and surprise, opened the door. He had been born too late to know the procession of white men and women who had once crossed this threshold.

"Is your mother or father here? I'm an old friend of theirs."

"Momma's here." But the boy did not stand aside to let Hux enter.

"Tell her it's Larry Hux. She'll know who that is."

The boy vanished into the house and a moment later returned with a heavy, middle-aged, very dark woman in a white terry-cloth bathrobe. She and Hux stared at each other without recognition.

"Bessie?"

"That's me. Who you say you are?"

"Larry Hux. For God's sake, Bessie, don't you remember me? I lived in this house for two whole weeks. Back in '64."

"So many people come in an' out those days. You put on weight?"

"I sure have." It was all Hux could do to keep from adding, "So have you." There was in her scarcely a trace of the glossy-skinned, supple-bodied, loud-laughing young woman whose image he had retained unaltered for a decade.

"You was *real* skinny. I remember you. You slep' in that back room.

157

I remember. Well, now, ain't that somethin'! What can I do for you?" She made no move to invite him in.

"I'm in Jackson just for the day and—well, I thought I'd just drop by to say hello to you—and to Junior, if he was at home."

"Junior ain't here. Junior's workin' down in Gulfport. We separated."

"I'm sorry. I didn't know that."

"I remember you real good now," said Bessie with just a trace of a smile. "You wanna come in, have a beer or somethin'?"

Hux no longer did. He wanted to flee. But there seemed no way now to turn down her invitation. He followed Bessie and the boy into the tiny, linoleum-floored living room, in which there was a large color television set toward which every piece of furniture, including a narrow bed, had been turned, as if drawn by a giant magnet. Bessie disappeared into the next of the successive rooms, arranged, Hux remembered, like a railway flat in New York; to get into his own shedlike room in the back, he had had to go through a rear door no more than five feet high. Turning to the boy, who had sat down and was awkwardly twisting one corner of his white T-shirt, Hux said, "I stayed here before you were born, so I don't know your name."

"My name Baxter."

"You have an older sister. She must be about twelve now."

"Got two. Ruth-Ann an' Denise. Reckon you talkin' 'bout Denise."

"That's right. Denise. She was just a toddler then. Is she here?"

"Naw, she live with Granma."

Hux did not pry into this arrangement. The lives of Negroes had always seemed mysterious to him when he was growing up in the South. But there had been nothing mysterious about the Wilcoxes in 1964; then he had seen them, perhaps idealized them, as a hardworking, loving, and brave young couple, willing to risk their jobs and their home and even their baby's safety at a time when blacks who took white agitators into their houses ran the risk of fire bombing and worse. A great sadness now filled him, and he could think of nothing else to say to Baxter.

Bessie returned with two cold cans of beer and a bag of potato chips. She was laughing—chuckling loudly to herself in the old way—but she did not at once reveal the source of her amusement. Instead, after handing Hux a moisture-beaded can, she asked what had brought him back to Jackson. His reply produced nods but no comment or even any real sign of interest in the fact that he had spent much of the day discussing matters of planning and financing at two black colleges. Then, in response to a question of his, Bessie said that she worked at the local veterans' hospital, on the seven-to-three-thirty shift. She worked on floor maintenance—whatever that meant. There seemed to be nothing more to say. Drinking his beer faster than usual, Hux tried to keep up a degree of conversation. He learned that Junior was now employed by an oil-drilling outfit in Gulfport and that he came back from time to time to see the children. When Baxter asked if he could watch "The Electric Company" on television, his mother instantly gave permission, and for the next ten minutes they all watched the frantic display of exuberance on the screen.

Hux had finished his beer and was about to leave when the slamming of the screen door made everybody jump. A tall, bald, coffee-brown man came in; he was wearing white coveralls with the words HIGHTOP BREAD stitched in red across the chest. Over the noise of the program Bessie introduced the man as Curtis and he and Hux shook hands. "He one of them stayed here back in '64," shouted Bessie by way of explanation. Curtis nodded, smiled in a friendly way, and sat down to watch. Standing up, Hux said loudly that he had to be leaving, gave Baxter a pat on the shoulder (the boy did not shift his eyes from the screen), and went out the front door. Following him, Bessie began to laugh again. "Sure I remember," she said. "I remember when me an' Junior had to pull you off that other man, the one who got shot. You looked like you was about to kill him yourself."

Hux vaguely knew but did not fully register what she was referring to. Making no reply, he held out his hand and after a second or two said, "Goodbye, Bessie. I'm glad I found you at home. If you ever see Junior these days, remember me to him."

"Lord knows when that'll be," said Bessie, shaking her head. "Round about Christmastime, I reckon. Okay, I'll tell him." She began to laugh, again in the old way. "Le's you an' me both promise to lose a little weight before we meet again. Then we won't have no trouble recognizin' each other next time we meet. You take care of yourself now, you hear? So long, Larry."

"So long, Bessie. Good to see you."

Hux hurried down the wooden steps of the porch and down the brick walk to his car, where he turned to wave. Bessie, still on the porch, waved back vigorously with one hand while holding her bathrobe closed with the other. An alphabet song from "The Electric Company" was pouring at high volume from the open door and window.

Chapter Twenty-three

Anne set up the evening with care. She arranged for Prudence to have supper and spend the night with a friend; though "sleepovers" on school nights were generally discouraged. Rushing from her job at the library to the supermarket, she bought the supplies needed for a creole chicken dish that she—not ordinarily an adventurous or inventive cook—had found in a New Orleans cookbook. By the time Larry arrived (only half an hour late), the apartment was filled with the pleasant steam of simmering onions, green peppers, and tomatoes, and Anne was dressed in a black silk blouse and a bright red skirt—the Spanish colors that went well with her eyes and her black hair, which tonight was pulled into a pony tail and tied with a thin red velvet ribbon. She was exhilarated, ready to have a good time with her odd, Yankeefied Southerner, not exactly nervous but a bit shivery with the first vibrations of anticipated lovemaking. For Anne could think of no reason why she should not admit this particular visiting fireman to her bed. Despite the tentativeness of their kiss at their last meeting, she had no real doubt as to how this evening would end; there was even a certain symmetry about the arrangement that excited her, quite apart from Larry's appeal in his own right. Clark's best friend . . .

Larry was neither distraught, as he had been last time, nor drunk, as Anne half expected him to be, but strangely solemn and unsmiling. He greeted her almost as if they were meeting at the funeral of an old friend—with a kiss on the cheek and a gentle pat on her arm. Still dressed as he had been for the day's meetings—in his tan poplin suit and a striped tie—he had even brought his briefcase along. Anne persuaded him to loosen his tie and to surrender his jacket, which she hung with care in the front closet. They had hardly settled down to their drinks (she had gone beyond her liquor budget to buy a bottle of Jack Daniel's for the occasion), when he said, "I have just paid a visit to the last place where I saw Clark alive—and it meant nothing to me at all." For several seconds he looked away dreamily, his lower jaw slack. Then he brought his gaze sharply back to Anne

and said, "My pilgrimage is pretty much a failure. I may as well finish up and head for New Orleans or back to New York. Bessie Wilcox
hardly even remembered Clark. The family has broken up. The place
looks different. . . . Everything that happened there might never
have happened at all—there's nothing left."

"That can't be true," said Anne with a touch of impatience. "Whatever happened that summer *did* make a difference—a real big difference. It's just what happened isn't neat, the difference doesn't have
an outline that you can easily trace. It's all messy, with lots of loose
ends. Like people's lives." She gave him one of her close, head-tilted
scrutinies. He seemed to be mulling over what she had said but with
a humorless, slightly petulant expression that annoyed her. Why had
her gaily projected evening taken such a serious turn right at the
start? Where was that streak of mischief, of playfulness, that she had
counted on to lighten the atmosphere, to keep the shadow of Clark
from spreading its wings over too much of the evening? "You're not
being fair," she resumed severely. "You want to keep the Wilcoxes
exactly as they were—or as you saw them—in 1964. Why can't you
allow them to change, to mess up their neat outlines? Think how
much you and I have changed since then—and not exactly in the
direction of neatness and order, either!"

"You're right," he said gloomily. He had hardly tasted his drink.
After a moment he got up and went to the closet where Anne had
hung his jacket. Returning, he held out a fat pink envelope. "Here.
You were asking what Linda Helmholtz is like. This will give you an
idea." While Anne was reading the letter, Larry got up twice and
paced around the small room. "Well?" he demanded, leaning over
her chair.

"What am I supposed to say? I don't know what you wrote to her."

"I wrote to her about visiting Tupelo. And this is the response I
get. I might just as well have written about a visit to the corner store.
Linda's a stupid cow. She never had any idea she was married to one
of the brightest men of his generation. As far as she's concerned,
Vance Johanssen is probably an improvement."

Anne felt uneasy; she doubted that she would like Linda, who certainly had the style of an overgrown Girl Scout, but she felt a sisterly
impulse to defend her against the scorn that was now curling Larry's
lips. "Has it ever occurred to you," she asked, handing back the letter, "that Vance Johanssen might *really* be an improvement? Bein'
married to an intellectual is not every woman's dream."

Larry looked angrily away. "You know damn well Clark wasn't

just an intellectual. He was a hell of a lot more than that."

"Don't get mad at me, Larry. You don't have to tell me what Clark was like. But I doubt if he was the easiest guy in the world to be married to." With that Anne got up and went into the kitchen to finish off the preparations for dinner. *I should tell him*, she thought. *Now.* But an instant later she was saying to herself, *Let it lie, let it lie.* Through the door she could see Larry hunched over his drink, deeply preoccupied. Was he even aware of what he was drinking? Was she going to have a goddamn crank on her hands all evening? It occurred to her, not for the first time, that Larry might be latently— actively?—homosexual, that he had been in love with Clark and therefore jealously resented Clark's wife. . . . Was she wasting her time, wasting this good food and expensive booze on a faggot? The idea chilled her, even while it did not seem probable. Of course the fact that he had been married once and was the father of a child proved nothing, one way or the other, but it did establish a certain probability. Besides, Larry did not give off gay vibrations, as did some of the university bachelors who were her dinner partners. Screwed up—God, yes!—but not that way, she concluded. . . .

Anne turned off the heat under the chicken, inspected the rice, and set about bringing the frozen green beans to a boil. Then she took a bottle of California vin rosé from the refrigerator and brought it with a corkscrew to Larry. "Would you open this for me? And please, for God's sake, stop eatin' your heart out over poor Linda's letter. Just the other night you told me you liked her—that she was a real good egg or somethin' like that."

"I'm sorry for the outburst," he said as he began to peel the magenta foil from the bottle's neck. "I had no business talking about her that way."

Larry continued to be preoccupied and mostly silent during the meal. Anne kept hoping that he would comment on the chicken, which seemed to her delicious, but he did not seem to notice what he was eating—though he consumed it eagerly enough. She made most of the conversation, telling him about a fight she had had that morning with the curator of Special Collections at the library. It concerned the proper display of a letter written in 1859 by Jefferson Davis to a portrait painter in Natchez, a brief note in which the future President of the Confederacy offered to put the painter in touch with a prospective client in Port Gibson. "From the way Mr. Rogerson was carryin' on," said Anne, "you'd have thought that little old note was the Magna Carta or somethin', and that I was tryin' to sabotage the exhibit by puttin' several *inferior* documents in the same display case. My God, the idiocy I have to put up with! Can't you get me a job in New York?"

"You can have mine," said Larry, lifting a forkful of tomato-flecked chicken to his lips.

"Only on the condition that it will never send me to Oxford, Mississippi, on any kind of mission!" She now began to complain about the life she led in Oxford. Her complaint, which soon became a diatribe, was really a form of flirtation, for Anne was determined to provoke him by exaggeration, to startle him into seeing what she offered as a woman.

"The fact is," she said, "I haven't any close friends here. Most of the women at the library are nice enough, but I can't see spending much of my time with them. And the men—" She made a rueful face, raising her eyebrows and puckering her wide mouth. "People tolerate me, and that's about it. I try to do all the right things for Prue—birthday parties, PTA, even church sometimes, God help me, but I make the other mothers uneasy. Prue isn't ostracized—I don't mean that—but she's definitely the child of an outsider, a maverick. Ray and Peggy are pretty good about havin' us over for Sunday dinners and all the big holidays. From time to time they invite me over to meet a single man they've dredged up from somewhere, usually a visitin' fireman like you." Her eyes flashing with humor, she waited for Larry's response.

"I don't mean I'm all *that* isolated," she continued. "People do hang around me at parties, especially the men. I shock them a little bit. They suspect I'm more women's lib than I really am. And they think I sleep around a lot—as if I had the chance!"

Larry frowned slightly, and for a moment Anne saw herself as disgusting to him, as a horrible, aggressive woman throwing herself at a reluctant man. She waited, and when Larry again made no comment, she said, as if with an afterthought, "Of course Prue's good company for me. Mostly. I do love her and . . . I try not to burden her with too many of my discontents. I try to be a decent mother. I guess that's the only reason you don't find me night after night sittin' at the bar of the Holiday Inn tryin' to pick up some sales representative from Little Rock. I don't mean that really, but sometimes I do get the feelin' that I'm always bein' forced to choose between Prue's welfare and mine. Not that pickin' up travelin' salesmen is my idea of the good life." She waited, again with the sense that she had gone too far—waited for the look of contempt she deserved.

Larry shook his head slowly, in a way that seemed more sympathetic than contemptuous. Then, as if he had heard nothing she had been saying, he asked if she had ever had a religious experience.

"What?" She had stood up to clear the table, and she now swung toward him, two plates and silverware clattering in her grip. "What do you mean 'religious experience'?"

"I mean—I guess I mean—a sort of inflowing of power or—or *energy*, something that takes you over, that flows through you—" He broke off, took a deep breath, and said, "I mean a feeling so overwhelming that you think it could only come from God."

Setting the dishes back on the table, Anne looked down at her guest, her hands on her thin waist. "The answer to that is *no*. Why do you ask? Have you had that kind of experience?"

He did not answer her immediately. Finally he shook his head and said, "No, I never have. But I sometimes wonder what it would be like—how I would deal with it."

Relieved, Anne picked up the dishes again and carried them to the kitchen sink. Then she took their dessert—vanilla ice cream topped with crushed strawberries—to the table and said, "I'm the wrong person to ask. All I've had is what you might call an *un*-religious experience. When I was about fourteen, an aunt of mine died, and people were talkin' about her bein' in Heaven, with God, and all that. All of a sudden the whole business just struck me as pure nonsense—Aunt Kate was dead and that was that. All the rest was about on the level of tellin' children that babies are brought by the stork. It made me furious to have to listen to all that stuff—and I've been a hard-core atheist ever since. Even though I kept on goin' to church till I was eighteen—mainly to please my father."

"And now you go for Prue's sake?"

"Right. I show my face to the congregation three or four times a year and I loath every minute of it, I can tell you."

"Have you ever wished that you *could* believe?" asked Larry, who was inattentively but vigorously spooning up his ice cream and strawberries.

"Not for a moment! If I believed in God, I'd have to give Him hell—for all the rotten tricks He's played on us. Really give Him hell."

"Seriously . . ." All at once Larry shook his head and began to laugh. Anne laughed too, and for the first time the solemnity of the evening was breached. After Anne brought in coffee, they talked in a relaxed way about Larry's impressions of the people he had met in Oxford and laughed again over his visit of apology to Carruthers Halsey. When they returned, carrying their cups, to the main part of the little living room, Larry at last gave Anne the compliment she had been waiting for. "Terrific dinner," he said with an easy and charming smile that made her want to hug him. "You must have gone to a lot of trouble. The chicken was spectacular." But they had hardly settled into this new era of good feeling when Larry perversely re-evoked the ghost of Clark. "Oh," he said, jumping up from his seat, "I brought along some of Clark's old letters I thought you might like to see. And some snapshots." And he fetched his briefcase and laid it on the table in front of the couch. "Here," he said, extracting the packet of letters. "Have a look at these."

"No!" cried Anne, recoiling, raising both hands as if to push away what he was offering. "I don't want to read Clark's letters. I don't want to see pictures of him!" Her dark eyes flashed with tears. "Make your damn pilgrimage if you have to, but for God's sake don't involve me in it."

Startled, shaken, Larry apologized as he gathered up his mementos. "I'm sorry, you're right. You're absolutely right. It's my pilgrimage, not yours. But I thought you'd like to read what Clark said about you. He—"

"Why should I? Why should I want to know what a man who's been dead ten years had to say about me?" Part of her, of course, did want to know—was dying to know—but Anne was (for the moment) determined to keep the past and all its attendant emotions in their own locked compartment. She had no intention of letting Larry seduce her into a sentimental wallow that she was certain to regret. "You're the strangest man," she protested. "I've never met anybody like you before. Never!"

Larry looked hurt. He was about to shut the lid of his case when Anne suddenly relented. 'Look, I'm overreacting," she said, reaching out and touching his arm. "Why shouldn't you want to share your feelin's about Clark with someone who knew him? Let me look at the stuff you brought."

"You don't have to."

"I want to. Clark meant a lot to me too. Did you bring all these with you just in case you ran into somebody who would want to see them?"

"Not exactly."

Nearly an hour later, Larry was lying stretched out on the couch, shoeless, his head in Anne's lap. Absently touching his hair with her fingers, she was staring across the room to the dining area, where the dessert plates and napkins still lay on the table. She had not only examined the snapshots and read the references to herself in the letters, but she had also listened to Larry's fantasy of producing all of this material for the benefit of Claiborne Herne. He had just told her that he had actually gone so far as to drive over to Alhambra on Sunday.

"I found out where the Hernes live," he said. "They've moved from their old house. So I just went up to their front door and rang the bell. Claiborne Herne himself opened the door and—"

"My God! What on earth did you say to him?"

He smiled up at her amazement. "I pretended I'd come to the wrong house. He gave me a funny look and slammed the door. I think he was drunk." Larry in turn gave her an odd look. "And that," he continued, "was the tiny little outcome of my great big fantasy. I never got to show him the pictures and letters of the man he killed."

"I'd say you went pretty far with that fantasy. But what does he look like?"

"A broken-down old drunk. Full of anger. Mean . . ."

Anne was silent. Her fingers continued to ruffle Larry's hair, which felt like fine-spun wire. "So," she said at last, "nothing has worked out the way you expected. Are you sorry you came to Mississippi?"

"No," he said, again smiling up at her. "If I hadn't come, I wouldn't have met you. Thanks for listening to me—and for putting up with all my foolishness." He sat up, swinging his feet over the side of the couch. "I'd better be going."

"Don't," she whispered, "not yet."

"I'd better. I'm worn out. I've been through too much today and I—"

"Never apologize, never explain," Anne snapped. "By all means go on home. You're under no obligation to hang around here. Like I said the first time I asked you over for a drink, there are no strings."

Larry reached out and caught her by the shoulders. Anne did not move away but she would not look at him. "It's been a real good evening. You've put me in a much better mood than I thought was possible. I have so many things on my mind, Anne, so many things . . ." His face puckered. "I guess I'm not in very good shape. That must be obvious to you."

Now Anne shrugged beneath his grasp. Yes, she thought, *you can say that again.*

"But will you give me another chance? Will you come out with me on Saturday—on Saturday night? Come on, we'll have a good time. I promise I won't be such a drag."

"You don't want to see me. Stop pretending."

"Oh, yes I do!" he nearly shouted, pulling her to his chest. She stiffened and again averted her face, but Larry caught her under the chin and forced her face around so that he could kiss her on the lips. Raked and scratched across the cheek by his day's growth of whisker, Anne kept her lips tight and was about to push him away with both hands when suddenly she thought: *it's only a kiss, for God's sake.* . . . Why was she now resisting him when she had been so eager just a short while before? She could not shake free of the feeling that his whole performance was forced, was being faked. . . . But she let herself go loose in his grip and opened her lips to his mouth. His kiss was ravenous, too gross and thrusting, and she wanted to pull away. Then, as he was clinging to her, she felt the prodding of his erection. A shudder ran through him, and he pulled back his thighs and groin while letting his chin rest upon her shoulder, a dead weight. He backed away from her and turned.

Seeing him thus, hulking and disheveled, one corner of his shirt pulled out, Anne could not stop herself from laughing aloud. "You look so weird! Like a baffled rapist or somethin'." She was angry again.

"I'm baffled all right," he murmured. Then, in a stronger voice, he said, "What the hell," and faced her again. "I'm going to go now and see if ten hours' sleep will put my head and body together. You still haven't answered me about Saturday. Will you give me another chance?" He crossed the room to the chair where he had hung his jacket. "Will you?" he asked, putting it on.

"I'm not in the mood to spend another evenin' with the ghost of Clark Helmholtz."

"I promise not even to mention his name."

"All right then. But call me later in the week. You might want to change your mind."

"Not a chance. But I'll call you anyway late Friday night when I get back from Starkville—if not before. Just to talk."

"Suit yourself."

Anne went downstairs with Larry and outside to his car, which was parked some distance up University Avenue in the yellow glare of a sodium street lamp. The night was soft, like a warm, wet compress against her forehead. Since it was still early, there was a fair amount of traffic up and down the avenue. At the car, Larry, who had been silent ever since leaving the apartment, turned to Anne as if to kiss her again but said, "I'm sick and tired of ghosts. They keep getting in the way."

"They sure do," said Anne after a moment's lapse. She had been distracted, having noticed for the first time, in the glare of the street lamp overhead, a wet-looking stain on the front of Larry's trousers. "But only if you ask them in."

"My ghosts are gate crashers. They don't always wait to be invited."

"Then you just have to drive them out." She waited, her lips parted, for a final kiss. It came—brief, unprobing, but tender—very different from the last. Then she watched as Larry, after lifting one hand in a wry salute, got into his car and drove away.

Chapter Twenty-four

Isabelle Herne sat dejectedly in the mahogany embrace of an old barrel chair while her brother stood above her, bent like a giant red-and-white stork preparing to stab a plump frog. "Lamar is your oldest and dearest friend in Alhambra," said Isabelle, who was close to tears. "You can't let him down on an occasion like this." They had just received a telephone call from the Pikes' daughter, Mary-Pinrose Hubbard, informing them that her mother, Evelyn Pike, who had been ailing for some time, had failed to wake up from her afternoon nap.

"Oldest and dearest? He's been draggin' my name through the mud for thirty years, and don't think—"

"Oh, Brother, little Brother! What fiend from hell ever planted that idea in your head? You have no more loyal friend in this world than Lamar and you know it. It's broken his heart the way you've turned against him." Resting her chin on her knuckles, Isabelle looked away, now actively blinking tears. She had begun to think that her brother might be entering one of his "good" periods; he had recently been much more outgoing and talkative, even kinder to her, and, as far as she could tell, he had had no contact with Rooney or Vicky since he sent them away last Sunday. But now he was being impossible again, refusing to call on the Pikes, saying that he would not even go to Evelyn's funeral, raging against poor Lamar. . . .

"There's nothin' to stop you from goin' over to the Pikes' right now," said Claiborne. "Nothin' in this world. I think I'm probably old enough to entertain myself while you're gone." He walked over to the drink tray, where he had left his glass when the telephone rang. "All this flapdoodle over Evelyn Pike's death infuriates me. She's an aging, disagreeable woman who's had the good sense to die. That's all. Why all the fuss?"

"What a dreadful, heartless thing to say. And you don't really mean it. I can't go by myself. It would be too humiliatin' to appear on their doorstep and have to make up some excuse for your absence." But Isabelle had other reasons for not wanting to leave him today. That familiar sly look, that mischievous glint . . . She clung to the idea that, if only she could keep a careful enough watch over him, she might be able to prolong the good period—"good" being the most relative of terms.

"If I showed up at the Pikes', Lamar might accuse me of havin' poisoned Evelyn. I wouldn't put it past him."

"Oh, be quiet! That's so silly it makes me sick." She recognized an oblique reference to another of his silly notions: that Lamar had never forgiven him for recommending a hysterectomy for Evelyn some thirty years ago—as if that operation had anything to do with her bad disposition and invalidism in recent years.

"You can do what you like," said Claiborne, taking up his drink and going with it into his bedroom.

A little later the telephone rang. Isabelle, who was still sitting pensively in the barrel chair, did not hear it. Then her brother stormed back into the living room, shouting, "For God's sake, answer the phone." She gave a startled jump and scurried into the hall, certain that someone was calling about poor Evelyn. When she overcame her deafness enough to realize that Ainsley Black was on the telephone, she let out a small shriek of excitement. "Ainsley, Ainsley, it's like a special providence havin' you call just now! I was thinkin' about you—I've been thinkin' about you since last Sunday and wonderin' what had happened. How I've wished that we could talk . . . and now here you are! Ainsley, somethin' very upsetting and sorrowful has happened. Our old friend Evelyn Pike—" Isabelle lowered her voice, certain that Claiborne was listening from the living-room doorway; but her loud whisper was perfectly audible as she told Ainsley about Evelyn's death. Evelyn Pike, she said, was a difficult person, not easy to be friends with, but Isabelle had loved her all the same—"for her own dear prickly self as well as for Lamar's sake." Then her voice sank still further into a breathy, rasping sound that carried just as well as the whisper while she described Claiborne's refusal to go to the Pikes' and the quandary that this put her into. "Darlin' Lamar needs his old friends to rally around at a time like this, but Brother's in sort of a funny mood and I'm unhappy about leavin' him alone tonight."

She had trouble hearing Ainsley's response. Had he said what she thought he had? Very slowly, as if repeating a message in order to confirm it, Isabelle said, "You mean you'll come here this evenin' and stay with Brother while I call on the Pikes?" She listened carefully and then gave two long sighs that were almost groans. "It's such a kind offer, Reverend Black—Ainsley—so kind. . . . But I'll have to ask Brother. He loved your visit last Sunday, but, as I say, he's been in sort of a funny mood—"

Striding into the hall, Claiborne grabbed the receiver from Isabelle, who uttered a small cry. When she tried to get it back, he gave her a hard push which sent her reeling backward so that she bumped hard against a table, hurting her thigh. Again she cried out. Claiborne meanwhile cleared his throat several times. In a harsh, phlegm-thickened voice he said, "Am I to understand, Reverend, that you've offered to pay me a social visit this evenin'?" He frowned. "What's that? No, nothin' fell—everything's fine here." Glowering at Isabelle, who stood rubbing her thigh through her dress, her soft face puckering between astonishment and pain, he said loudly, "Excellent! I'll be delighted to see you, Reverend. Come over about eight. It's mighty kind of you to offer to sit up with an old fella like me." And Claiborne Herne hung up without allowing his sister to speak to Ainsley Black again. "Why did you hesitate when he made his offer? Do you want to keep him to yourself? I know you've got a crush on this young fella, but I need company—*young* company—and you're not to keep me from havin' it!"

"You hurt me! You made me bang myself on that table. I'm goin' to—" What was she going to do—run and tell her mother? Isabelle stood quivering with rage and frustration. It was not often that she stood up to her brother. Nor was it often that he physically hurt her. Just now he was laughing; at any moment, she felt, he might stick out his tongue, just like a younger brother. Then, remembering poor Evelyn, she put the childish squabbling behind her and went to the kitchen to prepare the offering that she regularly presented to a newly bereaved family: a rich spice cake with a caramel icing that came from one of the recipes in the old, dog-eared "receipt book" that her mother had brought from Beulah as a bride.

So Ainsley was coming! Isabelle had been more disappointed than she would acknowledge to herself by his silence since Sunday. His explanation on the telephone had been that he had received unexpected assignments involving Brother Thurlow's coming mission to North Carolina. Nothing was said about the extraordinary occurrence at church, and Isabelle wondered if that had had something to do with the silence. Perhaps it led to a sort of retreat, to an interval of meditation and solitude. . . . But now he was coming! *The bridegroom cometh.* . . . And in the nick of time, too. The wonderful effect which Ainsley's presence, in some miraculous way, had had upon her brother was clearly wearing off: he had become sly, jeering; at any moment he might make a call to the Lees. . . . Isabelle, too, had felt a kind of blessing in his presence, a source of strength, a heightened power to endure—and even to hope; he had even made it easier for her to stand up to Claiborne. It was all very strange. . . . Though she yearned to be in his company, Isabelle was glad that she would be at the Pikes'; her very absence from home (an absence that she felt as a sacrifice) might provide an opportunity for Ainsley to reach her brother—to touch him—in a deeper, more intimate way than would be possible in her presence. Who could tell? As she got out the butter to soften and began to assemble the cloves and cinnamon and nutmeg that she would need for the cake, Isabelle prayed directly to God that through Ainsley's ministry her brother might at last be granted the peace that passeth understanding. . . . And for herself? She was selfish enough to know that her brother's peace would mean her own. It was peace she wanted, not the rapture and terror involved in a direct encounter with the Spirit such as she had witnessed last Sunday.

Somewhat later, as Isabelle was coming through the open door of the kitchen into the hall, she saw that her brother was making a telephone call. Was it the one she had most dreaded—was he making a Sunday-morning appointment with Vicky? She next perceived that Claiborne was arguing—arguing vehemently, his face flushed and twisted—and that he apparently had not sensed her presence. But she could not make sense out of what she only partially heard. Then there was a final, violent "No!"—followed by a slamming-down of the receiver. Before she could duck back into the kitchen, Claiborne wheeled around and saw her.

"You sneaky old fool!" he bellowed, just as if she had been ten and he five. "How long have you been standin' there?"

"Brother, I just came out to go to the bathroom. I didn't hear a single word. I promise!"

Chapter Twenty-five

Hux was twitchy with apprehension as he drove over to Alhambra in the sultry twilight. He had really let himself in for it. . . . But he had had no choice about calling. There was no way that he could drop the Alhambra mission, though its nature had changed, making it now seem full of peril for him. The old plan of revenge had been subtly modified—into what? He did not fully know. He now seemed committed to help Miss Isabelle without having any clear idea where such a project might lead. Having involved himself with her, having raised her expectations, he could not simply abandon her without a word. Was it still feasible to think that Dr. Herne could be brought to a realization of what he had done? Probably not. The man was old, drunk, crazy . . . and pathetic. But hateful, too—a vicious old man. A part of Hux still yearned to rub that arrogant, veinous old nose in the hideousness of the bloody mess he had made; but another part— more clamorous now—wanted never to lay eyes on the doctor again.

Hux shrank from the thought of once more putting on the clown suit of Ainsley Black. Far from seeming a protection, an armoring, that role now enhanced his feeling of vulnerability. In order to minimize the evangelical image, he had dressed as informally as possible in an Ivy Leaguish way: a red golf shirt, chinos, loafers. . . . Thank God Brother Thurlow was no longer physically present in Alhambra. Yet, as Hux approached the outskirts of the town, he began to sweat and his anxiety intensified, rippling through him as if at any moment the evangelist might rise before him and denounce his imposture. It was all he could do to stop himself from turning around, from heading straight back to Oxford—and to Anne. If only he could be with Anne, make love to her, make her love him, carry her off to New Orleans. . . . But the look of disappointment and dismay on Miss Isabelle's face rebuked this fantasy and kept him on course, passive as a robot at the wheel.

"Here you are!"
Despite the severe black-and-white dress she was wearing for her call of condolence, Miss Isabelle seemed oddly young and fluttery as

she opened the door for Hux—like an overweight girl who had rushed breathlessly through the house to let him in. "What a treat to see you!" Then, resorting to her loud, carrying whisper, she said, "It's like a miracle—for you to call just at this critical time and then to be able to come on such short notice. Brother's so pleased. He's waitin' for you in the living room. Are you sure you've had supper? There's lots of cold ham and potato salad. . . ."

Hux assured her that he had eaten. Through the open door came the delicious spicy smell of the freshly baked cake, its odor mingling with that rising from a gardenia bush by the stoop. They continued to stand outside while Miss Isabelle, putting a conspiratorial hand on Hux's wrist, said that she had been worried about her brother for the last few days. "He hasn't been his best self. I don't know how to put this, but sometimes it seems—well, it seems like a demon rises up in him. Refusin' to call on his oldest friend at a time like this—that's not the Claiborne I know and love best." She was holding her face close to Hux's, as if to make sure that he heard a whisper that could be heard twenty feet away. "Anyway, you've come at a good time. He *needs* you. But," she continued, tightening her hold on his wrist, "Ainsley, dear Ainsley, if you'll forgive me for tellin' you how to conduct your own business, don't press him too hard. Approach him real softly, sort of indirectly if you can—"

"Miss Isabelle, I'm not planning—"

She was not listening. "Reverend Thurlow's approach just wouldn't work with Brother. I hate to say it, but he's always been rather . . . rather *scornful* of evangelists. Approach him softly like I say. A gentle, indirect approach at the right moment—"

Hux forced her to listen to him. "Miss Isabelle, I'm not planning to bring up religion with your brother. I'm here as his guest, to listen to him. If the Holy Spirit—" He broke off, feeling himself beginning to quiver at the mere saying of the words.

"You'll do what's right. I know that. You don't need me to give advice when you've got the inspiration that comes—that comes directly from the Lord." She looked away shyly for a second, then said in her regular, non-whispering voice, "I expect I'll be back by ten—by ten-thirty at the latest. I'm sure Lamar's exhausted, poor darlin', but Mary-Pinrose—that's their married daughter—Mary-Pinrose Hubbard—she sounded so pleased when I called to say I'd come. She says I'm the only one who can remember the names of all the out-of-town cousins they'll have to get in touch with. And they'll need help gettin' ready for Alex and his family—he's their son, and they'll be arrivin' late tonight from Galveston—there'll be a real houseful by

tomorrow—Alex and Marjorie have *five* children—think of that!"
She paused for breath, her eyes bright with the prospect of all the
bustle that a death in a Southern family brings. "Anyway, there'll be
lots to do, and I'd better be on my way. Oh, my cake! Maybe you
could carry the cake to the car for me? It's on the hall table."

Claiborne Herne was waiting just inside the door from the hall to
the living room. Dressed up in a linen jacket and crisp white trousers, he looked, in the half light, more distinguished than ravaged,
his darkened features more sunburnt than vein-threaded. With a formal smile he shook hands with his guest. Exhaling whiskey fumes,
he ceremoniously led Hux into the living room and indicated a chair.
    "It's good of you to keep an old fella company," he said as he
lowered himself into his own Morris chair. He picked up the drink
that he had left on its shelf-like arm. "Of course, I suspect you of
havin' designs on my immortal soul, but I'm prepared to put up with
that for the sake of once again havin' a young face sitting opposite
me in this rather depressin' room."
    This speech sounded rehearsed to Hux, who distrusted the doctor's
geniality, which, as he had witnessed, could switch in an instant into
grinning malice. "Any talk about your immortal soul will have to be
initiated by you, Dr. Herne," he replied in a voice that did not sound
like Ainsley Black. Realizing this, he quickly added, in country tones,
"Heck, I'm happy just to be sittin' here, talkin' or listenin' as the
spirit moves us." He smiled an eager, country boy's smile.
    "How about drinkin'? Won't you go over to the tray and help
yourself?"
    "In a little while. Right now I just want to relax for a few minutes.
It's real peaceful here, and I've had what you might call a troublesome day."
    "Savin' souls or trackin' down criminals?"
    The first flick of the whip, thought Hux. Evidently the doctor had
not quite abandoned his notion of Hux as an FBI agent; it was there
to be revived when it suited him. "No," answered Hux, "I've been
busy tyin' up loose ends, you might say, and gettin' ready for the
next big move."
    "I apologize, Brother Black. You must forgive an old fella's impulse
to tease a young visitor. The truth is, I have very little idea what an
evangelist does when he's not preachin' or baptizin' or something
like that."
    "The same thing everyone else does."
    A silence fell upon them after that, a peaceful silence during

which the doctor sipped his drink, occasionally nodding as if in reply to some inaudible suggestion of his own, his watery blue eyes never shifting from his guest. Though conscious that the silence—and the doctor's scrutiny—would become awkward if continued beyond a certain point, Hux was relieved that he could play Ainsley Black in a lazy, offhand manner that did not involve him too deeply. He had not succeeded in shaking the feeling that he was being watched by Brother Thurlow—and he felt too that the preacher could somehow *get at* him through Ainsley Black. If he could only maintain a detachment from the role and carry it off with just enough attention to satisfy the doctor, then he ought to be able, he told himself, to get through the evening without serious danger. It was for this reason, too, that he had declined—or delayed accepting—a drink. Whiskey too often led to involvement.

How strange that he should be sitting here, he thought—sitting in this room of heavy furniture and worn rugs with the murderer of Clark. . . .

He wished that he could tell Anne about it. But lacking the courage to reveal the truth of the secret agenda to her, he had entangled himself in lies. Stupid, stupid! He longed to be open with Anne, to bind her to him as an ally, to tell her everything—even about his experience with Brother Thurlow. Would she laugh in his face? She must think he was pretty crazy already, after the way he had behaved on their last day, acting like a sick adolescent, coming in his pants. . . . How much had she noticed?

"You're lookin' mighty dreamy and thoughtful," said Claiborne Herne. "In the old days, when any of my boys looked that way, I used to tease them about havin' dirty thoughts about some girl. That always got their goat. They would stammer, turn red as a beet, indignantly deny everything—my goodness, what a fuss they used to make!"

The doctor chuckled, and Hux felt himself beginning to redden. He saw merriment glittering in the faded eyes, and hated the doctor more purely than he had ever done before.

"You're not a married man, are you, Brother Black?"

"No," answered Hux shortly, omitting the usual "sir."

"That's what I figured. Were you ever married?"

At the point of exploding in the doctor's face—and then storming out of the house—Hux hesitated, telling himself that, for Miss Isabelle's sake, he had to finish out the evening. He was tempted to answer "yes," but he had a hunch that to do so would involve him in a whole new script which he would have to improvise—a script that would lead him deeper into the part of Ainsley Black. So he said, "No, I never was."

"Just as well." Again the doctor's eyes glinted mischief. "I don't suppose it's fitting," he drawled, "to ask an earnest young preacher how he takes care of his animal needs. Perhaps you don't have any. Maybe you're pure as the driven snow, keepin' yourself that way for the sweet young thing you'll marry someday. Are you by any chance a virgin, Brother Black—a thirty-year-old virgin?"

Instead of laughing outright, Hux assumed the offended dignity of Ainsley Black. "Doctor, I don't consider that a proper question. You got no business askin' me about matters that are strictly between me and my Lord." It occurred to him that Dr. Herne must have treated the boys in his club this way—prying into their sex lives as well as teasing them about girls; but they probably would have been in no position to object. Hux got up and went over to the drink tray.

"I apologize," said Dr. Herne as Hux was pouring his drink. "You're absolutely right. Your sex life is none of my business." He then waited until Hux had returned to his chair, smiled, and said, "Did you know that I was once married? I was briefly married to a young woman, a hospital nurse, who turned out to be a whore." He watched narrowly for Hux's reaction and, receiving none, continued. "It turned out she was sleepin' with one of my colleagues, a married man, both before and after she married me. I have never remarried. Once was enough—I never had the slightest desire to repeat the experiment. It was the most wretched time of my life—my young life, that is—but I reckon you could say I learned my lesson once and for all about women. They may not all be whores, but they are naturally deceitful in the way no man or boy could ever be. Even my own dear sister, God bless her, is as deceitful as they come. Full of little subterfuges. They're mostly harmless, thank the Lord, but they're part of her nature just the same. Deeply ingrained. Nobody could call Isabelle a whore, but she's one hundred percent female."

"I think your sister is one of the loveliest people I ever met! You should be ashamed to mention her in such a context," said Hux in a ringing voice that did not sound like Ainsley Black.

"You speak like a chivalrous gentleman of the old school, Brother Black. But you don't know what she's capable of." Dr. Herne rapidly finished off the rest of his drink and immediately had a coughing fit. When he had recovered somewhat, his color having deepened to a dark, purplish red, he held out his glass and said, gasping for breath, "Would you mind? My legs are giving me trouble tonight." And when Hux got up and took the glass, the doctor gave him exact instructions: fill the glass with ice cubes and then pour over them two-and-one-half ounces of bourbon.

"I don't mind tellin' you," resumed the doctor after he had tasted his drink and nodded approval, "that *my* animal needs were powerful. But I kept them under control. You might say that I kept in strict training over the years. I allowed myself one overnight visit to Memphis every month. That was it. And there I consorted with women who were not only whores but never pretended to be anything else. That way I kept out of entanglements. Am I shocking you, Brother Black?"

"No, sir. In my line of work very little shocks me. Am I to understand, sir, that you take pride in this particular compact with the Devil?" This was an Ainsley question, one that had slipped out before Hux could think better of it.

Claiborne Herne gave an exultant "Ha!" and bared his yellowed teeth. "So I have shocked you after all. I suppose I meant to. But I take great pride in the discipline I was able to impose on my needs in those days. And I like to think I was able to help the youngsters in the Fellowship learn the value of self-discipline too. Nowadays"—he shook his head—"the young have no morals, no discipline, nothing. Present company excepted, Brother Black. And of course you're not *that* young, are you?" he added with his familiar cadaverous grin.

There was a pause. Hux held his glass between his knees. It was empty; he had drunk it much too fast—like lemonade on a hot day—and he felt a little dizzy. Minutes passed, nothing was said. Then the doctor slowly got to his feet. "I must excuse myself," he said. "By all means help yourself to another drink." And he walked unsteadily into his bedroom, closing the door behind him. Hux got up and went to the drink tray. Telling himself to take it easy, he poured a weak drink and stood with it by the table. Though the night was only moderately humid, Hux's shirt was soaked. The faint breeze coming in through the windows made him shiver. He crossed the room, intending to close them, but opened them wide instead. A twittering of night sounds wafted in with the breeze. Wishing that Miss Isabelle would return, he looked at his watch and saw that no more than an hour had passed.

As Dr. Herne came back into the living room, he lurched into the round parlor table, causing a framed photograph near the edge to fall to the floor and the fringed lamp to totter but not fall. Steadying himself, Dr. Herne pushed on single-mindedly toward his chair and his drink while Hux rushed over to deal with the photograph. The glass was cracked but not shattered. "Too bad," he murmured, placing the photograph back on the table. "The glass is cracked." Dr. Herne muttered something inaudible while Hux continued to gaze into the face of the young man in the photograph, a young man with a solemn expression, thin lips, and pale eyes that looked as if they had been lensed with a brittle transparency of glass. He was wearing a high-collared military tunic with a great many brass buttons.

"My father," croaked Dr. Herne from his chair. "It was taken at the time of the Spanish-American War."

"He looks mighty serious," said Hux, turning away from the table.

"What you call serious is what I'd call determined. We were talkin' about self-discipline—well, Papa had more of it than any man I've ever known. He could endure any amount of pain. I'm sure he never cried in his life after the age of five—not even when my mother died. I could talk for hours about Papa."

Hux returned to his chair and sat brooding over his weak drink. He was thinking of his own father, who was hardly the military type. Self-discipline? Well, he supposed it took a certain amount of self-discipline for a man with a hangover to drag himself to work every morning for nearly thirty years, to a bookkeeping job that he hated—and that paid hardly more than a foreman's wages at the cotton mill. . . .

"Let me tell you a story that illustrates Papa's character. Would you like to hear it?"

"I sure would. Your papa sounds like a mighty fine man." Fathers—fathers and sons . . . Hux was not sure he wanted to hear the story, but what was he to say? He had let Ainsley Black answer for him.

The two men faced each other across the patch of worn Brussels carpet that separated their chairs. Dr. Herne took his time, sipping, resting his glass on the chair arm, taking it up again, sipping. Hux got the impression that the doctor, having decided on a story, was almost reluctant to begin it.

"So, Reverend, you'd like to hear about my father, would you?"

Hux nodded, just as if he had first suggested the story.

"Well, like I said, Papa was a great believer in discipline. Self-discipline first of all. And after that he expected respect and obedience from his children—which he got—and responsibility on the part of those who worked for him. Which he also got. Even from the Nigras. Of course he couldn't expect *too* much responsibility from them—he realized they were like children—but he made damn sure he had their respect, and he got about as much work out of them as a reasonable man could hope for. He never cheated them, but there was a

179

limit to the amount of foolishness he was prepared to put up with."
The doctor's face had grown increasingly stern, as if he were imbib-
ing his father's spirit along with the whiskey.

"Well, when I was about twelve, I went with Papa to a little country store over near Beulah—near the land we still have over there. I
forget what it was he wanted, but anyway, here was this drunk nigger sitting on the porch steps with his head in his hands, blockin' the
way. Papa asked him to move, and the nigger just looked up with
bloodshot eyes and mumbled something. You couldn't exactly tell
what he was sayin', but it was clearly impudent. I saw Papa's lips go
kind of white—that was always a bad sign—but he controlled himself and asked the man again to move. The nigger just sat there,
lookin' up and mumblin'."

He paused and finished off his drink, his face concentrated fiercely
on Hux, who was already sure that he did not want to hear what was
coming.

"Without another word Papa whacked him as hard as he could on
the side of the head with his cane. I'll never forget the *swish* and then
the *crack* which that cane made." The doctor dropped his gaze and
shook his head, smiling slightly. Again he shook his head.

Hux let out his breath.

"The man keeled right over and I was sure Papa had killed him.
But Papa didn't wait to find out. He just went right into the store,
dragging me with him by the arm. He bought whatever it was he
needed and walked right out again and down the steps without
lookin' either to the right or the left. Of course I couldn't help lookin'.
I saw the nigger stretched out in the dust to the side of the porch and
a couple of other niggers leanin' over him. One of 'em was holdin' a
rag with a lot of blood on it. There was a pool of blood in the dust.
That blood made a stronger impression on me than any blood I ever
saw during all my years at the hospital. I never did find out what
happened to the man. . . . I'm fairly sure he wasn't killed, or I'd have
heard about it.

"Papa didn't say a word and he never mentioned the incident afterward. And I knew better than to ask questions. You see, Papa was
teachin' me a wordless lesson. And I absorbed it."

The coil of outrage that had been tightening in Hux now snapped
free, propelling him to his feet. The story had revived in him instantly that special Southern shame which had overwhelmed him again
and again during the late fifties and early sixties as each new report
of racial atrocity came his way. The self-congratulatory tone with
which Dr. Herne had finished was almost the hardest thing to bear.

"That's a terrible story, it makes me sick. My God—"

"Hold on, Brother Black, hold your horses." The doctor's expression was gleeful. "I believe you *are* shocked this time. But hold your horses. I haven't finished yet."

"You're right, I am shocked. That's an ugly story, doctor, and you don't even realize how disgusting it is."

"Be quiet!" shouted the doctor. "I haven't finished what I intend to say. I didn't think you revivalists got so worked up about the Nigra question. I thought you fellas mostly thought the Bible was right about the place of the Sons of Ham in the general order of things. You sound more like a goddamn Northern liberal to me," he said, screwing up his features as if he could not tolerate the smell of such a specimen. "I'll have you know, Brother Black, that I have always been a friend to the Nigra race and so was my father. They knew where they stood with us. We loved 'um, the good ones, and we protected them, got them out of scrapes, helped 'em where we could. But by God, let one of 'em—"

"Dr. Herne, I'm not going to argue with you—"

"Goddamn right, you're not!" Claiborne Herne pounded his fist on the arm of his chair, causing his whiskey glass and ashtray on the other arm to jump and nearly fall. "It's people like you who have caused all the trouble. You happen to be Southern, but you're just as bad as all those Yankees who come down here and fill their black heads with every kind of ridiculous notion under the sun. *You* think they can be educated, but goddamn it, I've lived with 'em longer and closer than you have, Brother Black, and I know from painful experience that a half-educated nigger is just about the most miserable— *and* the most dangerous—human bein' on the face of this earth."

Standing now in front of the mantel, Hux raised one hand, as if to block the old man's rage, which was now leaping like a fire in the branches of a dead pine tree. Miss Isabelle's words came rasping to his ear: *It seems like a demon rises up in him.* . . .

"You're about to interrupt me!" screamed the doctor. "Don't you dare interrupt me!"

Helplessly, Hux lowered his hand and shrugged. Again he was tempted to leave the house.

"You claim to be a good Christian," continued the doctor with a sly narrowing of his eyes, "a good Baptist preacher leadin' sick souls to salvation, but *I* know who's payin' your bills and it sure as hell ain't the Baptist church—"

"Dr. Herne—"

"Shut up! Now listen to me. I've experienced things at the hands of the colored race—men and women alike—that you haven't the remotest idea of in the world, and yet you have the gall to come into my house and drink my whiskey and tell me the Nigra vote is better than mine and any fat nigger whore has a better right to sit in our family pew at church than my own sister!"

At the word "sister" Dr. Herne began to cough so violently that his white hair fell over his forehead and his eyes began to stream. Suddenly he looked terrified, like a child choking on a fragment of bone, and Hux, strangely moved, rushed over to the chair and caught the doctor by the shoulders. As the fit subsided and Claiborne Herne raised his bleared eyes to Hux's face, Hux was stricken by pity so strong that it was like a tearing pain. The man's life lay before him— scorched, rubble-strewn, devastated. . . . Out of the pity came words, an upwelling of words that seemed unwilled and beyond his control. As he clung to the bony shoulders, gently rocking the old man back and forth in his chair, Hux heard himself say, "This hate is all wrong, Dr. Herne, all wrong. There's too much hate, so much hate. What we need is to give love a chance, to give it just the smallest opening." Aware that the doctor, still gasping for breath, was looking up at him in wonder, Hux said, "I'm not going to preach to you—I'll keep my promise—I'll only say this one thing—"

What was it? What was it he was going to say? Hux closed his eyes against the doctor's look, knowing that he had to go on, that he must not break the current which he felt flowing through his own arms and hands into the knobby shoulders of the old man. And after a moment the words came again, a kind of chant, a singsong of words coming from old sermons heard in his childhood, from old hymns sung. And Hux no longer listened to himself but let the words come, let them form in his throat and on his tongue and go outward, unchecked. The words flew outward as if summoned by an unseen conductor standing behind the doctor's chair. "Open your heart," he was saying. "Let love come into your heart. Let love replace all that hatred that has made your heart a barren place where nothing grows. Love that will not let you go. Hide yourself in it! That love is the rock of ages, cleft for thee. . . . Drink the precious waters, let the barren places in your heart turn green, let love come in!"

A name was forming on Hux's lips, a name that he had not yet voiced though he could feel its power working through every word that he had spoken. The name stuck, like a rock that could not be dislodged and sent forward on the torrent. At that level of his mind from which he could still observe, as from a great distance, what was happening to him, Hux was afraid of the name—afraid of what it might do to him once it passed his lips. But the pressure building up behind it was irresistible, and he let it come.

"Jesus," he murmured, "Jesus . . ."

Then Hux felt sharp, bony fingers gripping his wrist like a wrench, and he opened his eyes and said, loudly and clearly, "You must open your heart to Jesus Christ, your Lord and Redeemer."

Dr. Herne was still looking up at him, his mouth slightly open, flecks of spittle in the corners. His expression was bewildered, the look of a raptly listening, bewildered child, but it was not angry or scornful. Though the grip on Hux's wrist was strong, even painful, it did not seem intended as a protest or a command to stop the torrent of words—though the torrent had stopped; rather, it was the beseeching hold of a cripple whose legs had suddenly given way and who needed to be helped to his feet. The doctor was clearly very drunk.

The two men stared at each other for a moment. Quietness fell. Claiborne Herne let go of Hux's wrist, and Hux drew back. Then he said, in a voice vibrant with the intonations of Brother Thurlow, "There is no sin so black, no deed so foul—not even the shedding of an innocent man's life blood—that it cannot be expunged and wiped clean by the redeeming blood of the crucified Jesus."

Dr. Herne mumbled something which Hux did not catch, for his attention was distracted by a persistent ringing and banging from the direction of the kitchen. Dr. Herne's eyes cleared for an instant, and he raised his head, cocking it to one side. "The back door," he muttered, "the back door. Then, with an agility that seemed to belie his drunkenness, he propped himself against the chair arm and got to his feet. "Shtay here," he commanded in a slurred but unexpectedly powerful voice as he went lurching out of the room.

Chapter Twenty-six

Dr. Claiborne's telephone call that afternoon had infuriated Rooney by canceling, without adequate explanation, the after-dark visit that had been arranged—a visit that would take place after Miss Isabelle had gone to her bedroom and could not hear any comings-and-goings by way of the kitchen. Alerted that something was up, something possibly serious in its consequences for him, Rooney had decided to come anyway—without Vicky—and for the forty-five minutes before he began his ringing and knocking at the back door, he had been squatting among the shrubs outside the living-room windows, trying to make sense out of what was going on between Dr. Claiborne and the man he addressed as "Reverend." To his amazement, Rooney realized that this preacher, whom he had seen from his car last Sunday, was the prowler that he had spotted two weeks ago—for the preacher tonight was wearing the dark red sport shirt that the prowler had worn then. But eavesdropping had been difficult, for the Mississippi night was loud with chirpings, hummings, peepings, croakings, and scrapings, as well as with the thumpings of moths and large flying beetles against the window screens; then the preacher—looking so unlike a preacher—had come over to the windows and opened them wide while Rooney crouched in black shadow. After that he could hear everything, and his eavesdropping had been interrupted only once by the headlights of a car coming down Granada, which had sent him sprinting around the corner of the house; the car had turned out not to be Miss Isabelle's, which he had been expecting at any moment.

Rooney pounded again on the door, making the glass panes rattle. Then he pressed his thumb on the doorbell and held it there. He was quivering with rage—not so much at Dr. Claiborne for his story about his father and the drunk nigger (he had heard that before, several times) as at the preacher-prowler, whom he had heard the doctor call Brother Black. Though he hated preachers, Rooney had an almost superstitious notion of what they could do once they got their hooks in someone they wanted to convert. Miss Isabelle, he was sure,

had found this particular preacher and set him to work on her brother. It did not at all suit his plans to have Dr. Claiborne get religion.
For a while it looked as though the old man were getting the best of
his visitor, and he had silently cheered him on, willing to tolerate
even the references to half-educated niggers ("That's me!") and
whores for the sake of the outrage they produced in Brother Black.
But when the preacher caught Dr. Claiborne by the shoulders and
began to shake him while talking about love and when the doctor
looked up at Brother Black at the name of Jesus and caught him by
the wrist, Rooney knew that what he feared the most was about to
happen: in another moment the preacher would have the old man on
his knees, hugging the preacher's legs and crying like a baby. It was
then that Rooney had raced to the kitchen door, determined to raise
as much hell as he could, even at the risk of arousing the neighbors
down the street.

After what seemed to Rooney an interminable wait, the kitchen
light was finally switched on and Dr. Claiborne came unsteadily into
the room, supporting himself first on one of the counters and then
on the kitchen table. Slowly the doctor made his way to the door and
pulled it open.

"Go 'way," he said thickly. "I ordered you not to come. Now go
'way."

Rooney pushed past the doctor into the kitchen, where he stood
with the overhead light falling directly upon his huge turban of
steel-wool hair. Wide-shouldered, his arms akimbo, Rooney was like
a lightweight boxer in training, his hips so slim beneath his jeans
that he could almost have encircled them with his big hands; the
body-fitting yellow T-shirt which he was wearing pinched his biceps, which bulged where the short sleeves ended. His white sneakers were wet, stained with grass and mud. In a light, drawling voice,
he said, "Your half-educated nigger goin' to pay you a little visit.
Saw Miss Isabelle's car wasn't in the drive, so I jus' thought I'd drop
by to see how you was. I been kind of worried. You sound like you
was sick or somethin' when you telephone."

"I told you I was expecting a visitor"—the doctor slurred the word
into "vizhta." "Now you get the hell out of here. I don't want you
hangin' around."

"How you like your new baby-sitter? Tha's my old job. Ain't my
service good enough?"

"Stop talkin' like an illiterate. And leave this kitchen. You've already made enough noise to wake up the whole goddamn neighbor-

hood. I expect somebody's already called the police."

"Vicky send you her love. Say she got a little surprise for you next time. Somethin' new—and real fancy."

"Out!" screamed the doctor, his face dark with blood. "Out! If you don't leave, I'll—I'll horsewhip you, I'll kill you!" He swayed in front of Rooney, both hands slightly raised as if he intended to push him out the back door.

Rooney gave a high, cackling laugh and shook his head. "You real scary, Dr. Claib'n, you scare me half to death talkin' 'bout horsewhippin' and stuff like that. I scared to death of your whip. But I ain't got time to fool around right now. You jus' go back and tell your preacher–baby-sitter he's off duty as of right now. All that stuff 'bout love and Jesus—why you sit there listenin' to that kind of baby talk? You got more sense than that, drunk as you is." Again Rooney cackled, his unblemished, unscarred face now close to the doctor's. "Tell him he can leave quietly by the front door while Mr. Half-educated Nigger sneak in the back. You go on, now." And Rooney gave the doctor a slight push with both hands that sent him staggering backward to the counter, which he then leaned against, resting both elbows on the surface, his face twisted and his tongue working as if to dislodge a food particle caught in his teeth.

"What's going on here?" demanded a ringing voice from the door leading to the hall.

Rooney jumped when he heard the voice and made a half turn, his hand automatically going to the jeans pocket where he kept a switchblade knife. The preacher was facing him, squared off, his hands held like a wrestler's.

"If you know what's good for you, you'll get out of this house *fast*," said the preacher, his face exalted, his eyes level and unswerving. "And I mean fast!"

Rooney cocked his head and grinned at Brother Black, who was trying to intimidate him with that white man's blue-eyed glare of command. *Shit*, he thought, slipping his fingers into his pocket and halfway pulling out his knife. *Not now, not now. Too big a hassle—he'd have to kill them both. . . .* Instead, he decided to clown. "Yas suh, yas suh," he said, turning his pale palms outward. "Yas suh, I leavin'. This half-educated nigger's leavin' right now." Then he bent his knees outward, slapped his palms loudly against his thighs, and gave a wild, whooping laugh. Still laughing, he turned and performed a bent-kneed, shuffling dance to the kitchen door. "You take good care of Dr. Claib'n now, you heah? I mighty glad he in such good hands. Yas suh!" With another whoop, he went out, letting the screen door slam behind him. As he reached the corner of the house, Rooney saw the light by the kitchen door go on. Brother Black stepped outside. "Don't you worry none," called Rooney. "I leavin' right now." And he waved.

The preacher went back into the house and switched off the outside light. But Rooney did not leave. Instead, after walking noisily down the gravel drive to Granada Street, he darted back to his station at the living-room windows and crouched low.

Chapter Twenty-seven

Dr. Herne had collapsed into a kitchen chair, his head lolling forward, an idiot smile on his lips. "Who is that fellow?" asked Hux, coming toward him, too flushed with command, too exultant, to notice at once the doctor's condition. "Should I call the police?"

Slowly, with a sideways motion, the doctor raised his head and tried to steady it. "That nigger?" he muttered, frowning in his effort to fix upon Hux's question.

"Whoever he is, he looks mean as a snake. Does he come around here often?"

"Rooney?" Still frowning in his befuddled way, Dr. Herne said, very slowly, "Rooney's been . . . comin' . . . 'round for—for years." He nodded emphatically. "Old acquaintance. Gets drunk, comes 'round . . . lookin' for a handout."

"He didn't look drunk to me. Isn't he the same fella with the big white car? Your sister saw him last Sunday and got very upset."

Dr. Herne shrugged, then let his head drop and stared at the blotched, ruddy skin of his hands resting upon the spotless white of his neatly creased trousers. His white hair sparkled under the kitchen light. Again hunching his shoulders, he mumbled something that Hux could not catch.

"What did you say?"

"Said, how should I know?" He raised his eyes, came into sharp focus, and said, "Isabelle's a fool. Takes fright if a month-old rabbit looks at her sideways. Now help me to my room."

At last Hux realized that the doctor could not even stand without assistance. Catching him under the armpits, Hux lifted him out of the chair and, like a hospital attendant, helped him to the door of his bedroom, which opened directly into the kitchen. There Dr. Herne straightened himself and with a summoning of tattered dignity said, "I 'pologize—must 'pologize leavin' you here like this. I can get myself to bed. Izhabelle—*Isabelle*—ought to be here soon." Then, after opening the door, he suddenly caught Hux's wrist, as he had done before, and murmured, "Thank you. For helpin' me." He leaned and pulled his way into the bedroom and closed the door.

"God bless you, sir!" called Hux.

He did not have long to wait for Miss Isabelle, but still lifted high by his performance, he had little awareness of time. Sitting down in Dr. Herne's Morris chair in the living room, he closed his eyes and leaned his head back. The sense of power was still upon him, and it made him more than a little drunk. Full of wonder, he heard again the words that had come to him unbidden, that had sprung from his throat and tongue, words that had been transmitted, he was sure, to some hidden receptor in Dr. Herne; again he felt the old man's grip, saw the bewildered, yearning look in his eyes. . . .

The same mysterious infusion of power had enabled him to confront Rooney and drive him out. Hux had felt as fearless—and as thrilled—as some early saint facing a demon and ordering him to be gone. At the moment he was far too involved in both the role and the very being of Ainsley Black to draw back and try to analyze what had happened; he knew only that the full power had been conferred upon him *after* he had voiced the tabooed name of Jesus.

When a flash of headlights through the window signaled the arrival of Miss Isabelle, Hux rushed to the front door and flung it open. As she came into sight, he could hardly keep from running toward her across the grass and embracing her with both arms. But he waited, and she came to him, framed as he was in the lighted doorway, and clasped his right hand in both of hers. Together they went into the living room, while she poured out her gratitude to him for coming, for enabling her to go to the Pikes'. "There's something so wonderful about bein' with old friends again, even at a time of sorrow," she said. "I've missed my friends, Ainsley. I need to be with them more. Maybe—maybe—if Brother gets better, I won't have to stay with him *all* the time. And if that happens, I will never be able to thank you enough."

"*I'm* not the one you must thank, Miss Isabelle. I'm merely an agent, a messenger."

"You're an angel!" Sitting by his side on the Victorian settee, she again caught his hand and pressed it. Then, her face more solemn, she said, "How did things go here? Is Brother—?"

"He has gone to bed. He was very tired, and he'd—"

"I know. But earlier, was he—?"

"He was full of beans," said Hux with a grin. "A little cantankerous. But then his mood changed, he softened—and I think something I said reached him, got through to him. I sure hope it did."

Not seeming to hear, she said, "I was afraid that he might behave badly. I'm so glad that he didn't."

There was a pause. Then, looking straight at her, Hux said in a louder voice, "I think you ought to know that there was a little disturbance about half an hour ago. A black man—a man named Rooney—came round to the back door and acted kind of strange. I had to order him to leave."

Miss Isabelle sank back into her corner of the settee, her jaw and cheeks sagging. "I'm real sorry you had to deal with Rooney," she said. "It must have been unpleasant." Her voice was faint.

"It wasn't too bad, ma'am. He left when I told him to. But he had been usin' a real insolent tone with your brother. Who is this Rooney? I gather you all have known him a long time."

"His mother used to work for us," said Miss Isabelle with a bosomy sigh. "Used to do our laundry. We were always devoted to her. And Rooney was the most adorable little Nigra boy you ever saw. He didn't have a father. His father—they weren't married—was a nice young Nigra named Willie-Boy Combs who worked as a yard man for the Morgans. I think they might have gotten married if it hadn't been for the war. Anyway," she continued with another hefty sigh, "Willie-Boy got drafted and he was killed—out in the Pacific, I think. Rooney was just a baby at the time. He was always around the house with his mother, and Brother and I made sort of a pet out of him—he was so adorable, just the most precious-lookin' little thing! Later on, Brother helped send him to college, but you wouldn't know it now. He hasn't turned out at all well."

"Why does he keep comin' around?"

She answered evasively. "Oh, he's just a nuisance. Takes advantage of our old acquaintance. I believe Brother gives him a little money from time to time."

"Is he blackmailing the doctor?" asked Hux bluntly.

"Heavens, no. Nothing like that." Then, clearly determined to drop the subject, she said, "Did you . . . find an openin'"—she faltered over the words—"to bring up—well, to suggest to Brother where he might find help? Could you even introduce the idea of God without makin' him mad?"

"Oh, yes, ma'am!" said Hux eagerly. "Like I told you earlier—maybe you didn't hear—I think I got through to him with the message." The thought of it thrilled Hux, and again he felt a great surge of excitement, a sense of what he might do for the doctor, and he surrendered to it recklessly. "But I need another evenin' with your brother—the sooner the better. There's a spiritual ferment at work there, it's beginnin' to bubble. I spoke to your brother in the name of Jesus and something in him responded—that I'm sure of. But then

Rooney interrupted us, and after that the doctor—well, he was worn out and ready for bed. But if we could just have more time together . . . Could I maybe come over on Sunday?" he said, plunging ahead, unable to check himself despite the warning whisper that he was rushing things, that there might be something else he preferred to do on Sunday. . . . Had he made some engagement? Had he planned to be with Anne? But the offer had tumbled out—and of course it was accepted.

"Oh, yes!" cried Miss Isabelle, clapping her hands. "Oh, please come, come have Sunday dinner with us. Stay as long as you can!"

"Perhaps I could stay with him while you go to church," said Hux, who no longer heard even the whisper of a warning. He felt only a great desire to be with the doctor again, to get his hands on him. . . . What if he could bring him to his knees! "I will pray to the Lord to prepare the way," he said, rising from the settee and starting toward the hall, "to make the rough places smooth."

Miss Isabelle followed him into the hall. "Yes," she said, "that would be a comfort for me, a relief. Brother's seemed so much better—on the whole—since you came into our lives, but I still worry about leavin' him alone, especially on Sunday mornin's. Then you could stay on for dinner and maybe for supper too, if we can persuade you. Spend the whole day! What a treat that would be for us." At the front door she rested one hand on his shoulder, stood on tiptoes, and timidly kissed Hux on the cheek. "How I wished I could tell the Pikes about our dear new friend, Ainsley Black. But I didn't. I thought maybe you wanted to continue workin' quietly for a while—known only to us."

"You were right, Miss Isabelle. I work best as a secret agent. And now I must go. Goodnight, and God bless you. May He bestow His peace upon this house." He raised his right hand, preacherlike, and then let it drop to his side.

"Amen," said Miss Isabelle, bowing her head.

"Pray for me, Miss Isabelle," said Hux fervently. "Pray for me. I need your prayers too."

"What did you say?" Looking startled, she strained to hear.

"I'm askin' you to pray for me. I need your prayers."

"Yes," she replied, at first uncertainly. "Yes. Of course I will!"

Still in the grip of his performance, Hux drove back to Oxford through a night suffused with the milky gray light shed by an almost full moon riding behind a thin covering of barred clouds. His mood was still too exalted, his sense of quivering, unused power too strong, for him to draw back from his role. He wanted nothing less than—in the voice and person of Ainsley Black—to bring Claiborne Herne to awareness and repentance, to force the pitiful, hateful old man onto his knees before God. He had at the moment no doubt of his capacity to open Claiborne Herne's eyes to the state of his own soul and to open his heart to the forgiveness and divine comfort promised to all who believe. . . .

Yet Hux did not, in any real sense, believe the words he had spoken. They had come to him independently of belief, and their effect upon him—and presumably upon Dr. Herne—had nothing to do with belief. It was as if the name *Jesus*—the mere syllables—could work a spell upon both him and his listener that bore no relation to all the doctrines in which Hux had been reared and which he had discarded, like the outworn clothes of his childhood, nearly twenty years before. It seemed to him that he could, if he wished, draw upon the names of the doctrines too—Incarnation, Redemption, Grace, the Holy Trinity—and upon all the events associated with them—the miracles, the Crucifixion, Resurrection, and the Ascension; he was like a man who had uncovered an enormous hoard of buried words and symbols with which he could perform miracles, cast out devils, and bring souls to God.

This discrepancy between felt power and actual belief did not bother Hux or even strike him as odd so long as his exaltation lasted. But before he reached Oxford, it began to subside, and the first premonitions of a spiritual hangover manifested themselves in the form of an uneasiness, a vague anxiety over the degree to which he had surrendered control. The recollection of what he had said—and the voice in which he had spoken—now made him tremble slightly, as if he had gone too far. . . . Then fatigue set in, and he became so sleepy that his eyes watered and stung; the headlights of other cars now hurt his eyes, particularly the lights of a car reflected in his rear-view mirror. The inspiration that had filled him left him feeling muddy and deficient as it drained away, taking with it even more vital energy than it had brought.

At the motel he could barely pull himself up the outside stairs to his room. He went immediately to bed. Just before sleep overwhelmed him, Hux saw the face that had not materialized in Alhambra, though he had dreaded it in advance. Thurlow's face—heavy and sullen—did not frighten him into wakefulness; now drifting faster toward sleep, Hux sensed that it had been there all along, concealed like the moon behind thin clouds.

Chapter Twenty-eight

The lunch meeting scheduled at Mississippi State never took place. Hux awoke from a night of lurid dreams of which he could remember little except the dizzying mood swings—from fear and revulsion to moments of floating euphoria. While taking a shower he retrieved one image: of himself crawling through a cobwebby tunnel, knife in hand, under orders to kill. . . . But the object of his murderous impulse had disappeared. He was now in the full grip of the reaction that had set in last night. All traces of his exaltation had vanished, and he remembered with shame the torrent of words, the illusions of power, the desire to play God with the bruised and degraded psyche of Claiborne Herne. The spiritual hangover manifested itself physically in a headache and a cruddy tongue—symptoms that did not bode well for a full day of academic conferences in Starkville. He had not even the excuse of having drunk too much.

In the dining room of the motel his waitress, Jackie Sue, said, while pouring coffee, "You look like you had yourself a fine ol' time last night. Right?"

"I wish I had."

She paid no attention to his reply, and for the next few minutes Hux had to listen to her account of the drinking exploits of her stepfather, who worked in a sawmill over near Laurel. While she went to get his eggs, he sat motionless, staring out the window, which was streaked with the rain of an early-morning squall. By the time he set out with his briefcase for his car, the worst of the gusty storm had passed, leaving in its wake a steady downward needling of rain and broad puddles of oily water in the parking lot. As he approached his car, Hux sensed an oddness about it that he could not at first identify. The car seemed lower, squatter, than the similar models parked on either side. Then he saw that all four tires were flat—and not only flat but slashed. With water streaming from his hair, he gazed for more than a minute at the atrocity, telling himself that he had made a mistake, that this car could not possibly be the one he had rented. At last he noticed a piece of soggy lined paper under the left windshield wiper. Someone had written him a note, but the blue ink had run into an indecipherable smear. Though the paper disintegrated when Hux tried to draw it from under the wiper, he stood for some time in the rain trying to make out a message from the fragments. There seemed to be an *r* and an *e* in what had been the upper left-hand corner, but he could not be sure. Nothing made sense—neither the tires nor the note.

Hux continued to stand motionless beside the car, his hands dangling, one scrap of soaked paper still between his fingers. The rain was beginning to darken and penetrate the shoulders of his tan poplin raincoat; tiny rivulets ran from his hair across his forehead and face and down the back of his neck. Then, trembling with that special paranoiac desperation that men feel when their cars—even rented cars—have been savaged, Hux splashed through the puddles to the motel office to report the outrage and to call a garage. Next he placed a call to the officials of Mississippi State, alerting them that he would be late—possibly very late—for lunch.

It was not until Hux was on the highway, after the long delay spent in getting new tires, that Rooney Lee occurred to him as a possible culprit. He had considered other possibilities: aimless vandalism, a sneak attack by some motel employee whom he had unconsciously offended, an act of revenge based upon mistaken identity. . . . But nothing had seemed plausible until the mocking image of Rooney, with his wild afro and his boxer's frame, leapt before him, a figure from one of last night's nightmares that made Hux's mouth go dry. Rooney, he concluded, had trailed him back to Oxford—now Hux recalled the headlights in his rear-view mirror—and had slashed the tires as . . . as what? A punishment? Rooney certainly had reason to be angry with him over the confrontation in the kitchen—but to go to such lengths! A warning? But why? Obviously, Rooney was involved with the Hernes in a way that Hux could not fathom; the notion of blackmail again came to him, along with the memory of Miss Isabelle's evasiveness. Did Rooney see Hux as a threat to some scheme of his? There had been something very odd about the scene between Dr. Herne and Rooney in the kitchen, something suggesting a powerful bond or dependency beneath all the anger displayed on both sides. Hux wondered if Rooney could be a drug pusher—*that* might account for the flashy white car. Could Dr. Herne be a drug addict as well as a drinker? Hux then realized that he himself was seriously afraid of the black man and that his fear was suffused with an impression of the uncanny, an impression made stronger by his inability to assign a motive for either a warning or a punishment. Moreover, Hux was puzzled by a nagging sense of familiarity: Rooney, for all his menacing aspect, reminded him of someone else he had known or met—whether recently or in the far past he could not decide.

Repeatedly Hux told himself that he had very little to go on, that there was really no substantial reason to identify Rooney as the slasher. Yet the idea persisted—and with it the dread. Hux, who had always regarded himself as neither a dare-devil nor a craven when it came to physical courage, was surprised at the degree of his fear. Last night he had not been afraid of the knife Rooney had been fingering; today he saw it as poised to strike the moment he relaxed his guard. If a warning had been intended, it had its effect. Coming on top of the revulsion that had already set in, the tire slashing filled him with the most profound reluctance ever to set foot in Alhambra again. But he had already committed himself for Sunday. Could he invent an excuse or simply break his word? Again, it was the look on Miss Isabelle's face that rebuked his cowardice. . . . In his dilemma, Hux, without being aware of it, began repeating under his breath the name of Jesus.

He heard a sudden flapping, knocking sound from the motor. Pulling to the side of the highway, Hux raised the hood and found what he had expected—a broken fan belt. In his panic he imagined that Rooney was responsible—could there be other sabotage as well? But these possibilities aside, there was the immediate problem of what to do about the car on a deserted stretch of the highway that could well be twenty miles from the nearest garage or filling station. Hux flagged down the first pickup truck that came along.

Back in Oxford in the early afternoon—the Starkville appointments postponed until Monday—Hux telephoned Anne at the library and asked her to have dinner with him. He had to see her tonight—he couldn't wait until tomorrow. And when she hesitated, he felt another rush of dread at the prospect of being left alone all evening with his proliferating fantasies. . . .

"Do you really want to see me tonight *and* tomorrow night too?" Hux swore that he did. At last Anne agreed, provided the twelve-year-old in the next apartment was permitted to baby-sit; if not, she would telephone Hux, who could then pick up a steak and a bottle of wine to have at Anne's apartment.

"One more thing," said Anne. "Will you promise to leave Clark and all his relics behind at the motel? I don't want him sittin' between us at supper."

Hux laughed uneasily. "I promise." But he had in fact been thinking of Clark almost continuously ever since the pickup truck, driven by a slouch-hatted, fat-bellied, nigger-hating farmer, had stopped for him on the highway.

195

Chapter Twenty-nine

At Anne's suggestion they went to a steakhouse called Rosie's on the outskirts of Oxford. Red-carpeted, with red tablecloths, red napkins, and red-shaded lamps, the restaurant glowed with the murky crimson of an electric fire in a darkened room. "I know it looks depressin'," said Anne as they were being led to a table, "but they do have the best steaks and shrimps anywhere around Oxford. And in a little while there'll be a country-and-western group in red silk shirts to keep us entertained."

"Isn't the New South wonderful?" said Hux, squeezing her arm. "What it's lost in bigotry it's gained in graciousness." And with that he laughed so loudly that several diners turned around to stare. He was in a nervously elated mood, as if he had been granted a few hours' respite—a shore leave—from the turbulent waves by which he had been buffeted for days on end. From the huge red satin-textured menu, which was hard to read in the ruby light, Hux ordered an extravagant dinner for the two of them, insisting on the most expensive filets mignons and a bottle of Pomerol (the only French wine on the list) that was absurdly overpriced.

"You must have had a good day," said Anne, who herself looked somewhat tired, with brownish circles under her eyes that had turned violet in the weird light.

"On the contrary, it was a rotten day. One of the worst I've ever had. The only good part of it is right now." Hux then told her about the slashed tires and the fan belt and drew what nourishment he could from her outraged, puzzled, and sympathetic response. Again he was powerfully tempted to open himself to her, to tell her all about the secret agenda, about the Hernes and Ainsley Black, about Brother Thurlow and Rooney. He came very close to doing so, and when he checked the impulse, he felt ashamed of his very fear of being shamed.

"You're the *strangest* man," said Anne, reaching over and, as if absent-mindedly, resting her fingers lightly on the top of his hand. "I don't know you at all. You keep most of yourself hidden under water, and what shows above water doesn't make sense to me."

"What do you mean?" demanded Hux, feeling simultaneously hurt and guilty as charged. She was reading his mind again!

"For one thing, you're a father, and except for that first night at the Bensons', I've hardly heard you mention your son. Most parents I know are always talkin' about their children. I bore people to death talkin' about Prue."

"I love Tony very much," said Hux defensively. "But I know I'm not the world's greatest father. I don't seem to have the natural aptitude. I thought I had it for a while, but I guess I was mistaken," he concluded sadly. The evening was taking a serious turn that he did not like.

"And your ex-wife? What about her? I don't think you've ever told me her name. I know it only from Linda Helmholtz's letter."

"What is this? Why are you poking around at me like this?"

"Don't get mad." Then, more gently, Annie said, "It's because I like you. And you interest me—in a perverse kind of way." She grinned. "I guess I want to know you better."

The waitress arrived with their drinks, and when she had gone, Hux said, "I don't know myself these days. So there's no way I can make myself clear to someone else. Perhaps after I leave Mississippi, things will come together more, become a little clearer." *But they haven't come together for years,* he thought.

"Was it a mistake to come here?"

"I don't know. I don't know." Hux took a long swallow from his bourbon-on-the-rocks, wiped his mouth with his ketchup-colored napkin, and said recklessly, "I lied to you. I've been going over to Alhambra to see Claiborne Herne and his sister. I was there last night and I—I began—I found myself preaching to him. About Jesus ...And about—"

"*Preaching* to him?"

Hux thought he saw in Anne's face the unmistakable reflection of his insanity. *I've lost her,* he inwardly wailed, drawing in his breath with a sobbing sound. "Yes," he continued, determined to push ahead, damning all consequences, "yes, I started preaching to him. It's a long story. I'm not sure ... Do you remember the other night when I was asking you about religion?" Again he caught his breath. "Something very strange has been happening to me. I don't understand it at all. Anyway, I'd better start with—"

The empty glasses were taken away. Shrimp cocktails were brought on and for a long time lay untouched by either Hux or Anne. When the bottle of Pomerol appeared, Hux had to interrupt his narration for the ceremonial sip and nod of approval as the waitress stood by; the wine had been refrigerated to a taste-numbing chill, but Hux let it pass. Though the expensive filets were eaten, they were as tasteless as soggy paper to Hux, who, in a disjointed way, punctuated by soblike catchings in his throat, managed to lay most of his Mississippi story before Anne, omitting only the apparition that had set the whole enterprise into motion.

For some moments after he had finished, Anne sat toying with her food. Once or twice she raised her dark, luminous eyes to Hux, who assumed that she was struggling for the right, tactful words to conceal her full horror and distaste. The silence was protracted. Several times Anne leaned forward, as if about to speak, only to draw back again. At last Hux could stand it no longer and said, "What do you make of this? Do you think I am going out of my mind?"

"Honey," she replied, her brow puckered, "don't ask me. I—I don't understand religious experience—I'm the last person in the world to make any sense out of what happened to you with Brother Thurlow. And this other business ..." She gave him a helpless smile, shrugging and spreading her hands. "I guess I don't know what to say about that either. I understand—I think I understand—the deep way you felt about Clark's death. But involvin' yourself like this with those old people—that crazy old man—" Again Anne shrugged, smiled, as if asking him to help her out of her plight.

So far it had not been too bad, Hux thought. At least she had not left the table in horror.

"But, honey," Anne continued, repeating the surprising endearment, "I think you ought to stay away from Alhambra. I think you ought to finish up your business here just as fast as you can and head back to New York and—"

"And get help," supplied Hux. "Find a good shrink. That's what my wife has been saying for a long time."

Ruefully, Anne nodded. "I guess that's what I mean. I went to a therapist in New Haven when my marriage was breakin' up, and I think it helped. Some," she added, with a tiny, deprecatory downturning of the corners of her mouth. "Anyway, stay clear of Alhambra. Whether that Rooney was or was not the one who attacked your car, that town sounds like the wrong place for you to be hangin' out. The atmosphere's bad for you—gets you all wrought up."

Hux both welcomed and resented the humor that Anne had now brought into her voice. She was making a joke of the whole thing, telling him that she didn't see his situation as too desperate or crazy. On the other hand, she was patronizing him, treating him as a silly adolescent who had been experimenting with something that was bad for him. Trying to *humor* him out of it. . . . "I've got to go back at least one more time," he said soberly. "I promised Miss Isabelle. I can't simply drop her without a word."

"Why not? What has that old lady got to do with you? Why should you . . . *upset* yourself for her sake. Can't you just call up and make some sort of excuse that won't hurt her feelings?"

Hux pondered this possibility. "No," he said at last, "I can't. She *does* mean something to me—I can't exactly say what. I have to see her—them—on Sunday. But it will be the last time."

Anne grimaced. "And you're actually goin' to preach to him again—try to save his soul?"

Hux shook his head. "No, not that. I'm not sure what I'll do, but it won't be that." He stared thoughtfully past Anne to a platform across the room on which a man in a red jacket was testing a microphone and arranging chairs. With a shiver Hux recalled the platform and chairs at the Baptist church. . . .

"Get out of it. Stay clear. That's my advice."

"I appreciate it, believe me," he said, reaching over to take her hand. "I'll try to think of some excuse to get away right after dinner— get away fast." How sane she was—and how weird and mad the whole secret agenda now seemed to him! Perhaps the true explanation of Brother Thurlow's impact had to do simply with Hux's overexcited condition at that time. Ainsley Black clearly *had* been a dangerous identity for him to assume. . . .

"In another few minutes," said Anne, who had turned her head at the popping of the microphone across the room, "we're not goin' to be able to hear ourselves think, much less talk."

"Do you want dessert?" asked Hux. The waitress, who had somehow cleared away the dinner plates and wine glasses without his noticing, was now thrusting the big crimson menus at them again.

"Just coffee."

"Two coffees."

"You folks ought to try our Plantation Special Pecan Pie. It's mighty good. Comes with real whip-cream."

"Just coffee," said Hux as he handed back the menus.

For some reason, the arrival of the White Mules (as a sign on a tripod now announced the group) was delayed, and Hux and Anne continued to talk. Heavy fencing had been pulled down; Hux's secret life now lay exposed, and nothing terrible had happened. To the contrary, Hux felt an immense relief, as if he had received a favorable report on a biopsy after having feared the worst. *I can tell her anything,* he thought, reveling in his new freedom and the new intimacy that had begun to grow between them; when had he last been with a woman to whom he could tell anything? *She's lovely*, he decided, as if Anne's rather gaunt dancer's face, with its dark encircled eyes and wide mouth, had suddenly softened into that of a Bellini madonna.

"I'm going to finish up here early next week," he was saying. "By Wednesday at the latest. But I'm not going straight back to New York. I'm going first to New Orleans for a few days. I've never been there, and I've always wanted to go."

"You'll be disappointed. There's still some good jazz and a few good restaurants, but mostly the city—and especially the French Quarter—has been turned into a tourist trap aimed at the busloads of tourists from Houston."

"That's what I've been told, but I don't entirely believe it. Besides, I can't be disappointed if you're with me."

"What on earth are you talkin' about?"

"Take three days of your vacation," Hux said, now aflame with his bright idea. "Or pretend you're sick." His voice grew urgent. "We'll leave on Wednesday and you can be back at the library on Monday. Work it out any way you can, but please come. How about it? Even if New Orleans is as disappointing as you say, we can still have a good time. Say you'll come!"

Anne gave him a ferocious frown, her head tilted, her lips stretched wide. "You really are out of your mind. My God, we haven't even— What makes you think I'd come to New Orleans with you even if I could get away?"

"What have you got to lose? I think we could have a good time, a terrific time!"

"This is absurd," Anne said, but a smile had begun to play in the corners of her eyes and mouth. "It's impossible."

"I'm sure the library can spare you. You can't be the only one who knows how to display the Jefferson Davis letters. And—"

"But you've forgotten about Prudence! What's she supposed to be doin' while I'm gallivantin' around New Orleans with a madman?"

That stung Hux into momentary sobriety. *So she did think he was crazy. . . .*

"Honey, I didn't mean it that way," said Anne. "I wasn't even thinkin' about the—about all the other stuff. But you seem to have completely forgotten that I'm a mother and that I can't just take off for New Orleans on the spur of the moment."

Mollified by her explanation, encouraged by the fact that her objections were practical rather than moral or psychological, Hux pressed on. He suggested the Bensons—couldn't Prue stay with them? Anne shook her head; the Bensons were in Atlanta and wouldn't be back until early next week—too late to make arrangements.... Then Hux suggested a live-in baby-sitter, maybe a graduate student from the university. He was inventive, fertile with solutions, but nothing that he offered so eagerly seemed practical to Anne.

Suddenly a blast of sound wiped out the conversation. Unobserved by Hux and Anne, the White Mules had appeared on the platform, and now, with shattering amplification, they began a ballad, "My Cinder-Block Honkytonk Girl." Anne shouted something to Hux and then, laughing, got up, came around the table, and said in his ear, "I would love to come to New Orleans. *Probably* I can't, but it's nice to think about. Let me try to work something out, one step at a time. The first step is to get out of this awful racket!" She stood back, and Hux could see a red spark leaping in the pupil of each of her eyes. He caught her and kissed her. Across the room, bathed in a hot-pink spotlight, the White Mules sang.

> So she turned away—
> What more could I say?—
> In the light of a bright neon sign.
> She left me behind, to weep and repine,
> That cinder-block honkytonk sweetheart of mine.

The next step led not to Hux's motel, with its skimpy twin beds, but to the Bensons' house, to which Anne had a key. By the time they reached the house, they were already rumpled and hot from their embrace in the parking lot at Rosie's and from the quick grapplings that occurred whenever they had to stop at a traffic light during the twenty-minute drive. As Anne leaned over to unlock the front door, Hux ran his hand beneath the waistband of her skirt and caught one buttock in a gentle squeeze; to his fingers the silken globe seemed hardly bigger than the breast of a buxom woman—and nearly as soft. When his fingers probed further into the cleft, Anne gave a small yelp and straightened up. "Stop that, you idiot," she whispered, turning to him and offering her open mouth.

They pushed open the door and entered the house conspiratorially, not turning on a lamp, finding their way in the diffused light coming from the full moon outside. Up the stairs they bounded, Anne leading the way, one hand reaching back to hold Hux's and to keep it from further pawing. The guest bedroom, with its white muslin curtains and the white canopy over the double bed, seemed to glow with a white, interior light of its own, matching the glow of the night beyond the window panes with their undrawn shades. Anne immediately pulled back the bedspread, sat down on the snowy sheets, and kicked her feet free of their shoes, while Hux stood over her, trying to unbutton his shirt with fingers made inarticulate with lust. He kept telling himself to take it easy, not to rush—there was all the time in the world.

But his impatient flesh paid no heed and spent everything it had at the instant their bodies came together.

Nearly an hour later Hux was lying sleepily—belly up, toes up— next to Anne. With his hands clasped behind his head, one elbow poking the top of Anne's shoulder, he looked up into the glowing muslin cloud of the canopy and was conscious of deep happiness and relief—and of the fact that within a very few minutes they would have to get up. For some time neither of them had spoken, but slight movements of Anne's fingers—faint tracings on the surface of his stomach and chest—told him that she was not asleep. He wondered if she was as happy, as relieved, as he. But why should she be relieved? Why not just happy or pleased? She knew nothing of his sexual problems; she had seen nothing more than overeagerness when he leapt ahead of the wave, so to speak. And she had laughed good-humoredly about it, never doubting that he would rise on a new wave, never suspecting his agony during the interval between that first spill and the blessed moment when he felt himself surge forward again before losing himself in the process of which his body was simply an extension. Closing his eyes to the white muslin cloud, Hux drifted into sleep. He was sweating lightly in the warm air of the room.

When, only a minute or two later, he awoke, he saw that Anne was sitting on the edge of the bed. "Hel-lo," he murmured drowsily.

She leaned over him. "I was just about to wake you up. We've got about ten minutes to get dressed and back to my apartment."

Reaching out, Hux encircled her with one arm and pulled her down upon him.

"We've *got* to go. Really."

"Can't we call and say we've had a flat tire or something?"

"You've had enough go wrong with your car today. Don't be so *greedy*. Seriously, honey, Mary Lou's parents will be furious if we're late getting back. They're not real happy about havin' her baby-sit for me anyway." But contradicting her words, Anne ran her fingers over the damp tangle of Hux's belly curls and lowered the tip of her index finger into his navel. He turned, pressing into her flank, hardening as he pulled her closer. "Don't," she pleaded, moving away from him. "Don't. I didn't mean to start anything. We really can't stay another second."

"Then we'll save it for tomorrow," whispered Hux, kissing the top of her shoulder and the back of her neck, shoving the long hair aside with his face. "Promise me you'll come to New Orleans."

"I promise." Anne got up and began retrieving her scattered clothes from the floor. As she bent over, her breasts swayed and her hair fell across her face. "I'll work something out," she said, straightening herself and flipping back the mane of her hair. Holding her clothes to her breasts in the silvery room with its dense shadows, she reminded Hux of some etching he had once seen—or perhaps a charcoal drawing—of a model in a studio. . . . Degas? Courbet? Eakins? "If all else fails," she went on, "maybe I can make some sort of deal with Peggy when she gets back from Atlanta. Now get up and let me do something about that bed. I really ought to change the sheets but there isn't time."

Chapter Thirty

Anne was mostly silent as Hux drove her home through the leafy streets, the moonlight now nearly obliterated by street lamps and headlights. He turned on the car radio and found a station playing Negro work songs and blues. He sighed peacefully. "What a fantastic ending to one of the worst days in my life," he said.

They drove on, Anne still silent. Then, as they swung into University Avenue, she suddenly reached over and switched off the music and said, "There's something on my mind, sweetie, something I've been meanin' to tell you. It's a bit of ancient history about Clark and me that he didn't mention in his letters. Clark and I were lovers during the few weeks before he was shot. I slept with him the night before he died."

Hux said nothing. He drove on, feeling strangely fragile, as if he dared not move, as if he would shatter into glassy splinters if he even took a deep breath. He was more consciously aware of the strobic interchange of lights and shadows along the street than of the significance of Anne's words.

"Aren't you goin' to say anything? We're bein' open with each other, aren't we? I thought—" Her voice, breaking through the silence within which he had walled himself, sounded a little frightened. "Larry! Have I upset you?" Moments later, as they drew up in front of Anne's building, she touched his arm. "Larry, for God's sake—"

"Don't worry about it. Why should it upset me?"

"But, honey, your voice sounds like it's comin' from the tomb! It *does* matter to you, and it mustn't—not after ten years."

"You're the one who says it matters." Hux stopped the car and pulled on the handbrake but did not turn off the motor.

"Aren't you goin' to come up and have a drink or some coffee? I can't bear to say goodnight when you're actin' so strange and distant."

"I'm not upset. It's taken me by surprise, that's all. I'll just have to get used—get used to—to a whole new idea about—about Clark's marriage. That's all." His mouth was so dry that he could hardly get the words out.

"Oh, sugar, I have the most awful feelin' I've ruined everything. But nothing should be ruined—really. Clark was Clark. He's dead, and you're—oh, my sweet Larry!"

"Nothing's ruined, Annie. But I don't think I'll come up now. It's been a very long day, and since I can't spend the night with you . . ."

"Will I still see you tomorrow night?"

"Of course." Leaning over, Hux kissed her on the lips and felt the wetness of tears on her face. "Anne," he whispered, but she pulled away and jumped out of the car and ran to the door of her building.

Hux could not bear to return at once to the Holiday Inn. Instead, he drove to the Court House Square and then headed south out of Oxford, following the main highway as if driving to Jackson. But after eight miles or so he turned onto a paved country road which soon gave way to a crazy network of unpaved roads, some of them hardly more than tracks. Surrendering to the craziness, the lostness, not caring if he drove all night, Hux entered a whitened landscape, an undulating terrain of ribbed fields, of woods where trees, vine-looped, stood like black-velvet cutouts against the bleached sky; where, in a sudden clearing, the tin roof of a cabin blazed in the moonlight. He saw few lights, encountered no car. The full moon was of such equatorial brilliance that Hux was able to drive for miles with his headlights switched off. At one point he was tempted to remove his clothes, to let the mild air flow over his skin; but the fear of driving into the headlights of some beer-soaked farmer's pickup truck kept him sane. Now totally disoriented, he was unwilling to turn around or make the slightest effort to extricate himself from the web of little roads. He did have to stop and turn around once—when a single-lane road he had taken abruptly reduced itself to a pair of deep ruts leading to a tiny house surmounted by a towering television aerial; set back in a dirt yard full of stripped and rusted vehicles, the unlighted house was guarded by a hound that barked frenziedly at the car wheels as Hux backed and turned, expecting at any moment to have a tire ripped open by some spiky piece of derelict machinery or to receive a shotgun blast in the side of his head.

Nothing very coherent shaped itself in Hux's mind as he drove on, propelled by a febrile excitement that twitched and strummed his nerves. His clearest perception was that he was in no condition to sleep, that a return to the motel would be foolish. There were fleeting, triumphant moments when he relived, in Anne's arms, the sudden sweep of desire that had carried him on and on like a surfer, but mostly he was aware of something leaden and sorrowful pressing at

205

his consciousness, and he sensed the possibility of opening himself to a despair more desolating than any he had ever known. Once or twice he tried to focus on what Anne had revealed, telling himself that he had to grasp it, that it was, after all, no big deal. . . . But her words floated past him like bits of fluff. He could not picture her making love to Clark; instead, he saw her at Tupelo, cradling his friend's shattered head in her lap.

An intersection. A paved road. Hux held his wristwatch to the moon. He had been driving for more than two hours, and it was now time to turn back, to calm himself, to get the sleep he needed. Tomorrow he planned to draft a memorandum of his official findings in Mississippi and to map out the schedule for his last few days, a schedule that would now have to include the postponed visit to Starkville. Though there were no road signs at the intersection, Hux, following some obscure directional hunch, turned right. The road looked like the sort that would eventually lead to a bigger one, where there would be signs. Hux had no idea whether he was ten or fifty miles from Oxford. His mood having changed, he was now tired of—perhaps frightened by—the shimmering disorientation that had enveloped him for so long. Now the need to find a road or a village that he could locate on his highway map became urgent. Though he still could not pull his thoughts about Anne or Clark into any graspable shape, he was able to concentrate on the immediate situation, and he drove now with full attention to the road and to any variation of the terrain that might give him a clue.

Eventually Hux crossed a rattling bridge over a rather large stream. What river flowed here? Some feeder of the Tallahatchie or the Yazoo? He was on the point of stopping to examine his map when he became aware of the headlights of a car behind him. He drove on, realizing that to stop at this place, at this time, would certainly provoke an encounter of some sort. Even a friendly "Need any help?" was more than he felt able to cope with just now. After another mile or so, the road was crossed at a right-angle intersection by another road, slightly larger. Again Hux looked for signs and saw none. Once more following a hunch, he turned left and soon afterward realized that the other car had turned left too. Hux thought little of that except to wish that the car would either pass him or turn off the road, for the lights in the mirror kept breaking through the membrane of solitude that had enclosed him for so long. At the next intersection Hux found what he was looking for: a sign pointing to Route 7, which would, he knew, take him back to Oxford. Though it now made sense that the other driver would also want to reach Route 7, Hux experienced a jolt of fear when he once more saw the lights behind him. Telling himself that this was not the summer of '64, that he was neither a Northern freedom rider not a local black to dread a pursuing car on a country road, he none the less accelerated, and when he reached Route 7, he ignored the stop sign and blinker and swerved, with some screeching of tires, onto the highway.

For some time the headlights did not reappear, and Hux, driving north, let his shoulders relax. But then the lights were there, and soon they were closer behind him than they had any right to be. Hux did not trust himself—or his rented car—to a race; keeping to a steady sixty miles an hour, he could only hope that whoever was pursuing him (Rooney?—impossible!) would not attempt anything so rash as to try to cut him off on a two-lane highway that had its share of curves. No longer lifting his eyes to the mirror, he kept them fixed, self-hypnotically, on the white line down the middle of the road—as if the line were a ribbon that could magically draw him to safety. One truck passed, going south; otherwise Hux and his follower had the road to themselves for more than ten miles. Hux did not need the mirror to know that the other car was scarcely more than ten yards behind him. Again Rooney's image flashed through his mind—again to be dismissed even as it made his pulse accelerate.

A glow appeared over the horizon ahead: the lights of Oxford. Then, as Hux crested a low hill, he saw below him a major intersection, with a traffic light showing green. I have to make that light, he told himself as he sped forward; if he could make it, he would be able to reach the safety of Court House Square within minutes. But the light turned yellow and then, just as Hux was within braking distance, red. He had to stop, for another car was speeding toward the intersection from the left. Headlights flashed blindingly in his mirror, and for a moment Hux crouched over the steering wheel, paralyzed like a rabbit in the beam of a hunter's flashlight. Then he forced himself to turn and have a look.

Despite the glare of the headlights, Hux could see that the other car, which had stopped just behind him, was an old red Volkswagen, battered and dusty, with an out-of-state license plate. New Jersey . . . The car, the license plate, even the number on the plate, were instantly and overwhelmingly familiar. How could Clark's old VW—? Before he could register the implications of this astounding occurrence, he saw that a hand was signaling to him, waving back and forth across the windshield.

Hux flung open the car door and jumped out. In an instant he was at the driver's window of the Volkswagen, pulling at the door handle, and then he was looking into the broad face of a middle-aged woman who was smiling and nodding while her eyes bulged with something like fear—presumably from the expression on Hux's face.

After Hux had caught his breath and once again found his voice, he became aware, while mumbling an apology for the way he had leapt at the woman's car, that there was another passenger huddled in the back, and that the driver was saying something about a hospital. When he had calmed down enough to listen, he heard the woman say that her grandmother had taken sick and that she was trying to get her to the hospital. Did Hux know the way to the Oxford hospital? "I reckon I gave you a bad scare," said the woman, "but I live in Jersey now—my husband works in Bayonne—and I'm just down here on a visit to my granny—and I—well, I guess I don't remember all them back roads too well. Anyways, I got lost. So when I seen you, I thought maybe you could lead me out to the main road. I would have ast you but you never slowed down. Granny's got real bad chest pains—I cain't sit here talkin' any longer. You say you know the way to the hospital? I sure would appreciate—"

"I think I know where the hospital is," interrupted Hux. "You can follow me." He leaned against the car door, his legs still barely able to support him.

"You hear that?" the woman said loudly, looking over the seat back. "This gentleman knows the way. So don't you worry none, sweetheart. We'll be there in a jiffy."

There was a muffled sound from the back.

"She don't hear real good," said the woman, thrusting her head out the window toward Hux. Her hair was in curlers. "Granny's ninety-one an' she's the sweetest lamb you ever seen, jus' the sweetest little ol' thing. . . ." Then, as if resisting with a great effort the temptation to enjoy a good chat, she said, "Reckon we better git goin'. Sure do appreciate it. You're mighty kind to direct us."

But Hux's long day was not yet over. After pulling into the parking lot of the Holiday Inn, he sat for a while in the car, trying to quiet the tumult in his head, to calm himself before attempting sleep. But too much had happened, beginning with the slashed tires; unable to deal with this overload, Hux's mind kept rushing up against the events and then backing away, helpless before the many faces they presented. The red Volkswagen again appeared—and, as always, it was Clark's car, not the woman's. Hux tried to concentrate upon the woman's face and her words and upon the old woman in the back seat—all in an effort to restore the car to its rightful owner, so to speak. But it continued to reappear as Clark's car, license number and all.

After twenty minutes Hux decided to go up to his room and pour himself a good stiff drink as a possible aid to sleep. Also he needed badly to urinate. Though the moon-washed sky was still cloudless, a strong breeze was now sweeping in from the west, bending and shaking the treetops beyond the roofline of the motel. Hux's feet seemed leaden, his legs sinewless, as he climbed the outside steps to the upper deck. At the door to his room, he bent down to insert the key and at that moment heard a sound—a low and somehow familiar, though unidentifiable sound—that threw him into a state of quivering alertness—and dread. For several long seconds he stood fixed in the bleakly lit passageway, the key shaking in the fingers of his right hand, while the complex wiring of his nerves and glands hummed with a signal for flight which his legs could not have obeyed. But this was insane! The sound—whatever it was—must surely have come from an adjoining room or from the street on the far side of the motel. Hux wondered if, in the hurry of his departure to meet Anne, he might have left a window open.... After taking and expelling a deep breath, he forced himself to turn the key and then to give the door a shove. But he did not immediately switch on the light. Just as he thought, the window was open and the venetian blind was rattling in the strong cross-current of air.

Then he lowered his eyes to the farther twin bed, across which a thin strip of light fell from a street lamp outside the window. On the bed a man lay, face up, one arm dangling to the floor. He was wearing a long-sleeved white shirt, across which the light angled, and what appeared to be chino trousers. The head was in total darkness, but from the region of the pillow a black, irregular stain spread into the strip of light.

Moaning softly, his knees buckling, Hux lowered his face into his hands. Unable to look, he stood, squeezing his chest with his elbows, his fingertips touching his forehead, thinking, *It was your car, and now you're here....* His right trouser-leg was wet.

When Hux at last removed his hands and looked, the figure was still there, but it now met his eyes as a dummy, not a corpse. This new vision gave Hux the strength to reach for the light switch and flick it on. When the dazzle subsided, he saw a tangle of sheets with a pillow stuffed in the middle of the tangle, as if by an anguished or delirious sleeper. The bedspread, which was beige in color, was pulled halfway up, and the dark red sport shirt that he had worn yesterday at the Hernes' was flung across the top of the bed where the pillow would normally have been. Probably he had picked it up from the floor or a chair and thrown it there while changing his clothes before leaving to meet Anne.

Clark's presence was not immediately dispelled by the light. For a while it seemed to withdraw into the far corner of the room, near the bathroom door, while Hux sat collapsed in a chair, staring at the innocent tangle of sheets, one corner of which dangled to the floor; it did not leave altogether until Hux got up to go to the bathroom to expel what was left of the urine that had earlier spurted down his leg. Then he undressed, hung up his pants in the bathroom, wiped his right thigh and leg with a washcloth, and poured himself the stiff drink that he had originally planned.

Shock and terror had meanwhile given way to grief—to tearless but soblike spasms of grief. *You're dead, Clark,* he thought. *You've been dead a long time. And now I have your girl and you have nothing—you've been cut off with nothing at all. . . .* After a while he put down his drink and brought his briefcase over to the chair. Still dry-eyed but with an aching, unrelieved sadness, he stared at the pathetic remnants—the snapshots, the letters. He reread what Clark had written about Anne: *ugly-attractive . . . intelligent . . . quirky . . . fantastic. . . .* There was no outlet for Hux's grief. Clark's loss was total, his death senseless, his murderer a pitiable, drunken, and hateful old man against whom Hux now felt a vain and helpless flickering of rage. Hux's joy in Anne was shriveled, as if a scorching desert wind had blown over it. The proposed trip to New Orleans now seemed pointless, the city itself—his fantasized city—as degraded as a battered old slut.

The drink did not help him get to sleep. Lying in the bed on which he had seen Clark's body, Hux forced himself to go over every item of clothing, to analyze every trick of light and shadow that had created the illusion. Yet it was still Clark's body that he saw; his vision was fixed in that moment of purest horror, a vision that he had barely survived and that would not allow him to substitute the shadowed red sport shirt for a spreading stain of blood. He continued to see what he had seen and not what he knew to have been there. At last he got up, switched on the lamp, and poured himself another drink. There was no television at this hour, but he managed to get an all-night radio station in New Orleans and sat in his chair listening to Dixieland jazz until nearly four, when at last his eyelids began to droop. He was calmer now, able to hold for some moments a picture of Anne and himself without having it instantly shattered by Clark.

But once he gave way to sleep, Hux was handed over—like a prisoner bound and gagged, sweating, unable to scream, at times unable to breathe—to be tormented by a succession of nightmares, each following quickly upon the brief interval of wakefulness into which the last had thrown him.

Chapter Thirty-one

Between the time he fell asleep (if what he experienced could be called sleep) and the hour of his awakening (which was after ten in the morning), a subtle but decisive change took place in Hux's response to his visions of Clark. He surrendered to them. No longer did he have the will or the energy to explain away what he had seen. Even though he still knew, in some recess of his mind, that he could account rationally for every detail of these episodes, there was simply no point in making the attempt. What now seemed harshly clear to him was that Clark, the *real* Clark, was trying to reach him by means of the very phenomena that could be accounted for. Clark existed, actively existed, *behind* them and was making use of them—that was the appalling fact which Hux now had to accept. Clark had pursued him in the Volkswagen and had signaled to him by means of the woman driving it; he had animated the tangle of clothes and sheets on the bed. And he had spoken to Hux—given orders to him—through dreams. As Hux lay staring at the ceiling through the tawny light of the motel room, he knew exactly what Clark wanted from him.

The one nightmare that he could now recall with some coherence seemed to echo—and amplify—a dream fragment of the preceding night. In the dream that he now replayed he was a fugitive running through dense brush and vines along the bank of a river that he somehow knew to be the Tallahatchie. He was being pursued, like a runaway slave, by a pack of hounds whose baying he could hear far off. Ahead was a bridge which he had to reach, but the thickets were becoming more knotted and snarled and his pace was slowing almost to a crawl as he laboriously parted the heavy curtain of vines and leaves that blocked his way. In a knapsack strapped to his shoulders was what his pursuers wanted: the pale, unbloodied, waxlike head of Claiborne Herne. Hux could remember cutting it off in an earlier portion of the dream—or perhaps in another dream altogether. The knife had sliced easily through the neck until it reached the spinal column; this Hux had had to snap by kneeling on Claiborne Herne's chest and pushing hard against the chin as the head dangled back-wards over the edge of the bed. There had been no blood. . . . If only he could reach the bridge, he could drop the head into the muddy waters below and then he would be safe. He had to keep pushing his way forward; he could not give up. But by now the tangle was almost impenetrable. . . .

Hux was in no condition to theorize about his situation. There was only one way that the dream could be understood: He was under orders from Clark to kill Claiborne Herne. That all along had been the secret behind the secret agenda, a secret kept even from him un-til now. In some obscure way he had, he felt, forced Clark's hand by going to bed with Anne—had made him reveal the secret mission prematurely. He knew that he could not withstand another visitation from Clark. His heart would stop, he would fall in his tracks. Or go completely out of his mind. It had come to that. . . .

After a while Hux got up, took a long shower, and dressed with his usual care. Except for the slime of fear on his tongue, he was almost without sensation. Like a condemned criminal—a man condemned not to die but to kill—he went through the motions of his life, at last forcing himself to go downstairs, to eat a breakfast that he could not taste because of the fear in his mouth.

Afterwards, Hux returned to his room and lay down on his bed again. Perhaps he dozed a little, for suddenly he opened his eyes to the amber light and felt less desperate, less doomed—as if a possibili-ty had been revealed to him in sleep. Whatever it was, it seemed still to be there, hidden from him, just beyond his reach. Then abruptly, as if a dust sheet had been whisked away from a portrait, he saw the face of Archie B. Thurlow. And that face, despite its thunderous scowl, was so strangely reassuring that Hux almost wept with relief. If Clark was powerful, so was Brother Thurlow. One strength could oppose another. . . . Nothing was explicit to Hux; he did not specu-late or theorize or theologize. The name of Jesus did not shape itself upon his lips. Yet he sensed that behind Brother Thurlow stood an immense reserve of power, a force that could be raised like a flaming sword to oppose Clark's offensive.

Propping himself on his elbows, Hux let his mind race ahead. What was to stop him from leaving right away for North Carolina, for Fayetteville? It was absurd, he couldn't do it, couldn't leave Mis-sissippi just like that—but why not? Most of the day still lay ahead of him; there was plenty of time to get out of Oxford, to get out of

Mississippi. He was convinced, though he could not have accounted for his conviction, that Clark did not have the power to manifest himself in broad daylight. Outside, the sun was shining. If he could just get to Fayetteville . . . He would have to leave immediately, drive to Memphis, catch a plane.

As though he had already drawn upon the strength of Brother Thurlow, Hux was able suddenly to clear his mind and bring his thoughts under control. The motel room looked perfectly ordinary. He opened the heavy curtains and sunlight streamed into the room. There was the telephone. Clearly, efficiently, he ticked off the steps he had to take. He was determined to act responsibly, even though the thought of what he was going to do still seemed wild to him— wild and possibly dangerous. After attempting to telephone various airlines in Memphis and getting busy signals every time, he realized that he would do better to make flight arrangements after he got to the Memphis airport; to continue trying to do so from Oxford would simply take up too much time.

His next call was to Alhambra. There was a long wait before Miss Isabelle answered. "Hello, Miss Isabelle, this is Larry," he said.

"Who?" came the quavering, rasping voice.

"Larry, Larry Hux."

"Who?"

Now realizing his mistake, Hux drew a deep breath and began again. He was sweating. "Miss Isabelle," he boomed out in an altered voice. "Can't you hear me? This is Ainsley—Ainsley Black."

There was a pause during which Hux could imagine Miss Isabelle trying to adjust her hearing aid after the booming sound of his voice. "Oh, it's Ainsley!" she cried, now making *his* eardrum wince. "Something's wrong with my wretched contraption. I simply didn't recognize your voice at all. It seems all right now, so don't speak *too* loudly. How are you, my dear?"

Hux told her, as gently as he could, that he would not be able to come to Alhambra tomorrow. His excuse was the Lord's business: he had been called to Atlanta—he was not sure for how long—on a mission that he was not free to divulge. But he would be back, he assured her—probably when she least expected him. Meanwhile, she should try to help her brother persevere along the path he had begun.

Again there was a pause, followed by a crackling sigh. "I'm so disappointed about Sunday," she said in a voice that sounded close to tears. "I can't tell you how disappointed I am. And Brother will be too. He responded so—so wonderfully to your last visit. Bein' in your company, hearin' your words—he didn't talk about it, but he's been like a different person. He's actually agreed to go to Evelyn Pike's funeral this afternoon. Can you believe it?" She had now begun to cry—softly but audibly—into the telephone.

"Miss Isabelle . . ."

She did not hear him. "It will be the first time in years he's done something like that, the first time in years." She brought her crying under control and said, in one of her stage whispers that probably carried throughout the house, "I'm not goin' to tell him, Ainsley— about Sunday, that is. I don't want to upset him just before the funeral. Is that all right with you?" she asked with a catch in her voice.

"Do what you think best, Miss Isabelle."

"Then I won't tell him till afterwards. I hate to think how disappointed he's goin' to be. I need—but I mustn't be selfish," she continued more firmly. "May the Lord bless your work, Ainsley dear. And come back soon, please hurry back real soon. . . ."

The next call was much harder, but Hux could allow himself no hesitation. He dialed before he had even framed the excuse he would have to make.

Anne gave a joyous yelp when she heard his voice. "Oh, hi, sweetie! I tried to call you just a little while ago. How are you?"

"I had to go downstairs." Hux dug his fingernails into the palm of his free hand. What in God's name was he going to say? "I've got to leave Oxford. Right away."

"What do you mean?"

"I said I've got to leave. Go home." Closing his eyes, Hux waited a second or two for the kind of inspiration that had come to his aid before. Then he said, "Anne, something terrible has happened. Louise—my ex-wife—called a little while ago and—and Tony's in the hospital."

"Tony's in the hospital! What's wrong?"

"He was—he was hit by a car while running to catch a bus on Riverside Drive. My wife called a little while ago and—"

"Oh, my God!"

"They think he'll be all right," Hux continued, hating the direction his improvisation had taken but now having no choice but to plunge ahead. "They've taken him to St. Luke's Hospital and he's regained consciousness. But his shoulder's broken and—and—his right leg." Hux waited a second while he summoned up saliva to irrigate his dry mouth. "That's all they know for sure," he went on. "They don't think there are any serious head injuries, but they can't be sure until they've run more tests."

"Oh, *poor* Tony! Poor Larry! Do you want me to drive you to Memphis to catch a plane?"

The concern—the love—ringing in Anne's voice was a torment to Hux, and he struggled to think of a way to turn down her offer, which was now even more frightening to him than inconvenient. Thanking her, he mumbled something about turning in his rented car, which had been giving him some trouble, at the airport and getting another one when he returned.

"So you will be back?"

"Of course. Or—or—maybe I'll fly straight to New Orleans and meet you there." In his desperation to get away, to start for Memphis, Hux was willing to say anything. But there were other arrangements to be made. He asked Anne to telephone his secretary at her home so that she could cancel the various appointments scheduled for the coming week. Most of these were merely ceremonial anyway—thank-you-and-goodbye visits—and even the postponed trip to Starkville was a follow-up visit that was not strictly necessary. "I'll call you from New York in a day or two," said Hux, "and let you know how things stand."

"Oh, sweetie, I can't stand all this!"

"I know. Isn't it the worst luck? I'll be thinking about you all the time—and about last night. What awful timing! But we'll be together soon, Annie—just as soon as I can leave poor old Tony." How had he managed to entangle himself in such an elaborate lie? He had to get away! Babbling on, he was hardly aware of what either he or Anne was saying during the brief remainder of the conversation. By the time he hung up, his shirt was soggy with sweat.

In less than ten minutes Hux managed to pack both his suitcase and his briefcase. Then he checked out of the motel and dashed to the parking lot, where he half expected to find his car with slashed tires once again.

Scrutinizing the flight schedules at the airport, Hux found that while there was an immediate Delta flight to Atlanta, there was no connecting flight between Atlanta and Raleigh-Durham until late afternoon. That meant he would not reach Raleigh until nearly seven; then he would have to rent a car—or take a bus—for the remainder of the trip to Fayetteville, arriving there well after dark. A sudden breath of fear blew across him, making him shiver and look around

216

anxiously in the crowded terminal. Hux did not want to spend the night alone in a Fayetteville motel room until he had had a chance to see Brother Thurlow.

There was an alternative. Why not spend the night with his mother in Raleigh? He had no particular desire to see her, but in some way that he could not have defined, Hux knew—knew deeply—that he would be safe in her apartment. At least he would not be alone.... Then, on Sunday, he could drive on to Fayetteville, reaching it in plenty of time for the first service of the Rededication that evening. He hurried into a telephone booth and looked up his mother's number in his pocket address book.

Rachel Hux was at home. After Hux's somewhat breathless explanation, there was a notable pause before her response, a pause which led him to expect rejection of his plan. "My, this *is* a surprise," she said at last. "I wish you had given me just a *teeny* bit more notice, Lorenzo. There's hardly a thing to eat in the house. I was planning to have some of that Stouffer's macaroni and cheese for supper, since I try to avoid flesh these days. I'll have to go out—"

"Don't worry, Mother. I can pick up some—"

"Now let me see," she said, forgetting about the food problem. "How long has it been—five years?—six years? When was it you came to help me move? You must be prepared for some striking changes in your rapidly aging mother. Some of them distinct improvements, I'm glad to say." She laughed in the high, trilling way she had—a laugh that Hux had last heard when he telephoned her on Christmas Day.

"I've changed too," Hux replied, feeling, despite all that he had on his mind, the familiar letdown produced by his mother's lack of eagerness to see him. He told her that his plane was about to leave and hung up.

PART 4

Chapter Thirty-two

Rachel Stallings Hux had been watching from the living-room window. As soon as she saw her son drive up and park his car across the street, she rushed into the front hall and flung open the door. Standing framed in the doorway of the tan-painted, peeling, turn-of-the-century house where she had lived for the last five years, she looked on without so much as a wave of her hand while Larry lifted his bag and briefcase from the car. Despite the sweltering heat, she was wearing a monkish wide-sleeved gown of cinnamon-brown cotton, belted at the waist with a tasseled cord, and darkened under the armpits with sweat. Her gray-streaked hair, fixed with a tortoise-shell comb, was drawn into a huge knot on the top of her head, and she wore rimless glasses over which she contemplated her approaching son with weepy-looking brown eyes. Her lips were a slash of scarlet against the chalkiness of her powdered face.

When Larry was within a few feet of her, Rachel—as if recognizing him for the first time—darted toward him with both arms out-stretched. "Lorenzo, Lorenzo," she murmured, resting her chin on his shoulder and embracing him, "it's been so long." Then she abruptly drew back and retreated to the doorway, where she stood with her hands on her hips. Appalled by her son's appearance, she felt unable to move as Larry picked up his suitcase and briefcase from the sidewalk where she had hugged him and advanced toward the front stoop.

"Well, Mother," he said with a baffled look, "aren't you going to let me in?"

"I just can't get over the way you've changed, Lorenzo. I keep ask-ing myself, Who is this bloated stranger? What have you been stuff-ing yourself with? Whatever's happened to my slender, handsome boy?"

Larry gave an uneasy laugh. "Now come on, Mother, I haven't put on that much weight." And he pushed past her into the dim hall of the ground-floor apartment that she occupied. "You've always had the wonderful knack of making me feel welcome."

Ignoring his sarcasm, Rachel led him to the back room where he was to sleep. It was airless and hot, with frayed muslin curtains at the window. An amber-colored shade was pulled partway down. "I wouldn't open the window until it's cooled off a bit outside," she said. "Today's been a real scorcher, and tomorrow promises to be worse." Then, after pointing out the door to the bathroom down the hall, she told Larry that she would be waiting for him in the living room, which was a bit cooler.

They had their meal on trays in the living room, where the saturat-ed air was kept in motion by a large, silent, oscillating fan. "I can't stand the claustrophobic chill of air-conditioning," she explained. "It's a premature reminder of the tomb." Her scarlet lips parted in a ghostly smile as she wondered whether her son ever wished her dead and out of the way. Hardly pausing to lift food to her mouth, Rachel began an account of her day, which soon extended into many areas of her recent life. After Larry's telephone call from Memphis, she had ventured into the outdoor oven to get a package of frozen baked chicken breasts and some tomatoes, which she now served to him along with a Parker House roll and a glass of iced tea with lem-on. As she picked at her own macaroni and cheese, she explained that she had become a vegetarian—a *modified* vegetarian, for she al-lowed herself milk products and eggs; just the smell of roasting meat or frying chicken now made her ill. She had also been going to a yoga exercise class. . . .

"Yoga? Here in Raleigh?"

Rachel frowned over her granny glasses. "Do you really think we live in such a backwater, my darling? My goodness, what a New York smarty-pants my boy has become! So full of pity for us poor, benighted provincials . . ."

"You've got me all wrong, Mother," said Larry, a slight smile playing on his exhausted face. "I would have assumed just the opposite—that Raleigh was far too up-to-date for something like yoga."

Rachel felt herself recoiling from her son's tone; it went with his coarsened, dissipated look and those circles under his eyes. What had he been up to? He looked as if he had not had a good night's sleep for months. . . . Choosing once more to ignore his sarcasm, she went on to insist that the diet, the exercises, and the meditation had done her a world of good—really, she had never felt better. The leader of her group, she explained, was not a real Indian but a former dancing teacher from Charlotte who had studied with Swami Niktananda at his famous ashram in Santa Barbara. But yoga was far from being her only—or even her chief—interest these days. Triumphantly she informed her son that she was not only secretary of the Sir Walter Poetry Club but also chairperson of its recording committee. This committee had been set up to tape readings of famous English and American poems, which were then distributed without charge to English teachers in the public schools.

"Now that so many of the teachers are colored," she said, "it's especially important for the students to hear great poems read by cultured people with trained voices. Otherwise," she concluded with a gay laugh, "we're going to have a whole generation growing up with the impression that Shakespeare and Milton and little Emily D. all sound rather like Uncle Remus!" Rachel stood up, her mouth again split into a witty smile. But when her boy made no response, she picked up her tray and carried it into the kitchen, telling herself that he had never appreciated her sense of humor.

"You probably think," she said, returning from the kitchen with a plate of peanut-butter cookies, "that I'm a rather eccentric, lonely widow who joins yoga groups and poetry clubs for the sake of a little company. In fact, my problem is too many people. I positively have to fend them off. Otherwise, I'd get nothing done—none of the things that really matter. Like my reading. I've just reread every word Jane Austen ever wrote, including the letters. And there's my sewing. I make all my own dresses now." Looking toward her lap, she spread the full skirt of her gown. "I'm afraid your old mother's going in for self-improvement in a mighty big way. I have to keep reminding myself that at sixty-seven I'm almost an old lady. Though I can't say I feel it." She laughed and again waited for a response. Wasn't he at all impressed by her activities, her energies, her youthfulness? Didn't he believe her when she said her problem was too many people? What was he thinking? He had always been so secretive, even as a little boy. . . .

"How is that great big grandson of mine?" she suddenly demanded, her voice drawn taut with grievance.

Larry seemed to flush slightly. "He's fine," he said, "really fine. Getting ready to go to camp in a week or so."

"When am I going to get a chance to see him? I boast about him to all my friends. I buttonhole strangers on the bus to show them his picture. I even read aloud his thank-you notes on the rare occasions I receive one. But do you realize, I haven't actually laid eyes on that child since he was six months old!"

"You can see him any time you're willing to come to New York or ask him down here. You know that. He sees his Richmond grandmother several times a year."

Rolling her eyes with exasperation, Rachel said, "Oh, Lorenzo, Lorenzo, what a hypocrite you are. That child would be bored to distraction down here, as you know perfectly well. And I haven't been exactly overwhelmed with invitations to visit you in your new quarters. When you left Louise, I thought perhaps there might be a *little* room for me."

"There literally isn't any room. I live in a studio apartment. But you could stay at a hotel. Or stay with Louise and Tony."

"Lou-*ise*," she replied, drawing out the sibilant, "has always known how to make her mother-in-law—her *ex*-mother-in-law—feel at home."

"Mother, I'm sick and tired of defending Louise to you and I'm not going to do it again. You've never forgiven her for the way her mother behaved to you—or you *thought* she behaved to you—at our wedding." Larry's face was still a dull red. "Speaking of hypocrites," he went on, "since when have you given a damn about Tony? Or any of us? Do you realize I've been in this house for over two hours and you still haven't asked how I am or what I've been doing in Mississippi or why—"

"I know, I know," Rachel interrupted. Unable to deny his words, she still felt unjustly accused. "I plead guilty. I'm a thoughtless, self-centered old woman. You don't have to tell me. But, Lorenzo," she continued, her eyes filling with tears, "you've always shut *me* out. Even when you were a tiny baby you shut me out, you pushed me away. How can you expect . . ."

Larry came over to her and placed a hand on her shoulder. "Let's not quarrel, Mother. I'm worn out—I've been through a lot—and I came here hoping—" He broke off, his face contorted.

Rachel reached up and patted the hand on her shoulder. Already she felt better. He did love her, she told herself; underneath all his coldness and anger, he did love her—and she had brought him close to tears! Wiping her own eyes with her knuckle, she said, "I'm sorry, Lorenzo, sorry you've been having such a bad time. Do you want to tell me about it?"

Instead of answering her, he said, "Is there anything to drink in the house? I could use something tall and cool, like a gin and tonic. The heat is really getting to me."

"As you know perfectly well, there hasn't been a drop of alcohol in this house since your father died. Not even cooking sherry. But sit down, Son, and let me get you another glass of iced tea. That's a lot more cooling than something alcoholic."

For some time they were able to avoid acrimony. The fan hummed discreetly in its half-orbit, sweeping the room with its sterile breeze. Larry did not tell Rachel his troubles, and she did not press him. He remained mostly silent while she reminisced—complained rather—about their old life in Gastonia. How isolated she had been! Had Larry ever realized how much the women whose husbands worked in the offices of the Crawford Mills resented her superior education and culture? Fortunately, some of the older, *established* women in town had realized what she had to offer and had gradually included her in their little circle. "Believe it or not, Lorenzo, they even found me witty! But of course your father's drinking made it impossible for us to have any real social life as a couple. I absolutely refused to be one of those pathetic drinking men's wives, always smiling, being extra sweet, and pretending nothing was wrong. . . . Also, we were terribly poor! My success, such as it was, was purely a daytime affair. Lunches. Circle meetings. *My* ladies knew better than to invite us to their homes in the evening." She went on to tell Larry that only recently had she begun to value his father's good qualities—his gentleness, his patience, his love of gardening that had made their little back garden a wonder to behold every spring. Now she could appreciate such things. . . . But then! Well, she sometimes thought that even then she could have put up with his lack of ambition, his lack

223

of drive, his lack of social presence, if only it hadn't been for the drinking. She could never learn to tolerate that; it had spoiled everything. . . .

During all those years she had simply *lived* for the summer visits to her father's house here in Raleigh. They were the only thing that kept her going. "Even though poor Mother was dead, it was always such a homecoming for me, such a treat. To be waited on hand and foot, to enjoy the wonderful meals old Fanny used to cook—" Rachel drew a profound breath and released it slowly. "At the Retreat I felt I could breathe again. There was something about life in Gastonia that caused my very lungs to shrink!" Smiling and tilting her head, Rachel playfully shook her finger at Larry. "The only fly in the ointment on those visits was you, my dear. You were never very happy at the Retreat and I could never understand why. All those wonderful grounds to play in, the swimming pool . . ."

"You know exactly why."

"And your grandfather," she went on. "It's one of the great disappointments of my life that you never got close to him."

"It's very simple. I was scared of him." Larry plucked at his damp shirt, which was sticking to his chest.

"I know, I know," said Rachel sadly. "Scared of that wise and wonderful man. I know, but I'll never understand why. He did everything he could to win you over."

"That wise and wonderful man," said Larry, rising from his chair, "never once spoke to me without being teasing and ironical. How can a child be expected—"

"He had the most marvelous sense of humor!" Rachel's voice rang with protest.

"Maybe so. But a small child can't cope with sarcasm, even when it's meant to be funny. I never knew what to say." Walking across the room, Larry stood for a moment looking up at the portrait of Dr. Stallings that had been painted to hang in the reception room of the Stallings-Yarborough Retreat.

Rachel followed his gaze. Though very dignified, the portrait still managed to capture some of her father's sparkle, she thought—the gleam in his eye under those heavy brows, the hint of a smile beneath the mustache. . . . After her father's death, she had managed to spirit the portrait away and to resist all efforts to have it returned—a coup of which she was still immensely proud. Now it hung over that poor, sagging old sofa that she really had to do something about. . . . "You never appreciated him," she said bitterly. "Not even when you were old enough to know what a distinguished man he was. The

224

leading alienist in the entire state of North Carolina, and as far as you were concerned, he might as well have been some . . . florist or bank teller!"

Larry laughed and looked away, as if he had been rebuked by the portrait itself.

"Speaking of matters ironical," resumed Rachel, "isn't it peculiar that I—the daughter of a man renowned throughout the South for the treatment of alcoholics—should have married a man who quietly drank himself into a stupor almost every night of our lives?"

Larry turned on her furiously. "The way you talk about him makes me sick! You had no business getting married in the first place. You didn't really want a husband. Or a baby. Least of all a baby."

"Lorenzo!"

"No, you should never have married. You should have remained a vestal virgin all of your life, keeping house for the greatest alienist in North Carolina." Larry crossed the patch of plum-colored carpet and stood directly in front of the fan, spreading his arms as if to capture all the breeze. Then, facing Rachel again, he said, "Mother, I'm in great trouble. I didn't come here expecting help from you. I know better than that. But I—for some reason I wanted to see you before I went on to see a man who may be able to help me. I see now that it was a mistake—stopping here, I mean. I should have gone straight on to Fayetteville and—"

"What sort of trouble are you in?" demanded Rachel. Had he killed someone? Was it possible?

"It doesn't matter, it really doesn't." Suddenly Larry laughed and, as if he had read her thoughts, said, "Nothing criminal, Mother. You won't have to burn my fingers."

Burn my fingers—what could he mean? Rachel shrank back into her chair. There was something demented in his expression, something out of control, and it occurred to her that she might be in danger. "Larry," she said, for the first time dropping the Lorenzo, "Larry, you look so overwrought. Please sit down. You're making me nervous, standing there like that. Please sit down."

Abruptly he did so. "It was a mistake to come here. For me and for you. There's no point in getting you all upset. I think I'd better go to bed." He leaned forward.

"Who is the man you're going to see?"

"A preacher. An evangelist."

Rachel's lips parted but she said nothing, fearful that any response to this astounding revelation might set him off again. *An evangelist!*

"I heard him preach in Mississippi. I think he might have some-

225

thing to say to me. We'll see," he added with a tired smile. "And now I'm going to go to bed." He stood up.

"I think that's a good idea, Son," said Rachel. "You do look worn out." A note of concern had entered her voice. "I'm sorry you're in trouble, Son. You never let me help you—never."

At this Larry shrugged, spreading both hands. "Goodnight, Mother," he said with the merest smile, a smile which turned almost at once into a suppressed yawn.

"Sleep as long as you can, Larry. It will do you good." She wondered if he would kiss her on the cheek in the old way as he left the room.

He did not.

Hours later, at around three in the morning, Rachel got up to go to the bathroom. Making her way into the dark hall, she saw light coming from under the door to Larry's room. Should she knock—to see if he was all right? She tiptoed to the door and stood for a moment, holding her breath, her fist raised and closed, ready to knock. No sound came from the room. Suddenly timid, she crept back to the bathroom and used the toilet without flushing it, fearful of the noise it would make. Returning to her bedroom door, she glanced over her shoulder before going in. The light still burned.

Chapter Thirty-three

More than seven hours after his mother had seen the light under his door, Hux awoke abruptly, sitting upright in bed. A shaft of white sunlight, streaming through a jagged hole in the window shade, had inched its way across his pillow, finally striking his eyelids. He reached for his wristwatch on the bedside table and noticed that the lamp was still on, its light absorbed in the morning glare. Hux switched off the lamp and then stared at his watch in disbelief: half past ten! For some moments he was gripped by panic, sure that he was terribly late for something, that he had missed a crucial appointment. *I've really screwed up,* he thought, his fists clenched tight. Then a sense of relief settled over him, and he sank back into bed, telling himself that he had needed the sleep badly, that it was just as well. . . . After all, the evening service in Fayetteville would not begin until eight. While rested by nearly eleven hours of sleep, Hux at the same time felt weak-limbed and sluggish, as if recovering from a childhood illness. There was one great comfort: Clark had not come during the night. However much Hux had tried to convince himself that such an invasion of his mother's house was unlikely, he could not, in the face of Clark's evident determination to get to him, be sure; he had left the lamp on as an added deterrent. Now, in the hot light of day, the threat itself seemed remote, a little less than real.

For a long time Hux lay naked on top of the sheets, which smelled of mildew and dust; his skin was already damp. The day was going to be the scorcher that his mother had predicted, and the little room, which faced east, was beginning to bake in the accelerating heat. A fly buzzed between the amber shade and the window pane, probably caught in one of the cobwebs that Hux had noticed when he lowered the shade and opened the window last night. Although no longer sleepy, he saw no reason to get out of bed and get dressed. As long as he lay quietly, he felt safe not only from the terrors of the last few days but also from the spiritual turmoil that he would certainly encounter tonight. His resolution to seek help from Brother Thurlow was as strong as ever, but he dreaded the unknown depths into which he would have to plunge, and he welcomed this interlude of laziness, which made him feel as if he were rocking gently in a small boat. But even in this suspended state he was aware of a tension that kept his passivity from being truly restful. While his sleep had been profound, producing no dreams that he could remember, something had disturbed him just before his awakening, some memory or fear that seemed unconnected with Clark. Whatever it was, it hovered just beyond his threshold of recall, teasing him into pursuit but always eluding him. After a while he no longer tried to corner it.

The hot little room reminded Hux of his boyhood room in the rear of the narrow frame house they had lived in, one of many such houses built in Gastonia about the time of the First World War. Vague feelings of childish guilt now made him uneasy, as if he were malingering to avoid going to school, or had been caught in a lie. He wondered if his mother was up and about—he had heard a sound, possibly from the kitchen. . . . Suddenly he seemed to be watching a tableau, its figures intensely lifelike but at the same time diminutive and immobilized, as if framed in a lighted box. He stood, a boy of about seven, before his mother, who wore her brown hair piled up as she wore it now. They were in the kitchen, where his mother had just caught him with a handful of expensive crystallized fruit which she had bought as her contribution to the annual baking of Christmas fruitcakes sponsored by the ladies of the church. It was a Saturday in November, and his father, who had been quietly drinking since noon, was listening to a broadcast of a football game. The war was on. . . . Then the scale changed. Now frighteningly large, his mother pulled him by the wrist to the kitchen table, where he was made to open his hand to release sticky red cherries and chunks of pineapple and citron. She next hauled him to the sink, where she forced him to spit out what he had in his mouth. But she was not through with him yet. Still clutching his wrist, she dragged him to the electric stove and turned on one of the burners. The boy began to scream and struggle but was unable to break her grip. As he twisted and kicked, he glimpsed through his tears the dejected figure of his father standing helplessly in the doorway. . . .

Then Hux saw himself doubled over, sobbing, at the kitchen table. His mother came back into the room with gauze and a jar of Vaseline and proceeded to bandage the blistered fingers of the boy's right hand, all the while murmuring, "Forgive me, Lorenzo, forgive me." When she had finished the bandaging, she said, "Now watch," and went over to the stove where the burner, still on, glowed red. When Hux realized what she was about to do, he screamed louder than ever and covered his face. "Watch, Lorenzo, you've *got* to watch," said his mother. His father reappeared at the doorway. Did he say anything, do anything? Her jaw set, his mother spread the fingers of her right hand and placed them on the burner. She gasped. Then, without another word, she gathered up the gauze and Vaseline in her unburned hand and left the room.

Hux's father placed his arm around the shuddering boy. He smelled strongly of whiskey and pipe tobacco, and the boy shrank from the kisses now being lavished upon his cheek and forehead. He felt the wetness of his father's lips and the sandpaper touch of his chin. "You know how she is," said his father in a broken voice. "There's no stopping her. There's no way I can stop her." And Hux remembered feeling that his father's embrace was harder to endure than the continued smarting of his fingertips. He wanted his father to die. . . .

The strip of white sunlight now fell across Hux's chest. Sweating profusely, he told himself that he would probably be cooler if he got up, dressed, and left this airless box of a room. But his listlessness kept him sprawled upon the bed as if his wrists and ankles were weighted. Again he wondered whether his mother was up; he had heard no further sounds from the rest of the apartment. Poor woman, he thought—she should never have married. The idea no longer filled him with bitterness. He began to construct an alternative life for her—a life in which she ran an antique shop (or perhaps a bookshop in Chapel Hill), in which she was surrounded by brisk or bookish semi-lesbians instead of the company wives whom she scorned and who had found her so formidable and strange. He could imagine her living in England, growing roses, collecting china, taking long walks through the drizzle. In this single life she would have made no one unhappy—least of all herself. So engrossed did Hux become in reshaping his mother's life that half an hour went by without his thinking once of the terrors from which he had fled or of the unknown (and possibly terrifying) shape of what lay ahead.

There was a tap at the door, and Hux hastily covered himself with the top sheet. When the door opened, he saw that his mother, who was wearing a long-sleeved cotton nightgown, had released her hair, which now fell across her shoulders and down her back to the top of her buttocks. With her face as yet unpowdered, her lips unpainted, she looked like a wizened, slightly mad country woman in some old photograph. Peering over her granny glasses into the sunlight, she said that she was about to make herself some wheat-germ toast and tea—would he like some too? She had forgotten to buy coffee, which she never drank any more, but there was an egg if Hux wanted one.

Hux said that he would like a fried egg.

"Do you realize that lamp was burning most of the night?" said his mother in a mildly accusing voice.

"I know. I left it on."

"Why did you do that?"

Suddenly Hux began to laugh. "To keep away ghosts," he said. "The lamp kept away one kind but some other just got in." Seeing his mother's look of bewilderment, Hux laughed still harder. He was afraid that he might not be able to stop. "Here," he said, sitting up and holding out one hand—palm upward, fingers splayed—while clutching the sheet to his chest with the other. "I'm sorry I wasted your electricity. You can burn my fingers if you want to. Just turn on the light and let the bulb get hot enough."

"What on earth are you talking about?" His mother retreated to the door, the bewilderment in her eyes shifting into something like fear.

"Don't you remember—the time you burned my fingers and then burned your own?" He was now red-faced, nearly choking, from laughter.

"*Burned* your fingers? What is this nonsense?"

Sensing that she had indeed forgotten the whole episode, Larry tried harder to bring his laughter under control. "Never mind," he said. "It's just a private joke." Sweat was still pouring from his face and chest, but he had now managed to calm himself. "I think I'd better have a shower before breakfast," he said, dabbing at his chest and throat with the sheet.

"I never did understand your sense of humor," said his mother, shaking her head. "I'm afraid the shower isn't working," she added after a moment. "There's only the tub."

"A cold tub will be just fine."

After the frugal meal Hux decided, against his mother's advice, to take a walk. "You'll get a heat stroke," she said as he went out. "It's already about ninety-eight." Even so, the air felt fresh to Hux—fresh and breathable after the stale heat of the house. Keeping to the shady side of the street and walking very slowly, he noticed that the houses, mostly wooden, looked even shabbier than he had remembered from five years ago. He wondered if the neighborhood was becoming dangerous, given the continued spread of Raleigh's black population in that direction; probably not, since most of the black families buying houses on the margins of the district were clearly middle-class. But all that could change. . . . It was typical of his mother, who had a more than sufficient income from her father's estate and her husband's insurance, to give up a decent apartment in a decent section of town and move back to this unsatisfactory area just because of its associations with her childhood. At the corner he turned right and came to the grounds of the Stallings-Yarborough Retreat, which his grandfather had founded and for many years directed. It was still a going concern, though no longer, Hux gathered, Raleigh's leading private sanitarium for alcoholics and other mentally disturbed patients. Through the high iron fence he could see several new glassy buildings, as well as modern additions to some of the large brick "villas"—each with a name like that of a resort hotel—which he remembered. The trees—some of them—had now grown to an impressive size, but the lawns and flowerbeds looked poorly tended, as if suffering from the universal lack of cheap black labor, he supposed, lapsing into a momentary regret that was hardly in keeping with his principles.

When he reached the main gate, Hux considered going in. *I could commit myself,* he thought, smiling at the image of some half-baked Southern psychiatrist trying to explain away Hux's terror in terms of too much booze. When he observed the way the guard at the gate was staring at him, he moved away. He was now in sight of the director's house, where he had spent so many cautious weeks during his childhood. He had always thought of it as so much grander than the little frame house in Gastonia that he was surprised now by its relative modesty. A pink brick box with a green tiled roof, it had four bedrooms at most. . . . Trying to reconstruct the interior, he could summon little to his inner eye except his grandfather's study, lined with books and medical journals bound in black or dull red; he also managed a quick glimpse of his grandfather in his swivel chair—that bustling, opinionated walrus of a man whom he had never loved. . . . Through the fence Hux could see a few patients sitting, singly or in groups, on benches under the trees, and he remembered how strange and frightening they had seemed to him as a child: fluttery old ladies who made a fuss over the little blond boy, the heavy men with red veins in their faces who beckoned to him, offering mints or chewing gum. He wondered if it was still possible to hear the occasional shrieking of patients confined to the Villa Chalfonte, which had iron bars on its windows; most probably they no longer shrieked, having been drugged into silence and housed in one of those new air-conditioned buildings with TV sets in every room.

Beyond the grounds he turned right at the next corner and stopped at a candy store to buy a Sunday paper. Back at his mother's house, he took off his sopping shirt, put on a white T-shirt, and spent the next hour sitting in the darkened living room, in the direct path of the fan. For lunch his mother prepared a salad of tomatoes, lettuce, cucumbers, canned kidney beans, and wedges of cheddar cheese, which they ate with toasted wheat-germ bread and glasses of iced tea. While his mother worked on a crossword puzzle and occasionally asked his help on a word, Hux read the Sunday paper and leafed through several back issues of the *Saturday Review*.

At four-thirty he set off for Fayetteville in his rented Ford, waving to his mother as he drove away.

Chapter Thirty-four

"You cain't go in," said the guard who was leaning back in a chair at the outside door to Brother Thurlow's suite of rooms at the Sunrise Motel. A large, fat-cheeked young man in a white short-sleeved shirt, he looked menacing, needing only a low-slung cartridge belt and a holster to fit Hux's idea of a brutal deputy sheriff left over from the summer of '64. "No way. He don't see nobody this time of night. Visitin' hours tomorrow at ten. You come back here then." The guard's manner, however, was kindly, belying his appearance or, rather, transforming it suddenly into that of a shy, overweight country boy.

"Look—please—I've got to see Brother Thurlow. I can't wait till tomorrow."

"No way, brother. I'm sorry, but my instructions is definite. He don't see nobody this time of night."

Hux leaned back against the railing of the motel balcony and closed his eyes, in which tears were again springing. *This crying!* If he wasn't careful, he would break down and blubber in front of the cheerfully stupid yokel. Taking a deep, sobbing breath, Hux in a low voice said, "I'm in real bad trouble. Only Reverend Thurlow can help me now. What would you say if I told you I was on the point of killin' somebody?—that I'm scared if I don't see the Reverend I just might do it?"

"You tryin' to kid me?"

"I swear I'm not tryin' to kid you," replied Hux, who had, without thinking, lapsed into the accents of Ainsley Black. "I'm desperate." And he stared at the guard with wet, shiny eyes. After a moment the guard looked away, shaking his crew-cut head in perplexity. "I mean what I say," continued Hux. "I'm right at the point of killin' somebody—somebody who—well, never mind who. I can't help myself."

"All right," said the guard, lifting his bulk from the chair. "I reckon I better speak to Reverend Archie B. Now, don't you go away," he added, as if Hux might suddenly dash off to do what he had in mind.

Standing outside the door, Hux could hear a steady rumbling of voices, occasionally punctuated by cackling laughter. He felt both resolute and frightened. During the service at the Mt. Hebron Baptist Tabernacle, Hux had alternately wept and shivered but he had not joined the dozen or more sinners who came forward at the end nor had he tried to speak with Brother Thurlow after the service. The bustle, the crowding, was too great for a private audience. Instead, he had lurked outside the Tabernacle until Brother Thurlow, accompanied by half a dozen followers, came out the back entrance and crowded into three waiting cars; then, in his own car, Hux had followed the little motorcade back to the Sunrise Motel on the outskirts of Fayetteville. There he had waited in the parking lot to give the evangelist time to cool off, to collect himself after his ordeal (as Hux saw it) at the Tabernacle. At the end of twenty minutes Hux had then mounted the outside stairs of the motel to confront the guard. From inside the motel the sounds now gave the impression that a rowdy, all-night poker game was in progress. So powerful was this effect that when the fat boy opened the door and beckoned him inside, Hux, though he knew better, was for the moment surprised by the absence of cigarette smoke and whiskey fumes in the air-conditioned room.

Two men, wearing short-sleeved white shirts like the fat boy's, were seated at a table, going over what appeared to be a list of figures. Another man, who looked like a country doctor with his wavy gray hair and rimless glasses, was thumbing through a stack of index cards, checking something with a pencil. The noise and laughter were coming from four men sitting knee to knee on a couch; they were loudly—and good-humoredly—arguing about something while they drank Coca-Colas from cans. After they had all for an instant glanced up at Hux, who was dressed in his tan poplin suit and wearing a striped tie, they paid him no further attention. The guard knocked at the inner door of the suite. It was opened, and Hux could see Brother Thurlow lying shirtless and face-down on a bed. A buxom young woman was leaning over him, massaging his shoulders.

"Five more minutes," she said, lifting her head and shaking back the profusion of light brown ringlets that fell across her face.

The guard nodded and softly closed the door. "Five more minutes," he repeated, with a concerned look at Hux. "You jes' keep ahold of yourself five more minutes an' Reverend Archie B.'ll take care of you. He'll know what to do."

The preacher had pulled a T-shirt over his stocky torso and was standing by the bed. As Hux came in, the heavy young woman gave him a warm smile of encouragement and went out by the same door. "So you're thinkin' of killin' somebody," said Thurlow, who thrust out his hairy, well-muscled right arm and rested his hand heavily on Hux's shoulder.

Shaking his head slightly, Hux looked down, shamed by his lie. "I've dreamed of killing somebody," he whispered. And then: "I'm afraid."

His hand still on Hux's shoulder, Thurlow waited for more. But Hux was dumb; his knees shook and he had trouble drawing in his breath.

"Were you at the Tabernacle?"

Hux could only nod.

Then Thurlow placed the fingers of his free hand under Hux's chin and tipped it up, so that their eyes met. The blond professional man in his tan suit and the scowling black-haired preacher in his sweat-stained T-shirt and blue trousers stood face to face, the preacher's arm forming a bridge of flesh to Hux's shoulder. Thurlow's eyes were dark, purplish-brown like plums, angry and loving, and Hux felt most of the strength go out of his legs, leaving him barely able to stand.

"Have you been saved?" asked Thurlow at last, a faintly evangelical ring sounding in his voice. "Have you thrown yourself at the feet of our Lord Jesus Christ and asked Him to free your immortal soul from Satan's grip?" His own fingers dug bruisingly into Hux's shoulders.

"No!" cried Hux with a blind shaking of his head. And he sank as if pushed to the carpeted floor, his arms encircling Brother Thurlow's knees, his face against the shiny blue cloth of the preacher's pants. "Save me," he sobbed, "save me." Suffocating, nearly drowning, he let his head sink lower and lower until his forehead was pressed hard upon Thurlow's shinbones. A shock of Hux's hair which had fallen forward now almost brushed the tops of the bare feet and both ends of his striped tie were splayed on the carpet.

Thurlow's hand had moved from Hux's shoulder to his head, where its pressure was light. "The Spirit is workin' mightily within you," he intoned. "You will be saved." But as yet he made no move to lift Hux to his feet.

Later, when Hux's breathing had become regular, the preacher said, "Your sins are forgiven. Arise and sin no more."

Hux raised his streaked and reddened face, his eyes narrowed as if hurt by the light. Then he moved to a half-kneeling position, which he held for several seconds as if waiting for further permission to stand up. The preacher removed his hand from Hux's head, and Hux rose to his feet.

"What is your name?"

"Ainsley," Hux blurted out. Then, after a rasping breath, he said, "Hux. Lawrence Hux."

"Ainsley Lawrence Hux?"

"Just Lawrence Hux."

"Lawrence Hux, will you shake hands with me?"

Hux did so.

"Welcome to the fellowship of Our Blessed Savior, Jesus Christ." Thurlow paused expectantly and, when Hux said nothing, sounded a loud "A-men," with a prolonged and very flat "a."

"Amen," said Hux, pronouncing the word as the preacher had done but without the emphasis.

"You look worn out, my friend," said Thurlow, still clasping Hux's hand. "And troubled. Deeply troubled. Bruised in the depths of your soul—like the Devil's been using you as a punching bag. Am I right?"

Hux nodded.

The preacher released his hand and stood back. "Well, you've taken the first big step in the right direction, my friend. You've come to the right place. And now you must pray—pray and pray and pray to the Lord to strengthen you in your resolve. I don't know in what guise Satan's been visitin' you, but I'm sure he's been comin' around in one way or another—"

Hux shivered. *Clark*, he thought—*Clark* . . .

"Whether," continued the preacher, "he appears in the guise of lust or overindulgence in alcoholic drink or some kind of meanness to your loved ones or cheatin' somebody in business or dreamin' about killin' your enemy—" He paused, his dark eyes focusing steadily upon Hux as his head went up and down. "Whatever form he takes, I can tell he's been givin' you fits. Even temptin' you to commit murder. But you've reached the point where you're not goin' to take it any more." Now Thurlow pointed a thick finger at Hux and cried out in a voice rich with vibrato, "You're goin' to stand up and fight! You're goin' to put on the armor of Jesus Christ and defy that foul fiend to do his worst!"

Then, his voice dropping, he said, "Now go git yourself some rest and come back here at ten o'clock tomorrow mornin'. That's when I see visitors. I'll give you all the time you need, and we can git to the bottom of this thing—whatever it is—that's botherin' you. Meanwhile, you are safe in His hands. Sleepin' or wakin', no harm will befall you. And you're not goin' to harm anybody else. Got that straight?"

Hux nodded. "Thank you," he said humbly.

"Thank the Lord God Almighty. And now, before you go, I want you to promise me somethin'— By the way," he added, suddenly frowning, "are you in the habit of churchgoin'?"

"No," said Hux. "I haven't gone regularly since I was a boy."

"And how about prayin'? Are you in the habit of daily prayer?"

Hux gave a negative shake of his head.

"Well, startin' this very night," said Thurlow, his frown deepening, "I want you to get down on your knees by your bed like a little chile and beg the Lord's forgiveness for your sins and ask His blessin' on your resolve to lead a new life in His service. Will you promise me to do that?"

Hux nodded. The prospect was strangely and unimaginably thrilling.

"Then goodnight to you, my friend. I'll expect you at ten o'clock sharp."

Again they shook hands, and as they did so, the preacher's face sagged, as if something had suddenly gone out of him.

The group in the anteroom looked up as Hux passed through. The stout young woman with the ringlets was watching television in a corner. At the door Hux heard Brother Thurlow call out, "Thelma, you come on back in here, girl!"

No harm befell Hux that night; no apparitions or bad dreams came. Kneeling by his bed, his face buried in his arms, he prayed that night and again in the morning. The great, warm, orgasmic waves of emotion that he had experienced at Brother Thurlow's feet passed over him every time he invoked the name of Jesus. As the remembered words poured out from his childhood, Hux let them come. He did not question their source or try to analyze the state of his belief. The experience was everything; the understanding of it trivial. Whatever traces of revulsion or fear had been attached to the vulgar image of the preacher were now obliterated by Hux's overwhelming sense of the saving power emanating from the man—power that had its source in God. To this Hux's surrender was absolute.

237

Chapter Thirty-five

Though he had been up and busy since seven o'clock, Archie B. Thurlow was not yet dressed to meet his public at ten. Wearing a white T-shirt and beige double-knit leisure slacks with an elastic waistband, the preacher was seated, with a bath towel over his shoulders, at the dressing table in his motel room. His feet, thrust into a pair of laceless sneakers that he regularly used for slippers, were stretched out beneath the table while he leaned back in his chair to receive Sister Thelma McKinney's "improvements" on a recent haircut—a mangled job by a local barber. Dancing around him, she moved with surprising grace, clicking and lifting her scissors as if they were castanets; her weight, so evident in her hips and thighs and in her ballooning breasts, seemed to have nothing to do with her small, quick feet, which darted this way and that beneath the bell-bottomed pants of her green slack suit. On the screen of the color television set, which faced the improvised barber's chair from across the room, a colleague (and rival) of Brother Thurlow's—Reverend Scotty Biggers—was conducting his half-hour morning service from Dallas; it was a program that Brother Thurlow liked to watch—sometimes admiringly, always appraisingly—whenever his schedule permitted. Already that morning Brother Thurlow had conferred by telephone with his advance scout and trouble-shooter in New Orleans and had, during an early breakfast meeting with his two most trusted advisors, reached the prayerful decision to fire, at long last, his publicity man, Buddy Chalmers, who had once again miscalculated in his arrangements for a press conference, this time in Fayetteville. The decision was a painful one, and Archie Thurlow had brooded over it during the lengthy shower and shampoo that preceded the hair trim in progress.

The suddenly impassioned voice of Reverend Scotty Biggers now filled the room. The preacher—an emaciated, narrow-eyed figure who conformed roughly to Brother Thurlow's mental image of John the Baptist in the wilderness—was rounding out his half hour with a fiery denunciation of those congressmen who were busy houndin' an' vilifyin' one of the few truly Christian Presidents this country

238

had ever had. Though Brother Thurlow emphatically agreed with Reverend Biggers's views, he was rather scornful of the evangelist's style, which he found antiquated, much too countrified for today's viewing public. No need to sound like such a hick, he thought, recalling that he had heard nigger preachers with a more educated delivery. Yet he also knew that Scotty Biggers's audience numbered in the millions. Brother Thurlow had recently begun negotiations for a television program of his own.

Above the rasp and twang of Scotty Biggers's Texan voice came the sound of rapping. Sister Thelma held her scissors in midair. "Thel, see who that is," said Brother Thurlow as he extinguished Reverend Scotty Biggers with the electronic control that he held in his hand.

"It's that man who come last evenin'," said Sister Thelma after she had opened and closed the door. "Name of Hux. Said you tol' him to come back at ten."

"It cain't be ten yet." Brother Thurlow lifted an arm to glance at his wristwatch, thereby dislodging snippets of hair from the towel. "Sure is," he said, shaking his head. "Right on the dot. Thel, sugar, would you jus' tell him to wait ten, maybe fifteen minutes? Tell him it's been one of those mornin's. . . ."

Brother Thurlow had by no means forgotten his appointment with Lawrence Hux. He had indeed thought about it several different times that morning—and always with surprise, for he had never had a man of Hux's type at his feet before. This type he would have described, with some vagueness, as "Ivy League" or even "Northern liberal": terms that he would have clung to despite the fact that Hux had said little that could have revealed his education or politics and had spoken with a diminished but still recognizable Southern accent. Still, Brother Thurlow *knew* the type, and it was one that he had always associated with the enemies of the Lord and of poor boys like himself, a type that was likely to be at once atheistic, communistic, elitist, nigger-loving, and rich. If Brother Thurlow had been astonished by the touch of the man's hair and tears upon his bare feet, he had also been moved—and awed. During the ten years of his ministry he had known the workings of the Lord to take many strange turns; yet God managed to surprise him every time. What could the Lord mean by sending such a man to grovel at his feet like Mary Magdalen? The Lord's got something up His sleeve, he thought, phrasing it that way to himself without the slightest qualm of irreverence.

But whatever the Lord's plan (and Brother Thurlow did not doubt that He had one—or that it involved him as well as Lawrence Ains-

239

ley Hux), there was an immediate problem to be dealt with. From the looks of him, the man was in a bad way. Afraid that he might kill somebody . . . probably his wife. What Brother Thurlow had done last night was to apply the Lord's first aid; today he would have to probe the wound. "Tell that fella I'll see him now," he said to Sister Thelma, who had removed the towel and shaken the hair clippings into the wastebasket. "And tell the boys outside I don't want to hear a peep out of 'em for the next hour. No visitors, no phone calls, nothin'." Brother Thurlow picked up a short-sleeved shirt from the foot of the bed and put it on, stuffing its tails unevenly into the waistband of his pants; then he pulled on a pair of white socks and stuck his feet into the well-shined black shoes that he had worn at the service last night.

Sister Thelma ushered in the visitor, who, though pale, looked less distraught than he had before. With a little wave of her fingers and a cheerful nod which set all her ringlets bobbing, she tiptoed out and silently closed the door behind her.

"Well, brother," said the preacher as he held out his hand, "I can see that the good Lord's given you the rest you so sorely needed."

As the hour wore on, Brother Thurlow had to resort more and more to strong-armed pumping, for the flow of his visitor's story had a tendency to dry up. At times the poor man's reluctance or embarrassment became so intense that he would hang his head and close his eyes for long intervals before he could be made to resume. The preacher was fascinated by what was being brought up, sometimes in rushes, often in mere trickles. He himself well remembered the killing of Clark Helmholtz and the sensation it caused. Though he had forgotten the name of Claiborne Herne, he had retained an image of the man from newspaper photographs of the time. Listening to Hux's account of his self-transformation into Ainsley Black and his experience at the Rededication service, Brother Thurlow could hardly contain his excitement. At one point when his visitor had lowered his head and was biting his lip, the preacher jumped up from the bed where he had been sitting and crossed over to Hux's chair; then, placing both hands on his visitor's shoulders and pushing him back in the chair, he leaned forward, like a dentist, his face close to Hux's upraised face, and said, "Brother, are you aware of what the Lord's been up to? Who do you think inspired you to become Ainsley Black? Who do you think led you into my congregation? Who do you think caused the powerful and holy current of grace to pass from me to you? Praise the Lord, brother, praise Him for His wondrous works!"

240

Hux silently stared up at him, the lids of his blue eyes quivering. "It's hard for me," he mumbled—"hard for me to take it all in. It's all too new."

Brother Thurlow released his grip on Hux's shoulders and went back to sit on the bed, his whole being alert to the Lord's purpose. "Now," he said, "I want you to tell me—word for word if you can— exactly what you said to Claiborne Herne that Sunday after the Holy Spirit had twisted the arm of your soul."

"I said very little. I was too wrung out. Too overwhelmed. All I could think about was—well, all I could think about was *you*—and what had happened to me."

"Try hard," said the preacher. "You must have said somethin'. It might be real important. There you were—you'd been livin' the lie of Ainsley Black and suddenly you got stung with the truth. . . ." He slowly shook his head, once again bemused by the wonder of it all. "I reckon you could say Jesus had found a new trumpet to declare His holy word."

"I had no voice then. I was too stunned. The voice didn't come until later in the week—last Thursday—when I stayed with Dr. Herne while his sister went out. . . . And I began to—" At this moment Hux's chest began to heave, and he had to pull himself together. "I began to speak the name of Jesus." Another silence ensued.

A few minutes before noon, Brother Thurlow went to the door of his bedroom and opened it. There was an instant clamor in the room beyond, where eight or ten people jumped to their feet and advanced toward the preacher. "No!" he shouted, blocking the doorway. "Cain't see you all now. Whatever you all got on your minds will just have to keep for another hour. Where's Thelma?"

She moved through the expostulating men almost as if she were swimming, a plump mermaid in green, her face bright with a dimpling smile. "Why, Archie B.," she said, "what in this wide world has been keepin' you? Couldn't you use a little lunch? I sure could!"

"That is exactly why I am here," said Brother Thurlow, who was suddenly ravenous. He instructed her to order two cheeseburgers with side orders of french fries, a grilled cheese sandwich with tomato slices, a piece of apple pie, and one coffee, black.

"But what about *me*?" Thelma wailed, smiling and frowning at once. "Don't I git to join you?"

"Not this time, Thel. That fella in there and I still got lots of ground to cover. You have yourself a nice lunch down in the restaurant, and I'll see you around two. Okay, boys," he said, raising his voice to the onlookers. "Time for a lunch break. We'll git down to business this afternoon. You all better be ready for me—that's all I got to say!"

After lifting his right hand as though to bless—or ward off—his retainers, the preacher turned back to his bedroom, where his visitor still sat in a lounge chair, looking pale, drawn, and, above all, submissive. The sight of Lawrence Hux filled Brother Thurlow with exultation. *It's a case of total surrender,* he told himself. *He's putty in my hands—I can mold him into any shape the Lord directs, put him to any use. . . .*

During their lunch, which Hux scarcely touched (relinquishing half of his cheeseburger and all of his french fries to his still-famished host), Brother Thurlow began a new line of questioning, often interrupted by the necessities of chewing and swallowing. Now that he had heard the Mississippi story, including the last two appearances of Clark Helmholtz (about which he reserved comment), he was avid for the details of Hux's background and education and profession. Chapel Hill, Princeton, the Woodrow Wilson School, the Morrow Foundation—these names reverberated in the preacher's mind like the temple gongs of some great, exotic, and wicked city: Babylon, perhaps, or Nineveh. What an edifice of pride and vainglory they represented! While his visitor was describing his work as educational director at the Foundation, Brother Thurlow suddenly cried out, "Education! What has it done for you, my friend? You've been privileged to attend all these great institutions of higher learnin' and yet look at you! A man at the end of his rope, steeped in sin and wretchedness, grovelin' in the dust of a ruined life, a hopeless case if the good Lord hadn't taken compassion on you and opened the door to salvation! It wasn't education that brought you to kneel at the footstool of the Lord."

Lawrence Hux seemed about to protest but compressed his mouth and said nothing. "I quit high school when I was fourteen," continued the preacher. "I would've been kicked out anyhow, but that's another story. The only educatin' I've had since that day has been in the great school of life and hard work, startin' with the Shelbyville Millin' and Lumber Company, where I went to work full-time the day after I quit school. I did have one measly year at the Burpee Bible Institute in Little Rock after I was called, but that was mostly a waste of time. Brother, you'd be astounded, let me tell you, at all the readin' I've done on my own. Astounded." Here Brother Thurlow scowled, as if he expected some denial or refutation of what he had said. "I've read tons of books I bet you never even heard of—books on philosophy, books on the secret religion of the Egyptians, on the ancient cities of the Holy Land, all kinds of stuff about the American Indians, which is a special hobby of mine—I've got a few drops of Cherokee blood myself—and everything I can find about the Lost Tribes of Israel. I bet I know every theory there is about the Lost Tribes and I don't believe a single one of 'em! But, Brother Hux—" and again his look grew fierce—"I'm tellin' you right now and you better believe me, all book learnin'—howsoever you come by it—unless it's been leavened and elevated by faith, is *mere chaff in the sight of the Lord!*"

The preacher rose from the bed and stalked around the air-conditioned room, his hands clasped behind his back. Then, swinging abruptly toward Hux, he jabbed at him with a thick finger. "I'd bet my bottom dollar there's one book you haven't cracked very often in the last twenty years. The one and only book—"

"You're referring to the Bible," interrupted Hux with a look that struck Brother Thurlow as less than submissive. "And you're right. I haven't looked at it very much, I've had no reason to—"

"No reason to! My friend, if you had made a daily practice of consultin' the Holy Writ of God, I assure you, you would not be in the miserable, pitiful condition in which you was in last night."

Hux spread his hands in a gesture more helpless than defiant. "The Bible," he said, "can't ever again mean to me what it means to you. I'll have to approach it—*re*-approach it from another angle."

"I reckon you think you've been educated beyond it," said Brother Thurlow with a sneer. Then he relented. "I'll tell you somethin', Lawrence Hux. Nobody respects learnin', the right kind of learnin', more'n I do. A good education is a mighty weapon in the service of the Lord. I wish I'd had a better one, I truly do," he added, with the hint of a pang in his voice. "But I'll tell you this. Your number-one job right now is to tear down the mighty edifice of pride you have built upon your privileged education. You must humble your intellect, Brother Hux, and become like a little chile, humble and contrite. Then maybe you'll learn somethin'. Maybe you'll learn that the Devil is real, the father of lies. Then maybe you'll be able to reject the Devil, once and for all, and dedicate all the learnin' you've acquired to the service of your Redeemer. Otherwise it's all chaff—worse'n that, it's the dried-up shit of the Devil that will be swept away by the terrible sweepin' broom of God's wrath!"

Brother Thurlow's voice had risen, had boomed out as if he were speaking in a cavernous auditorium. Now slightly out of breath, he contemplated his convert, who sat quietly, offering no response or resistance to what the preacher had been sure would elicit some kind of protest. "You're lookin' mighty drawn and tired, Brother Hux," he said. "You've been through a lot and there's a lot more to come. Now here's what I want you to do."

243

For the first time that day Hux spoke up independently of the preacher's questioning and prodding. Lifting his blue eyes, which were strained, a little watery, he said, "All I ask is that you don't lay too heavy a burden on me right now. As you say, I've been through a lot. I've felt I was losing my mind. I'm better now, thanks to—to something I can't begin to understand. And thanks to you."

"And to the Lord God Almighty."

"Yes," said Hux. "Yes, thanks to God Almighty. But," he continued in a weary voice, "I'm not up to much right now. My life is changing—unbelievably—and I guess I need a little more time to get my bearings."

"That's exactly what's on my mind. Now here's what I want you to do. I want you to set out right now, this very evenin', while there's still plenty of daylight, and drive to one of the beaches—Wrightsville Beach, Myrtle Beach—somewhere fairly close by—and I want you to lie in the sun for three whole days and swim and walk—git yourself some exercise." Brother Thurlow's excitement was growing, as if he had devised this prescription for his own benefit. "I want you to try real hard, hard as you can, to keep your mind a blank. No broodin' over the past or takin' thought for the future. Don't try to understand what the Lord's done for you. Just accept His grace as the greatest gift you've ever been given and leave it at that for the time bein'. I know that sounds impossible, but I want you to try. Okay?"

Hux nodded, his expression now less strained, as if some of the anticipated burden had been shifted to one side. "I'll do my best," he said.

The preacher studied him. "One of the best ways to empty your mind," he resumed, "is to fill it with prayer. Not the kind of prayer where you're askin' the Lord to do you a favor but the kind that's just thanksgivin' for the gifts He's bestowed—maybe somethin' like 'Blessed be the name of the Lord,' or a few lines from the Psalms, repeated over and over until your mind's filled with their sound and nothin' else. Do you remember any of the Psalms?"

"I guess I still remember the Twenty-third. I had to memorize it in Sunday school."

"Great! That's perfect. 'The Lord is my shepherd, I shall not want.' Jus' those two lines. Jus' keep repeatin' 'em about a thousand times every day, while you're lyin' in the sun or joggin' up the beach. Let 'em seep into every cell of your brain, every fiber of your bein'. And another thing . . ." Here Brother Thurlow paused, his dark eyes narrowing, his heavy lips contracting momentarily into almost a pout. "No sex and not one single drop of booze. Not even a glass of beer

244

when you're hot and pantin' with thirst. You hear me?"

Lawrence Hux simply stared.

"You hadn't counted on that, had you?" said the preacher with a triumphant sneer. "You were thinkin' about all those girls—practically nekkid—rompin' up and down the beach, and about gittin' loaded and laid every night—"

"No, that's not what I was thinking."

"Maybe not right now. But in a couple of hours, while you're drivin' down to the beach, drivin' along and thinkin' about— Well, I'm tellin' it to you straight, brother. The good Lord won't buy that—you cain't have it both ways with the Lord. My instructions—*His* instructions—is that you've got to purify your mind and your body, and that means refrainin' from sex until you can once again participate in a sanctified Christian union. No sex and no cigarettes and no liquor. You clear about that?"

"I don't smoke," said Hux with a slight smile.

Now the preacher's face softened. "I'm not pretendin' it won't be hard. I reckon I know the temptations of the flesh and the bottle as well as any man alive, but I also know the strengthenin' power of Jesus's name. When you feel the urge comin' on, just say 'Jesus, Jesus' about thirty times while you hold your breath and shut your eyes. Or keep repeatin' those words from the psalm. You'll be surprised."

Hux gave a nearly imperceptible nod, his expression as empty as his mind was supposed to become.

"Good! You hear me!" shouted the preacher, coming over to where Hux was sitting and clapping a meaty hand on his shoulder. "Now, le's see. Today's Monday. I want you back here in this room, all rested and restored, no later than ten o'clock Friday mornin'. I'll be thinkin' and prayin' about you, and when we git together Friday we'll work somethin' out. The Lord's got a plan for you—that's sure as shootin'—and by then we'll have more than an inklin' of what it might be." The hand was pressed down, then lifted. "So goodbye, my friend. Git yourself a good rest but watch out for that sun! I don't want no boiled crab crawlin' back here all blistered and sore on Friday."

Lawrence Hux stood up, and Brother Thurlow shook his hand, pumping it heartily up and down. Then he walked with his visitor across the room, opened the door, gave him a farewell clap on the shoulder, and bellowed out, "Thelma! You come on in here, girl. The rest of you," he said, scowling around the little room into which nearly a dozen people were crowded, "jus' hold your horses. I'll git round to each one of you in the Lord's good time."

245

Chapter Thirty-six

As if it had left the white print of a hand, Hux again and again felt the *whack* of Brother Thurlow's farewell clap on his shoulder—a shoulder which, after a day and a half on the beach, was already turning an ominous red. That hand clap had in some mysterious way confirmed, once and for all, Hux's access to the apparently inexhaustible flow of power, energy, nourishment—whatever it was—that the preacher had channeled in his direction. He had never felt more totally alive. The effects of the infusion seemed to be as much physical as spiritual; he moved with a lightness, an efficiency, that he had not known since the collapse of his marriage. In spite of—because of?—the prohibition on sex, he felt secretly, curiously, potent. The tan or rosy girls sauntered by, their oiled legs glistening, their breasts and buttocks suspended in cups of bright fabric, and Hux blessed them as they passed. He did not yearn or pant after them; he was able to stop any oncoming fantasy in its tracks, and yet he delighted in their presence and in the sense of reserved excitement that their presence conferred.

Despite the preacher's warning, Hux was reckless with the sun, reveling in its warmth and in the shock—stinging, then exhilarating—of the salt water upon his overheated skin. After three hours of sunbaking, a cold beer or an ice-tinkling gin-and-tonic would have tasted indescribably good—though hardly better than the Coke or Dr. Pepper that he drank at a hot-dog stand when he came up from the beach. Hux was not lonely. Staying away from bars, dining by himself at the counter of a rough-and-ready but adequate seafood restaurant he had wandered into on his first night at Wrightsville Beach, he enjoyed the taste of his isolation as he consumed fried shrimp and hush puppies and cole slaw. After dinner on his first two nights he took a long walk along the firm sand at the surf's edge and watched the late rising of the now lopsided, honey-colored moon, which was still full enough to spangle the waters. Then he returned to his motel room and read several chapters from St. Matthew (he was systematically working his way through the New Testament he had bought before leaving Fayetteville), undressed, stared sleepily at the television screen for a little while, said his prayers, climbed into bed, and fell almost instantly into nearly dreamless sleep.

Though successful in his abstinences, Hux encountered much difficulty in "emptying" his mind. It seemed impossible to avoid a certain amount of brooding over the past and speculation about the future. He would try conscientiously to keep the words of the psalm running through his head, but his powers of concentration were as yet weak and unreliable, and he found that after a minute or two the litany would simply fade out of his awareness, to be replaced by the familiar, often urgent concerns of his recent life. Then sternly he would banish these thoughts and again try to restore the steady drone of the sacred text: "The Lord is my shepherd, I shall not want." Often he narrowed down the incantation, repeating merely "the Lord, the Lord," or else substituting the name of Jesus. But none of this worked very well or for very long.

Most often it was the image of Archie B. Thurlow that dominated Hux's consciousness. While he was able to obey the preacher's injunction against trying to understand what had happened to him, he was powerless against the commanding presence of the man himself. And Hux's response to this presence was neither fear nor love but a gratitude so pure and so direct that it became as intense as any emotion Hux had ever felt for another person in his adult existence—as strong as his first love for Louise or his guilt-ridden grief for Clark. The man had saved his sanity, and probably saved his life itself—and perhaps the life of Claiborne Herne as well. In the glow of this gratitude, what could have been obstacles to Hux's acceptance of the preacher—his vulgarity, his narrow literalism—melted into insignificance. As yet Hux could scarcely get past the immense figure of Thurlow in the foreground, could catch only glimpses of what lay behind and beyond. God the Father, Jesus Christ the Redeemer, and the Holy Ghost that had wrestled him to the ground—these presences or concepts were still not very real to Hux, though he had found himself brought close to tears by the gospel story of St. Matthew, which he had not read since his boyhood. He had forgotten how astonishing the words and acts of Jesus really were! In any case he did not doubt that God—whether in the Christian version or some other—existed as the ultimate source of that irradiating current that had flowed toward and through him from the preacher. This towering intermediary blocked out most of his view, and Hux was for the present content to remain quietly in the shadow of the colossus, though he knew that sooner or later he would need to see beyond. There would be time, plenty of time. Meanwhile the gift was his, and he could hold it close, grateful beyond speech or thought.

By the morning of his third day at Wrightsville Beach, Hux knew that he could take no more sun. He bought a green-visored golfer's hat to shield his hot-pink nose, wore a long-sleeved shirt to the beach, and covered his stinging knees and thighs with a towel. The scarlet tops of his feet were now so sore that he could barely stuff them into untied sneakers. But how soothing the water felt, once the initial shock was over! Coming out after a brief dip, during which he kept himself submerged as much as possible, Hux covered himself again and sat for a long time watching some children playing with pails and shovels in the wet sand. It was a familiar, even banal, sight, yet moving to Hux in his present condition. One little boy of about two—a blond, serious-looking child with tiny striped bathing trunks and pudgy arms and legs—reminded him of Tony at the Jersey shore during their last year in Princeton. . . .

After lunch Hux retreated from the quivering heat of the sand and the streets into the numbing chill of his motel room, where he slept heavily for an hour. Awaking, he thought of Anne for almost the first time since arriving in North Carolina. She seemed very far away, nearly a stranger. . . . Wistfully, he summoned her face and voice, as if from a childhood memory. A scorched and smoldering trench, wide as a canyon, seemed to lie between him and the interlude of happiness, of lovemaking and tenderness, that he had experienced on the other side. He had no recollection of leaving Oxford, of the frantic drive to Memphis; it was as if he had emerged from a continuous bombardment of nightmares to find himself at his mother's house. It seemed to Hux remarkable that he had made the trip, that he had survived the terrors that rained upon him; only the image of Brother Thurlow, carried like a secret badge or a precious medal, had seen him through. And Anne was back there, far away on the other side—a face bending over him, a wide-mouthed smile, a voice. . . . Then, even more blurred, as if through a screen of frosted glass, came the face of Miss Isabelle.

Don't think about them, he commanded himself, suddenly aware of a seepage of melancholy into the liquid brightness of his mood. Both belonged to that past, at once immediate and remote, over which he was forbidden to brood. And the future—did they belong in his future too? Could he approach Anne again, changed as he was, changed as their relationship would have to be? The impossibility of it squeezed his heart. Again he tried to shut off his thoughts and this time he succeeded. Leaping from his bed, he pulled up the venetian blind and flooded his room with the strong light of the afternoon.

At four-thirty the sand was still too hot for Hux to walk across it barefoot. Before leaving the motel he had heard that the temperature had reached a hundred and one at three o'clock. What a heat wave!— apparently it extended all over the East and South. . . . Covered against the sun, he made his way to the damp, packed sand at the water's edge and sat down, letting the wetness soak through his chinos and the trunks underneath. A delicate, low-flying breeze was now coming in from the ocean, and he was not uncomfortable. In a few minutes he would be ready for the shock of the water on his stinging skin, but for the moment he was reluctant to bare his shoulders and thighs to the sun. The Lord is my shepherd, I shall not want. . . . Gradually the residue of his earlier sadness faded away.

The little boy he had noticed that morning was there again, playing with two slightly older children. How chubby his little arms and legs were, what delectable baby fat! Again Tony came to mind—Tony dancing, tripping, dashing, squatting on the beach at Mantoloking, New Jersey. Hux saw himself and Louise lying on adjacent striped beach towels, belly-down, with their chins propped on their arms, watching together and sometimes laughing at their child disporting himself ten yards in front of them. Whenever Tony got close to the curling edges of the surf, Louise, who was a worrier, would raise herself on her elbows and call to him to come back. After a while Hux would get up and, holding the child's hand, lead him up to his knees in the whirling water and sand. Tony was afraid of the breakers and would not go beyond them even when Hux offered to carry him on his shoulders.

As he watched the little boy, who was now hooting and crowing as he stamped around, brandishing his small green spade, Hux was touched by a yearning tenderness, a mixture of nostalgia and regret that tightened his throat. Yet he felt a deep happiness along with a sense of unbearable loss. He *had* loved Tony! And he had loved Louise too, as she rose to her elbows and called to the child in the fullness of her maternal concern. He *had* loved them; he had been capable, once, of that. Then a wild possibility occurred to him: what if he went back to Tony and Louise, told them that his life had changed, profoundly, and that he wanted to live with them again, wanted to build up, on a new basis that reflected his change, the love and trust that he had allowed to disintegrate. . . .

But Hux's rising euphoria was abruptly cut down. From the nightmarish jumble of his flight from Oxford the memory came, precise and starkly lit: he had made up a terrible, hurtful lie about Tony, had come close, so close, to wishing him dead, and he had told that lie to

Anne. How had such a lie found its way to his lips? The shame of it made him groan aloud. *Jesus,* he whispered, *Jesus.*

Then, just as abruptly, Hux felt better. He was not helpless. He could recognize what he had done and feel sorry for it. And tonight he would telephone Tony and tell the boy that he loved him, that he missed him. . . .

Standing up, he dropped his various coverings to the sand and strode into the ocean.

Chapter Thirty-seven

Shortly after seven-thirty on Thursday evening, Louise Hux pressed the button to start the dishwasher and left the humid kitchen, taking with her a stack of towels that she had removed from the dryer and carefully folded. Tony had gone out a few minutes earlier, taking advantage of the prolonged daylight to spend an hour with a school friend who lived a safe half block down West End Avenue. Tired and perspiring, Louise looked uncharacteristically frail, her eyes pouched and tendrils of dark blond hair sticking to her pale forehead. On such a hot night the kitchen was worse than a tropical rain forest, and Louise was eager to get to her bedroom, which was air-conditioned, and to take off the green-and-white cotton dress that had looked so crisp and pretty when she had set out for work and was now such a bedraggled mess. But more than the heat and fatigue of a complicated day at her editing job was oppressing Louise. Just before dinner she had received a long-distance telephone call from a woman—Anne something—in Mississippi, a woman with a Deep Southern accent who said she had been trying to reach Larry Hux in New York for the last two days; she hated to disturb Louise, she said, but Larry had promised to call and tell her how Tony was getting along.

"*Tony?* What's this about Tony?"

The woman, obviously perplexed, had said something incoherent about an accident; in a faltering voice she mentioned possible head injuries, x-rays. . . .

"Why that—that's just crazy!" cried Louise, who at the same instant was terrified that perhaps there had been an accident—but no, Tony was right there in the apartment; she had seen him only a few minutes ago, when he had come into the kitchen to ask if he had time to take a shower before dinner. . . . "But Tony's fine," insisted Louise, finding her voice again. "There's been some mistake. Did you say Larry told you he was coming to New York because Tony had been in an accident?"

"That's what he said." The voice had become faint. "I guess Larry must have been playin' a joke or somethin'. Anyway, I'm mighty glad Tony's all right. And I'm real sorry I upset you. It's—well, goodbye." And before Louise could ask further questions, the woman had hung up. . . .

Louise began to rank the clean towels according to size on the shelves of the linen closet. More than an hour afterwards, the telephone call still puzzled and horrified her. A *joke*, the woman had said—what a rotten joke. . . . Despite her own past troubles with Larry, despite her indignation toward him in Tony's behalf, Louise had never before felt hatred for her ex-husband. But that was what she was trying to handle now—a thin, keen blade of hatred for a man who could joke about a nearly fatal accident to his own son. Head injuries! Compressing her lips, she closed the folding doors of the linen closet and turned toward her room—once *their* room—with the conviction that she was a fool, a naïve fool, for not having imagined that Larry could do something so heartless. So absolute, so pure was this new hatred for Larry that she could not even feel curious about the woman who had called—this Anne something-or-other. Just after the call, Louise, breathless with rage, had tried to telephone Larry at his apartment. No answer. Throughout the meal with Tony she had had to conceal her rage and its cause, and the strain, even more than the heat, had left her limp. Several times during dinner she had noticed that Tony was looking at her oddly.

Now, with her hand on the knob of the closed door to the bedroom, Louise decided that she would once more try to telephone Larry—though probably he had not come to New York at all. As she pushed open the door and felt the gust of chilled air against her face, she heard the ringing of the telephone on her bedside table. *Philip*, she said to herself, sure that it was Philip Crocker calling to ask her for another date. In the few seconds it took her to answer the phone, a dozen conflicting thoughts and images raced through her mind: Philip, whom she had met at an East Side dinner party, struck her as something of a jackass with his braying voice and military (or financier's?) mustache; on the other hand he was lively, knew lots of people in sets that she had never entered, and seemed eager to introduce her to his friends; she had not been exactly bored on her one previous date, but she had hated his jokes and most of his social assumptions; his marital record was not good, but she mustn't judge him prematurely—she knew too little; above and beneath all, she was teased by a perverse sexual curiosity—what would it be like to go to bed with a man that looked like that, bristling eyebrows, fierce mustache, and all? Mentally set to deal with a mixture of bluster, flattery, and schoolboy impetuosity, she did not realize for several seconds that the voice on the line was not Philip Crocker's but her exhusband's.

"Is Tony there?" he was saying. And then: "Louise, I said I want to speak to Tony. Can't you hear me?"

"Where are you?" she demanded, nearly strangled with fury. "Are you in New York?"

"I'm down at Wrightsville Beach, in North Carolina. Louise, I've had an amazing experience. I'll tell you all about it as soon as I get home." His voice sounded higher pitched than usual, excited and a little breathless. "Right now, there's something I want to say to Tony. Is he there?"

At that point Louise nearly hung up on him. But then it occurred to her that the caller from Mississippi might have been playing some kind of bizarre prank, some unbelievably cruel joke. "Did you tell someone Tony had an accident—a serious accident?"

After a protracted pause, Louise heard a sound that came across the line as a whistling sigh. "I'll have to—well, I'll try to explain." There was another pause, and then: "How—what did you hear?"

"A little more than an hour ago, at around six-twenty," said Louise in a tone of steely precision, "I got a call from some woman named Anne something-or-other from Mississippi, who told me—"

"I know," said Larry, sounding very depressed. "I'm very sorry she called and upset you. It's my fault, not hers—a misunderstanding— that is," he continued with an obvious struggle, "it's because of something I told her—very wrongly, it's completely my fault—and she—"

"A misunderstanding! Is that what you call it? You told that woman you had to come to New York because Tony had suffered serious injuries—*head* injuries—in an accident. Is that right? Is that what you told her?"

"Yes."

Louise, whose throat and neck had flushed rose-red, expelled her breath. "I have no idea what was behind such a dreadful lie—such a cruel, vindictive lie—about your own son, but I do know this: You are not fit to be Tony's father. You never have been. And I'm going to take legal steps to protect him from you. I can never trust you to be alone with him again."

"You don't know what you're saying. Please, Louise, give me time to—" And then: "Is Tony there? Can he hear what you're saying?"

"No, Tony's gone over to Ivan Baumbach's. Thank God." Louise now felt herself on the point of sobbing aloud with rage and bafflement. "I don't want you to call him."

"Louise, I called to tell Tony that I loved him, that I was eager to see him again. I can't explain everything now," he continued, quickly, urgently—as if afraid she would hang up on him. "All I can tell you is that I was out of my head when I said what I said to Anne Schlamm. Out of my head. Frightened and desperate—desperate to get away—and that was the first excuse that came to mind—"

"Excuse!"

"It's too complicated to tell you about now. But I *am* better. A big change has taken place. I've experienced something that puts a whole new perspective on everything. You have to believe that, Louise."

"I don't know what you're talking about."

"I have found someone who has helped me a great deal—"

"Are you seeing a psychiatrist?" *In Wrightsville Beach!*

"No."

Louise waited, her anxiety rising. Was Larry crazy? Would she have to deal with a psychotic ex-husband, a psychotic father of her son?

"This is hard to say, Louise. I know how weird this is going to sound to you—but I've met a man—a minister—a preacher, you'd call him—who has helped—who has enabled me to open myself to something—" Larry's breathing at the other end was now audible. "Well, I'll just call it a kind of *force*, a force so great, so tremendous— I know how this must sound to you—but I can only think of it as coming from God."

"Larry!" *Crazy*, she thought, holding the receiver at almost an arm's length from her ear.

"You must believe that I'm better," came the voice from a great distance. "I will be all right. We will all be all right. I'm going to hang up now. I'll be back in New York soon—I don't know exactly when but soon—and I'll come to see you right away—"

She brought the receiver back and said, "No."

"Yes!" The word rang out with confidence. Then, in a lower register, Larry said, "I can't tell you how sorry I am that you got that call. It's entirely my fault. I should have expected it might happen— should have called you first. But all that's in the past. Please believe that, Louise. It was part of my desperation—my craziness. Everything is different now. Goodnight, dearie. Tell Tony I called. Please tell him." After waiting several seconds for her response, he said in a suddenly anxious voice, "Does he know about your conversation with Anne? Does he know what I told her?"

"No, I haven't told him."

"Thank God for that! You've used your head, Louise."

"Did you really think for an instant that I'd tell Tony such a terrible thing?"

"No, I was sure you wouldn't. But I was afraid he might have been there when Anne called."

"He was in his room. The bedroom door was closed. But afterwards I could hardly control myself. He must have noticed something."

"But he doesn't *know*. That's the main thing. Thank God for your good sense and self-control. You're a good woman, Louise. I love you."

"Don't say that!" she cried, nearly choking with bitterness.

"It's true. Goodnight, dearie. I'm so sorry about all this. I'll be in touch soon."

Louise sat at her bedroom window, which looked west to Riverside Drive and the river. Between two towering apartment houses on the drive, she could see the glittering water and the New Jersey Palisades and the sky. Inky-blue clouds were piling up fast, obliterating the sun, which, until a few minutes before, had hung luridly over the Palisades and the glassy slabs of the high-rise apartments thrusting upward from the cliff tops. The river shimmered with the silvery light that always preceded a storm in summer. Oppressed by the airless chill of the bedroom, Louise after a while went into the living room, which also faced west. There she opened both windows wide, allowing the curtains to billow in the strong gales that were beginning to sweep across the river, corrugating its surface with little whitecaps. The heat wave, which had lasted more than a week, was already broken, well before the first flash of lightning had torn through the clouds, which were now advancing in purple-black outriders almost to the top of the sky.

The room had suddenly darkened, but Louise did not turn on a lamp. Still at the wide-open window, she let the strong currents of air blow over her, while the curtains flapped on either side. Then a sharp pattering of rain forced her to close both windows in a hurry, but not before the sills were spotted with raindrops. Pulling up a chair, she sat by the streaming window panes, unable now to see the Jersey cliffs through the sheets of rain racing across the river and over the rooftops. She hoped that Tony had had the good sense to stay at the Baumbachs' and hadn't set out to reach home before the storm broke. Should she telephone to make sure? No, she was being overanxious; Tony was a sensible boy.

With a crazy father . . . She turned her face inward to the room, now so dark that she could barely make out the shapes of the furniture. So he's found God, she told herself. It was inconceivable. Larry had never shown the faintest trace of religious feeling, not the slightest nostalgia for his churchgoing childhood. On the contrary, the Larry she knew was not only unsympathetic but downright hostile to the mild and undemanding low-church Episcopalianism in which she had been raised in Virginia; he had refused even to consider her mother's plea—a polite suggestion, really—that they have Tony christened. *The Larry she knew* . . . But what in fact did she know? She had no idea what he was doing in Wrightsville Beach. Why wasn't he in Mississippi where he was supposed to be? Had he quit his job to follow some crackpot preacher? She knew nothing, and she realized that she had known nothing about him—really—for a very long time. His periodic visits to West End Avenue had revealed little except that he was troubled and unhappy. There was nothing new in that. Recently he had put on a lot of weight. He showed less and less interest in Tony. So far as she was aware, he did not have a steady girlfriend. His apartment, according to Tony, was a mess. . . .

But crazy? Out of his mind? Fantasizing a nearly fatal accident for Tony one day and turning to God the next!

Of course the whole involvement with Clark in Mississippi had had its crazy aspect. Once, not long after Clark was killed, when Larry was attacking her for having dragged him back from Mississippi, Louise, reaching for any weapon to defend herself, had accused him of having fallen in love with Clark—platonically but still homosexually in love with him. Larry had gone wild, denouncing her for trying to cheapen his friendship, finally reaching such a pitch of outrage that he had swept the lamp and books off the tabletop next to him before storming out of the house. That had been crazy. He had even told her of his conviction that he could have saved Clark if he had been present at Tupelo. That was crazy—pure megalomania. Yet in all those years she had not thought of him as crazy, had always imagined herself to be dealing with a man who, however disturbed some of his behavior, was basically sane, a man to be reasoned with, to be argued with, occasionally (and increasingly) to be fought with. But now— Apparently she had been wrong all along, willfully blind to the true state of affairs.

She should have known. Memories of that most terrible of fights now came back to her. He had berated himself for being a coward, for having let her pussy-whip him into coming home. *Pussy-whip*—what an expression! And he had used it just after she had pleaded her desperate, frantic need for him—tried to tell him what it was like, once the nurse had left, to be cooped up alone, night after night, with a baby who seemed to have trouble digesting his food, a baby who cried much of the night.

Louise had now become almost oblivious of the storm outside that periodically whitened the room with lightning and made the windows rattle with thunder. She was thinking of the radiant and humorous young man she had married, the best actor in the Carolina Playmakers, the marvelous mimic who also happened to have a first-rate analytical mind, the graduate student with a need to know the secret history of every public political event, the young husband who could be so much fun, in bed and out, who— *What a waste! What a wretched, miserable waste.* With a sob she jumped up from her chair and lunged toward the nearest table to turn on a lamp. Instantly the room glowed. She turned on lamp after lamp—all the lamps—and stood in the middle of the room, orienting herself, glancing now at the paintings in their gilded frames on the walls, now at the amber, rose, and indigo pattern in the Chinese carpet at her feet. Then Louise went back to the window. Though it was still raining, the clouds had lifted on the New Jersey side of the river, revealing a clear, copper-green strip of twilight sky She would telephone the Baumbachs and tell Tony it was time to come home. *Poor boy,* she thought, already gathering him into her sheltering arms. She had seldom felt worse.

Chapter Thirty-eight

The conversation with Louise was at first devastating to Hux. Her bitter voice stung him and he could only repeat to himself (as if rubbing the spot where he had been slapped) that he deserved what he got and should have expected it. He had been a fool to think that he would not have to pay. And he would have to pay more: he would have to explain things, one way or another, to Anne. It would be wrong to leave her in the confusion and hurt that must have followed her call to Louise. Hux could barely bring himself to imagine what she must be feeling—and he cringed at the thought of how she might respond to his confession.

But though full of pain, he was not tempted to despair. Repentance, confession, reparation—these were part of the new burden placed upon him, and he felt able to shoulder it. He would write to Anne—no, telephone her—to write would be evasive, cowardly—and endure whatever she chose to lay upon him. Hux was still much puzzled by the form his lie had taken; that was one of the many things he wanted to explore with Brother Thurlow in the morning. There was much that he had not yet told the preacher.

That night, his last in Wrightsville Beach, Hux took one of his long walks on the packed sand. He would have to get up early to reach Fayetteville by ten, but he knew that he was too keyed up to get to sleep easily unless he had some exercise first. His sunburn was now a problem. Even the cotton-mesh sportshirt that he wore made the skin of his neck and blistered shoulders smart, and the hot-pink skin of his face was sore, despite repeated applications of Noxzema. The night's breath was so chilling as it blew across him that he wondered if he had a fever. Tired or not, he would have trouble sleeping because of the pain inflicted by every change of position in bed.

As he walked along the beach, past the straggling cottages at the far end, Hux felt a kind of joy in the very blankness of his future. It was as if a cottony fog had rolled in from the ocean, obscuring anything more than five feet in front of him. He was a new man, an Adam with his eyes just opened before the morning mist had lifted, the world before him unknown, not even seen, much less named. . . .

Despite his wistful fantasy of a reunion with Louise and Tony and his resolution to call Anne, Hux had no real idea of what lay ahead. Would he follow Brother Thurlow to New Orleans?—a New Orleans hugely different from his earlier images of it. Or would he go right away to New York? Would he keep his job, quit his job, or be fired from it? He could not know, and for the moment he was content to obey Brother Thurlow's command against speculation. Tomorrow he would have some of the answers. Meanwhile, there was something to be enjoyed in the very opacity of the fog. *The Lord is my shepherd, I shall not want.*

Returning, Hux left the beach, put on his sneakers (tying them as loosely as he could), and walked along the main street toward his motel. As he was passing the Town Pump Bar and Grill, the door of the tavern flew open and a shirtless, bleeding young man dashed out, screaming curses. He was followed by two other men, one of them carrying a stick about the size of a policeman's billy. The screaming young man stumbled as he stepped from the sidewalk into the street, and his two pursuers jumped upon him, one of them pummeling him with his fists while the other tried to land a blow with his club. Without thought or hesitation, Hux ran forward and grabbed the wrist of the man wielding the club. An instant later Hux found himself sitting on the pavement, felled by a blow that caught him just under the left eye, splitting the skin over his cheekbone. Blood streamed down his face and between the fingers of the hand raised to his cheek. He was groggily aware of a crowd pressing around him and then heard the siren of a police car.

The cut under his eye continued to bleed through the paper towels that the police provided. For a while it looked as though he might be arrested on a charge of disorderly conduct, but a bystander managed to persuade the police that Hux had tried to break up the fight. Eventually the police drove him in their car to the emergency room of the Keenan Memorial Hospital in Wilmington, where a young resident stitched up the cut and covered half of Hux's face with a grotesque bandage. Then, after he had been issued some Darvon to help with the pain, the police, with whom he was now on almost an old-buddy basis, drove him back to Wrightsville Beach and his motel. The Darvon was strong enough to provide Hux with a good night's sleep despite the sunburn and the aching of his swollen cheek. He got up at six-thirty to drive to Fayetteville.

Chapter Thirty-nine

"What in the name of the Lord has happened to you?" Brother Thurlow jumped up from the bed where he had been sitting and advanced upon Hux, whom Sister Thelma had escorted into the room. "You're the sorriest-lookin' mess I ever laid eyes on," said the preacher, now face to face with his visitor. The face like an overripe tomato about to burst its skin, the thick white bandage with the purple bruise spreading beneath it, the dyed look of the sun-bleached hair—these details coalesced into an image that Brother Thurlow found hateful: Florida beach bum, degenerate, brawling surfer.... "Now, what have you been up to?" he demanded.

"I jumped in to break up a barroom fight," said Hux, grinning crookedly, his voice surprisingly vigorous. "Jumped right in and sat right down." He laughed. "I still don't know whether I got hit by a fist or a stick."

"Whatever it was," said Sister Thelma, who had been shaking her head and clicking her tongue, "it sure lef' you lookin' worse than somethin' the cat drug in."

"I won't be needin' you right now, Thel," said Brother Thurlow. "Check in with me about twelve and maybe we can git some of the boys together and go over to Red Sam's for some of that good barbecue." He waited until Thelma, in her floating, ballooning way, left the room. "Now you tell me this," he said, turning with a furious scowl toward Hux. "You been drinkin'?"

"Not a drop." He sounded unrepentant, unabashed. "Let me tell you what happened."

As he listened, Brother Thurlow nodded several times, his conviction growing that he was being told the truth. When Hux finished, the preacher said jovially, "I was on the point of kickin' you right out of this room, but I believe you. How-ever, it sounds to me like you're a little too full of the Spirit for your own safety. I cain't afford to let you git killed bein' a Good Samaritan before I even put you to work! Slow down, Brother Hux. The Lord don't require you to git your head busted wide open savin' riffraff in a fight that ain't none of your business to start with."

"I didn't even think about what I was doing. I just jumped right in."

"Sounds like the kind of stuff I used to git messed up in. Only I was full of the Devil—and I mean the Devil. Now sit down and tell me what else you've done to disobey my orders—like turnin' yourself into a steamed crab with all that sun." He sat down himself and propped his bare feet on a chair. Brother Thurlow was pleased by his convert's new tone. The change was amazing, even to someone who had witnessed the miraculous workings of the Spirit many times. Less than a week ago, Lawrence Hux, with all his privileges, had been little better than a beaten mongrel with his tail between his legs. Now he was full of fight—joyous fight, the Lord's fight—and raring to go. At the conclusion of Hux's brief account, Brother Thurlow was beaming as if he had made the man over with his own hands. "And now," said the preacher, "what are you goin' to do now? What thoughts came to you while you were roastin' yourself on the sand?"

Hux drew back in surprise. "I thought you told me not to speculate about the future."

"I did, I did, but that don't keep thoughts—or visions—from comin' anyway. Fact is, if you empty your mind, a vision is more likely to come."

"None came," said Hux as he delicately fingered his bandage, as though the skin were itching underneath. Then he said, "The rest of the work in Mississippi can be taken care of by phone or mail. I have some vacation coming to me which I can take now if I want to. I could come to New Orleans—" He broke off, smiled tentatively, and added: "*If* you'd like me to." He waited, but Brother Thurlow chose not to respond. Then Hux said, "I'll have to be back in New York no later than the twentieth."

"Are you eager to git back? Git back to the office, see your son?"

For the first time that morning, a look of the old dejection crossed his convert's face. "You mentioned visions," he said. "I did have a kind of vision—really just a brief fantasy. I saw myself living again with my wife and Tony—it seemed possible—but when I called—" Hux shook his head. "You see, I'd done a very dumb thing just before I left Oxford, and Louise heard about it."

"What kind of dumb thing did you do?"

When Hux told him, Brother Thurlow cocked his large head to one side and covered his upper lip with his fleshy lower lip. Then he drew his lips apart with a smacking sound and said, "You mean to tell me the words jus' came to you, jus' popped into your head?"

Hux nodded.

"Boy, it's a good thing you got here when you did. Looks to me like Satan was right on your back, whisperin' in your ear." Now Brother Thurlow frowned. "This Anne—you been sleepin' with her?"

"We made love once."

"And you wanna do it agin?"

Hux drew back, bristling a little. "I feel very bad about Anne. Ashamed of myself. I'm going to call her and—"

"Answer my question!" yelled the preacher. He saw Hux go pale beneath his sunburn as the line of his jaw tightened in defiance.

"That's my business. And Anne's."

Brother Thurlow pounded the table next to his chair. "Your business is *my* business, Brother, and my business is the Lord's! And the Lord's not goin' to stand for that kind of evasion and pre-varication. *Say* you want to sleep with her agin—say it right out—and then pray to God to give you the strength to refrain. Sex is blessed and holy in a sanctified Christian marriage. But as fornication and adultery, it is vile, and the Lord has set his seal against it. I know the power of temptation—oh, my, how I know it!—and what it means to struggle against it." The preacher's chest swelled froglike beneath the loose-fitting blue tunic of his leisure suit, and his face darkened. Then, exhaling loudly, he said in a quieter voice, "And I also know the strength the Lord gives those who pray for it, the strength to resist the worst and strongest temptations the Devil can send in your direction."

Hux nodded, his expression no longer defiant but hooded, thoughtful.

The preacher sat silently too. *Now?* he asked himself—was this the time? He glanced narrowly at Hux and then gave an imperceptible nod to himself. *Now* . . . "You mention New Orleans," he said, "and you mention New York, but you don't say one little word about Oxford. I guess you're not plannin' to go back there. Am I right?"

"No, I'm not goin' back. There's no need—"

"And what about that pitiful ol' man and his sister? You jus' gonna leave that ol' man danglin' between salvation and damnation? You've planted the seed of savin' grace, but it don't look like you plan to water it and make it grow. Am I right?"

"I can't go back."

The preacher ignored him. "And that sister of his—from what you told me, you raised her hopes, you won her affection and trust. And now you're jus' goin' to leave her—maybe worse off than she was before, with her hopes raised and then dashed and—"

"I'm planning to write her—"

"Write her!" Again Brother Thurlow pounded the table, so abrupt-ly that his convert jumped. "That's the weakest, yellowest thing I ever heard in my whole life!"

"But what do you expect me to do?" cried Hux, his face anguished. "I can't go back. If I go back, I'm afraid—"

"Afraid your friend's ghost is goin' to come again and scare you straight into the insane asylum? Is that what you're afraid of?"

Hux spread his hands.

"Man, where is your new-found faith in the livin' God? What do you think is the meanin' of all that's been happenin' to you in the last week?" A look of weary exasperation passed over the preacher's face. Then he leaned forward, his eyes flashing their dark light, and shouted out, "Oh, ye of little faith!" Seeing Hux quail physically, he drew back and said, in a voice full of scorn, "Can you sit there and tell me you're afraid the good Lord isn't strong enough to protect you from some measly ol' ghost fit to scare children on Halloween— that the Lord brought you this far and then intends to hand you over to the Devil to drive insane or else do some terrible thing, like kill that pitiful ol' man? Is that what you mean to tell me?"

Again Hux raised his hand and adjusted the edge of his bandage. His lips moved—he wet them with the tip of his tongue—but he did not yet speak.

"Don't jus' sit there like a dummy. Answer me!"

"You keep talking about the Devil. Do you really—literally—be-lieve in the Devil?"

"You're evadin' my question, but I'll answer you anyhow." Again leaning forward and spreading his knees so that his blue slacks hitched up, revealing his bare ankles, the preacher said ringingly, "Yes, the Devil is as real as you are, sittin' right there in front of me with that foolish look of disbelief on that foolish, beat-up face of yours. I've *seen* him once, and I've come close enough to seein' him several other times, close enough to smell his stinkin' breath and to feel it cold and clammy on my skin. And Lord knows I've had to deal with him hundreds and hundreds of times, even when he didn't git close enough to feel him or smell him." Brother Thurlow let his hand drop to his knee. "I'll tell you somethin' that'll shock you. The Dev-il's every bit as real as Jesus."

"That does shock me. How can you believe that?"

"I said as 'real.' Not as powerful. God can destroy him—He permits him to exist so as to try and test mankind. That's what free will is all about. But as long as Satan is permitted to exist, he's plenty powerful. We need every bit of Jesus's help we can git to withstand him. He is *the* Adversary."

Hux nodded, but whether in agreement or bemusement, the preacher, who was eying him closely, could not tell. After letting the words sink in, Brother Thurlow said, "I've been doin' some thinkin' about your case since las' Monday. I cain't be sure, but I think there's a good chance you've seen the Devil too."

"You mean Clark?"

"Like I said, I cain't be sure. I don't believe in ghosts, but I do believe in the legions of Hell. I think there's a mighty good possibility that the Adversary or one of his legion appeared to you in the shape of your dead friend."

"But why?" cried Hux, his face now mottled as if fingers had pressed pale spots upon his sunburned skin.

"We cain't be sure," said Brother Thurlow, who was enjoying the impact of what he had said. His convert had looked first panic-stricken, then stupefied. "Maybe he wanted to tempt you into murder. You tol' me you dreamed you killed the old man." Then, before Hux could respond, he said, "Of course there's another possibility."

"Which is?" asked Hux, as if he had suddenly snapped out of a trance.

"That what you kept seein' was an angel of the Lord!" At this the preacher laughed aloud and shook his finger at Hux. "Surprised you, didn't I? You think I'm kiddin' you, but I'm not. I think there's a equally good chance the Lord sent his angel in the shape of your dead friend to summon you to Oxford, Mississippi, to save the soul of a miserable ol' sinner. Now what do you think of that?" he concluded gleefully.

"But—"

"Think about it for a minute. Who do you think inspired you to become Ainsley Black and meet up with the ol' sister and make your way into Dr. Herne's house and confront him with the word of the Lord?" Brother Thurlow was now smiling at Hux, as if encouraging a slow student. "I know, I know," he continued. "Your dead friend was frightenin' to you, terrifyin'. And he seemed evil, at least that last time, and you cain't associate somethin' frightenin' and evil with an angel."

"Miss Isabelle acted like she thought *I* was an angel."

"And we know better'n that, don't we?" said the preacher with a grin. "I reckon you don't believe in angels anyway."

"I don't. At least, I haven't."

"We'll fix that. Anyways, there's a third possibility. But before I go into that, I'm goin' to have me a Coke. You like to join me?"

"Yes," said Hux. "My mouth is dry. I think all that sunburn may have given me a little fever."

"Wouldn't be a-tall surprised," said Brother Thurlow. He got up and walked across the deep-piled carpet but instead of going to the kitchenette with its refrigerator, he entered the bathroom, leaving the door open. There he urinated noisily, splashing the toilet seat in the process. *I've got him hooked*, he thought as he shook his fat, uncircumcised penis and tucked it into his slacks, leaving a trail of droplets down the front. He decided to play Hux for a while before reeling him in. Next he took two cans of Coke out of the tiny refrigerator, popped them open, and, without bothering with glasses or ice, brought them into the part of the room where Hux was sitting.

"What's the third possibility?"

Brother Thurlow took several deep gulps of his Coke while frowning at Hux over the rim of the tilted can. Then he smacked his lips and said, "The third possibility is that the good Lord's plannin' to turn the tables on ol' Satan, usin' me as His agent." He emitted a prolonged belch and continued. "It goes like this. The Devil really sets out to destroy you, appearin' as your friend Clark and temptin' you to murder that ol' man. That is, Clark really *is* the Devil, frightenin' and evil, and not an angel at all—at least only a fallen angel. But the good Lord gets wind of Satan's little plot and decides to play a trick on him. There's nothin' God loves better than playin' a little trick on the Adversary. You git the drift of what I'm suggestin'?"

"I'm not sure." Hux was listening intently, his one visible eye fixed unswervingly on the preacher's face.

"So the Devil summons you to Mississippi to commit murder, but the Lord steps in and sends you all unexpectin' and unprepared to hear me preach. And lo and behold, you git knocked off your feet by the Spirit. So instead of killin' Dr. Herne, you're goin' to end up bein' the agent of his salvation. Pretty neat, huh?"

"So according to what you're saying," said Hux very slowly, "it makes no difference whether Clark is a devil or an angel. It comes to the same thing in the end."

"Right! That's the Lord's scenario, as they say. Takin' somethin' evil and turnin' it into good." Baring his teeth, the preacher gave an exultant toss of his head. "You cain't beat the Lord. He'll win out every time."

"That's too simple," protested Hux. "Evil wins out too." He hesitat-

265

ed. "Dr. Herne may be a broken old man, but he did a purely evil thing—a *final* thing. He killed a man in the prime of life, a man who was doing what any Christian would have to consider the Lord's work."

"Don't you be too sure, boy." The preacher was scowling. "There's plenty of good Christians would say all those outside agitators swarmin' down here that summer were the very spawn of Satan."

"Are you among them?" cried Hux, starting forward in his chair. "I was part of that swarm, part of that spawn. And I consider that *I* was doing the Lord's work—just as Clark was—though it would never have occurred to me to put it that way. My only regret is that I had to leave, that I—" He broke off, breathing heavily, his visible eye narrowed to an angry slit.

"Now hold your horses," said the preacher. "Jus' hold your horses. I'm not goin' to git into the rights and wrongs of all that. I've known some mighty good niggers in my time and I believe in treatin' 'em right. They're God's children, same as you and me. But I also believe God ordained the separation of the races and that He's mapped out a different destiny for the Sons of Ham." Suddenly he laughed. "I can see from the look in that one baby-blue eye of yours that I'd have a hard time convincin' you of that. And I ain't even goin' to try!"

Brother Thurlow finished off his Coke and expertly tossed the can into a wastebasket halfway across the room. Exasperated as he was by the knee-jerk reactions of this Ivy League liberal, he warned himself not to go too far. He was fairly confident that his fish was securely hooked, but he did not want to risk losing him on such an issue. "When you talk about evil things winnin' out," he resumed, hauling the conversation back into quieter waters, "don't forgit you haven't got the whole picture. Your friend's death in the long run might be the means of savin' at least two souls—your own and Dr. Herne's— and maybe hundreds more before you git through. Lookin' at it that way, maybe your friend's death—terrible and hateful like it was— could be considered a sacrifice for a higher cause."

"I thought sacrifices had to be voluntary before they could have any spiritual meaning. And what about Clark's soul?" Hux demanded. "And what about his *life* and all that it meant to the people who loved him?"

"Who knows? Maybe his soul was already damned. You tol' me he rejected the Christian preachin' of his father."

Surprisingly, Hux offered no protest. He simply kept his gaze fixed on the preacher. Several times his lips parted, but he seemed to draw back from whatever he was on the point of saying. The preacher decided he had best let his line go slack for a while. No use hurrying things. A little prayer, a little silent communion—that was what was needed. Lowering his head and covering his face with one hand, as if about to take a catnap, he said, "I want you to join me in five minutes of silent prayer. Jus' stay where you are—we won't kneel this time— and let your mind play aroun' with what I've been sayin'—about goin' back to Oxford and finishin' up and all that. Don't force your thoughts. Jus' let your mind play around while you listen for anything Jesus might whisper to you. I'll do the same."

Five minutes passed, and another three. Brother Thurlow removed his hand from his brow and looked at Hux. The man's single eye was closed, and the fingers of his right hand were touching his lowered forehead. His lips moved from time to time. Then, as if feeling the preacher's scrutiny, Hux looked up, his lips parting further into a slow smile.

"I'll go," he said. "It's the least I can do in view of what God—and you—have done for me."

"Praise the Lord," said Brother Thurlow, coming over to Hux to shake his hand. "You go and you'll succeed. You'll wrestle that ol' man to the ground and you'll twist his arm until he opens up his heart to Jesus and cries out for mercy!"

"It may not happen like that."

"Never mind *how* it happens," said the preacher as he clapped Hux on his tender shoulder, making him wince. "I want you to give yourself one week, no longer. See him every day if you have to. Jus' keep up the pressure. And don't let a thing distract you. Don't go near that girlfriend of yours—don't even call her up—until you got that ol' man's soul in your pocket. You hear me?" When Hux nodded, Brother Thurlow said, "Now, my hunch is, it won't even take a week. With the power of the Spirit workin' through you, inspirin' your every word, I wouldn't be a-tall surprised if he didn't surrender everything he's got before you've been at him even for one hour. Wouldn't surprise me one teeny bit." He chuckled, envying Hux his assignment, wishing that he could have a go at the old man.

"And when I leave Oxford?"

"I want you to come straight to New Orleans. There I intend to put you to work in a humble and lowly capacity. I'm goin' to test you further. At the end you may decide to return to New York and your family." The preacher hesitated, his thoughts leaping into the future. Should he say what had occurred to him after his first session with Lawrence Hux? Would there be any danger in that? Would his ideas scare the man, put him off? Looking at Hux, whose comically battered face seemed to glow with expectation, Brother Thurlow decided to trust the spirit that was impelling him forward. "Or," he continued, standing massively by Hux's chair, his hand still resting (lightly) on Hux's shoulder, "maybe you'll decide to remain with me. An educated man, with your capacities for writin' and speakin', could be mighty valuable for the Lord's work. Who knows?—you might even end up bein' in charge of publicity and press releases for the Archie B. Thurlow Mission of Rededication. You might even look pretty good on TV!" He laughed and gave Hux a little push on his sore back. "Now that ain't a promise but it sure is a possibility."

PART 5

Chapter Forty

On Friday night Rooney waited with Vicky in his parked car until the lights went out in the Hernes' living room and went on, a minute or so later, in Miss Isabelle's bedroom. Then, after telling his wife not to leave the car until he got back, he sprinted soundlessly toward the house. Rounding the corner past Dr. Claiborne's workroom, he headed for the kitchen entrance, where, following the instructions whispered to him over the telephone by the doctor, he waited a full five minutes before trying the door. The grass of the back lawn had been cut and its fragrance hung thickly in the warm air. The door had indeed been left unlocked. After tiptoeing through the dark kitchen, telling himself that it was unnecessary to tiptoe, that Miss Isabelle wouldn't even hear a bomb going off, Rooney entered the hall, where he could see light coming through the crack under Dr. Claiborne's bedroom door. He did not knock but slowly turned the knob and pushed. The door was locked from the inside.

"Dr. Claib'n," he called softly. "It's me. Open up."

"Go away. I've changed my mind."

"Now come on. Don't give me that stuff." Rooney leaned his shoulder against the flimsy door, making it creak. "Vicky waitin' in the car."

"I mean it. Go away." There was a long pause. "I've changed my mind."

"Your preacher friend come back?"

"No, I just don't want to see Vicky. I don't want to get involved in all that again." Though the doctor's voice was muffled, his words were clear enough; he did not sound as drunk as Rooney had expected him to be.

"That ain't the way you sounded on the phone this mornin'. You said you couldn't hold out till Sunday. Had too big a load on your mind. Needed her right away. That's what you said." Rooney waited for the words to penetrate the old man's skull, which was thicker than this door, which you could practically poke your finger through. One good push would send it crashing from its hinges—that's all it would take. . . . "Now come on, Dr. Claib'n," he said. "I broke a date in Memphis to bring her over here tonight. Real important date—could cost me five hundred dollars, easy. Could even git me in bad trouble. So we ain't about to go away. Now you jus' open that door, you hear?" Drawing back, Rooney stood for a moment with his thumbs hooked in his belt, as if to keep his hands from battering the thin plywood in front of him. "I'm gonna count to three," he said, feeling his neck and shoulders go rigid with anger. "If that door ain't open—"

The lock clicked and the door was pulled back. The sudden burst of light for a moment blinded Rooney, whose pupils had grown wide and tender in the darkness. Dr. Claiborne stood just inside the door, his hair white as a cloud where the light struck it, his face shadowed. Stripped to the waist, the doctor's torso was still well-muscled for a man of his age; only his arms and throat looked stringy. His feet were bare and the color of yellowed ivory beneath the white trousers. From his right hand dangled a snaky length of braided rawhide, with a wooden handle.

"That's better," said Rooney as he stepped into the room.

The doctor twisted his face into a scowl that was almost a crooked grin and raised his whip. "If you don't get out of here in one second flat," he said, "I'm going to take every inch of skin off your back."

"Is that right?" Rooney's hand shot forward and caught the doctor's wrist. For a moment the two men strained against each other in a kind of Indian wrestling, the doctor's face and throat darkening to purple above the pale skin of his shoulders. There was no sound except for the doctor's breathing as the brown arm inexorably brought the white arm down. The whip dropped to the floor.

"Prayer meetin' time, Dr. Claib'n. Prayer meetin' time." Rooney performed a little shuffling dance before reaching down to pick up the whip, which he placed on the white counterpane of the bed. Then he went to fetch Vicky, who was feeling nervous about her first nighttime visit to the doctor.

Rooney sat restless in the humming night, sometimes tapping on the car's dashboard with his fingertips. He was in trouble with the Memphis boys, probably in danger. He might have to go away for a while. Since he needed money—at least a thousand—and needed it fast, he had felt desperate when Dr. Claiborne balked—desperate and furious. How easily he could have killed the old man! At one moment while they were Indian wrestling, Rooney had felt a barely controllable urge to let go of the doctor's wrist and go for his throat. If Dr. Claiborne hadn't given in when he did . . . The possibility made Rooney shiver. A murder rap was the last thing he needed.

Vicky was approaching, her white nurse's uniform gleaming softly in the diminished moonlight. Rooney leaned across the front seat and opened the car door.

"Everything cool?" he asked.

Vicky slung her black satchel into the back seat before answering. "He needed it real bad," she said. "Wouldn't let go of my knees—jes' beggin' for it like a ol' hound dog. That ol' man's the biggest mess I ever hope to see." Vicky laughed and gave a heaving sigh.

"Don't you talk 'bout Dr. Claib'n like that." Rooney started the car but did not turn on the headlights. "How much he give you?"

"Forty."

Rooney said nothing. The big car, its motor purring, moved slowly down Granada. No lights showed in the Hernes' house. Vicky settled into her seat like a giant marshmallow, her knees spread, her bosom rising and falling beneath the starched white of her uniform.

"You think you got him back where you want him?"

"Unh hunh," said Vicky noncommittally. She unwrapped two sticks of chewing gum and thrust them into her mouth. Soon the odor of spearmint mingled with the rank odor of exertion that rose from her body and the hospital smell of Clorox that clung to her uniform.

"You damn well better have him lickin' your hand," said Rooney.

271

"I'll let it sink in for a couple of days and soften him up real good. Then I'll pay him a visit. He want to see you again on Sunday?"

"Sunday too soon," said Vicky, her jaws working slowly. "He still be too raw on Sunday."

Rooney switched on the headlights and the car radio as well. Pushing the selection buttons on the panel, he at last got what he wanted—an all-night station in Memphis that played nothing but rock. Edgy and restless, he decided to drop Vicky off at home and then head west to Clarksdale. He needed the roar and swish of the highway and the rush of wind even more than whatever action awaited him there.

Chapter Forty-one

Isabelle sat at the front window of the living room, half concealing herself behind the white curtains, unwilling to be seen from the street. White cloth daisies with yellow centers adorned her new navy-blue Sunday hat, which she had forgotten to take off; it was now tilted back, pushed a little to one side, giving her the air of someone who had just returned, somewhat unsteadily, from an Irish bar. She had, in fact, just returned from the Presbyterian church. Even at the open window Isabelle was aware of the smell of a roasting guinea hen and steaming onions—smells that, however appetizing, seemed excessive to her, a little vulgar. She missed the old house, where the kitchen was so far from the front rooms that even the odor of boiling turnip greens and salt pork could seldom penetrate them. Claiborne was in his bedroom, where he had remained all morning—and where he had remained yesterday as well, refusing to come out for meals. The pain—the intense pain—caused by her brother's relapse was partly offset for Isabelle by her excitement over the impending arrival of Ainsley Black. Already he was a little late, and Isabelle sat in dread of the ringing of the telephone, feeling that she could not survive the disappointment if he should call to say that the Lord had suddenly made other plans for him.

His call yesterday had come, providentially, at a moment of wild despair. Puzzled by Claiborne's refusal to leave his room for breakfast, she had returned to the kitchen, where, for the first time, she noticed a tracking of newly cut grass and the unmistakable print of a sneaker's tread on the polished linoleum just inside the kitchen door. Sinking into a chair, she had leaned across the kitchen table and wept, her whole body convulsed. Rooney and Vicky had entered the house—*her* house—during the night! Sickened by the violation, she did not for some time become aware of the ringing of the telephone. . . .

Ainsley was now almost twenty minutes late. When Isabelle heard an approaching car, she pressed a hand to her bosom and held her breath. But it was only the McCutchins from down the street returning from the Baptist church. If only Ainsley hadn't gone away! If only he could have come last Sunday to reinforce the progress her brother had made, to help him take another faltering step toward God! But the Lord had other plans for him—and for her. She must learn to accept that fact, to bear no resentment. It was hard. . . . Though she longed to be able to tell Ainsley that during his absence the Spirit had descended, Isabelle felt that her brother was further from the Lord's sanctifying touch than ever. And her own thoughts were foul: again and again at church this morning—even when her lips were moving with prayer—she had found herself wishing that Rooney Lee might die. . . .

A crash came from the kitchen, a crash so loud that even Isabelle heard it. What, she wondered, had Europa dropped this time? Isabelle hoped it was not the roasting guinea hen. Having Europa in the kitchen was a mixed blessing these days. When the old woman, who had worked for the Hernes for twenty-six years before retiring to live with her married granddaughter in Memphis, called to say that she was going to be in Alhambra on Sunday and would like to cook dinner for the Hernes, Isabelle had hesitated to accept the offer. She told Europa that while they would of course love to see her, they didn't want her to feel that she needed to cook for them every time she visited her niece Sharon in Alhambra. But Europa had not only insisted that she wanted to cook Sunday dinner for her old employers but also promised to make up a batch of her Texas-style chili con carne for them to warm up for Sunday-night supper. Isabelle gave in, wondering if the old woman badly needed the big tip she got whenever she paid them one of her cooking visits. Then, of course, when Ainsley called, she had been delighted that she could ask him to share their treat. There had never been a cook like Europa, she said, urging him to stay for supper as well. When Ainsley not only agreed to stay for supper but also volunteered to spend the evening with Claiborne while Isabelle went to a meeting of the Women's Auxiliary at church, she had experienced a sudden, horrible misgiving: what if Ainsley didn't like chili? But he assured her that he loved it—the hotter, the better. Now Isabelle was worried that Europa, who had become very unsteady, might spoil the dinner, a meal that promised to be difficult enough as it was, given Claiborne's condition. She did not know which possibility she dreaded most: a refusal by Claiborne to leave his room or a dinner table dominated by his scowling, silent presence.

She comforted herself with the thought that Ainsley was one of those gifted people who could handle any situation. How wonderful his voice had sounded, how her heart had leapt! Sickened as she was by Rooney's pollution of the house, she had begun to cry with tears of relief when she realized that her dear Ainsley was back from Atlanta, ready to come to her, ready to help her pick up the pieces. . . .

Why was he so late? Isabelle glanced at her wristwatch—it was now nearly one o'clock. Once more she pushed back the curtain to get a better view of the street, and as she did so, a memory suddenly made her skin prickle with embarrassment. Last night she had dreamt that Ainsley was a little boy and that she was giving him his bath. . . . The joy which she remembered experiencing in the dream now filled her with shame. What if Ainsley could read her thoughts? She would die, simply shrivel up and die. Shuddering, Isabelle withdrew behind the curtains, her face hot as she glimpsed the happy yellow-haired child splashing about and felt his shoulders and slender arms slippery beneath her gliding, soapy fingers. . . . At that moment she heard a car pull up and stop in front of the house. Scurrying into the hall, she stood before the front door, her right hand splayed across her heaving breast. She waited—one, two, three—and then flung open the door and advanced with outstretched arms toward her blond savior. When he saw her, Ainsley, who looked so nicely dressed in his blue seersucker suit and striped tie, waved his hand in the air and called out her name.

The next thing that Isabelle noticed was that he was carrying a briefcase in his other hand. Then, seeing his face, she gave a little yelping cry. The sunburn, now peeling, was startling enough—patches of pink against tan—but his eye, his eye! "Oh, Ainsley, my dear, what on earth happened to your poor eye?" she said, taking another step toward him as he strode up the front walk.

He laughed gaily, raised two fingers to touch the yellow-green bruise extending beyond the bandage, and said, "I've wrestled with many a sinner in my day, but this is the first time I ever got knocked down by one. I wish I could say, 'You should have seen the other fella,' but I hardly saw him myself!"

"Oh, Ainsley!" Hugging him, pressing her forehead against his shoulder, Isabelle felt the heavy case bang against her leg. "Oh, Ainsley, I've needed you so. Brother's been having one of his bad spells and—well, you're here, that's the main thing. And Europa got here just before I went to church, and she's still her same old precious self. I'm afraid the cookin' odors are pretty overwhelmin' but you won't mind that, will you? These dinky modern houses just don't allow any privacy when it comes to cookin'!" Smiling in a way that made her cheeks seem to wobble, she let him hold the screen door open for her as she went in. Then she turned toward him in the hall, longing to put her finger on the discolored cheekbone, to touch lightly the bandage. . . . Instead, Isabelle removed her hat, which had been knocked to one side of her head during the hug.

"Ainsley, will you ask the blessing?"

The table was covered with a white lace cloth and the silver and glassware sparkled as if Europa had devoted all morning to them instead of to the food. Claiborne was at one end of the table, holding his shoulders rigid in a posture of military attention. But at least he had come to the table—Isabelle was thankful for that. And he had accepted Ainsley's handshake, though he had not said a word. Europa stood by the kitchen door in her freshly starched white uniform, waiting for the blessing to be said. Her white-tufted head was bowed, her eyes closed, her sunken mouth set grimly—as if at any moment she expected a blow on the back of her neck.

"O God, we ask Thy blessing," intoned Ainsley, "upon those who partake of the bounty of this table on this, Thy holy Sabbath. May we arise from it with a replenished sense of Thy goodness and Thy infinite mercy to all who open their hearts unto Thee. Amen."

"A-men!" said Europa so loudly that even Isabelle, who had been leaning forward to hear, gave a little jump.

There was plenty to make Isabelle nervous at the beginning of the meal. When Europa tottered in with the beautifully browned and succulent-looking guinea hen on a silver platter, Claiborne, with a wave of his hand, refused to carve. Ainsley then instructed Europa to set the platter in front of him. Ignoring Claiborne's contemptuous look, he managed the carving well enough, despite one brown sliver of fowl that landed on the white cloth. After carving, Ainsley joked about his sunburn, puzzling Isabelle, who wondered how he had contrived to burn himself so badly in a place like Atlanta. Then, with a look of wonderful courtesy, he turned to Isabelle and inquired loudly how she had been spending the past week. Grateful to him for keeping the conversation rolling, she responded by talking about a packet of old family letters she had received on Thursday from Cousin Gracie Roberts, who lived in St. Francisville.

Europa, who was then passing the gravy boat to Claiborne, interrupted loudly enough for Isabelle to hear. "She the one with all that red hair pile up on her head?"

"That's right, Europa. My, what a good memory you have! Cousin Gracie hasn't set foot in Alhambra for at least twenty years."

"Never took much shine to her, some reason or 'nother," said Europa.

Isabelle was on the point of gently rebuking her but let it pass. The poor old thing seemed a bit senile. . . . As Isabelle went on about the letters, one of which, written during the siege of Vicksburg, had been so rain-soaked as to be barely legible, she had the painful conviction that she was boring Ainsley—though he looked alert and interested. She was also aware of the angry-eyed glances that her brother kept firing in her direction. Would he suddenly pound his fist on the table, rattling the plates and the glasses? On and on she went, digressing more and more.

There was an interruption, but not from Claiborne. "What's that, Europa?" Isabelle looked up with a mild frown. "What did you say?"

The old woman stopped in her tracks, clutching in her gnarled fingers the plate of hot biscuits she was passing for the second time. "I say, times is changed." Her cracked voice was loud with exasperation. "Folks got no business botherin' with a bunch of ol' wet letters."

"Why, Europa!" Isabelle was hurt. "Old letters are a hobby of mine," she continued, hearing the loud clink of her brother's knife and fork as he laid them across his plate. She began to blush, feeling not only his furious stare but what she interpreted as the impatient gaze of Ainsley as well. "It may be a foolish hobby, but it does no one any harm."

"Nobody say it do," grumbled Europa.

"Go on about your great-uncle's letter," said Ainsley. "I find it fascinatin'."

"I doubt if it's very interestin' to anybody outside the family," said Isabelle, who at that moment felt for Ainsley a love that far transcended her gratitude for his encouragement, a love that she flung toward him coil by coil, wishing that she could bind him to her forever. If only she and Claiborne could legally adopt him as their son—make him a real part of the family! Simultaneously, she wished that she were younger, years younger, and less ugly. . . . Getting a new grip on her narration, she said, "It is an amazin' letter when you stop to think that a young man of twenty-three took the time—in the middle of that dreadful siege and all that hardship—to write to his ten-year-old nephew. And such a high-spirited, cheerful letter when you think about what was goin' on. I wouldn't have thought it was still possible to get a letter through the Yankee lines by that time, but I was never very good at rememberin' all the dates and details of the siege. Let's see, that was in late May, sixty-three, and—"

What she saw was that Claiborne had pushed back his chair and was standing up. He grasped one corner of his napkin as if he were trying to strangle a snowy bird. Then he let the napkin flutter to the floor, turned around, and strode out of the dining room.

"Brother! Brother!" cried Isabelle. "Aren't you goin' to stay for dessert? Europa's baked one of her lemon chess pies."

"Let him go," said Europa, who had come in to clear away the dishes. "He jes' actin' like a two-year-old, same as always."

"I kept hopin' I'd have good news for you," said Isabelle. "I kept hopin' I'd be able to tell you that Brother was still makin' progress while you were in Atlanta."

She and Ainsley were sitting side by side on reclining lawn chairs near the only tree—a six-year-old pecan tree—in the Hernes' back yard. The sky was like soft gray cotton, the air still and humid but not uncomfortably hot. The wet smell of the mown grass mingled with the overripe sweetness exhaled by the few remaining blossoms—now turning brown at the edges—of the cape-jasmine bushes at the side of the house. Beyond the border of the lawn was a weedy lot and beyond that an acre or so of young corn, planted by the owner of the cotton fields stretching into the distance. The cotton plants themselves were strung like tiny green beads in straight rows across the flat, mocha-brown earth.

"But the way Brother's been actin' . . ." She sighed. "At church this mornin' I was so distracted I couldn't concentrate at all, not even when I prayed for the Lord's help. I surely need it. Brother's setback has put me in a terrible frame of mind." Again she sighed, wishing that she could confess to Ainsley some of the foulness of some of her thoughts—and in that same instant she caught another glimpse of Rooney's mangled corpse. She knew that her only hope of cleansing her spirit was to pour out the whole story of Rooney; yet she could not bring herself to do that—especially when she did not know what the whole story was. . . .

Isabelle waited for some response, but Ainsley, looking thoughtful, was silent. Then, unable to check herself, she said, "What a pity you had to go away. If only you could have come last Sunday to reinforce the progress you had made with Brother and help him take another step toward a reconciliation with God. If only . . . "

Now he swung toward her, exposing again the discoloration of his face, which had been hidden from her as they sat. "Miss Isabelle, the Lord's schedule in these matters doesn't always coincide with our wishes." Then, with a gentle smile, he said, "I hate to tell you, but my stay in this part of the world is nearin' its end."

"Oh, no! You're not leavin' for good?"

"The Lord hasn't sent me my ticket yet, but in the nature of things it won't be too long now."

"Then we mustn't waste a moment! Time's too precious."

"Your brother—"

Damn my brother, she thought with a sudden flaring of jealousy— why must everything revolve around her brother? Instantly, she was ashamed of herself. "Poor Brother!" she wailed.

"Frankly, Miss Isabelle, I'm not too worried about your brother. His lamp is filled with oil. It will be lit. Just be patient, and it will be lit. When I'm alone with your brother tonight—while you're at your meeting, I'm goin' to make an all-out effort to strike the spark that will light his lamp. I won't be around to watch it glow and shed light, but at least I want to see it ignited. To do that, I have to know everything. Have you heard me?"

Isabelle nodded, though she was having difficulty in hearing him, for the expression in his unshielded eye made her uneasy; it seemed unnaturally bright, the eye of someone with a fever. His voice, too, was strange: deeper and more resonant than she remembered it—and less countrified. What did he mean by "everything"?—had he learned something about Rooney?

"Now, Miss Isabelle, I'm goin' to ask you a question that may cause you pain. But before I do, I want you to close your eyes and pray with me for a moment. I want us both to pray for guidance. Have you heard me?"

She nodded. His eye! Was he going to ask her about Rooney? But what could she tell him? She had nothing to go on but her own suspicions—awful suspicions—about the blasphemy of those prayer meetings.

"Now close your eyes. Let us pray silently together."

Dear God, she prayed, *give me the strength to rise above shame, to face the truth regardless of what it points to. This I ask as Thy weakest child, awaiting the baptism of my dear brother in Thy Holy Spirit. Amen.*

"Amen!" said Ainsley Black loudly. Then he tugged his chair a foot or so across the grass and leaned toward Isabelle. "Miss Isabelle, with the Lord God as your witness, answer me this: did you ever, even for a single moment, doubt your brother's innocence in the shooting of Clark Helmholtz?"

The words reached her like a distant shout heard through the roar of an oncoming freight train, a deepening roar that beat against her ears. Was she about to have a stroke? So be it. . . .

"Did you ever have any doubts?"

Had he raised his left eyebrow slightly or was she imagining it? The roaring had begun to subside. Though unwavering, Ainsley's cyclopic gaze was kindly after all, Isabelle decided. She felt a surge of trust. God was with her. She could say anything. . . . "Yes, I had my doubts. For just a little while. Brother was goin' through a bad time, a mighty bad time. I've often wondered if he wasn't on the verge of some sort of nervous breakdown. I was worried sick about him. You don't know what it was like in those days."

"Sure I do. Go on."

"There was so much pressure. He had to close down the Fellowship—the boys were afraid to belong any more, afraid they'd be called nigger lovers because of all the good work the Fellowship had done with the Nigras in the past. And when Brother wouldn't join the White Citizens Council, there was a lot of talk. . . ." All at once depleted, Isabelle let her shoulders go slack. Convinced that her brother was watching from his bedroom window, she turned in her chair and looked toward the house. He was not at the window; the shade was drawn. "He began his heavy drinkin' about that time—secretly at first, in his bedroom. The pressure was so terrible all those years—ever since the Supreme Court ruled against separate but equal. . . . It was a bad time for everybody, especially for people who felt there was a lot wrong with the old way."

"Like you?"

She nodded. "Yes. I felt that. There were a lot of things I couldn't square with my conscience as a Christian. And Brother—we didn't see eye to eye and we didn't say much to each other, but I could tell he was troubled too. He had been so good to the Nigras—they all loved him. . . ." She paused, biting her lower lip. "But when James Meredith tried to enter Ole Miss, it just about drove Brother wild. He couldn't bear it, even though he had spent a lot of money to send two Nigra boys to college. But it was a *Nigra* college, not Ole Miss, not his alma mater. . . . And then, a year or so later, when all those radicals started pourin' into the state—"

"Can you tell me exactly what happened on the day Clark Helmholtz was shot?"

"What did you say?" When he repeated his words, confirming what she thought she had heard, Isabelle tried to laugh them off. "Why, Ainsley, you sound just like one of those lawyers at the trial!"

But Ainsley was relentless. "Tell me about that day, Miss Isabelle."

She felt crowded, pushed into the corner of an airless room. This wasn't like Ainsley, to put such pressure on her. Despite her resentment, she forced herself to begin. She told him how Claiborne had left the house that morning after breakfast without saying a word to her or Europa. He had taken the car—he still drove then—and was gone all day. When he returned about six-thirty in the evening, he told her he had driven over to Beulah to look over a piece of their family land he was thinking of selling. "I'll never forget how awful he looked when he came into the house—the long drive had exhausted him and he must have taken a bottle of whiskey with him in the car."

"And you didn't doubt his story?" asked Ainsley, his smile gentler than ever.

"Of course I didn't. Brother's a truthful man. And everything he said was proved at the trial. There wasn't any witness at Beulah—nobody lives on that land any more—but . . ." Isabelle fell silent as she sensed the danger of what she was about to say next. She lifted her eyes to her interrogator, silently begging to be let off. His expression was tender, encouraging, implacable. There was no escape for her. "Someone," she began, "a Nigra who knew Brother, came forward and testified he had seen Brother in Cleveland, which is fairly close to Beulah, at exactly the time the shooting took place in Tupelo. And of course Tupelo must be about a hundred miles from Cleveland—maybe more—and in the opposite direction from Alhambra. There's no way Brother could have been in both places."

"But wasn't he seen in Tupelo by a lot of people?"

Isabelle looked hurt. Indignantly she said, "Why, the only evidence he might have been in Tupelo was the testimony of two of the agitators at that meetin'—both of them Nigras from Alhambra—who *thought* they recognized Brother and his car."

"But the jury didn't believe them?"

"Of course not! Those Nigras didn't get the license number. Besides, it was too far away for them to see anything clearly. And there wasn't enough left of that bullet to prove it came from one of Brother's guns, even though he did own a high-powered rifle like the one the murderer used. The so-called experts disagreed." Giving Ainsley a look that was as defiant and triumphant as her pouchy face could produce, Isabelle said, "They couldn't prove a thing! There was no way they could prove he cleaned and oiled his collection of guns just before he was arrested to cover up the traces. Brother was always cleanin' and oilin' those guns—at least once a week. In spite of the way the trial was reported up North, they never had a good case against Brother."

"Then what made you change your mind?"

"Why, Ainsley! I never said I changed my mind."

"But you admitted you had doubts. What caused them?"

Isabelle looked away. The fields shimmered, rose, and dipped in the brightness of her tears. Why, she asked herself bitterly, is he hurting me like this? Then, wiping her eyes childishly with the back of her hand, she said, "Those came later, those doubts. I had them because somethin' had ruined Brother's life. Somethin' that had to be even worse than the trial, bad as that was. Somethin' that was able to turn that wonderful, active, public-spirited man into what you've seen today!"

"But you said—I thought you said—things were going badly before the killing or the trial—that you thought he was having some kind of nervous breakdown."

Isabelle could only nod. She had said that. But she hadn't meant to connect those thoughts with her doubts. Or had she? She felt confused, cornered as she was by this *stranger* who was suddenly acting just like one of those lawyers. . . . "I never really—at any time— thought he killed that fellow. I'm tryin' to be as truthful as I can, Ainsley."

"I believe you."

"I did have some doubts for a while. Because I couldn't understand how Brother could have changed from bein' a troubled man to a totally *ruined* man, who isn't always quite right in his mind, unless— But then I realized the change must have been connected to somethin' entirely different, somethin' that had nothin' to do with the trial at all."

"Something to do with that colored fellow with the white Buick?"

He's read my mind again, she thought, feeling more trapped, more crowded than ever. "No," she lied. "Oh no. He just comes around to borrow money. No, I think it may be somethin' hereditary. Somethin' *physical*," she added, hating her cowardice, sure that God would now close His door against herself and her brother forever. I *will* tell him, she thought, I have to tell him. . . . "That colored fellow you mentioned—Rooney Lee—well, he was the one who saw Brother over in Cleveland and testified at the trial."

"And has been blackmailing him ever since!"

"Oh no. Not that. It's somethin' else. It's—"

But Ainsley was no longer listening. In his excitement he had jumped up and was standing directly over her. "Miss Isabelle," he said, his eye like a blue jet of flame, "whether you know it or not, you have already helped your brother more in this one afternoon than in the past ten years. I think I see a way of opening him to God." Then, in a less exalted voice, he said, "But you must be prepared for the possibility of losing him, too. He is not well. It may be that God will first open his heart and then gather him into His own abode."

"Then let God take me too!" she wailed, covering her face. "What would be left for me with Brother gone?"

Isabelle felt his hand on her shoulder, and when she looked up, she saw a radiance in his face that made her clutch his hand with both of hers. "God will see you through," he said. "Whatever happens. In helping me to help your brother, you have helped yourself too."

"Have I? Have I really?" Isabelle held his hand fast, pulling on it so that Ainsley had to lean forward a bit. Was he the angel of death? What a soft hand he had. . . . And how beautiful he was, despite the bandage and the bruise; there was something thrilling about his face, something that reminded her of the face of the young Alexander, a face from one of her old textbooks on the ancient world.

Though a faint drizzle was now falling, neither of them made a move to go inside. To Isabelle they seemed to be enclosed in a bubble of perfect stillness, a bubble that she hated to shatter.

It was broken by Europa, who appeared at the kitchen door. "When you all comin' in? Fixin' to pour," she called—so loudly that Isabelle heard the sound though not the words. "You got to drive me back to Sharon's before it begin to pour."

As Isabelle scurried toward the house, followed by Ainsley, she saw that the shade of her brother's bedroom window had been raised.

Chapter Forty-two

Europa was tired and out of sorts. She had changed from her white uniform into a green-and-blue print dress and put on a lime-green, floppy-brimmed hat—the kind of costume a mannequin might have worn in a department-store window in Memphis. As Isabelle stepped into the kitchen, Europa began to grumble about the church supper her niece was forcing her to attend that evening. "Cain't cook an' clean an' polish all mornin' *an'* serve *an'* wash all them dishes an' still 'spect to be fresh as a daisy with ever'body crowdin' round you sayin', 'My, don't you look *good*, Sister Europa, you look younger ev-ery day, I swear to God.'"

"Oh, Europa," said Isabelle, hugging the old woman, whose body sagged lumpily beneath her gay apparel. "Look what we've done to you! We've worn you out and now we've kept you waiting. It isn't fair!"

"Same like it always is," said Europa, straightening her hat, which had been knocked slightly askew by Isabelle's embrace. "Never mind."

"But it was such a good dinner, such a treat for us all, wasn't it, Reverend Black?" Isabelle looked over her shoulder to Ainsley, who was standing just inside the kitchen door. "And now we've got the chili to look forward to tonight."

"Never mind. Jes' git goin' before the bottom drops out of them clouds."

Ainsley stepped into the middle of the kitchen. "I'd like to come too," he said. "I have a special reason for asking. After we drop Euro-pa off, I want to drive by your old house. Do you realize I've never seen it? We can go in my car."

"But," faltered Isabelle, her fingers spread against her bosom, "but what about Brother? I don't think—"

"Never mind yo' brother," said Europa. "Dr. Claib'n feelin' better. He in his workroom right now, foolin' with one of his ships. Jes' fix hisself a drink. So le's us git goin'."

While Isabelle was struggling into her summer raincoat, Claiborne, in shirt sleeves, strode into the hall. He was carrying his drink. "Where are you goin'?" he demanded, blocking her way from the hall closet.

"We're just goin' to drive Europa to Sharon's and then take a quick look at the old house. Ainsley's never seen it. We won't be long."

Turning abruptly, Claiborne confronted Ainsley. "You've been with my sister long enough. I saw you out there on the lawn together, holdin' hands, carryin' on like a couple of teenagers—"

"Brother, for heaven's sake!"

"Be quiet, Isabelle. Now it's my turn for some of this young man's company. I'm comin' too." Setting his drink on the hall table, he commanded Isabelle to hand him his umbrella from the closet.

By the time they reached the niece's little wooden house, the rain had become steady and hard. Carrying Claiborne's umbrella, Ainsley carefully sheltered the old woman and her hat as he helped her along the already slippery brick walk; he also carried the suitcase that contained her uniform. Isabelle watched them mount the rickety steps to the front porch and saw Ainsley shake Europa's hand while the niece took the suitcase and held open the door. She found something touching in the sight and turned with a smile toward her brother, who was sitting rigidly, his shoulders not touching the back seat of the car, his eyes fixed straight ahead. Though he had demanded to join them on their drive, he had not since spoken or relaxed the hooded arrogance of his bearing. How amazing that he had come— and what a tribute to Ainsley's presence . . .

She followed Claiborne's gaze, which had shifted to the two-story brick building across the street. The rain was now pounding hard against the roof of the car and popping with thousands of tiny explosions against the surface of the street. Through the veiling of water Isabelle could see a large white car parked in the drive by the side entrance to the building. She sharply drew in her breath and closed her eyes. Then she remembered what the building was—and who lived there. . . . As if she had perceived a cloud of noxious gas rolling toward them, she lowered the window a crack and called out, "Ainsley, hurry! We haven't much time," so loudly that her brother turned and stared at her.

The car door opened and Ainsley climbed in, thrusting the dripping, half-furled umbrella in front of him. "Which way now?"

"The other way, the other way!" cried Isabelle. Bringing her voice under control, she instructed Ainsley to go back to Main Street, turn right, and follow Main to the Episcopal church, where he was to turn left on Saville Street.

It was impossible to see much of the old house. The spindly columns and fancy scrollwork of the verandah were largely screened by the dark cedars, pecan trees, and oaks that stood like shuddering, droop-shouldered giants beneath the slashing rain. A wind had come up, whisking gauzy curtains of rain across the lawn and producing a hail-like clatter of water pellets against the metal of the car.

"There's a wooden sign over the front steps that says 'Holton Retirement Home,'" said Isabelle, "but I can't even see it through all this downpour. They've added a brick wing—sort of modernistic—to the back," she continued. "Everybody says it's the only really good old people's home between Memphis and Greenville. They say the management's real decent, and that's mighty rare this day and age, I can tell you."

Since it was impossible to lower a window or open a side vent more than half an inch without admitting a torrent, they had to endure the steaminess of the car and the clouding of the glass. Still, Ainsley seemed in no hurry to leave. From time to time he cleared a space on the window with his handkerchief and stared through the downpour, as if waiting for the rain to stop and the trees to part. "Have you been back since you sold the house?" he asked.

Isabelle did not hear his words and asked him to repeat his question, which he did, turning in his seat.

"Oh, yes. Three or four times. Several older friends of ours are staying there, and I've been to see them. Of course everything's so changed I can hardly imagine I ever lived there. The wallpaper's gone in the front parlor—everything's painted green—and they have that awful plastic furniture. Still, they do say it's well run." She, too, cleared a space on her window, which steamed up again almost at once. "Wouldn't it be funny if Brother and I ended up there someday? Back at our old house . . . I'm not sure I'd like that one bit!"

They sat for another few minutes in the wet heat. Neither Ainsley nor Claiborne said a word.

"There's nothing like a good Delta downpour," said Isabelle to break the silence, which had begun to oppress her. "When it's over and we can open the windows, there'll be the most wonderful wet-dirt and green-growin' smell. I was scared of thunder and lightnin' as a child, but even so, I welcomed the storms—even the worst ones—for the sake of that good smell."

Suddenly Claiborne made a sound that was partly a gasp, partly a clearing of his throat, a sound that reached Isabelle, frightening her. When she turned her head, she saw that his mouth was contorted and that his dark cheeks were twitching, as if with repeated stabbings of neuralgia. "Brother! What is it?" she cried, afraid that he was having a stroke.

"Nothing," he said thickly. "I want to go home."

Chapter Forty-three

After his brief foray, Dr. Herne withdrew once more into silence, refusing to leave his room to have supper with Isabelle and Reverend Ainsley Black. But later he emerged from his retreat and stood at the living-room window to watch the preacher escort Isabelle to her car. The shower had passed, and an eerie light, seeping from a blood-red fissure that had opened at the bottom of the leaden clouds to the west, now dyed the trees and the lush grass with its crimson wash. The end of the world, thought Claiborne Herne, wishing that it could be.

Only a cataclysm could rescue him now; nothing else—will power, self-disgust—was of any use. For a while he had been able, for some reason obscurely connected with Ainsley Black's presence, to resist, but this brief holding-out had only made the surrender more demoralizing. And disgusting—for something new had occurred during the last session with Vicky, something grossly physical and embarrassing that had come close to happening several times before and never had. The recollection of it made him sick. Losing all self-control, his self-discipline crumbling, he had turned his penance into a mockery, had made a disgusting fool of himself in Vicky's presence. She had pretended not to notice, but Claiborne was sure that she had noticed—and sure too that she had told Rooney, whose cackle he could almost hear.

More than anything else, Claiborne Herne wished that he could die. Only Isabelle stood in his way. Many times he had worked out the details of his death, worked them out as meticulously as if he had been constructing a complex model; but always the thought of Isabelle and her horror of suicide had spoiled his fantasy. Given his physical disabilities, he saw no way by which he could disguise a suicide, pass it off as a car accident or an accidental drowning. As he now watched his sister back her car slowly out of the drive onto Granada and then head, still slowly, down the street toward the center of town, he felt a spasm of pure hatred and cursed Isabelle under his breath as the chief impediment to his salvation. Goddamn the woman, why should he hold back for her sake? Why should she be pampered at his expense?

Ainsley was crossing the soggy green lawn, his form dark against the lurid streak in the sky. Claiborne ducked behind the white curtains. Then, carrying the drink he had poured himself after supper, he walked over to his Morris chair and sat down, wincing as his shoulders touched the chair back. He was determined to sit there silently, whatever the preacher said or did. The words would buzz harmlessly around his head. After another drink or two he would hardly hear them. Ainsley, he had noticed, was not drinking tonight.

When the preacher came into the room and sat down, Dr. Herne simply stared at him without even a nod. How grotesque the fellow looked, with that mottled, peeling face and gruesome eye! Everything about him that had attracted Claiborne earlier was now gone. The change in Ainsley's appearance had renewed the doctor's old suspicions, leaving him half convinced that the fellow was indeed an FBI agent, a drinking Irishman who had been beaten up in a barroom brawl. Part of Claiborne of course knew better, but it suited him in his present mood to think the worst. After several minutes of mutual staring, Ainsley said, "I know you don't feel like talking tonight and that's a mighty big disappointment for me. For a while I thought you were feeling better. I see I was wrong." He waited, hunched expectantly forward, his hands clasped in his lap. Then he tried again. "I enjoyed the conversations we had before I went away, and I was looking forward to more of the same."

Sweet chance, thought the doctor. When Ainsley got no reply at all, he grinned and shrugged, gestures that Claiborne interpreted, with grim satisfaction, as evidence of his own power to make the preacher writhe. Then Ainsley stood up. "I think I'll get myself a drink of water," he said, going over to the drink tray. "Europa's hot chili has left me with a tremendous thirst. Last time I was with you I drank some of your good whiskey. Tonight I'm strictly on the water wagon." He returned to his chair with a glass of water.

Inwardly jeering, Claiborne decided that Ainsley had gotten into bad trouble in Atlanta and had had to swear off booze for a while. He did not permit himself even a faint twitch of response. Then the telephone in the hall rang. After several rings Ainsley realized that the doctor was not going to answer; he jumped up himself and ran into the hall. The doctor heard several "hellos?," then the click of the receiver. Evidently a wrong number—or Rooney . . .

"Whoever it was wouldn't speak," said Ainsley. "And he wouldn't hang up either. So I hung up."

In the long silence that ensued, Claiborne grew tired of staring and allowed his eyes and mind to wander. He saw the old house again—piercingly familiar, hopelessly lost, a blurred presence behind the curtains of rain. When he closed his eyes, he noticed that the ticking of the Seth Thomas clock on the mantelpiece grew louder; when he opened them, the sound diminished. He had never observed the phenomenon before and he tested it several times, always with the same result. Vaguely he wondered if someone had been tinkering with the clock, and he shot a glance toward Ainsley, who had turned in his chair and was looking out the window. Again closing his eyes, Dr. Herne remembered that in the old house the clock had stood on one of the glass-fronted bookcases in the library. None of the old things looked right in the new house, nothing was in its right place. *Mama,* he whispered, glimpsing his mother in a long gray dress—*Mama. . . .* We should never have left the house, he thought; we should have stuck it out in spite of everything. He saw the basement gym—and Rooney, a skinny, golden-brown boy in trunks jabbing at the punching bag. . . .

"Dr. Herne!" came the ringing voice, making the old man jump. "The last time I was sitting here I agreed not to preach to you about the state of your immortal soul. Tonight I cannot afford that luxury. I am about to leave Alhambra, perhaps forever, but I cannot leave until—"

Furiously the doctor rose from his chair. Despite his earlier resolution to endure the preacher's buzzing, he realized that he could not bear to sit there and be harangued by the fool. . . . But before he could even take the first step toward his bedroom, Ainsley Black had bounded across the space separating them and pushed Claiborne Herne firmly back into his chair. The pain across his shoulders brought tears to the old man's eyes. "Isabelle!" he called out, breaking his silence. Then, more plaintively, "Isabelle?"

"She's not here, as you perfectly well know. Now you sit there and hear me out. By the good Lord, I'll tie you to the chair if I have to!"

Claiborne Herne sat quivering, his eyes fixed on the preacher, who was pacing up and down in what seemed to be a frenzy of impatience. Now that he had surrendered the power of his silence, the doctor felt as helpless as if he had already been lashed to his chair. "Will you fix me another drink?" he pleaded, pointing to his empty glass on the table next to his chair.

"No, sir, I will *not* pour you another drink until you've heard me out. Nor will I let you leave that chair to pour your own. You've had more than enough already."

"Why—why—" the doctor quavered—"why do you want to torment me like this?"

"Because I mean to bring you to your knees." Brother Black had now sat down again but on the very edge of his chair, prepared to spring forward at any moment. "Doctor, you are obviously a sick man. There's no way of knowing how much time you have left. I want you to come clean and make your peace with God before I leave this room."

Come clean . . . The doctor leaned back, ignoring his pain. Dimly he sensed that his adversary had been transformed, that even his voice and language were not those of the Ainsley Black he had known. *Come clean* . . . He shook his head, trying to shake off a fantasy that had already gripped him. In an instant he saw himself lying on the floor of a cell, slung there by a brutal guard who had torn him from the arms of his weeping sister. He heard the clang of a metal door. His relief was enormous: there was no way Rooney could get to him now. . . .

"Dr. Herne"—the voice seemed to boom at him from all sides—"you will be forgiven. Whether innocent or guilty, you will be forgiven. I can make that promise in the name of the highest authority, the ultimate judge. But only if you bare your soul before His tribunal."

"You've been talkin' to Isabelle," snarled the doctor. "She's been tellin' you things. I saw you out the window. She's—"

"Dr. Herne, that's all beside the point! I'm not talking about any earthly tribunal or court. Whatever you say, I'm not going to report you to the police or the FBI. My lips are sealed."

"Please give me a drink. Please, Brother Black."

"No!"

The doctor started to rise from his chair but sank back before Ainsley even made a move. The preacher was grinning at him in a way that unstrung his muscles and left him as weak as a convalescent child. "I want to die," he muttered aloud.

"That's in the Lord's hands, not yours. When He's good and ready, He'll take you, not before."

Again Claiborne Herne glimpsed the bare cell, felt the guard's grip on his shoulder, felt himself pitch forward, a splintered toy flung into a corner by an angry boy. He lay very quietly, face down on the floor, bleeding, his mouth cut. Safe at last . . . But he roused himself to say, "Did Isabelle tell you I shot that fella?"

"No, she believes you're innocent."

"Isabelle is a fool," said Claiborne. "She never gets anything straight. Never has, never will." The doctor's vision was beginning to play tricks on him, encircling Ainsley's head and the lamp behind him with rings of light. Again closing his eyes, he could still see the rings revolving slowly in the shadowy crimson space behind his eyelids. He had a sense that his life itself would, if he let go, drift off like a balloon. Why should he try to hold on to it? Why not let it go?

"All right," he said in an accusatory tone. "All right! I did shoot that fella. I hadn't planned to, but I did. It was a kind of accident."

He saw Ainsley's face change color beneath its peeling skin. *Good,* he thought, relishing for an instant his old sense of power. *I've surprised him.* Ainsley, he knew, was going to be very cautious, fearful that too quick a response would undo everything. Claiborne was close to laughing aloud.

"A kind of accident?" asked the preacher in almost a whisper.

"That's right. I really wanted to shoot the nigger."

"The nigger?"

"That's right. I couldn't stand that nigger. Funny, I can't even remember his name. He kept poppin' up all over the state."

"Was it Franklin Mosby?"

"That's the one! Franklin Mosby. How the devil did you know?"

"An inspired guess."

The doctor gave Ainsley a narrowed look, then said, "Franklin Mosby. That black son of a bitch!"

"Do you still want a drink?" The preacher was on his feet.

"Yes," said Claiborne, with a sudden dryness of his mouth. "I could use a drink."

When Ainsley handed him the glass, Claiborne held it carefully in both hands, a consecrated vessel. The first sip seemed to roll through him, to reach every extremity and set it tingling. *He can have anything he wants from me,* thought the doctor—*anything at all....* His vision was still playing tricks on him, so that Ainsley, who continued to stand, seemed outlined with a thin band of flame from the table lamp behind him. The doctor took another drink, a profound drink, and set down his glass. How beautiful Ainsley looked. Even the rather soiled bandage over his eye was glowing with a white radiance.

"Go on, Dr. Herne," said Ainsley in a voice like a summoning trumpet. "Tell me why you wanted to shoot Franklin Mosby." Once more the preacher sat down and once more he seemed to loom in his chair, outlined with fire, larger than life.

There was no holding back. The words came in a rush, often tripping over his tongue, which was less thickened than usual by drink at this time of night. As he spoke, Claiborne Herne saw, on a small screen, the replay of everything he described—and felt that he was seeing it for the last time. Anger rose up and collapsed, leaving him momentarily shaken and out of breath. With every sentence spoken he had the sense that he was clearing away all the accumulation, all the junk and impedimenta, that stood between him and his death.

The story began with the appearance of Franklin Mosby in Alhambra a week before the shooting. He had spoken at a rally in front of the post office, where Dr. Herne was among the onlookers. With Mosby was a white girl. "Somebody," said the doctor, "told me she was one of the Sibthorpes from Greenville, but she looked like a Cuban whore to me, a real slut if I ever saw one."

"Go on," said Ainsley, even though Dr. Herne had shown no sign of pausing.

"You should have heard the way that nigger was carryin' on before the sheriff arrested him. In the old days he wouldn't have lasted two minutes. High-yellow nigger, cocky as they come—" Anger nearly choked him. Pulling a snowy handkerchief from his pocket, Dr. Herne wiped away the frothy spittle that had collected in the corners of his mouth. "But the way things were that summer," he went on, "'specially after those killin's over in Neshoba County—and with all those FBI agents and federal marshals hangin' around—why, they had that nigger out of jail in less than twenty-four hours, and the next thing I knew, he was slated to speak at a rally over in Tupelo. Posters all over the place. I couldn't stand it. I just couldn't stand it."

Again lifting his handkerchief, this time to blow his nose, he saw Ainsley jump up and make a circuit of the living room, pounding one hand against the other in his excitement.

"Go on!" cried the preacher. "I'm listening." Sitting down abruptly, he said, "But why did Franklin Mosby upset you so? There were dozens like him, speaking all over the state."

"But Mosby's the one I *saw*. And I couldn't stand the way he looked, couldn't stand that swagger, that high-yellow impudence, that—" Here Claiborne Herne began to cough uncontrollably and once again flecks appeared in the corners of his mouth. Gasping for breath, he took a deep swallow of whiskey, choked on it, and nearly lost consciousness. When he recovered, he realized that Brother Black was standing over him, patting his back. In pain he cried out and twisted his shoulders away from the preacher's touch. It was some time before he could pick up the scattered pieces of his story and proceed. "Soon as I knew Mosby was goin' to be speakin' at Tupelo, I *knew* I was goin' to go there and take a shot at him. Don't ask me why." Raising one hand to ward off the impending question from Ainsley, who was sitting opposite him again, he repeated, "Don't ask me why. I didn't even ask myself why. I hardly thought about it, even when I was makin' preparations. I just knew I was goin' to do it."

"But you shot Clark Helmholtz!" cried the preacher, again pounding his hands. "You shot Clark Helmholtz!"

"I know, I know!" The old man finished off what was left in his glass but did not immediately ask for another drink. More slowly now, with longer pauses to catch his breath and to hold back a sudden need to sob, he told how he had driven over to Tupelo, a town he did not know very well, and how he had lost time trying to locate the school where the rally was being held. Then he had lost more time—precious time—trying to find a place to park in the area—a place to which he could return quickly for his getaway, a place where he would not be hemmed in by other cars. After a long search he had decided on a dirt road that ran through pine trees to a field in front of the school. All that took precious time—a phrase the doctor kept repeating. Then he broke off his narration to say, with a lopsided grin, "If you ever planned to kill a man, Brother Black, you'd soon find out how many things have to be considered and how long it all takes."

"Go on!"

"Well, the crowd was in front of me, facin' the platform. Lord knows somebody on that platform could have spotted me with the rifle, which I couldn't completely conceal, but nobody did. Mosby was sittin' down, next to that Sibthorpe girl, and that fella Helmholtz was speakin'. From what he was sayin' over the loudspeaker system, it sounded like he was the last speaker and I'd come too late to hear the nigger. Helmholtz was tellin' 'em to march in an orderly way to the courthouse and demand the right to register. Somethin' like that—I only took in the gist of it and not the exact words. But it was clear the rally was about to break up and I had lost my chance. You see—" He sighed heavily and shook his head; one tear trickled from his left eye. After he had taken a deep, shuddering breath, he said, "You see, there was no way I could get a clear bead on Mosby. Just no way. Helmholtz was standin' half in front of him and that slut was leanin' with her head practically touching the nigger's. In a moment they'd all be gettin' up and movin' off the platform and joinin' the crowd and I—"

Claiborne Herne paused and drew his white sleeve across his eyes. Then, lifting his old warrior's face, he said, "So I shot Helmholtz."

"Oh, my God!" Ainsley gasped. "Just like that, just like that. You shot the wrong man. Just like that."

"Just like that," repeated Dr. Herne. Suddenly exhausted, he let his chin drop to his breastbone—as if he had been dealt a karate chop at the back of his head. Spittle again appeared in the corners of his mouth. "Help me," he muttered, "help me to my room. I'm very tired. Isabelle will be back any minute. I don't want her to see me now. My legs—I'm very tired."

From the depths of the overstuffed bedroom chair into which he had collapsed, Dr. Herne stared upward at Ainsley and said, "I'm all right now. Don't need you now. You can go."

But the preacher leaned over him and said, "Are you sure you're all right?"

"Perfectly sure." Raising himself in his chair and keeping his gaze fixed upon Ainsley, Claiborne began to undo the buttons of his shirt. His face was still dark red and his fingers were awkward and trembling at their task. Ainsley made no move to leave the room but watched him closely, saying nothing. At last the final button was undone. With an abrupt movement the doctor pulled his shirt open at the chest and down from his shoulders. He was not wearing an undershirt. Slumping forward, his head nearly between his knees, he revealed the cross-hatching of dull crimson stripes on the skin of his shoulders and back. Beneath the stripes was a tissue of whitened scars, a contour map of deadened pain.

Ainsley drew back with a sharp intake of breath. After a moment he said, "Have you done all this to yourself?"

"What?" Dr. Herne raised his head.

"These—these welts and scars."

Dr. Herne shook his head but said nothing. Let him feast his eyes, he thought.

"Rooney?"

Claiborne Herne did not reply directly. "Haven't I been punished enough?" he mumbled. "What more does God want from me? Why doesn't God kill Rooney Lee?" he demanded in a bellow of rage and sorrow. "I would if I could!"

"Rooney has done this to you? Rooney whips you?"

"No," said Claiborne Herne with a violent shake of his head. Then he muttered, "I've asked for it. I've been very bad." And then loudly: "Why haven't I killed Rooney Lee? I killed somebody I didn't even know, but I can't kill Rooney."

"There's been enough killing," said Ainsley Black, drawing closer. "Killing's not the answer." Now standing directly over the doctor, he said, "The answer is to put yourself in the hands of the living God. He will protect you from Rooney. And He will forgive you. There's

294

nothing he can't forgive, including the murder of an innocent man."

"Killing that fella meant nothing to me," said the doctor, raising his bloodshot eyes to the preacher's face.

"Not true! Not true!" Ainsley moved forward, his hands spread as if about to grab Claiborne by both arms in an effort to shake some sense into him. "Look at you, just look at you," he said with an edge of disgust in his voice. "You don't even know what you've done. Well, I'm going to show you. By the living God, I'm going to show you!" He turned and ran out of the bedroom.

It occurred to Claiborne Herne that he should get up and lock the door. But he felt too weak, too passive. He was certain that his legs would not support him. Lowering his bare shoulders against the soft chair back, he glanced across the room to his gun rack on the opposite wall. Only last week he had cleaned and oiled the rifle that had killed Clark Helmholtz.

Ainsley Black came running into the room, carrying his briefcase. "I'm going to show you a picture of the man you shot," he said, his voice alive with excitement.

"No," said Claiborne Herne.

Ainsley laid his briefcase on the snowy coverlet of the bed and unsnapped the latch. After taking out a handful of photographs, he approached the doctor, who, like a child refusing his medicine, closed his eyes and shook his head.

"Now look."

"No."

Claiborne's wrist was seized and cruelly twisted. With a little yelp of pain the doctor opened his eyes while still averting his head.

"Now look!"

After another sharp twist, Dr. Herne's wrist was released. The doctor obeyed orders and faced the photograph which Ainsley was now holding directly in front of his eyes. It was a black-and-white snapshot of a grinning, strong-featured young man with dark curly hair sprouting low on his forehead. After some moments Dr. Herne said, "That's not the nigger. I don't know that fella."

"You know him very well. You shot him through the skull."

"I don't know him. I never saw him before."

"You know him all right. Didn't you ever see his picture during the trial or in the newspapers?"

"Never." This was true. Dr. Herne had never read the newspaper accounts of his arrest or trial.

Exasperatedly, Ainsley thrust the picture even closer to Claiborne's eyes. "Well, you're looking at him now. Clark was my closest friend."

Though dimly puzzled, Claiborne Herne made no response to this revelation. His lips were drawn tight as he pulled his head back slightly from the photograph, as if it had been cutting off his air.

"Clark Helmholtz was twenty-seven years old when you shattered his skull. He was a man of tremendous promise. But you killed him without knowing who he was, what he was like—anything." There was a soblike catch in Ainsley's voice. "Now," he continued, "you're going to look at a picture of his wife and little girl."

The doctor looked. Then he raised his eyes to the preacher and said, "I didn't know them. They didn't mean anything to me."

"Look again. And keep looking. The girl—Susie—was five when you killed her father. They had been very close. You've never had a child, so I don't suppose you know the feelings involved."

"My mother died," whispered the doctor, "when I was four." Then, in a burst of anger, he muttered, "Goddamn Yankee agitator."

"What did you say? I couldn't hear you."

"What was he doin' in Mississippi? Why didn't he stay with his family where he belonged?"

"Don't try to shift the blame!" yelled Ainsley Black. "Look at that child, look at that woman. You're not too crazy to understand what you did to them. And to him . . . And to me!"

Claiborne Herne felt a bolt of terror shoot through him. "You don't sound like Ainsley Black. You—you've changed. . . . " And then in a small voice he said, "Are you goin' to kill me? Haven't I been punished enough already? Just look at my back!" Then, in what was no more than a whisper, he added, "I deserve to die."

"No, I am going to pray with you. Come over here." Using both hands, Ainsley pulled the half-naked doctor from the depths of his chair. "Over here. By the bed. I want you to kneel at the side of your bed like a little child."

Chapter Forty-four

Claiborne Herne put up no resistance. Moving quickly, Hux guided the old man across the room and held his arm as he lowered himself with some difficulty to his knees, the white shirt flapping around his waist. In this close contact, Hux briefly marveled at the human ordinariness of the man's skin, his hair, the whorls of his ears; even the red criss-cross on the man's back seemed not lurid but merely ordinary, pitiful, human. How extraordinary that the arm he was grasping had held the rifle that had killed Clark.

Now Hux lowered himself beside the doctor, resting his elbows on the white spread and pressing his palms together in the classic attitude of prayer. But before he had emptied his mind to pray, he glimpsed, as on a brightly lit screen, the figure of Claiborne Herne as he hurried down the dusty track, the spindly pine trees on either side, the rifle swinging in his hand, the roars and screams of the shattered crowd in his ears. There was the car just ahead. . . . A chill passed over Hux. He turned his head to glance at the old man at his side—an exhausted, drunken, half-crazed old man with a vaccination scar puckering the yellowed skin of his upper arm. Then Hux closed his eyes, and as he did so he experienced a swelling of warmth within, a euphoric tingling of his lips and fingertips and ears—the descent of the Spirit! The words came, poured from a source beyond himself, funneled through his throat and mouth. He did not—could not—resist his inspiration.

In a resonant voice Hux prayed for the gift of God's grace to Claiborne Herne, his fellow sinner. He prayed that Claiborne's heart might be softened and his mind enlightened so that he might comprehend his deed in all its dimensions. "Let him become truly contrite, O Lord," Hux intoned, "let him be made humble and quiet at the center of his being so that he may catch the first whisperings of Thy voice, the first intimations of Thy forgiveness. Then let his soul burst forth in a song of thanksgiving, a song of triumph in the assurance not only of Thy forgiveness but of his salvation."

Hux paused, his own words humming and then dying away in his mind. After the last vibration, self-conciousness suddenly filled the silence, and he wished that Brother Thurlow could see him now. He wished, too, that Dr. Herne had made some slight sound—if not an assenting "amen," then a murmur or sigh to show that he had been reached. Then, as if a new chord had been struck, he banished all such thoughts and let the words come again. "Strengthen him with Thy Holy Spirit," he prayed. "Strengthen him, O Lord, that he may resist the forces of evil that have led him into harmful and unnatural practices that stem from an overburdened conscience. Instruct him that Thy mercy is freely given to those who seek it and that it is not contingent upon extremes of penance and self-mortification. Rub the balm of Thy loving kindness upon his wounds, which are wounds of the soul even more than the body."

Again Hux waited, catching his breath after this spate of words, which amazed him by the shape they had taken. He heard nothing beyond the rise and fall of Claiborne Herne's own breathing. He checked an impulse to open his eyes and turn toward the old man before going on.

"I beseech Thee, O Lord, that Thy servant Claiborne's time upon this earth—however long or short its allotment may be—that this time may be blessed by a spirit of love and reconciliation, that he and his beloved sister may live together in affectionate harmony, that together they may—"

There was a low, strangled sound from the doctor, but Hux felt himself being swept toward a climax and did not try to stop or resist the onward rush. He prayed—so fervently that his frowning brow ached—that on this very night Claiborne might accept Jesus Christ as his Savior and Redeemer and that he might rise from his bed in the morning as a man born again through God's grace—born into that eternal day that will never fade. "Amen!" he cried out. "Amen!"

What he heard, as the reverberations of his voice left his ears, was the sound of sobbing. Turning, he saw that Claiborne Herne had thrown himself forward on the bed, his forehead resting upon his crossed arms. His weeping was violent, noisy. Gently Hux laid his hand upon the heaving shoulder, whereupon the doctor gave an angry twitch, and Hux removed his hand. He stood up. "Let it come," he said. "You've got a lot to cry over. Let it come." The weeping continued, less torrential now, more spasmodic.

Hux heard the sound of a car outside the window. Once again he ventured to touch Dr. Herne's shoulder. "Your sister's here," he said. "I'm going to leave you now. I'll be back to see you tomorrow." Standing away from the bed, he gazed with tenderness, awe, and subdued joy at the penitential figure of the doctor, whose exposed back seemed to quiver in expectation of further lashings. "Don't try to resist the workings of the Spirit," he counseled in a hushed voice. "What you are experiencing is the death agony of the cast-off self. Pray again before you climb into bed. The Lord will give you strength." Hux crossed to the door leading to the living room and turned once more to look. Dr. Herne had not moved. "You're well on your way. I bet it will be all over by the time I get here tomorrow. There'll be nothing left for me to do but congratulate you in the name of the Lord—and shake your hand. Goodnight, Dr. Herne."

Closing the door behind him, Hux stood exultant for a moment in the living room. Then he went to greet Miss Isabelle as she entered the house. He walked right up to her and caught her in his arms. Startled, she gave a little laugh, said, "My *good*ness," and responded to his hug with several tentative pats on the small of his back. "What about Brother?" she asked, pulling away. "Has Brother gone to bed?" And when Hux nodded, she smiled and said, "It's turned into such a beautiful night. Real clear—just like a winter sky with all the stars shinin' bright. How did things go? Did Brother come out of his room? Did he speak?"

"Indeed he did, Miss Isabelle," said Hux, hugging her again, almost lifting her from her feet. "Indeed he did. He talked and I preached—not too much—and then we prayed. He's goin' to be all right, Miss Isabelle. I'm positive of it."

"Are you? Are you really?"

"I can tell you this much," said Hux, moving toward the front door. "His resistance has crumbled. I prayed with him and he wept. He cried like a little boy, cried and cried."

"Did he, did he—" She broke off, her eyes wide.

"Yes," said Hux, "he told me—" He checked himself; he had no right to reveal her brother's confession. "He let me see—see how unhappy he was. I spoke to him about God's love, His Mercy, His forgiveness—and he listened."

"He what?" She leaned forward to hear.

"He listened. He took it all in. And he wept. Miss Isabelle," he continued, "I may be all wrong, but I honestly think that your brother is ripe for the descent of the Spirit. He seems to me chastened, open, vulnerable in the best sense. All that anger and all that arrogance just seemed to drain away while he was weeping. I think you're going to find your brother a new man tomorrow. I can't guarantee that it will all happen that fast, but I'll be surprised if it doesn't. The well-watered plant is about to flower."

"I hardly dare hope," said Miss Isabelle. "It would be too—almost too wonderful. I can hardly imagine . . ."

"Don't be afraid to hope, Miss Isabelle. Hope and pray. I'll be back tomorrow afternoon—probably late—to see how he is. I'll be praying too." He smiled at her, his confidence high.

"And then you'll be leavin'," she said sorrowfully. "Leavin' for good."

"Yes," said Hux, "but I fully expect to see the lighting of the lamp before I go. I have to leave, but part of me will never leave. You'll feel the presence of my prayers—and my love." Suddenly on the point of tears himself, he looked down at her, smiling and spreading both hands—as if to apologize for the meagerness of his offering compared to the fullness of her love. "And I'll come back someday, I promise. But let's not think about all that now," he continued briskly. "Goodnight, and I'll see you tomorrow." Hux went to her, bent down, and kissed her on the forehead. Timidly Miss Isabelle reached up and touched the bandage over his eye. Then Hux left the house.

It was just a little over a week since he had driven under the full moon, weaving his way through the Mississippi countryside, half insane from his lovemaking and the revelation that followed. The past week had been the most tumultuous in his life, even wilder in its extremes than the one in which he had learned of Clark's murder. Now, driving back to Oxford before the rising of the shrunken moon, he realized, with some surprise, that he was supremely happy. It was not a condition that he was accustomed to. Moments of happiness, of great pleasure—yes; but what he was experiencing now was at once higher and deeper than anything he had previously known. Above all, it had a quality of serenity to it, of confidence and satisfaction that he had never associated with what he had thought of as happiness before. It's all due to Brother Thurlow, he thought with a burst of gratitude. Thanks to him, he had been able to accomplish the secret agenda; he had been able, just as he had planned, to rub Claiborne Herne's face in what he had done—but in a spirit of love, not vengeance. He had been able to repay Miss Isabelle's kindness and trust. He hoped—he believed—that her brother's salvation was at hand.

But why did Hux thank Brother Thurlow and not God for this turn of events? God still seemed too abstract compared to the fleshly bulk and flashing eyes of Brother Thurlow. Though he constantly invoked God and spoke in the name of Jesus Christ and the Holy Spirit, Hux had not yet figured out exactly the terms of his belief. But this did not worry him; the Trinitarian theology could wait. Meanwhile, he did accept the existence of God as both absolute and immediate, not only as a mighty source that he could draw upon but as a living presence made manifest in and through Brother Thurlow, a force that actively made use of Hux himself. He had been *used* by God! God had put words into his mouth. The words of course were known to Hux, but the pattern, the combination, even the voice—these were not his. Nor were they exactly Brother Thurlow's. Yet it was Brother Thurlow whom he thanked.

Hux had no fears for the future. He looked no further ahead than to New Orleans. Tomorrow he would wind up the official agenda, have a doctor look at the cut over his eye, and pay what he expected to be his final visit to the Hernes. Next he would call Anne and make his confession; he would not worry about the outcome—let it be, let it be. And then New Orleans! He could hardly wait to report to Brother Thurlow it was by far the most exciting prospect that had ever confronted him. He felt that he was in the bright infancy of a new life; its shape was still unknown to him, but in New Orleans he would catch his first glimpse of what lay ahead. *New Orleans . . .*

So caught up was Hux in his happiness that he was nearly in Oxford before he became fully conscious that for some time he had been experiencing stomach cramps—and that they were growing in intensity. A faint nausea had gathered in his mouth. By the time he reached the motel, this nausea was so strong that he barely made it to the bathroom before vomiting copiously. Something had apparently gone badly wrong with Europa's chili con carne. Still, he was happy. *Bad carne, bad kharma,* he thought, grinning between bouts of vomiting. And even the onset of diarrhea, which several times roused him from his bed during the night, could not diminish his conviction that all was well, supremely well.

Chapter Forty-five

Hux developed a slight fever toward morning and had many vivid dreams. At one point he was tiptoeing toward Claiborne Herne's bed, a flashlight in one hand, a small revolver in the other. Slowly he played the flashlight beam across the narrow bed with its rumpled sheet and stained, blue-striped mattress. Claiborne was lying there, with his knees drawn up beneath the sheet, which also covered his head. After sticking his pistol into his belt, Hux pulled back the sheet with his free hand and saw his mistake. "Clark!" he shouted, rolling over and opening his eyes. The clatter of morning, along with one thin strip of sunlight at the edge of the drawn curtains, had begun to penetrate the airless hush of the motel room. Turning his face to the wall, Hux subsided into a sweaty sleep that continued until nearly ten.

Fully awake at last, he guessed that his temperature was nearly normal, but he was still foul-tongued and damp. While telling himself that he had a dozen things to do, that he couldn't afford to lose the entire morning, he knew very well that he was in no condition to get up and go out. Food poisoning or intestinal flu—whatever it was, his sickness had unstrung his muscles so that he staggered when he went to the bathroom. Well, so be it, he thought; perhaps later he could make some telephone calls. His increasingly dirty bandage would have to remain unchanged; his visit to the Hernes would have to wait until tomorrow and his departure for New Orleans would be delayed by a day or two. So be it. Though the extreme pitch of last night's euphoria had not survived the repeated attacks of nausea and diarrhea, Hux's spirits were still high. This illness was the most temporary of setbacks; it could almost be ignored.

The dream about Clark had not terrified him. He was not afraid of another encounter. But his mind kept returning to the odd detail of the mattress—that cheap, narrow, blue-striped mattress that had taken the place of Claiborne Herne's vast snowy bed. Then, as if the upheavals of the last week had dislodged an accumulation of covering earth, Hux found himself staring, as from a great height, at a

302

buried stratum of his life that he had neither forgotten entirely nor completely remembered, a miraculously preserved deposit that he had chosen, half consciously, to leave unexplored. With a rising excitement that was a compound of exhilaration and fear, he began to recover details, one by one. Then a mass of them came all at once and coalesced into a scene. He saw—and heard—himself arguing with Clark in the shedlike back room of Junior Wilcox's house in Jackson.

Arguing was hardly the word for it. They were rigid with fury. Clark, seated on the sagging iron bed with its blue-striped mattress, faced Hux, who was standing against the unplastered lathes of the wall, fists at his sides, his head nearly touching the ceiling, his face only inches from the dangling, unshaded lightbulb. Insects flung themselves against the window screen.

"Don't try to pin this on Louise," Clark was saying in a voice rasped hoarse by speechmaking. Despite his weathered, suntanned look of health, he was haggard with fatigue, having just returned with Hux to Jackson after three nearly sleepless days and nights in and around Meridian. "She can make out if she has to. Of course she's exhausted—new babies who cry all night *are* exhausting. Of course it's too bad the nurse had to quit. But don't kid yourself that the problem's a *serious* one. It just isn't. Compared to what we're facing down here, it's a problem of *very small* dimensions. Louise can find other help or go to her mother's. If you pull out of here now, with everything that's going on, you'll never forgive yourself—or Louise. Women have had to take care of their new babies without the presence of their menfolk since the beginning of time, for Christ's sake!"

"I warn you. Don't put pressure on me. I can't take it—"

"Precisely," said Clark, curling his thick lips. "You can't take it. Louise and the baby are just an excuse, and you're too intelligent to pretend otherwise."

Hux leaned back, pressing his shoulders against the splintery board of the wall. "What are you implying?"

"I'm not implying *anything*, for Christ's sake. I'm simply stating a *fact*. You can't take it, so you've decided to pull out."

"I'm a father!" cried Hux. "My wife is desperate—you should have heard her on the phone just now—she sounds like she's on the verge of a breakdown. She *needs* me. I'm a husband too, goddamn you! I've been here six weeks, I've done—"

"You're a pathetic, pussy-whipped son of a bitch."

As he sprang forward, Hux somehow struck the dangling lightbulb, which exploded with a loud *pop* and a shower of glass. Rolling and twisting, both men fell across the bed. At one point Clark was on top of Hux, pummeling his head and shoulders. But Hux, with his eyes shut, found Clark's throat with his hands. Exulting in the counterpressure of cartilage, veins, and tendons within the circuit of his hands, Hux knew that nothing could break his grip. The pummeling increased, became wild, they crashed from the bed to the floor—and still the grip held. . . .

Then the door had burst open, and the strong hands of Junior and Bessie Wilcox pulled the grappling men apart. Clark sat on the floor within the triangle of light from the open door, his hands at his throat, his face blood-dark, as he struggled for breath. Still gasping for his own breath, Hux could hardly hear—much less answer—the demands of Junior and Bessie to know what the hell was going on. When at last they released his arms, he walked out of the room and never again saw Clark alive.

Face up, motionless, Hux stared into the orange-tawny light and tried to hold on to what he had recovered. For a few seconds he was able to retain—mostly in the sensations of his fingers and throat—a sensory awareness of what must have been the most passionate moment of his existence. Then it began to fade, just as it had within days—even hours—of the actual event. By the time Hux, back in Princeton, had written to Clark to apologize for the quarrel, the sense-memory of it had completely vanished; only the bare fact of the quarrel had remained, and that too, in a very short time, had shriveled into something trivial. Clark, in his magnanimity, had never mentioned what he must have known: that his best friend had tried, with all his strength, to kill him.

Unsought, another memory came: the interior of a tumble-down shack outside of Meridian, a straw-filled mattress on the floor, covered with stained cotton. It was their last night in the area; he and Clark, undressing by flashlight, were to share the mattress, for the only bed was occupied by the wheezing but brave old black man who owned the shack. Worn out, made tense by the rumor of a marauding band of Klansmen in the area, Hux longed, as he lay down, to rest his head on Clark's chest, to cling to him for comfort as a frightened child might cling to his father, to feel himself held by strong arms. . . . That longing came back to him, as did the intensity of his recoil from such intimacy. He had rolled to the far side of the mattress, where he lay sleepless and sweating heavily for hours, his damp undershorts cutting into his crotch, afraid that the slightest

alteration of his cramped position would cause him to touch Clark—
if only with his foot or shoulder. In the loud, thick darkness he
sensed that Clark was awake too, registering every sound from the
woods outside. They had left for Jackson the next day, driving in
exhausted silence over back roads.

"Forgive me, Clark, I tried to kill you," murmured Hux, as if
Clark's spirit—now harmless, even benign—were somewhere in the
room. "I wanted to kill you. Forgive me."

Then, reaching over, he turned on the clock radio by his bed. A
lugubrious country voice was singing.

> Swee-eet Jee-sus, cool my brow,
> Swee-eet Jee-sus, wipe my face,
> Precious Jee-sus, show me how—

Hux switched it off. Then, before drifting once more into sleep, he
offered up his own prayer for the conversion of Claiborne Herne and
asked a special blessing for Miss Isabelle. He was repeating soundlessly the name of Jesus when sleep overcame him.

If only he could call Anne . . . Still weak and dehydrated when he
finally got up around three, Hux made the necessary phone calls to
set up appointments for tomorrow. He was debating whether he felt
strong enough to go to the Hernes'—perhaps, if he could find something bland enough to eat in the restaurant, he would then feel up to
it; in any case, he had not yet called Miss Isabelle. While he was
deciding what to do, he was seized by a longing to make things right
with Anne, a longing so urgent that it nearly drove the unfinished
business with the Hernes out of his mind. Even in his present mood,
the thought of his lie to Anne was deeply shaming. How seriously
should he take Brother Thurlow's prohibition on calling her until
everything in Alhambra was wrapped up? Did he have to obey the
preacher in every detail?

No! Hux reached for the telephone. If Anne hung up on him, he
would call again. If she still refused to have anything to do with him,
he would write her a letter—a straightforward, uncringing expression of his sorrow for what he had done. Meanwhile, he would defy
the letter of the preacher's injunction and call *now*. Beyond the apology, Hux yearned to tell Anne about Fayetteville and all that it meant
for his future. Probably she would refuse to listen to him. So be it.
He felt strong enough to withstand a total rejection. . . .

But as he began to dial the number of the University Library, Hux

305

noticed that he had developed an erection—though none of his thoughts about Anne had been consciously sexual. This gave him pause. Perhaps Brother Thurlow knew more than Hux knew. Still . . . with his hand on the receiver, Hux waited for detumescence. After all, he told himself, he was merely going to telephone; he would not try to see her until afterwards. . . . Having thus rationalized the matter, he completed his call, only to be told that Anne had taken the afternoon off from work to keep a dental appointment.

At a quarter past five, just as he was about to leave for the Hernes', Hux tried again, this time dialing her home number. He was answered by a man with a Southwestern twang to his voice who said that Anne was busy in the kitchen—could he take a message?

"No," said Hux, "I have to speak to her now. I'll hold on."

In the background, he could hear a record playing country music. Anne, he concluded, was entertaining a visiting fireman from Little Rock or Tulsa. Hux felt slightly sick again, though he told himself that he had no right to be jealous, that he had forfeited all claims on Anne. Besides, there was Brother Thurlow's prohibition. . . . He drew a deep breath. So be it.

"Hello?" Anne's voice sounded impatient, annoyed at the interruption.

Hux had prepared no script. Afraid that she would hang up, he rushed to tell her how sorry he was about—about—his lie and about the embarrassment he had caused her when she telephoned Louise.

Anne made no comment but said, "Where are you?"

"I'm here—right here in Oxford."

"I don't want to see you. Stay away from me."

"I don't blame you. All that I can say is that I was pretty crazy at the time and that I'm better now. I want—"

She had hung up on him. Hux dialed again and waited while the phone rang perhaps a dozen times before it was picked up. The visiting fireman said, "Look here, buddy, I don't know who the hell you are, but Anne don't want to speak to you. So buzz off, okay?"

"Then just give her a message. Tell her I'm leaving Oxford for good in a day or so and that I'll call once more. There are some things I have to explain. Will you tell her that?" He waited for some response. He could hear voices in the background over the plaintive song on the record.

Then Anne was on the phone. "Larry," she said in what seemed to him a softened voice, "you haven't heard the news, have you?"

"What news?"

"Claiborne Herne shot himself."

"Oh, no . . ." In the black storm that followed, Hux could hardly shape his tongue and lips to say, "When?—when?—when did you hear?"

"It's been on the news all afternoon."

"Oh, no. Oh, my God, my God." And a second later: "Is he dead?"

"Yes. Look, I thought you ought to know, but I don't want to get involved in any way or see you or talk to you again. I'm sorry about all your troubles, but there's nothing I can do about them. Goodbye."

"I'll call again!" he cried, just as she hung up.

After sitting stunned on the bed for five or more minutes, Hux got up and went to the television set, thinking there might be a news program at five-thirty. There was none. He then switched on the radio and, after much turning of the dial, at last got what he wanted. The newscaster, from a station in Clarksdale, was cheerful and folksy as he relayed the latest news on Watergate and President Nixon's trip to China Then he said, "I reckon you good people out there all remember Dr. Claiborne Herne. Well, he was found dead at his home in Alhambra this mornin'—a self-inflicted gunshot wound, the police say. Apparently, that is." Then, as if deciding to stick to his script, he continued more formally. "A spokesman for the family said he had been in bad health for some time. Dr. Herne was charged in 1964 with the slayin' of civil-rights worker Clark Helmholtz. After a trial that attracted nation-wide interest, Herne was acquitted and has since lived in retirement in Alhambra.

"Last night over in Batesville two white teenagers got themselves arrested—"

Hux turned off the radio and sat for a moment with his face in his hands. Then, snatching the car keys from the dresser top, he rushed from the room on legs almost too weak to support him.

Chapter Forty-six

By five-thirty on Monday afternoon, Isabelle, who had held up so beautifully, looked ready to crumple. Her face was chalky except for the purplish-brown staining of the skin around her strained and bulging eyes; postponing funeral black until the service tomorrow, she was dressed as if for church in navy blue trimmed with white, but her hair was disarrayed and one stocking sagged. From the old black horsehair sofa on which she had temporarily collapsed, she looked up at the little cluster of Alhambra ladies who had been with her almost continuously since midmorning (when the news got out) and who were now coaxing her, very gently, to take a nap. She should get a little rest, they said; tomorrow would be a big day, what with the funeral in the late morning and then all the out-of-town relatives and friends to deal with; she must try to conserve her strength. But Isabelle, like an exhausted and overstimulated child, pleaded that she was not tired, not sleepy at all, and that she did not want to lie down. There was a chance that her cousins Charlie and Kate Buford might arrive from Greenville before supper, and she wanted to be up to greet them. Other relatives had already come.

"But we'll call you," insisted Mary Gordon Munce, the minister's wife. "We'll call you the minute they get here."

Isabelle gave way—not because she was sleepy but because suddenly the living room seemed intolerably crowded and hot (though the air-conditioner was turned on) and her own wide bed, with its lacy spread and canopy, a refuge from the well-intentioned. "I think maybe I'll have another glass of iced tea," she said, "and then I'll lie down for a little while. I won't promise to sleep."

"You do whatever you want to, darlin'," said Cornelia Pike, who, as Lamar Pike's unmarried sister, was freshly acquainted with the whims of the bereaved. She hurried to the side table where Claiborne's drink tray now held a pitcher of iced tea, tall glasses, and a silver sugar bowl.

When Isabelle lay down in her room, where the blinds were closed against the western sun, she had the sensation that she and her bed were floating like an unanchored barge down a great river at twilight. Death was the mighty launcher, and the survivor, once set in motion, could only submit, will-lessly, to being carried downstream many miles before being deposited at an unfamiliar landing. The consultations with Dr. Ben Morgan, the police, Mr. Haig the undertaker, the long talk with Mr. Munce, the constant ringing of the telephone and the doorbell, the arrival of old friends, the clamoring of reporters—all these were events along the riverbank which she witnessed or heard from a distance as the barge slipped along, sustained on the majestic current. Tomorrow would find her much further downstream, witnessing the far-off funeral and the drive to the cemetery.

Meanwhile, food kept appearing, as if from a hidden cornucopia: vast platters of fried chicken, hams, covered dishes of meat and vegetables, cakes, pies, ice cream. . . . Isabelle had hardly set foot in the kitchen since she had put on the coffeepot at eight—just before knocking on Claiborne's door. This afternoon old Europa's niece Sharon, accompanied by Sharon's daughter, had arrived to help out; tomorrow, joined by Europa herself (who was resting from Sunday's exertions) and assisted by the Alhambra ladies, they would produce the lunch for the out-of-town visitors and old family friends who would flock back to the house after the burial. Then the crowd would disperse, and by tomorrow night she would perhaps be alone if she could dissuade the well-intentioned from staying with her.

She knew that, once ashore, she would have to make her way back by foot—a long wearying journey back to what once was familiar and would never truly be so again. The strange voyage and the slow return were a process she had often witnessed but not experienced intimately since the death of her father more than thirty years ago. And on that voyage her little brother had been with her every inch of the way.

Now Brother had dropped out of sight. Tomorrow he would briefly return, invisible in a closed coffin, before being dropped from sight forever. She wondered if Rooney would dare show up for the funeral. An hour or so earlier, she had stepped into the kitchen to greet Sharon and had found him sitting at the kitchen table, talking to the two black women. Abruptly he had started toward her, his face contorted. Isabelle had hurried back through the swinging door into the hall, where she collapsed into the arms of Cornelia Pike, sobbing, "I don't want that man in my kitchen. Tell him to go away!" The memory of his face sent a long shudder through her frame.

Brother had no right, she thought, with a flickering of the despairing anger that had been her first reaction to this morning's discovery. At that moment, when the meaning of what confronted her first became clear to her dull and resistant sight, Isabelle had cried out in her rage, denouncing her brother for doing such a horrible, thoughtless, selfish thing to her, for running away from her, for deserting her like that, leaving her high and dry. "How could you, how could you!" she had wailed, kneeling at the side of the bed, her anger beating like a child's fists against her brother—and against her Creator and Ainsley Black as well. It was this dark rush of emotion, sweeping through her uncontrollably, obliterating the first stirrings of grief, that had kept her from telephoning Ben Morgan for nearly an hour after she had knocked, knocked again, and then, with great trepidation, entered Claiborne's room. By the time Ben arrived, her swelling grief had pushed the anger out of sight, and she had greeted the good doctor by falling into his arms and soaking the shoulder of his jacket with tears. At that point the strange floating had begun, leaving both anger and grief trailing somewhere behind. Then the Alhambra ladies took over, and, buoyed by their kindness, she had drifted still further from the event that had set so much into motion. Yet still she greeted each new arrival with an embrace and a small fountain of perfectly real tears switched on by a mechanism that seemed beyond her reach or control. The latest had been Cousin Gracie Roberts, who had promptly hired a young man to drive her all the way from St. Francisville when she heard the news and who was now at the Pikes', resting from the five-hour drive.

Lying shoeless upon her bed, Isabelle felt as if the current carrying her had slackened, that she was spinning slowly in an eddy before resuming her downstream voyage. Her mind was purged to a near-blankness. Only a retinal image kept intruding, the same image, now bleached nearly white, drained of all horror, that had flashed like an optometrist's card across her vision a thousand times since it had first struck her eyes through the shades-drawn ghostliness of Claiborne's room.

Then something new occurred: the idea that she had been set free. Now there was nothing to stop her from seeing her friends whenever she wanted to. Nothing to stop her from selling this dinky modern house and moving into the second-floor apartment in Elsie Adamson's house next to the Pikes'. She could visit Cousin Gracie, who was already urging her to come to St. Francisville. And, when the time came, she could even move back as a paying guest into the house where she had been born. These thoughts brought with them no great elation and as yet produced no guilt. They were more like pleasant memories than anticipations, more comforting than exciting. They relaxed Isabelle, lapping against her consciousness as she fell asleep.

Cousin Gracie stood over her, her rouged and wrinkled face grimacing with tenderness beneath her improbable pompadour of red hair going white. *What on earth is she doing here?* Isabelle wondered as she looked up with startled eyes. *Why am I in bed?* There was a loud ringing in her ears.

Cousin Gracie was saying something about the arrival of an out-of-town visitor. Missing half the words, Isabelle gathered that the person urgently wanted to see her. Now her cousin's voice was clearer. "I said you were restin', but I'd see if you were awake."

Groggily Isabelle lowered herself over the side of the bed and felt for her shoes. "I'll be right out," she muttered, thinking wearily of all those embraces, all those tears. Cousin Gracie closed the bedroom door just as Isabelle thought to ask the visitor's name.

When she saw a man standing in the hall, with the light from the front door behind him, his face in shadow, Isabelle gasped and raised her right hand to her breast. Then she retreated toward her bedroom door, shaking her head violently. "No," she said, "no."

He stepped forward, holding out his arms. "Miss Isabelle—"

Isabelle backed up against her closed door, her hand on the knob. "No, I don't want to see you," she said in a barely audible voice. Cornelia Pike's face had appeared at the living-room door. Should she call to her? She turned the knob with a backhanded twist, but for some reason the door would not open.

"Miss Isabelle, I'm so sorry. I can't tell you how sorry I am."

"Don't say things like that! I can't stand it." Isabelle's voice was still faint, but she shrank from Ainsley Black with a look of horror and tried desperately to turn the knob. His arms were still spread—as if he expected her to rush into his embrace!

"Isabelle?" Cornelia Pike called uncertainly from the living room door, but Isabelle did not hear her.

"*You* put him up to it. You were the last one to see him, and you put him up to it."

Ainsley Black's arms dropped to his side. Slowly he shook his head.

"You were the last person to see him alive. . . . What did you say to him?" she shrieked. "What could you have said to make him do such a thing?" She could see over Ainsley's shoulder that Mary Gordon Munce and Cousin Gracie had joined Cornelia at the entrance to the living room. In a moment they would rush to her, surround her, beat off the intruder. Suddenly her bedroom door swung wide open and she backed in, unsteadily. Ainsley stood in the doorway for a moment, biting his lower lip. Then he followed her into the bedroom and closed the door behind him. He looked ill, stricken, his face a dirty yellow beneath the sunburn, his bandage dirty and yellowish too. There he stood with his back pressed against the door, his arms spread, like a fugitive flattening himself against a wall. After sucking in his cheeks several times, as if trying to collect enough saliva to wet his tongue, he said, "Miss Isabelle, when I left your brother last night, I—I . . . Well, this is the last thing I could ever imagine happening. We—we'd prayed together, the two of us, right there on the rug at the side of his bed—"

"I don't believe you!" By now Isabelle had backed up against her bed, but she did not sit down upon it. Instead, she took a faltering step toward the preacher, then stopped in her tracks.

"Miss Isabelle, when I said goodnight to your brother, he was like a man on the verge of making peace with himself and the Lord. Something must have happened later, something only he and the Lord God know about. But when I last saw him, I saw a man whose heart had begun to melt under the touch of redeeming grace. I was so full of hope when I left his room!"

She saw that his eyes were filling with tears. How she longed to absolve him! But again her anger rose, a wild anger scorching her lungs and throat. "But you must have done somethin', said somethin', to make him despair! If the Lord had touched him, there was no need for him to despair."

"I despaired when I heard the news," he said simply, not bothering to lift his hand to wipe the tears that were brimming over. "I wondered if the Devil had led me into making some terrible miscalculation. It could be, Miss Isabelle. It could be. Maybe I urged your brother too strongly, maybe I—"

Isabelle's anger abruptly gave way and she rushed to comfort him, crying out his name. How drawn he looked, how sad, as he came to meet her. "You mustn't blame yourself," she sobbed against his chest. "You mustn't cry. You did the best you could. It was awful of me to say what I said. Awful!"

He hugged her close, his head raised toward the ceiling. "I feel I've been betrayed," he said. "I feel I've been misled, that I was given an assignment too big—too difficult—for me to handle."

"Not by God," she whispered.

"No, not by God. I think I was summoned here by the Enemy," he added in a low voice.

"What did you say?" Isabelle was certain that she had misheard him. When Ainsley remained silent, she said, "We must try not to be bitter. This is no time for bitterness. Grief and sorrow, yes, but not bitterness. I've been both bitter and angry, and it's a waste, a terrible waste!"

"You're a better Christian than I am, Miss Isabelle. Your faith is stronger. I am still a prey to bitter and despairing thoughts."

Later, as they sat side by side on the lacy, crocheted bedspread, Isabelle told him the whole story, from that first hesitant knock on Claiborne's door after she had waited fifteen minutes for him to come into the kitchen for breakfast. She had found him lying with his knees drawn up, with two pillows pulled over his head, hiding it. The pistol was still in his hand. "I think he wanted to spare me as much as he could," she said with a sudden catch in her voice. "He didn't use one of his high-powered rifles or shotguns but a tiny pistol, one that had belonged to Papa. Everything was so neat. I think he was tryin' to be considerate."

Ainsley was looking away, his throat muscles moving slightly, as if he were trying to swallow and couldn't. *Poor man*, she thought—*poor, dear man, he's grieving too. And he thinks he's failed me. . . .* She saw again how pale he was beneath the ugly mottling of his faded sunburn.

"I'm sure the Lord had something to do with it," he said. "I think the merciful Lord wants to spare you as much as he could."

"Do you mean—"

At last he looked at her. "I mean—what I mean is," he began, as if each word had to be pushed out with enormous effort, "I think we Christians need to rethink our whole attitude toward suicide. I believe there may be occasions when the inspiration comes from God, not the Devil."

"You do? Aren't you making all this up on the spur of the moment just to comfort me—and yourself?"

"It's a new thought, Miss Isabelle—I admit that. I haven't tested it, but it strikes something deep inside me. I think it might be true. It seems to me there may be cases—and your brother could be one of them—where the Lord decides to use the fastest means possible to bring about the release of a tormented soul—short of a bolt out of Heaven, that is." He gave her a smile so sad that she was sure that she was right—that he was trying to comfort himself as well as her.

Still, she listened with an intensity that was like a holding of her breath. "I think," Ainsley continued, "the fact that your brother was so careful about appearances is a sign—a definite sign—of where his inspiration had its source."

"If only I could believe that!"

He stood up. His forehead was beaded with sweat and the front of his shirt looked damp. "*I* believe it, Miss Isabelle. It rings true to me. Absolutely true. But now I've got to be leaving."

Isabelle pleaded with him to stay for supper. His presence meant so much to her—couldn't he stay a couple more hours? She wanted him to meet her relatives and all her friends—everybody who had been so wonderful. . . . Couldn't he spend the night? Weeping, smiling, she caught his hand, pulled his arm toward her, and with an awkward ducking of her head, kissed the top of his hand.

"You're mighty kind, Miss Isabelle," he said in a strangled voice. "But you look worn-out. You've got to conserve your strength and get some rest. I'll be back for the funeral and I'll see you afterwards. For a little while." Putting his arm on her shoulder, he continued in a firmer tone. "I've been called to New Orleans. I have to get there as soon as I can, especially now that this has happened. I'm new to this—to this kind of Christianity, Miss Isabelle, and there's still a lot that I have to learn. I feel that I'm being tested, that I'm—" He broke off, shaking his head, frowning slightly. Then, as if focusing upon the desolation that had seized her, he said, "But New Orleans is not so far away."

"Oh, but it is! A million miles away."

"Not so far that I can't come back to see you. I will. I promise." He moved toward the door. "Meanwhile, we must pray for each other."

Chapter Forty-seven

From the back seat of Miss Isabelle's car, which was in the drive where she had left it last night, Rooney had an unobstructed view of the comings and goings at the Hernes' front door. Since the venetian blinds of the living room and Dr. Claiborne's bedroom had been drawn in customary respect for the dead, there was little chance of anyone's seeing Rooney as he peeped out of the car window, taking care to duck whenever a new arrival went up the front walk. Rooney had taken refuge in the car nearly two hours before when old Miss Cornelia Pike, acting on Miss Isabelle's orders, had told him to leave the kitchen. His own car—dangerously conspicuous now—had been left in the garage behind the funeral parlor, where it would remain until the heat from Memphis had been lowered. Miss Isabelle's car was shaded from the late afternoon sun by the house and by a clump of privet bushes; with all the windows open, it was not intolerably hot. From his hiding place Rooney had observed the arrival of Lawrence Hux, alias Ainsley Black, in a green Ford Falcon instead of the Plymouth he had been driving before; now he was waiting—and would wait as long as he had to—for the fake preacher to emerge.

It had been a bitter day for Rooney, the bitterest of his life. It had begun with an early-morning phone call from Slocum Turner, the only one of the Memphis boys he could trust, telling him that his time had run out, that the boys would give him until ten o'clock tonight to make his delivery *in cash* to the back room of Mungo's Blackstrap Bar in West Memphis. The sum was crazy, much worse than he had expected, far more than he could hope to raise from Dr. Claiborne and his other sources. When he protested, Sloke had told him that if he couldn't come up with the money, he'd better run his own ass out of town—and keep it out. Maybe Rooney could go to New Orleans and try to get Sanchez to cut him in on a deal; if that paid off, maybe he could settle with Memphis and rejoin that outfit—it was a possibility, Sloke thought. . . . Rooney was left in despair. Somehow he would have to get to Dr. Claiborne this morning, even if he had to walk over Miss Isabelle's dead body to do it; he had to raise at least five hundred just to get to New Orleans and keep

himself there while he tried to work out something with Sanchez—
he was that broke. . . . Then, a little after ten, while Rooney was still
pondering his next move, his brother-in-law had come running up
the outside stairs and into the apartment, his eyes rolling, with the
news that Dr. Claiborne had shot himself. "They jus' taken him over
to L. C. Haig's," he said, naming the white undertakers; he had heard
it from Bleek, a limousine driver who worked for both the black and
the white establishments. With a long wailing cry Rooney had gone
down on one knee, pounding the floor with his fists. . . .

Rooney heard voices from the Hernes' front door and peeped over
the rim of the rear window. But it was one of the old ladies, not the
preacher, who was leaving. Kneeling between the front and back
seats, Rooney fingered the pistol stuffed under his belt beneath the
dashiki shirt that he was wearing and lowered his mushroom of hair
out of sight. Maybe Ainsley-Hux would stay for supper, stay until
bedtime—Rooney was prepared to wait. Meanwhile, if the old lady
had turned out to be Miss Cornelia Pike, Rooney would have been
almost tempted to take a shot at her. The thought of his humiliation
in the kitchen made him shake with rage. He was uncertain why he
had gone there in the first place, presenting himself at the back door
like some old nigger coming to pay his respects to the dead master.
And why had he stayed on, when Sharon, who made it clear that she
regarded him as trash, gave him a contemptuous look whenever he
said how good Dr. Claiborne had been to him or how much he
would miss him? Rooney's grief was real—as real as his fury at the
doctor's slipping away from him—and he resented having it dispar-
aged by this uppity woman who barely tolerated his presence in the
kitchen. After a while he addressed most of his comments to Sharon's
daughter Edith, who, though she said little, at least refrained from
tossing her head or releasing audible hisses of disbelief. Rooney in
his time had hated the old man as much as he had loved him; had
exploited him, depended on him, victimized him, and rescued him;
had pandered to his secret tastes and had wanted many times to kill
him. But just now his loss, his grief, was uppermost, and this is what
he wanted the two women to acknowledge. So he rambled on about
Dr. Claiborne in the face of their silence, feeling more rotten all the
time. And then Miss Isabelle had come in—and had run right out
again before he could tell her how sorry he was. He had *wanted* to
tell her, he had nearly cried when he saw her!

The preacher was standing at the front door, saying goodbye to
someone Rooney could not see because of the bushes. Then he

316

turned and started down the front walk, his head lowered, his shoulders slightly stooped. Rooney waited until Hux was almost at his car, which was parked about sixty feet down Granada, and then leaped out of Miss Isabelle's car, letting the door remain open to avoid any noise. Sprinting soundlessly across the grass in his sneakers, avoiding the pavement, he reached the green Falcon just as Hux was letting himself in on the driver's side. Rooney climbed in at the other side and pulled out his pistol. He held it at seat level, pointed toward Hux's chest. "Don't open your mouth," said Rooney just as Hux seemed about to do so. The startled look on that one-eyed face made Rooney tingle with a thrill of power.

As he crouched down into the space in front of the seat, keeping the gun pointing upward, Rooney said, "You gonna drive to my place. I'll tell you how to git there. Now start up and drive past Dr. Claib'n's house lookin' straight ahead. If you too scared to drive, I'll shoot you right now and drive away before anybody even come to the window. Okay? And don't open your mouth. No need to talk, just do like I say."

Hux was slow to react. He simply sat there, holding the car keys, staring at Rooney with his uncovered eye. Then Rooney waved the pistol barrel in a three-inch arc, saying between nearly closed lips, "I see you too scared to drive. I'm goin' to shoot you in the face right now." Hux put the key into the ignition and switched it on.

"Where are you taking me?" Hux asked, speaking for the first time. They were on a country road, hardly more than a track cutting through a stand of tall pine trees. The sun, which had nearly set, splashed red paint on the shaggy trunks of the pines.

"I thought I tol' you to keep your mouth shut. You ain't been given permission to talk." Rooney was now sitting next to the preacher, the muzzle of the pistol about two inches from the man's ribs. "Jus' keep drivin'. We nearly there."

They came to a small clearing in which sat an abandoned trailer, its sides rusted and peeling. Rooney ordered the preacher to stop the car and give him the keys. Then, after getting out, he kept the pistol pointed at Hux until the latter had slid across the front seat and stood beside him, his hands raised. "I reckon you got sense enough not to try anything funny," said Rooney. "Now come on in. You go first." When they were inside the trailer, he made his captive sit down on an unpainted wooden chair. Then he took a length of cord from a pile of litter under a built-in bed and tied the preacher tightly to the chair, causing him to gasp with pain as the cord cut into his wrist.

The inside of the trailer was stifling, the stale air smelling of mildewed bedding, rust, and rotting linoleum. When he had finished, Rooney stuck the pistol into his belt and stood back to survey his work. "That'll do for now," he said with a flashing grin. "Welcome to my cabin in the pines, my home-away-from-home. Got all the comforts of home and nobody to bother us. We gonna wait here till it gits good an' dark. You can talk now. Yell your head off if you want to—ain't nobody goin' to hear you."

"Why are you doing this to me?" Hux's forehead was red and beaded with sweat, but his voice was stronger, less terrified, than Rooney would have liked.

"I'll tell you, you motherfucker!" screamed Rooney, raising his right hand as if to slap Hux. "You killed the best friend I ever had. You killed him jus' the same as you had shot him through the head."

"No," said Hux with a violent shake of his own head. "No."

"You jus' as good as kill him. You talk him into it."

"I did nothing of the kind."

"Don't you lie to me, Reverend Black. Or Mister Lawrence Hux or whatever you call yourself. You were there—las' night—an' you did somethin'—said somethin'—made that ol' man kill himself."

It was now nearly dark inside the trailer, which was unconnected with electric power or a source of water. The bandage over Hux's eye seemed to glow in the half light despite its stains and dirt. "No," he said, "you are wrong. I prayed with him. You are the one who made him take his life. He killed himself out of shame. I saw what you had done to his poor back."

Rooney slapped Hux across the cheek, just under the bandage. Suddenly he laughed. "His poor back! Shit, man, Dr. Claib'n would crawl on his hands an' knees beggin' to have a lady tickle his back with a little whip. Not shoot himself." Then angrily: "It's you who got him all stirred up. All that Jesus stuff you been feedin' him, all that shit!" He began to shake the preacher by the shoulders, so hard that the chair nearly tipped over. "What did you say to Dr. Claib'n?" he demanded in a choked voice.

"Don't," Hux gasped. "Please don't. The cord is cutting me."

"Is that right?" Rooney abruptly let the man go and crossed the floor to a shelf that projected over the bed. There he lit a candle which was stuck into a yellow plastic cup. The flame leaped to a whiskey bottle next to the candle and danced on the clouded surfaces of two dirty glasses. Looking over his shoulder, Rooney saw the dark place on the man's cheek where he had been slapped. He seemed to be breathing hard, his exposed eye surprisingly bright in the candlelight. Rooney splashed whiskey into both glasses. "We got another hour's wait," he said, approaching the bound man and holding out one of the glasses. "So we might as well have us a little party. You jus' open your mouth and I'll feed it to you like a little baby bird."

"No, I don't want a drink."

"Don't shit me. You're a drinkin' preacher. I watched you once—through the window."

"No," Hux repeated, turning his face away as Rooney thrust the glass to his lips.

"You too good to drink my whiskey? Here, have a taste." With a high cackling laugh, Rooney dashed the whiskey into Hux's face. Then he tossed back his own drink and smacked his lips.

Hux sat rigidly, his eye closed while the whiskey dripped from his cheeks and chin, wetting his shirt and jacket. Rooney saw his lips move, and it occurred to him that the man was praying—a possibility so enraging that Rooney barely controlled an impulse to slap the man senseless.

Opening his eye and blinking rapidly as if to get rid of the sting of alcohol, Hux said, "I have about three hundred dollars in my wallet. Will you take that and let me go? I promise not to report you to the police. I'm leaving the state—I'm going to New Orleans and I don't expect to return to this part of the country." As he spoke, he kept wetting his lips and swallowing, but he looked Rooney in the eye.

"New Or-leens!" yelled Rooney. "Tha's where I'm goin'. Goin' to take me a vacation in New Orleans. In your car! Town ain't big enough to hold us both." Laughing, he returned to the whiskey bottle and poured himself another drink. "But I'll accept the offer of your money. Mighty kind of you." Again he laughed. The whiskey had begun to buzz in his head (he had eaten almost nothing) and he felt better than he had all day. "You with the FBI?" he suddenly asked.

"No. Look, how long are you going to keep me here?"

"How come you got two names? I followed you home couple of weeks ago. All the way to Oxford. Looked through your glove compartment, saw your car-rentin' papers an' some other stuff. Mr. Lawrence Hux, New York City. Don't sound much like a preacher to me." He narrowed his agate-brown eyes. "I lef' you a note tellin' you to stop messin' round with Dr. Claib'n. You git that note?"

Hux shook his head. "The rain blurred the ink. You slashed my tires, didn't you?"

"You right. I did. I cannot tell a lie." Rooney giggled.

"And you're right too. I'm not a preacher. Not yet." He tried to shift his position slightly and winced with pain. "Look," he said, "couldn't you loosen this cord? It's cutting off the circulation in my arms."

"If you had some of this whiskey, you wouldn't mind it so much."

"Then you're not going to loosen the cord?"

"Right. You're gonna stay jus' the way you are till we git ready to move."

Hux closed his eyes and sat quietly for some moments. Then, after again wetting his lips, he said, "Do you believe in God?"

Running over to the chair, Rooney caught him by both shoulders and tipped the chair back. Hux cried out with pain. Leaning over him, Rooney said, "Don't you try to start that shit with me. I ain't Dr. Claib'n. You hear? One more word about God an' I'll knock the shit out of you."

"Go ahead," said Hux with a kind of sob. "Go right ahead. Unless you beat me senseless, there's no way you can stop me from saying the name of God."

Rooney slapped him twice—hard—across the face. Then he grabbed a dirty towel hanging on the back rail of the bed, stuffed it into Hux's mouth, and secured it with another strip of cloth. "Now try sayin' the name of God." After pouring himself another drink, he stood back and contemplated his work. The figure of Hux reminded him of scenes from movies and television shows that he had watched over the years: a dimly lit room or cave or cell; a bandaged prisoner bound and gagged, his face defiant though taut with pain. For a few moments he played with the idea of trying out a few of the things he had seen done in such scenes. It was fun to get drunk this way, but he warned himself not to get carried away—he had a long drive ahead of him.

A little later Rooney went through Hux's pockets, taking out his wallet, his traveler's checks, his keys, and anything else that might be used for identification. He thought of taking off Hux's seersucker suit, but that would have involved untying him, and Rooney was not ready to do that. Meanwhile, as he prowled restlessly around the trailer, circling his prisoner, he talked and sometimes laughed aloud or snapped his fingers. His talk was rambling, full of sudden leaps and trailings-off. Mostly he talked for his own benefit, for much of what he said could have made no sense to Hux. But once he turned directly to his captive audience and said, jeeringly, "That ol' man used to crawl up to Memphis 'bout once a month to git the skin taken off his back. I found out about it—I got connections in Memphis—plenty of connections—too many!" He gave a whooping laugh and slapped his thighs with both hands. "Too many—Lord knows, too many—so when I heard he got himself a big black momma in Memphis to take the skin off his back, I figured he didn't need to crawl all the way to Memphis for *that*. No, suh. Fix him up with somethin' closer to home." A few minutes later, after another shot of whiskey, he was crying over Dr. Claiborne, saying, "He's the bes' friend I ever had. Without'n him I'd be jus' one more skinny nigger headin' up North to look for work. You could call him my benefactor. I call him my gravy train. Yes, suh, that ol' gravy train. The Dr. Claib'n Special. Lent me money, sent me three years to a no-good nigger college, got me started in business, sent me to De-troit . . . Been derailed a few times but I always managed to git it back on the tracks, you might say. Till now." Rooney made a face, jutting out his lower lip; tears had come to his eyes, and he wiped them away with the back of his hand.

Suddenly he began dancing around the narrow space, jabbing at the air. "Didn't know I was a boxer, did you?" he said, grazing his prisoner's cheek with his fist. "Used to fight in the Memphis Golden Glove tournament. Dr. Claib'n taught me. That ol' man taught me 'most everything I know. When I was 'bout twelve or thirteen, he started trainin' me—down in that gym he rigged up in the basement of the ol' house. Shit, I was good, real good. He use to match me with another nigger kid name' Lewis. Down in that gym. The white boys used it all the time, but he had to be kind of careful—those days— lettin' us niggers use it. You know how it is."

He looked expectantly—and accusingly—at Hux, who did not make the slightest movement. "Shit," he said, making a right jab at nothing, "Dr. Claib'n woulda been run out of town if they knowed me an' Lewis was using the same shower an' toilet those nice lily-white boys was usin'. I don't have to tell *you*." Again he paused for an affirmation. "When I was 'bout sixteen," he went on, "I started boxin' with Dr. Claib'n himself. 'Course we had to keep it a secret— didn't even tell Lewis. He was a lot taller than me, had the reach all over me, but before long I could git inside his guard and knock the shit out of him." Rooney shook his head and grinned. "Guess what happened the first time I knocked him out. I'd already split his lip wide open and then I landed a right hook an' down he went. I was scared shitless. I went runnin' over to him an' raised him up an' wiped his face an' all that an' he started cussin' me. But you know what? That day, jus' before I lef', Dr. Claib'n shook hands with me an' slipped me a ten-dollar bill!"

Rooney had stopped directly in front of Hux. "Tha's when the gravy train first left the station," he said. "An' now it's off the track for good. Mighty bad havin' that train derailed right now when I'm kind of overextended, you might say." Rooney crouched over, his face level with Hux's. "You the railway man pulled the wrong switch and derailed my gravy train." He lifted his fist, saw Hux blink convulsively several times, and, still in a boxer's crouch, turned on his heels with a laugh.

After taking a swig directly from the bottle, Rooney said, "Gittin' close to leavin' time. Got me a little job to do." He rummaged through several cardboard boxes that lined the wall opposite the bed and from one of them drew out a pair of Mississippi license plates. After further searching he found a screwdriver and a pair of pliers. He went outside. When he returned he put the Tennessee license plates from Hux's rented car into the box and wiped his hands on a rag. "Time to git goin'. Got to be in New Orleens by mornin'." He grinned at Hux. "Since you cain't go to New Orleens with me, how'd you like to take your vacation over at Cobb's Creek? They're buildin' a dam over there. Lots of excavatin', lots of loose dirt. Jus' like the place them Ku Kluxers found for Chaney an' the two white boys over in Neshoba County. Ten years ago." Rooney's grin widened. "Hell, Reverend, don' look so sick. I'm jus' puttin' you on. You shit in your pants yet?"

Rooney got more cord to tie Hux's wrists more securely and to hobble his ankles. Then he cut the cord binding Hux's arms to the chair. "Stand up," he commanded. When Hux refused to move and made several throaty sounds through the gag, Rooney stood back for a moment, his hands on his slim hips, his dashiki half pulled off one shoulder. "I don't like the look in your one good eye," he said. "Le's see what the other one looks like." And reaching out, he clawed the dirty bandage from Hux's face.

322

Chapter Forty-eight

Though she had told him not to call, Anne was perversely disappointed when she failed to hear from Larry on Tuesday. Still, what else could she expect after the erratic way he had been behaving? After his lie about Tony—a lie as peculiar as it was hateful—she had tried to dismiss him as a seriously disturbed person, as more than a little psychotic. Badly hurt as well as embarrassed and horrified by the consequences of the lie, she had berated herself for ignoring all the early warning signs of his instability; she was a fool ever to have thought that anything good could come from getting involved with a man who had traveled all the way to Mississippi on such a mission. And yet she had gone right ahead and raised a crazy-built structure of hope—only to be nearly crushed by its collapse. When would she ever learn? She was furious at herself.

But she was also furious at Larry's unreliability. She could hear him crying out, just as she hung up, that he would call her. And she was at the same time consumed with a desire to see him, to hear in detail why he had lied to her, and—as if it were a television serial—to catch the final episode of his pursuit of Claiborne Herne. She kept glimpsing Larry's face, his odd smile, the way his brass-colored hair framed his forehead like a helmet. He had let her down horribly. She should wipe him out of her mind. . . . Yet Anne stayed up late watching television, hoping that he might call and hating her need for him to do so. At eleven-thirty she lost control of herself and telephoned the Holiday Inn, which informed her that Mr. Hux was not in his room. When she heard on the midnight news that an unidentified white man had been found badly beaten in a roadside ditch near Batesville, she paid little attention and made no connection. Shortly afterwards she went to bed.

There was a much fuller account of the incident in the paper the next morning. Anne put down her coffee cup and stared blankly at Prudence, who had asked her a question. After she had finally been able to focus sufficiently upon Prue's question to answer it, she re-read the article. It stated that the injured man found outside Batesville had been taken to the university hospital in Oxford, where he

323

was described as suffering from severe head injuries (including a possible skull fracture and concussion) as well as from a broken shoulder, several broken ribs, and facial and bodily contusions. His condition was listed as critical. Since he was unable to respond to questioning, police were awaiting a report on fingerprints in an effort to establish his identity. The man, who had been bound and gagged and apparently thrown from a moving car, had been discovered by a local farmer, Samuel J. Lunsford, 38, shortly after noon on Tuesday. Lunsford had been driving along a back road from Batesville to Alhambra when he noticed the man's foot and leg projecting above the rim of the ditch. Observing that the man was breathing but badly injured, Lunsford drove to a service station, where he telephoned the state police. The injured man was described as about forty years of age, of medium build, with dark blond hair. He had recently suffered a cut above his right eye that had necessitated stitches. He was wearing a blue seersucker suit with the label of a New York store, Brooks Brothers. . . . Police speculated . . .

"I have to get a real early start this mornin'," said Anne, rising from the kitchen table and carefully folding the paper. "So I'll be leavin' before the school bus picks you up."

Prue, who was simultaneously eating cereal and poring over a copy of *Mad* magazine, nodded without looking up.

One eye was open, its pupil much dilated. The other was covered by the snowy bandage that enveloped most of his skull. His vital signs were good, Anne was told, and his condition was now listed as serious but stabilized. Though his puffed-up lips moved, he could as yet make no intelligible sound, and he remained unresponsive to anything said to him. It would take a while, said the attending doctor, for them to be sure, but it was certainly well within the range of possibility that he would make a good recovery—without permanent brain damage of any consequence. He repeated that it was still much too early to tell. . . .

Anne spent more than an hour with the local and state police. She gave a somewhat laundered account of the man she identified as Lawrence Hux. The offices of the Morrow Foundation and the president of the University of Mississippi were called at once; there was no answer to the telephone of Louise Hux, and Anne could not remember where it was that she worked. Emphasizing Larry's official mission, she made no reference to either Clark Helmholtz or Claiborne Herne, even though she told herself that there could conceivably be some connection between Larry's abduction and Dr. Herne's suicide. If the police uncovered something involving the Hernes, that would be their business, not hers. And of course she could flatly—and with good conscience—deny any knowledge of drug consumption or drug dealing on Larry's part. She was questioned on this subject at some length, as if the local police had some stake in viewing the crime as drug-related.

"Why do you boys keep comin' back to that?" she asked, exasperated at last. "Both his money and his car are missin'. Looks like a plain case of old-fashioned robbery to me."

"Well now, ma'am," said one of the men, "you know good as I do these smart-ass New York executive types cain't git along without their regular sniff of coke."

Shortly afterwards she heard one of the sheriff's men say something to one of the state patrolmen about a Klan meeting that had taken place outside of Batesville on Monday night. . . .

Later in the day Anne suddenly remembered that Louise Hux worked at Columbia University Press. She hurried to the nearest pay phone in the library. Probably the Morrow Foundation had already been in touch with Louise, but she needed to make her own call.

Chapter Forty-nine

"Larry, this is Anne. Can you hear me?"

Yes, he could hear her, despite the constant buzzing and ringing of his ears. But her words were like bright drops of sound, falling separately. He could make out part of her face in the dazzling kaleidoscope that assaulted him whenever he opened his eye—a jumble of blurred images that refused to come together. It was easier to shut out all that light and return to the cemetery, where the grass was a soft green and the dappled sunlight fell gently through the canopy of old trees. He held Miss Isabelle tightly by the arm as the coffin was lowered. . . .

"Larry, Louise is comin' this afternoon. I called her yesterday, and she's arrivin' in Memphis at three-thirty-five. She's goin' to rent a car and drive straight to the hospital. So you'll be seein' her late this afternoon. Can you understand what I'm sayin'? Can you hear me?"

Yes, he could hear her, but he also heard, from a great distance, the sounds of a band playing "Onward, Christian Soldiers." He had to go, he had to leave—why couldn't she understand that? Why was her face hanging over the bed, along with the bottles and tubes and the blinding light on the ceiling? The sky, too, was blinding when he looked up. He turned his head violently, shutting his eye. Again he heard the distant band and knew that he had to hurry. . . .

"You better leave now," said the black woman in white. "He gittin' too excited."

"Larry, can you hear me? Try to understand me. Louise is on her way. You're goin' to be just fine, you're—"

"You really got to leave now. He got to be kept real quiet."

"Goodbye, Larry. Louise will be here this afternoon. Try to remember that. And I'll be back to see you. Now you do what they tell you. Lie still now, you hear? Lie still!"

He had no time to lose. The sky was blinding when he looked up—not a cloud to be seen. There were banners everywhere, thousands of them, and loudspeakers on every balcony. People were standing on the balconies, leaning over the railings, which were like iron lace, and a crowd was pushing through the narrow streets, moving toward the sound of the band. He had to reach Brother Thurlow in time to warn him, to save him. The danger was great—it could happen at any moment—he had to get there in time. . . . Feeling his pocket to make sure that Claiborne Herne's little pistol was still there, he plunged into the crowd, pushing his way toward the source of the sound. People jostled him, sending sharp stabs of pain through his shoulder and chest, pain so sharp that he yelled out. Everything was so slow, so slow . . . how would he ever get there in time? He wanted to cry with frustration and grief. Too late, he would be too late! And then he was being carried along, lifted from his feet almost as the mob surged forward and poured into the square. Thousands and thousands of people filled the square, all of them facing the cathedral. Arms were raised, scarlet balloons were floating like fireballs in the blinding light. Moving toward the distant cathedral, he felt his sore chest expand with relief. He would not be too late. He began to wave his arms and cry out as he saw Brother Thurlow standing on a crowded platform in front of the cathedral. Brother Thurlow was preaching, his voice booming out over the loudspeakers.

Now he was at the foot of the platform, and Brother Thurlow recognized him and waved his hand. It was then that he saw what he had known he would see: Clark was crouched just a few paces behind Brother Thurlow—crouched wrestler-like, his fingers extended like hooks, his thumbs drawn back, ready to spring! Already he was moving toward the preacher, so low that he was almost crawling, and no one on the platform tried to stop him or even saw him.

Hux pulled out the .22 and fired two shots into Clark. Suddenly everyone was shouting, and Hux, to his dumb horror, saw Brother Thurlow stagger, clutching his chest, and fall at the foot of the podium.

Clark had vanished.

Finding his voice, Hux screamed out, "Oh, no! Oh, no!" He climbed out of the bed, dragging the apparatus of tubes with him. The plastic bottles fell to the floor, spilling their liquid.

"Hey, you!" yelled the grizzled old farmer with the broken hip who occupied the other bed in the room. "You git back in yo' bed!" He began to ring for the nurse.

Still pulling the tubes behind him, Hux staggered toward the door. He sank to his knees as he reached it, bowed down, defeated, nearly annihilated by the pain in his padded skull, his strapped chest, his strapped shoulder and arm. Dizziness swept over him in a buzzing black swarm, and he did not hear the nurse come into the room, exclaiming, "Oh, Lord God Almighty! Good Lord have mercy!" Nor was he conscious when the nurse, with the aid of two orderlies, lifted him back into bed and the resident reinstated the apparatus.

Chapter Fifty

By the fifth day (after Louise had come and gone) Anne thought she could detect some improvement in Larry's condition. He still looked imbecilic—his face puffed-up and livid, his one visible eye unfocused, his mouth gentian-violet, two front teeth missing—but there were now intervals when he seemed to be speaking coherently. It was hard to tell, for his sutured lips and injured jaw made him almost impossible to understand. He called Anne by name several times, and she would lean close to him, trying to piece together the muffled words. He was evidently very agitated about Brother Thurlow, whose name she finally extracted from something that sounded like "brub'thlow."

"What about Brother Thurlow?" she asked, but Larry, though he screwed up his face, closing his eye and working his tongue behind his missing teeth, was unable to answer. She was just as glad. She wanted nothing to do with the preacher, whom she associated with the worst of Larry's aberrations.

It was not always convenient for her to come to the hospital, yet she did not miss a day. She would sit for ten or fifteen minutes by his bed while he mumbled on, sometimes gesturing with his free arm, once calling out, with almost perfect clarity, "All right, Newbie, you stuffed-shirt shit!" Once he began to sob, with tears rolling across his bruised cheeks. Anne leaned over and held his hand while he continued to sob, and then she wiped his eyes and running nose with a Kleenex; but he said nothing and did not seem to recognize her. He was evidently in pain much of the time. Whenever Anne came in, the old farmer in the other bed would cackle and say, "Girlfriend time! Wake up, sonny, it's girlfriend time."

On the seventh day she could tell immediately that Larry's mind had cleared overnight. His eyes, both now unbandaged, seemed bluer than ever against the still-discolored skin that surrounded them, and they greeted her with a flash of full recognition. "You've been here before," he said. "I'm sure I saw you."

"I've dropped by every day." She wanted to kiss his forehead in gratitude.

"They tell me I've been here a week." His speech, too, had cleared

328

considerably, but the missing teeth gave an unfamiliar sibilance to his voice.

Anne nodded. Pulling up her chair, she observed with relief that the old farmer was gone and that his bed had not yet been filled. I have him to myself, she thought joyously. He's come back, he's here. . . . But Larry seemed tired and extraordinarily remote, as if he wanted to stay within the shadowy cave of his thoughts, making only a few outward excursions into speech. Anne felt an obligation to talk, to entertain him, while at the same time she was hesitant to ask all the questions that crowded the front of her mind. Easy, she told herself—take it easy, don't rush him. . . . Noticing a huge basket of salmon-colored roses and pink and white carnations, she said, "Aren't they gorgeous?" But she did not ask who had sent them, and Larry did not offer the information. When she was about to leave, he suddenly frowned and said, "Was Louise here?"

"She was here for two days. Talked to all the doctors. Made arrangements and—"

"I don't remember her."

"That's hardly surprisin'. You were totally out of your head." She felt a small, unworthy glow of triumph. Louise had politely and civilly snubbed her, declining Anne's invitation to have dinner on her first night in Oxford, showing no interest in meeting her despite their telephone conversations.

Larry's voice again emerged from the recesses of his thoughts. "There's . . . so much . . . I can't remember," he said haltingly. "I lie here trying to fill in the gaps."

"I wouldn't worry about it."

There was an extended silence. Then: "They tell me I was beaten up and dumped from a moving car. The police were here this morning asking questions. But I can't remember a single thing that happened after Claiborne Herne's funeral. Who would want to beat me up?"

"You weren't at Claiborne Herne's funeral," said Anne. "You were brought into the hospital in the mornin', before the funeral."

Larry received this in silence. He seemed to stare past Anne toward some distant scene as he pondered her words. At last he said, "It was very real. The funeral, I mean."

"You'll get it all sorted out. Don't worry about it now."

Another sigh. "You'll have—to help me. But I'm too tired right now. And I've got a headache."

Anne stood up. "I'll see you tomorrow. Anything you want me to bring you?"

He shook his head slightly, his eyes already closed.

By the next day Larry had reoccupied more ground. "Did anyone get in touch with Brother Thurlow?" he asked as Anne entered the room.

"No. Why?"

"I was supposed to join Brother Thurlow in New Orleans. I—am sure of that. Positive."

Overcoming her revulsion, Anne said, "Do you want me to try to call him?"

"Would you? Would you?" His strength seemed to ebb suddenly, and he was barely able to get out the words. "Tell him—just tell him what happened to me. And not to worry. Tell him—" He broke off, wrinkling his brow, his mouth half open, exposing the gap that Anne hated to see. "Tell him—tell him I'll call when I get my strength back."

"Do you know where he can be reached?"

"The Mount Calvary Baptist Church. In New Orleans. I remember that very clearly."

"I'll try." She spoke out of a sheer sense of duty, dreading the whole task. Perhaps by this time Brother Thurlow would have left New Orleans and she would be unable to trace him. In that case Larry could perhaps be weaned away. . . . He now seemed to her perfectly sane, but so far off, even when he was talking about the preacher.

Toward the end of her visit, he said, "I got a get-well card from Tony. It's there on the stand."

"And those gorgeous flowers—did Louise and Tony send you the flowers?"

He shook his head. "Newbold Jenkins."

"Who's that?" She was sure she had heard the name mentioned before.

"My boss. He's a kind man," added Larry, his eyes suddenly brimming with tears. "I think you'd better go. I'm so tired."

Anne was unable to reach the evangelist that night. He had driven over to Mobile on business, she was told, and wouldn't be back until the next afternoon. But she managed to talk to a woman who identified herself as Sister Thelma something-or-other, who said she knew Larry and promised to give the message to Brother Thurlow. "That poor boy!" said Sister Thelma. "Now who in this world would want to do a thing like that? You tell him he'll be in Archie B.'s prayers for a speedy recovery the minute he hears about it—and mine too. Tell him not to worry hisself about one little thing. Ever'thing will be taken care of in the Lord's good time. You be sure an' tell him that, honey." Anne hung up feeling sick. How could Larry have become involved with such a trashy outfit? Crazy as he was, he ought to have better taste! Then it occurred to her that she was perfectly willing to put up with—even sympathize with—any amount of this evangelical business from blacks but not from whites.

Although she relayed Sister Thelma's message to Larry, she did not comment on it or bring up Brother Thurlow's name for another week. Larry said nothing. He still seemed remote to her: perfectly coherent, willing to respond to her questions, apparently glad to see her, but keeping most of himself concealed. His appearance distressed her. When the head bandage was removed, she was shocked to see that the helmet of tarnished brass was gone, revealing a shaved skull on which recently healed cuts had left irregular scars. With his now much thinner face, the shaved head, and the missing teeth, he reminded her of a tortured political prisoner—or a criminal prepared for the electric chair. She wanted to clasp his poor head to her breast, to run her fingers over the returning fuzz and the scars. At the same time she was repelled.

Meanwhile, the missing slabs of memory were being recovered. "It was Rooney Lee," he told her one day. "The same man who slashed my tires."

"Have you told the police?"

"No," he said, after probing the gap between his teeth with the tip of his tongue in what had now become almost a tic, "and I'm not going to. I hope they never find out."

Anne was outraged. "After what he did to you? My God! Aren't you carryin' Christian forgiveness a little too far? That man's a killer—he's got to be locked up."

"Rooney will get caught sooner or later—but for something else. Right now, all I care about is protecting Miss Isabelle. If I put the police on Rooney's trail, she'll get dragged in. They'll question her and she'll have to learn all kinds of things about Rooney and her brother that I'd rather she didn't know."

"What kind of things?"

"I'll tell you one of these days. Right now I haven't got the strength to go into it."

Anne was silenced—and left a little angry. But at least, she told herself, his motive was saner than simple forgiveness would have been.

Then one day Anne could stand his remoteness no longer. She had come in with an armful of flowers wrapped in wax paper—delphinium, columbine, larkspur, and other summer flowers she had cut from Peggy Benson's garden. While putting the flowers into one of the hospital vases, she noticed on his bedside stand a large greeting card with a picture of Jesus as the Good Shepherd on its cover.

"Is this from Brother Thurlow?" she demanded, picking up the card.

"Yes," he replied—and offered nothing more.

In a quivering voice—she was very angry—she said, "Do you still consider yourself a convert—a new-born or reborn or twice-born Christian? Or did Rooney Lee knock some sense into your head when he beat you up?"

"Don't be angry," he said. "I know what I owe you. I want to tell you everything but my own thoughts aren't clear. I need time."

"What you owe me! You don't owe me a goddamn thing!" This she felt was not true, but it was what she had to say. Clumsily she went about stuffing the flowers into the vase, snapping off stems that were too long, scattering a few petals on the table. "I guess I'm no good at handlin' invalids. I ought to keep tiptoein' around you, handlin' you with kid gloves—or else stay away."

His eyes were troubled, full of pain. "No," he said, "don't stay away."

"I get the feelin' there isn't room in here for both me and Brother Thurlow. He's the one who made you run off and make up that terrible lie about Tony. He's the one who made you act so crazy." Anne could not stop herself. All of these hospital visits had piled up, were tumbling over her, and she could not help crying out in her own pain. "He's the one who drove us apart."

"No," he said, "it was Brother Thurlow who saved my life. He saved my life. Oh, Anne, give me time, give me time!"

"Do you remember making love to me? Or is that one of the chunks of your memory that's still missin'?" And then seeing his mouth tremble, his eyes shimmer, she was stricken with shame. "Oh, Larry, honey!" she cried. "I don't mean to be such a bully. You aren't well yet. I'm sorry, I'm so sorry." And she kissed him on the forehead, squeezed his hand, and left the room before he could do more than call out her name.

She did not return for more than ten days. On a postcard she wrote: "I don't want to behave badly again, so am staying away. Get in touch before you leave. Love, Anne."

He called her at the library, and Anne walked all the way to the hospital that afternoon through the steamy heat. She didn't care how damp and disheveled she looked. She found Larry sitting, in his blue hospital robe and slippers, in the little lounge for ambulatory patients. A temporary bridge now replaced the missing teeth—and his hair had grown out to crew-cut length, partly concealing the scars. How thin he was! His new appearance, while an improvement over what she had last seen, would take getting used to; the Larry she had once known showed no signs of returning. He was now exercising regularly, he said—up and down the corridors. Although a firm date had not been set, he expected to be leaving shortly, perhaps in three or four days.

"So you called me back before you were ready to go," she said glumly.

"Does it matter? I wanted to see you. I'll be leaving soon enough."

"For New Orleans?"

"No, for New York."

He then told her that Louise had offered him the use of the West End Avenue apartment for the rest of his convalescence.

Anne's face must have revealed something, for Larry quickly said, "Louise won't be there. She's going to her mother's place on Squam Lake." They were now sitting face to face on plastic chairs, their knees almost touching. Anne wished that she had taken the time to wash her face and run a comb through her hair. "I forgot what you told me," continued Larry. "Did you see Louise or just talk to her on the phone?"

"I didn't meet her, but I saw her come out of your room. She was with Dr. Shaw," Anne added, "and I felt very excluded from their conversation, which was obviously about you. She looked pale and tense, and I wanted to say somethin' to her, but of course I didn't. She had made it plenty clear that she wasn't interested in meeting me." What she did not say was that Louise had looked both older and prettier than she had expected—and that she had instantly hated everything about her: her cool summer dress, her pallor, the dark gold of her hair, which was curiously like Larry's, and the intensity with which she was speaking with Dr. Shaw.

After the silence that fell between them, Anne said, "So you're not goin' to New Orleans. Are you disillusioned with your preacher friend?"

"Please don't be so sarcastic. You were more sympathetic once."

"So were you. You hadn't told me lies."

Larry spoke very slowly. "I think I was having a breakdown. I was in very bad shape. When I left town, I was running away from all kinds of things—from Clark, from the Hernes, from you. And I was running—running frantically—toward the one person who could help me. He took hold of my life—took hold of *me*—and he turned me around." His words were coming out more slowly still. "I keep saying 'he,' but what turned me around was much more than Brother Thurlow. I don't even want to give it a name."

"You found Jesus. Brother Thurlow opened your heart to Jesus."

Larry grinned at her, and Anne had the sense that, despite his earlier complaint, he was in some deep and real way beyond the reach of her scorn. There was something fixed about him, rocklike, and she was swirling around him like angry water.

"Jesus was the name I spoke, the name I prayed to. But the name doesn't seem necessary to me now, maybe not even useful any more. It's at the center of Brother Thurlow's whole system, but I'm not sure how much I'm committed to it." He stared at Anne and beyond her. Then he frowned. "All I can say right now is that the name and everything built around it strike me as an effort to tie down something that is a lot bigger and a lot simpler—well, 'simpler' isn't the word I want—than whatever Brother Thurlow has to say about it." Suddenly he laughed. "You know, my mother's been taking yoga exercise classes in Raleigh. The instructor isn't even Indian—I picture him as some kind of dancing teacher who's gone Oriental. What occurred to me just now is that he might even have a name for what happened to me which, for all I know, could be just as valid as Brother Thurlow's."

"At least you no longer sound like a Jesus freak. That's all to the good."

Larry shook his head. "But I've been changed, Anne. You mustn't underestimate that. I've been turned around and turned upside down and *shaken*"—he began to laugh—"and lots of loose change has dropped out of my pockets!" Putting his hand over his forehead, he began to laugh silently, as if he had said something extraordinarily funny.

Anne laughed too, but uneasily. He's not well yet, she thought. At the same time she was stirred by what he had said.

"And now I've been put on my feet again, pointed in a new direction, and told to march." Though still a little red in the face, Larry seemed to have recovered from his spasm of hilarity. "That's what Brother Thurlow did for me—saved my life. But I'm not sure I need him around to give me marching orders any more. Something in me seems to have pulled loose from him." Slowly he smiled again, as if at a private joke. "Maybe that beating I got snapped a link."

Again Anne thought, *he's not well yet, he isn't out of the woods.*

"I have no long-term plans," he said, anticipating the question on her lips. "I don't know what direction I'm going to take." He spread his hands palm upward and cocked his head in a gesture of mock apology. "I honestly don't know—all that will have to wait."

"For what?" Anne demanded impatiently. "Some still small voice? Some command from on high?"

"Don't," said Larry, shaking his finger at her. "You're being sarcastic again. I'm not well enough to take sarcasm. But while I've been lying in bed," he continued, "thinking about a million and one things, a few things have become clear to me. You could call them priorities. The first has to do with Tony. I've got to start building there and build as fast and as well as I can. For reasons I won't go into now—I'm not very clear about them myself—I think I'll now be able to build something with Tony. I don't think it's too late. . . ."

"It's not goin' to be easy," said Anne, who was suddenly jealous of Tony.

"And then," he said, ignoring her, "my next priority is to take three months' sick leave from the Foundation. I have it coming to me. I want to be my own think tank for a while—and look around. One of the things I'll do is come South again, probably in September. I want to see Brother Thurlow. I may even try to see Miss Isabelle, though I'm not sure about that. I'm not eager to play Ainsley Black again."

"God, I should hope not," said Anne. Then, turning down the corners of her wide mouth, she said glumly, "I suppose I'm number three on your Southern list. Is that it?"

"That's entirely up to you. The invitation to go to New Orleans still stands."

Was he kidding or what? Suddenly Anne felt outraged. Jumping up from her chair, she started to walk out of the room but turned instead toward the window. Outside, the landscaped grounds of the hospital seemed to quiver in the late-afternoon heat. She then swung around toward Larry so fast that her black hair seemed to float above her shoulders. "If you think I'm goin' to share you with Brother Thurlow in New Orleans, you're out of your fuckin' mind!"

"Don't be ridiculous. Come back here and sit down. Brother Thurlow won't be in New Orleans. In fact he's already left. He's in Knoxville now and Lord knows where he'll be in September."

"Lord knows where *I'll* be in September," said Anne, who was somewhat appeased but in no hurry to sit down. "I'm not waitin' around. Suppose you get marchin' orders to go to India or somethin' like that—then where would I be?" Larry got up and came toward her and put his arms around her. "Right now," she said, resting her head on his good shoulder, "I know exactly where I've got to be. I've got to go home and start fixin' supper for my starvin' child." He kissed her, and Anne, gripping his arms above the elbows with both hands, felt how thin he was.

They walked down the corridor together, and at the door to his room Larry asked if she would come again tomorrow. "Yes," she said, "and the next day too. And the one after that if you're still here. We might as well drag this out to the bitter end."

"I've got lots of stories to tell you," he whispered. "But they'll have to wait until September. I haven't the strength to go into them now."

They kissed again, and Anne said, "Do you realize this is the first time we've been together like this when Clark hasn't intruded?"

He looked startled. Then, drawing back a little from their embrace, he said, "You're right." His eyes were perfectly still, more somber than Anne had ever seen them. "You are right," Larry repeated, and his gaze began to relax its grip. "I don't think he'll have to come back that way again."

About the Author

Robert Towers was born in Richmond, Virginia. From 1945 to 1947 he served as a vice consul in Calcutta, India, the setting of his first novel, *The Necklace of Kali* (1960). A second novel, *The Monkey Watcher*, was published in 1964. Towers received his doctorate from Princeton and teaches at Queens College in New York. A frequent contributor to *The New York Review of Books* and *The New York Times Book Review*, he lives with his wife and daughter in New York City.